Surviving the Lion's Den

Books by Matt Scott

SURVIVING THE LION'S DEN SERIES
Surviving the Lion's Den

COMING SOON!
The Iranian Deception
The Ayatollah Takedown

Surviving the Lion's Den

Matt Scott

SPEAKING VOLUMES, LLC
NAPLES, FLORIDA
2021

Surviving the Lion's Den

Cover design by Hannah Linder

ISBN 978-1-64540-576-4

To the men and women of the CIA
who courageously put their lives on the line each day
for the sake of protecting our great nation, and
to the people of Iran who yearn to be free.

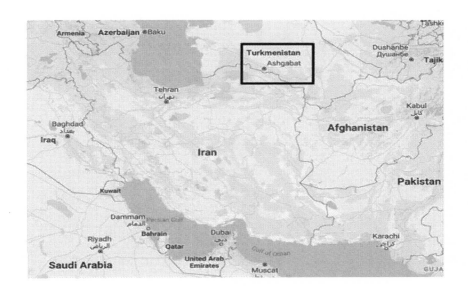

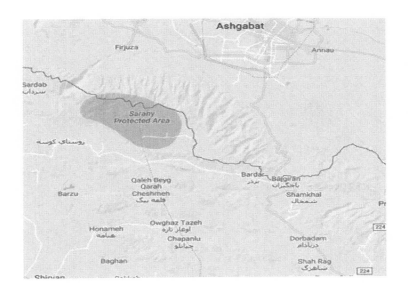

Characters

Americans

Kirk Kurruthers..............................American of Iranian heritage

Cameron Kurruthers, a.k.a. Kamran Kabiri.............Kirk's grandfather

Tom Delang, a.k.a. Marvin Meadows, code name *Merlin*.... kidnapped CIA agent

Beth Jenkins... CIA station chief

Ben Thrasher, code name *Jaybird*......CIA Counterterrorism operative

Vivian Walsh......U.S. Senator, chairman of the Senate Armed Services Committee

Devonte Spinx.......................................Secretary of Defense

Iranians

Farhad Khorsandi.................................smuggler, Kirk's guide

Simin Dehghani..…............................. Farhad's business partner

Capt. Azam Aslani..........Iranian Revolutionary Guard Corps (IRGC)

Major General Rahim Shirazi...commander of the Iranian Revolutionary Guard Corps (IRGC)

Lt. Mahmoud Yazdani......Iranian Revolutionary Guard Corps (IRGC)

Marzban Shir-Del.............head member of Iran's Guardian Council

Rasoul Haddadi.........former member of Iranian Revolutionary Guard Corps (IRGC)

Saudis

Tariq al-Masari..........Saudi Arabia Ambassador to the United States

Yasser Al-Zoubi...................Tariq al-Masari's director of security

Others

Mazaen Al-Jaffari, a.k.a. "Moz".................Delang's longtime source

Maxim Petrov...President of Russia

Kazeem al-Nashou.............................Basra, Iraq Chief of Police

Mustafa Shamekh...Iraqi terrorist

Prologue

Stuck in a narrow alley between two local theaters, Kirk Kurruthers wiped the sweat from his face and rose up slowly from behind a dumpster. He could see the gates of the American Embassy just two hundred yards away. Two Marines stood post on each side, holding their rifles. State Department workers flowed in and out, chatting, as if they didn't have a worry in the world. Smog from passing cars and dirt swirling in the air distorted Kirk's view of the stars and stripes, waving proudly through a congested sky.

His lungs burned and his throat scraped like sandpaper as he swallowed the parched desert wind. The two companions hunkered down next to him were also suffering. Their escape through the mountains had been laborious and demanding. They desperately needed water, but there was no time for pain, excuses, or fundamental desires. All that mattered was getting through the gates and entering the free space of the embassy.

Two Iranian Revolutionary Guardsmen were trying to prevent that. They had been hunting Kirk and his associates for the last three days. He'd been cornered by one named Azam a few days earlier in Tehran at a fancy dinner in the home of a Revolutionary Guard leader.

His mind wandered back to the banquet they had offered him, which became his last full meal until he escaped. Kirk knew that if he and his friends didn't make it through the embassy gates, the only food they would see any time soon would be rat burgers at Tehran's infamous Evin Prison, and that was thinking optimistically.

"Did they see us?"

Farhad rasped with a mouth as dry as paper as he tried to catch his breath.

"No, I don't think so," said Kirk. "They're looking for us, though, for sure."

Squatting behind Kirk with a hand on his shoulder was their injured, scruffy looking companion, whose unexpected rescue from a torture facility had hastened their escape from Iran. He suddenly began making sniffing sounds as a pungent odor from inside the dumpster crept into his nose.

"Man, the cumin in this dumpster smells good . . ."

Kirk and Farhad glared at the man they hoped to escort through the embassy gates.

Farhad could only stare in amazement. Kirk made no effort to show any understanding. The frustration from the last few days finally caught up with him, and he snapped. In one motion, he seized him by the collar, nearly lifting him off his feet, and slammed him against the wall. Too weak from months of torture and malnutrition, the older man was unable to resist.

"Really, numb nuts? Those fuckers over there want our heads on *Al-Jazeera* and you're talking about food?"

"Kirk, get down!"

Farhad yanked his friend down by the tail of his grungy t-shirt. As he did, the older man collapsed to his hands and knees.

It was too late. The Revolutionary Guardsmen heard the commotion and were looking in their direction. One of them pointed directly at the dumpster.

Kirk's eyes widened in panic. He watched Azam and his goon walk toward them with steadfast purpose. There was no more escaping. No more running. Their time was up.

Chapter One

DAMMAM, SAUDI ARABIA
APRIL 2020

As the elevator dinged on the first floor of the Novotel Hotel, a man traveling under the name Marvin Meadows yawned and wiped the sleep from his eyes. In spite of all his years of traveling, jet lag never failed to affect him.

When the doors opened, his eyes swept across the open layout of the lobby, from the water fountain in the left-hand corner across the swirling pattern of the carpet, adorned with brown leather couches, to the luminous front desk, with smiling employees assisting the half dozen guests standing in front of them. Meadows saw no sign of anyone who alarmed him or who might be watching his every move.

He noticed the morning newspaper on a side table next to one of the club chairs along the wall, so he decided to take a seat. As he opened the Arabic edition and kept it below his eye level, Meadows perused the paper for anything that might be of interest on his short visit to the city. Every so often he glanced over the top of the pages to see if he was being watched. Ten minutes later, he folded the paper and left it on the table, wiped his hands down his new, blue pinstriped suit and made his way to the front door.

Before he reached the exit, Meadows pulled his cell phone from his belt clip to his ear and said, "Hello?" He turned to face the lobby, affecting a look of confusion. He glanced at his gold Omega wristwatch, which read 11:13 a.m. He hadn't received a phone call. Looking at his watch was an old school trick Meadows had learned to rely on through his years as a spy. If anyone else looked at their watch after he looked at his, it was a sure bet he was being followed. Satisfied that there was no surveillance, he pretended to finish the call and exited through the bronze revolving door.

The April heat slammed him like a runaway train as he stepped outside. Summer in Saudi Arabia made him wish he was back home in Bethesda, Maryland, reclining in his La-Z-Boy, watching the Masters golf tournament on his 70-inch flat screen with a sloppy meatball sub in his lap and a chilled Miller Lite bubbling next to him.

Unfortunately, his boss had been oddly unwavering about him taking this trip. Luckily, his limousine service arrived before he began to sweat. He noticed right away that the driver was his usual contact, who in traditional fashion walked to the back and opened the door for his passenger.

After getting on the road, the driver lowered the window to the back seat and handed a holstered Glock 26 9mm to Meadows, who ejected the magazine to check for bullets before sliding it back in and tucking it into the back of his waistband.

"Good to see you again, Boss."

"Good to see you, too, Moz. How's your family?"

"Very good, boss, very good. My sister is getting married."

"Oh, good for her. Please pass along my congratulations."

Meadows made a mental note to send a gift to Moz's sister, Aliya.

Meadows had known Moz for more than ten years. They met during Meadows's first assignment in the Middle East. He had been stationed in Jalalabad, Pakistan, post-9/11, assigned to track down high value Al-Qaeda targets. It was grueling work with long, thankless overnight shifts.

On one night in 2002, as Meadows was burning the midnight oil, he went to the kitchen inside the CIA compound, seeking a caffeine fix. Since the cupboards were bare, he decided to go for a short run, thinking it could provide a much-needed adrenaline rush. He didn't make it far before three hoodlums jumped him as he rounded a corner. He tried to dodge, but the kid with a knife, who Meadows assumed was the leader, swiped the blade at him and made a four-inch cut from just above the corner of his mouth to slightly below the corner of his right eye.

That's when Meadows remembered what his station chief had told him.

"Never leave the compound alone."

The rookie operative found out the hard way that the compound was always being watched. Al-Qaeda operatives paid top dollar for a captured CIA spy.

Thankfully, the hoodlums were teenagers and Meadows's training kicked in. When the kid with the knife lunged at his midsection, Meadows caught his aggressor by the wrist and twisted it behind the kid's back, dislocating his shoulder. The kid screamed in pain and flopped to the ground.

Seeing his friend in trouble, a second kid ran at Meadows like a linebacker trying to tackle the quarterback. Meadows turned his body olé style and rammed the second kid's face into the corner post of a chain link fence. The third kid looked to be the youngest and stood frozen in amazement and fear. While the first two hoods lay on the ground moaning, Meadows kept a sharp eye on the boy, who couldn't have been older than thirteen.

"What's your name?" Meadows asked in Arabic.

"Mazen Al-Jafari," the kid said.

Meadows had no desire to hurt him. He had seen enough in his short time in the Middle East to know that the young ones could be as dangerous as the adults, but he made a judgment call that the kid wasn't going to harm him. He snatched the knife, cut a portion of his shirt across the torso, ripped it off and threw it on the ground. He wiped some of the blood from his face and smeared a blood trail down the edge of the blade to make it appear to the kid's friends that he had put up a good fight. The kid looked stunned when Meadows handed the knife back to him, handle first.

"Tell them you cut me with the knife before I ran off. Meet me back here tomorrow night at the same time and don't make me come looking for you."

Meadows stared at the stunned kid to ensure that his message was being taken seriously. He did not turn his back on the kid for at least twenty feet before jogging back to the station.

The next night, sporting forty stitches taped up on his right cheek, Meadows left the compound and leaned against the fence where he'd been attacked. He wasn't sure if the kid would show, but his gut told him he would. Sure enough, two cigarettes later, the kid turned the corner and approached Meadows with his hands in his pockets, eyes cast down at the ground.

"Take your hands out of your pockets."

The kid did as he was told, and Meadows lifted his arms to search him but found nothing.

"What was your name again?"

"Mazen."

"Okay, Moz. Who hired you to watch our building?"

"I do not know his name. I needed money and my friends knew a man who would pay."

"What did he look like?"

"A bald man with bad teeth."

Meadows squinted. It didn't sound like anyone his team knew. He took a picture from his back pocket, showing three terrorists seated around a table and held it in front of the kid's face.

"Do you see the man in this picture?"

Moz shook his head.

"You're sure?"

"No, I do not see him. But I recognize that man."

Moz pointed to another person in the picture with a full head of hair, a long beard, and large rimmed glasses.

Meadows's jaw dropped. Could he be this lucky? He tapped the picture with his finger, trying to contain his excitement.

"You're positive that you saw *this* man?"

"Yes. He was at the house of the man who paid us."

"You better not be lying to me about this, kid."

"I swear to you, Boss, it's him. He had terrible breath."

Bingo. Meadows had a lead on a big fish. He grabbed whatever money he had on him. It was only a thousand Pakistani Rupee, which wasn't even ten US dollars and shoved the money into the kid's pocket.

"Meet me here again tomorrow night. Same time."

The kid nodded in confusion as Meadows sprinted back to the station.

The CIA station chief was waiting for Meadows, clearly upset that the junior officer had left the compound again without authorization or additional personnel. His fury dissipated when Meadows told him that he may have a line on the whereabouts of Abu Zubaydah, Al-Qaeda's travel agent to the terrorist cause.

Two weeks later, a CIA team raided Zubaydah's apartment. The terrorist was badly injured, including a bullet to the testicle. The CIA doctor on site couldn't guarantee that he would survive, but luckily, the bastard pulled through. Zubaydah was subsequently waterboarded eighty-three times and became the face of the CIA's enhanced interrogation program of the early 2000's. While his mental stability and high value would later be questioned by doubters and the mainstream media, CIA officers milked him for all his valuable information.

Despite the circumstances, Meadows found Moz to be a worthy source and kept him around. Their nightly meetings led to an exchange of phone numbers. Meadows even started to like the kid, though he was never sure if the boy liked him for not killing him or because he doled out money for his information. He tended to think the latter, but they became friendly, and safety was never a concern. Moz wasn't about to let his golden goose get killed.

Meadows wasn't able to use Moz on every case that he worked in Pakistan, but whenever he was stuck and didn't know where to turn, the kid provided him with a valuable tip. Moz may have been the one getting paid, but the information he supplied made Meadows a rising star in the Near East division.

A few weeks ago, Meadows had asked Moz if he knew of anyone he could trust in Dammam. The kid, now twenty-nine years old, told Meadows that he was in luck because he had decided to stay with friends in Riyadh after making their pilgrimage to the holy city of Mecca a few months earlier. He could make the trip over to pick him up.

Meadows considered the information.

Too lucky?

Normally, he didn't like coincidences, but he decided to take his trusted asset at his word. He could have gotten another driver, but he relied on Moz's expanding list of contacts.

"Boss, we're here."

They pulled up to the front door of the Dharan International Exhibitions Center, where Meadows told Moz to sit tight and wait for his call within the hour. He strolled into the Saudi Arabia International Oil & Gas Exhibition, looking fresh and tanned in his polished Louis Vuitton loafers. With one hand in his pants pocket to expose his Cartier cuff links, he held his head high and oozed the confidence of the oil executive he pretended to be.

Making his way around the floor, Meadows shook hands and offered fake business cards to the hosts of the various exhibits. If anyone called to check up on him, they would be routed to a CIA station in Riyadh, where a junior officer would back up Meadows's identity.

After twenty minutes of mingling, Meadows spotted his contact. The man wore a traditional Saudi outfit, a white thobe and ghutra. It took a few seconds for them to see one another because the Saudi was surrounded in a group discussion. He smiled and laughed with the others, which Meadows took as a sign that he was in a good mood.

Once they locked eyes, his contact politely excused himself and discreetly entered Room 103. Meadows stalled for a minute, checking his phone, and when he felt it was safe, he casually made his way to the door and slipped inside.

Chapter Two

As Meadows closed the door, he immediately saw his man, who nodded to his security detail, indicating they should wait outside. Yasser and Abdullah, the bulky security team, looked like NFL linemen. Meadows knew them well. They smiled and shook his hand before exiting.

"Tom, it's so good to see you again," Tariq Al-Masari said.

Never knowing where a listening device might be planted, Delang was uneasy about hearing his real name used in the field.

"Hello, my friend," he said with a smile.

As usual, he was struck by his contact's silvery and modulated voice though he had seen it change abruptly to guttural and gruff when he grew angry or annoyed.

Tariq Al-Masari was one of the few people outside the CIA who knew that Marvin Meadows was an alias for Tom Delang. They had met years ago, when Tariq was an up-and-comer with the Saudi Diplomatic Service and Delang was a star salesman with Avent, a supplier of computer motherboards, prior to joining the CIA.

Delang covered their handshake with his left hand, a move that never seemed to fail.

"Still fighting jet lag, I see," Tariq said, noticing the shadows under his friend's eyes.

"You got me pegged, Tariq," said Delang, laughing. "I should work on my poker face."

"Poker face? I thought you CIA people had masks and make-up experts."

"Make-up, yes, but if we do have masks, they've never given me one. I think they save those for *Mission: Impossible* movies."

"Ah, yes. I'm a big fan of those films. I tried my best to get them to shoot one of them here, but it did not work out."

"Hollywood turned *you* down?"

"Not Hollywood. The King. I'm not sure if he has a crystal ball, but I think the latest events may not have played out well for the film's shooting schedule."

"Now that you mention it, what's the latest?"

Tariq sighed.

"Let's sit."

Delang knew that it couldn't possibly be good. The meeting room setting was no accident. Sitting next to someone rather than across from them and placing his hand on their forearm was Tariq's 'go-to' move.

The latest scuffle necessitating a meeting between these two friends involved an attempted Shia uprising in neighboring Bahrain, a situation the Sunni Saudis monitored carefully. The Shia had long complained of discrimination, and they had a fair point. With assistance from the Saudis, the Sunni-supported Bahraini government was openly using torture and gerrymandering to quell its Shia citizens.

Inspired by the successful Arab Spring uprising in Egypt that led to the resignation of Hosni Mubarak, the Bahraini Shia decided that enough was enough and began protesting in February. They were immediately met with a mix of tear gas and rubber bullets by government forces.

The next few weeks marked a vicious cycle of tragic events, as the protests grew, and the government beat them back. By the next morning, tens of thousands gathered for the funerals of those who perished in the previous day's protests. By night, the protests grew bigger, only to be challenged by government authorities. At its peak, the protestors numbered nearly three hundred thousand and began to cross the King Fahd Causeway bridge that connects Saudi Arabia and Bahrain, which left

Saudi officials no choice but to send troops over the bridge to protect their interests.

The protests lasted more than a month. They became a black eye on the Sunni government and an eye-opening experience for the rest of the world, who witnessed the upheaval on news and social media.

Beyond the human rights tragedies, Bahrain was also the headquarters of the United States Navy's Fifth Fleet, which gave Uncle Sam a commanding presence in the Persian Gulf, capable of responding quickly, provoked or not, to nearly any situation in the area. While the U.S. played no part in the Bahraini uprising, its military base put them on the playing field.

It was the key to protecting all interests in the region and American officials would not permit it to be threatened. Since Bahraini officials couldn't be depended on for a straight answer, Tariq was the most objective third party. For this reason, Delang had been instructed to get his ass to Saudi Arabia to meet with his old friend and report back.

"Tom, our Sunni friends in Bahrain aren't letting up."

"Tariq, this can't go on. They can't keep torturing their people."

"Don't pretend they are innocent, Tom. The Shiites have been trying to overthrow the Sunnis since before we were born. Let's not forget, they were the ones who started the protests."

"Okay, let me ask you this: if you were experiencing their treatment, would you and your fellow Sunnis act any differently?"

This statement gave Tariq pause.

"Look, Tariq, they want to be treated fairly. This torture and messing in local elections has to stop. Frankly, these people deserve a fair piece of the pie."

Tariq glared at Delang. He removed his hand from Delang's forearm and put his fingertips together with space between each one and the palms of his hands. This was Tariq's 'get serious' gesture, but it always reminded Delang of the Mr. Burns character from *The Simpsons*.

"First of all," Tariq said, "your country should know better than most that the harmony between Sunnis and Shiites is the most difficult in history to negotiate."

He was referring to America's recent inability to negotiate peace between the two sides in Iraq, which had disastrous results.

"Second, is your country really in a position to tell mine if we should be involved in another's' elections? Your CIA wrote the book on that."

This time, Delang paused. Tariq was referencing the CIA's 1953 coup in Iran, so he raised his hands and conceded the point.

"Look, you're not hearing anything from me that you won't hear from the State Department. From me, the message is delivered a little softer than it will be from the Secretary of State when she visits in a couple weeks. I know that you get my point, and as much as the human rights implications are relevant to my visit, I'm really here about the naval base. Are the protests posing any threat that might require our intervention?"

"Bahrain has its own agenda, Tom. Their government will not suffer Egypt's fate. Quite separately, in addition to the five thousand soldiers dispatched to the Causeway, the Minister of Defense will be sending two hundred members of the Special Security Forces to assist your navy. Off the record, we sent some of our own clandestine operatives from the General Intelligence Directorate to sniff around."

"Nice. Sniffing for what? You've got that look in your eye, Tariq."

"Iranian involvement."

Delang closed his eyes. It was exactly what he did not want to hear.

"You have proof?"

"Come on, Tom, since when does the CIA need a smoking gun? This isn't a trial, my friend. You know as well as I do that the absence of evidence is not evidence of absence. Shades of grey rule the Middle East."

"You may be right, Tariq. But the last time we gave the 'known unknowns' speech, we got our asses handed to us when we couldn't find Saddam's WMDs."

"Okay, fair enough. Call it a hunch. One of my friends at the Bahrain airport noticed some Iranians flying into their country. Not just run of the mill guys. He swears to me that he saw a member of Hezbollah that we thought we killed two years ago."

"Do you have a picture? I need something to take back to Langley we can run through our database."

"I'm working on it. Can you stay in country another day or two?"

"I'll make it work."

They sat in silence for a moment. Tariq then put his hand back on Delang's forearm, signaling that the tension was over.

"Tariq, do you think this cold war between your country and Iran will ever end?"

"I don't know. I'll fight for my country until my dying breath, but geopolitics is so poisonous. Sometimes, there isn't any fresh fruit from the tree. In the meantime, I have some back-channel communications going on, and I made a deal with them that may help improve relations. But with the Iranians, I've learned to keep a pen in one hand and a gun in the other."

That raised Delang's eyebrows.

"Anything I should know about?"

Tariq looked his friend straight in the eye.

"Trust me. You don't want to know."

Delang nodded. Whatever it was, he knew better than to inquire further.

"Thanks for taking time out of your day, Tariq. You know where I'll be."

Tariq patted his friend's wrist and stood. As he turned to leave, Delang held up a hand.

"Let me go out first. The most important man always leaves the room last."

Delang winked, referring to an old custom in Muslim culture.

Tariq grinned. As he watched Delang leave, he realized that it was this type of warmth, unnecessary after so many years, that kept their friendship alive.

Instead of mingling in the conference a little longer, Delang called Moz and made his way toward the door. He needed to touch base with some other contacts before his next meeting with Tariq. If he hurried, he could get Moz to drop him at the hotel so he could change and make his next meeting before afternoon prayers began. As soon as he stepped outside, Delang saw Moz had the door open. He entered the limo still looking at his phone. Hearing the driver's door close, he called to Moz without looking up.

"Back to the hotel, Kiddo. We need to switch cars before our next stop."

As the last word left his lips, Delang sensed that he was not alone in the back of the limo. He looked up and saw a well-dressed man wearing aviator Ray Bans, pointing a revolver at him.

"Who are you?"

The man said nothing. Moz rolled down the window. Delang stared ahead, knowing he had been betrayed by his long-time asset. He tried to put his phone back on his belt and slyly go for his Glock, but Moz shook his head.

"I removed the firing pin before I gave it to you."

Delang nodded in anger, at Moz and himself. It was standard agency procedure to have CIA personnel deliver a gun to an agent's room, but Delang had come to rely on Moz, who had provided him with functional weapons dozens of times.

Rookie mistake.

He hastily surveyed his surroundings and gazed out the window. People were leaving the conference. Delang thought about making a break for it, but he wasn't sure if the man in the sunglasses would shoot him or if this was a traditional kidnapping for ransom. If it was, perhaps he would have a chance when Tariq came looking for him, after failing to show for their next meeting.

Delang tried to bump the door open with his shoulder, but it wouldn't budge.

Moz must have engaged the childproof lock. It could only be opened from outside.

"Why, Moz?"

"Sorry, boss. Sometimes you have to pick a side. Plus, they pay better."

Suddenly, both passenger doors opened, and two more men got in, sandwiching Delang between them. The fat man to his left reared back and cracked him in the jaw. Not a second later, the man to his right nailed Delang in his gut and shoved him down by the back of his head. As the car drove off, he slumped on the floor, doubled over in pain as a canvas bag was thrust over his head.

Chapter Three

Summer in the Carolinas was scorching hot, and the air conditioning was busted in Kirk Kurruthers's truck. He had every window rolled down, but he was still sweating up a storm by the time he reached his grandfather Cameron's house. Thankfully, the AC in Cameron's Toyota worked fine so they could take his car to the game.

As he looked at the house, Kirk was reminded of the fact that he didn't like ninety-one-year-old Cameron living two and half hours away. The left railing on the steps was loose. The columns supporting the porch were cracked and needed to be patched and painted. The screens were peppered with holes from birds constantly flying into them.

Kirk knew he needed to do a better job helping his grandfather maintain the house, but he kept finding ways to avoid it. He had tried to convince his grandfather to move closer to his home in Charlotte, where he could keep an eye on him, but the old man dug in his heels and told Kirk that he was fine.

This didn't stop Kirk from visiting regularly, usually twice a month, and it would never keep him from their tradition of going to a baseball game on Fourth of July weekend.

Asheville was home to the Tourists, a minor league Class A affiliate of the Houston Astros. While McCormick Field was a far stretch from the big-league majesty of Minute Maid Park, any real fan knew that minor league baseball had a more personal touch than its major league counterpart. There was something special about cheap beer, overcooked hotdogs and the billboard for a pawn shop hanging from the left field fence.

Kirk and his grandfather were loyal fans and hadn't missed the post-game fireworks on Independence Day weekend in twenty-five years. For a man born in Iran, Cameron surely loved America's favorite pastime.

As Kirk made his way up to the house, he noticed that the bird feeder had fallen, and the sunflower seeds had spilled. Robins, cardinals, and squirrels had eagerly congregated on the porch to enjoy their snack. Kirk stopped a second.

This feels odd.

He wasn't much of a bird watcher, but Cameron was, and Kirk grinned at the memory of his grandfather, sitting on a bench next to the door, enjoying the birds. On this day, though, Kirk knew something was amiss because Cameron coveted his time with the birds, especially the cardinals, which were his favorite.

Kicking some of the seed away from the doorstep, Kirk sorted through his keys to unlock the front door and noticed it was cracked open.

Something's not right.

Cameron was a stickler for security and always kept the doors locked.

As soon as he entered the house, Kirk noticed a picture frame on the floor, a faded picture of him and Cameron at the first baseball game they attended. It was taken when he was twelve, only two weeks after his parents had tragically perished in a car accident during a torrential downpour. Cameron was the only family Kirk had left and he took his grandson to a game to cheer him up. The picture was one of Cameron's prize possessions and he proudly displayed it on the front table.

Kirk's stomach tightened.

"Pap?"

He hurried into an empty living room and continued through the screen door to the outdoor garage that he and his grandfather had built several years ago.

The old man found his sanity in refinishing furniture for his neighbors and friends, but Kirk didn't hear any power tools and it was dark inside.

What the hell?

Kirk headed toward Pap's bedroom and was relieved to see shadows moving in the room.

"Hey, you ready? We better get going if we're gonna beat the . . ."

Kirk froze as soon as he turned the corner and saw his grandfather flat on his belly, crawling through some kind of spilled liquid toward a lockbox he kept under his bed. A strong, nauseating, chemical smell filled the room.

"Pap!"

Kirk screamed as he dove to his grandfather's aid. He felt a burning sensation in the palms of his hands when he touched the floor. His eyes popped when he saw Cameron's face. His skin was heavily flushed; there were dark circles under his eyes, his lips had turned black, and the area around his mustache and goatee were blistered and purple. Blood and bile spewed from his mouth, pooling down the front of his shirt.

"Pap! What happened?"

The old man tried to speak but could barely whisper. He tugged on Kirk's shirt to pull him close.

"Rasoul . . . Haddadi . . ."

Panicked and confused, Kirk had no idea what Pap was saying.

"Hang on, Pap. I'm gonna get some help."

Kirk reached for his phone, but his grandfather grabbed his hand and pulled it toward the lockbox as he whispered to his grandson.

"Rasoul Haddadi . . . Iran . . . you, too . . ."

He got those words out before collapsing.

"Pap!"

Kirk screamed in anguish as he watched his beloved grandfather take his last breath. As he called 911, tears fell from his eyes as he tried to explain what happened. Kirk clutched Pap's body in his lap and just stared at his role model and best friend. The liquid from the floor continued to burn his skin, but his body was numb to the pain.

When the ambulance arrived, Kirk slyly grabbed the lockbox before anyone noticed. Since the technicians were busy trying to save Pap, neither of them noticed when Kirk dropped it through the lowered window of his truck as he followed the stretcher outside.

Pap was DOA at the hospital.

The burn marks around his mouth drew a considerable amount of bewildered attention from the doctors and nurses. Judging by the look on one doctor's face, it was apparent that he had never seen anything like it. One of the nurses noticed that Kirk's hands were starting to blister, so she gently dressed his wounds. After acknowledging her kindness, Kirk asked to see his grandfather's body once more before it was taken to the morgue, where he insisted that an autopsy be performed.

Kirk had never seen his grandfather so lifeless. Pap had always been spunky and bubbly, glad to be alive and living happily in America for sixty-plus years. Now, he was just a slab of meat on a table. Kirk reached out to grab his hand and was shocked by how quickly it had turned cold. Overcome with grief, Kirk leaned down and kissed Pap's chilly forehead.

Before the detectives arrived, Kirk took an Uber back to Pap's house and was immediately met by a crowd of curious neighbors. Over the next hour, Kirk kept reliving the incident as he explained to each of them as best as he could. Seeing that he was too distraught to drive home,

Chris and Jeanie, Pap's closest neighbors, invited Kirk to stay at their house.

After everyone had fallen asleep, Kirk grabbed some rubber cleaning gloves and snuck outside to grab the lockbox. Relieved that the cops had not asked about his car when they taped off the crime scene, Kirk sprayed it clean with a hose. Satisfied that it smelled somewhat respectable, he brought it back inside to examine it up close. After jimmying it open, he found a wilted manila envelope containing a spiral notebook and black and white photographs, which he had never seen.

Thumbing through the pages carefully, as his hands were still bandaged and tender, Kirk saw that the notebook was some kind of diary, handwritten in Farsi from his grandfather's time in Iran. From what Kirk could tell, the entries were dated July and August 1953, but Cameron had managed to write at least one entry every year since then and most of them said "No Surveillance" in English under the date.

Surveillance? Who would be watching Pap?

The most recent entries specified that he was seeing the same cars following him around downtown Ashville as he ran errands. He noted the vehicles' plate numbers. More people than usual were interacting with him on the street. The final entry was dated three months ago.

He closed it by simply writing, "Burned?"

Underneath was a small color photo taken in 2013, showing his grandfather and a white man Kirk had never seen with their arms wrapped around each other. The man appeared to be in his fifties with a beard that almost concealed a distinctive scar on the right side of his face.

A Post-It note on the back of the photo read, "They got him."

They? Who? Got who?

Tucked into the back of the notebook was an envelope addressed to the man whose name Pap had uttered during his final moments—Rasoul

Haddadi. The envelope was unsealed, so Kirk hastily read the letter inside.

> *Rasoul,*
>
> *If you're reading this, then you have succeeded in tracking me down and finally killing me. For the sake of what was once a solid friendship, please let your quest for retribution end with me. My family knows nothing of the event that changed our lives.*
>
> *You should know that I often wondered if I did the right thing or simply delayed the inevitable. Perhaps it was destined to end this way.*
>
> *See you on the other side, my friend.*
> *Kamran*

Kamran. It was the only time Kirk had seen written evidence of his grandfather referring to himself by his Iranian name.

What thing *was he talking about?*

Though his injured hands were throbbing, Kirk continued sorting through the box and found an old black and white photo of several men sitting around a conference table. He recognized a younger version of Cameron, aka Kamran. The names of each man were handwritten above their heads, enabling Kirk to put a face with the name Rasoul Haddadi.

Is this the man who murdered Pap?
Why did he track him down?
What happened between them?
Why did this happen now?
Why had Pap kept this a secret?

Kirk didn't know who Rasoul Haddadi was, but for his grandfather's sake, he was sure as hell going to find out.

Chapter Four

WASHINGTON, D.C.
OCTOBER 2020

Angel Mavares sat alone at an outdoor table at Penn Quarter Sports Tavern on the corner of 7th St. and Pennsylvania Ave. Though he pretended to be reading the latest copy of *Golf Digest*, he was keeping a close eye on the Capital Grille across the street. The target sat at his table two rows beyond the main window. The man was still eating his meal, so there was enough time left to either abort or initiate the plan.

Then Mavares's phone rang. Manssor Arbabsiar was on the other end. By looking at the man, one wouldn't think he was anything more than he appeared, an average, fifty-six-year-old, tax-paying Texan who owned a painting company and made trips to Mexico once a month to make a little drug money on the side.

But the Iranian government kept special tabs on their citizens living in America. The fact that Arbabsiar held Iranian and U.S. passports made him unique for their national interests. Thinking that Arbabsiar's naturalized citizenship would help him fly below the U.S. intelligence community's radar, Revolutionary Guard Lt. Col. Rahim Shirazi had secretly recruited the man to assassinate Saudi Ambassador Tariq Al-Masari, who had been a thorn in the Iranian side for far too long. The time had come to remove him for good.

Elated to be part of a special plan to help his homeland, Arbabsiar accepted the task. There was only one problem: Shirazi insisted that the assassination take place via an explosion, and Arbabsiar knew nothing about bombs. However, during his trips to Mexico, he played pool with Angel Mavares, an associate of an international drug cartel with considerable bomb making experience. The two weren't best friends but got along well enough that Mavares trusted him to repaint his wife's kitchen. Mavares had informed him that the explosives were wired to a car parked outside the restaurant. Once the ambassador stepped outside, Mavares would phone in the signal and boom.

"It's nearly closing time. I wasn't sure you'd call," Mavares said.

The mission to kill the ambassador had been named Chevrolet, so the two spoke in code, with Mavares playing the salesman.

"A good customer ensures that the car he wants is still available. My apologies for not being able to meet you in Mexico yesterday," Arbabsiar said.

They were supposed to meet in Guadalupe so Mavares could be paid one hundred thousand dollars of the hit fee up front. The move also allowed Arbabsiar to serve as his own collateral for final payment. But Arbabsiar had trouble with his passport and was refused entry. The Mexican authorities promptly put him on a flight to New York. Arbabsiar sat at the terminal gate waiting to board his flight back to Texas when he called Mavares.

Mavares was annoyed that he had not received payment in person.

"There may be a problem. The lot is crowded with other customers," he said, referencing innocent bystanders who could be killed by the blast.

"If a hundred go with him, fuck 'em. No big deal."

This enraged Mavares, but he kept his cool.

"Do you have my payment?"

"Not until the sale is complete."

"That's not how this works. Payment is due *now* or I walk, and you can find someone else," Mavares said.

"Half now and half after its done."

"No. Adios."

"All right, all right. I'm wiring the money now. Call me when it's done."

Mavares hung up and went straight to his bank app. His pulse quickened as the adrenaline pumped through his veins. This was the toughest part. Before the money was sent, the mission could be aborted, but there was no turning back once it was received.

Once detonated, bombs couldn't be unexploded. The burning question was whether or not the painter had the money he claimed to have from his Iranian handler. If he did, the job was real. If not, he was another nut with a grudge.

Mavares closed his eyes and took a deep breath. When he looked, the phone was refreshing its data. Then he saw it. All one point five million sat in his account.

Diverting his eyes from his phone, he saw Tariq Al-Masari getting up from his table. He shook hands with those who had joined him. Mavares immediately scrolled through his contact list to the number he needed. The ambassador made his way toward the revolving door. One member of the man's security detail was now on the street. Any second, al-Masari would follow. Mavares tapped away at the smartphone and hit "Send."

***

Arbabsiar sat with his elbows on his knees, palms sweating, and stared at the phone, anticipating the call he wanted. Nervously biting his bottom lip, he visualized calling Shirazi to give him the good news.

"FBI! Freeze!"

Startled, Arbabsiar dropped his phone and frantically looked up. His head jerked left and right until he saw he was surrounded by a dozen agents with their trademark blue jackets and credentials hanging from their necks, all of them pointing their guns at him.

"Manssor Arbabsiar," Special Agent Aaron Bailey said, as he stepped forward with handcuffs ready. "You're under arrest for conspiracy to murder the Saudi Ambassador to the United States. Stand up and put your hands behind your back."

Bailey barely gave the man a chance to comply as he yanked Arbabsiar up by the arm and turned him around. Outside, Bailey put the traitor in the back of a car and slapped the roof, letting the driver know all was secure. As the car drove away, Bailey looked at a text message he had received from Mavares minutes earlier.

Money in. Take him.

The sheer presence of the message made him smile. He would surely get a promotion for this. Bailey would need to call his friend at DEA to thank him for loaning out his source, but first he needed to call his counterpart agent in Washington, D.C.

***

Before coming through the restaurant's revolving door, Tariq Al-Masari was stopped in the lobby by Senator Jimmy Williams, who he'd known for years. After chatting about Williams's upcoming trip to Saudi Arabia, Al-Masari finally made it through the door and emerged on the street with his security detail, Yasser and Abdullah, glued to his sides. He was immediately met by Special Agent Brenda Gabriel.

"Mr. Ambassador?"

"Is it done?" Al-Masari asked.

"Yes, sir. The agent in New York just called. Arbabsiar has been arrested and is now in FBI custody."

25

Al-Masari sighed in relief. Gabriel had requested a meeting with him weeks before and briefed him about the assassination plot. While his security detail adamantly objected, the ambassador surprised Gabriel when he agreed to play along with the FBI's plan to be at the restaurant.

"Thank you, Special Agent Gabriel. Please let me know if you need anything else."

He reached out to shake her hand.

"Absolutely. Thank you again," she said, returning the gesture.

When Al-Masari entered his limousine, he sat back, closed his eyes, and groaned. He'd been perfectly willing to go along with the FBI's plan, but what he couldn't be sure of was if the Iranians had a backup plan in case the first one failed. It had been entirely possible that a sniper could have struck him down as he stepped outside. He had barely touched his roasted lamb during the nerve-racking dinner.

Not that the last six months had been filled with rainbows and sunshine. His friend, Tom Delang, had a strong history of being punctual for their meetings. When he didn't show for the second meeting in Dammam, Tariq knew there was a problem. Tom's reliable source, Moz, was in the wind as well. Had he been killed or had Moz betrayed Tom? Tariq's gut told him it was the latter, that Tom had been kidnapped. But by whom? Surely, Tom's disappearance and today's attempt on his own life were no coincidence.

As he opened his eyes, he saw his trusted chief of security, Yasser, staring at him.

"Any word about Tom from the GID?"

Yasser shook his head.

"When we get back to the embassy, get the Crown Prince on the phone. He will no doubt want to know that Iran is up to something."

Yasser nodded.

As he looked out the window at the Washington Monument, Al-Masari had a sickening feeling in the pit of his stomach.

Chapter Five

REVOLUTIONARY GUARD BLACK SITE
QOM, IRAN

Tom Delang laid on a dirty floor with what could barely be called a blanket. The scratchy wool irritated his bruises and was so thin he could poke his fingers right through it, but that mattered little because he could barely use his hands.

Worse, he was pulled out of his cell at random times, dragged down the hall, and strapped to a chair, palms up, where his captors took turns whipping his palms with a rubber hose. When they were nothing more than blood and welts, his captors tipped the chair over on its back and began doing the same to the bottoms of his feet. As if that weren't enough, they unstrapped him and made him run to one side of the room and back, over and over.

Delang had heard about this method of torture. Running on bloody feet supposedly keeps the swelling down, but he doubted that his captors were concerned about that. They enjoyed laughing at the hobbling, powerless American after they made bets as to how fast it would take him to make it across the room each time. To them, he was no more than a circus animal.

After the beatings and exhaustive questioning about other CIA assets in the region, he wouldn't see the prison guards for days except when they provided him with shitty meals and a new bucket that served as his toilet.

They opened the small window in his door and made belittling comments, such as "Death to America," "CIA scum," and his favorite, "Your mother is a whore." Each statement was followed by them spitting at him through the window. Those were the good days, the days he hoped for.

The remarks were window dressing, though. They would wait for him to heal and then drag him out of the cell to punch him in the face or gut. Delang knew that he had a couple of busted ribs. Once those wounds looked better, they would rip his shirt off and lash his back.

Torturing him seemed to be their gym routine. Monday was feet and hands. Tuesday was face and torso. Wednesday was back.

Not that he had any concept of time. His cell had no windows. All he knew for sure was that it must be nighttime when the temperature dropped. His best estimates were that he had been wherever he was for at least a few months. The sweltering hot days had turned cooler and breezy refreshing nights had become bone chilling cold. The seasons must have changed.

After having a hood put over his head in Dammam, Delang passed out after several blows to the head. The first thing he remembered was being put on a plane for what seemed like an hour. Upon landing, it was a short ride to what he now called his home, where he was dragged down a set of steps and thrown headfirst into his cell.

Who are my captors?

When his eyes weren't swollen shut, Delang observed that they never wore uniforms that were identifiable. Since his previous mission had ended in a shootout with Syrian authorities, when he narrowly extracted a general from the Military Intelligence Directorate in Damascus, there was a high probability that his captors were Syrian. But there was something about the way words rolled off their tongues that made him think they were Iranian.

As Delang contemplated his situation, he couldn't understand why Moz had betrayed him.

What was it he said in the car? They pay better.

Delang remembered paying Moz handsomely. At least he thought he had. Apparently, he hadn't. The question of who had turned Moz burned in his belly. What stung the most was that Delang considered himself to be an excellent judge of character. His instincts invariably served him well in detecting the trustworthy versus the weaseling scum of society. It's why he had not only survived in the spy business for so long but excelled. Moz had flown successfully below his radar, swaddling him in a blanket of false security. His only thoughts of comfort were those that he had about putting a bullet in Moz's head. That was his happy place, what made him smile with what was left of his face.

But the human mind is a powerful processor, and it isn't always used for good. Too often, Delang's mind wandered to the dark places of his soul.

Is Tariq okay? Surely, my friends back at Langley are looking for me, right?

Can I expect the SEALs to come bursting through the door at any minute?

What about Abagail? My wife must be worried sick.

Delang made every effort not to let his mind stray, but all he had was a limitless amount of time for the demons in his mind to play games with him.

Suddenly, his cell door unlocked. Delang opened his eyes but didn't have the energy to lift his head. The guard set his 'gourmet' dinner of stale naan bread and murky water on the floor and gave him the customary spit loogie. This time it landed in his ever-growing beard. He slammed the door, which made Delang shudder. Then the window at the top opened.

"Your Saudi friend is dead," he lied. "You will die here, too, you American pig."

The guard smiled before shutting the window. Delang could hear his heavy laughs continuing down the hall.

Could it be true? They got Tariq? No. There is no way. Tariq's security is too good.

Delang had no reason to trust what he was being told.

If they can kidnap me, isn't it possible they killed Tariq, too?

What the hell is going on?

He couldn't stand not knowing. Even worse, he couldn't stand not being able to do a damn thing about it.

Delang couldn't repress his anger anymore. With the lungs of a grizzly bear, he let loose a scream of agony, which had built up inside him. He kept screaming until his throat tightened and there was no air left in his chest to disperse.

Chapter Six

As Kirk stood over the burial plot, a crisp winter breeze sent dead leaves tumbling across his feet. His jet-black hair flapped across his face, but he didn't bother brushing it aside. A thousand thoughts raced through his mind as he stared blankly at the name on the gravestone.

CAMERON KURRUTHERS
March 22, 1929 – July 4, 2020

His grandfather didn't want his Iranian birth name engraved on his headstone. He had gotten it legally changed decades ago.

Cameron Kurruthers spent most of his adult life suppressing his Iranian roots. After immigrating in 1954, America became his new home. He taught his son, Kirk's father, Kyle, to do the same, and until his untimely death, Kyle ensured that Kirk also ignored his heritage.

Cameron rarely spoke about his early life in Iran. On rare occasions, he would relive a silly moment from his childhood or educate those who asked about a historical landmark. Each of these limited conversations about his home country concluded them with a first promise he was adamant about Kirk keeping:

Never, *ever* go to Iran.

Though he didn't say so, as Cameron watched the Iranian threat to America grow every day since the revolution of 1979, he knew his judgment was correct.

When Kirk's parents unexpectedly died, his grandfather became the dominant male figure in his life. So his sudden death, especially under such gruesome circumstances, was like taking a two by four to the gut for Kirk. Barely able to eat, Kirk had lost twelve pounds since the incident.

Staring at his grandfather's headstone, Kirk remembered sitting on Pap's lap doing word search puzzles. He grinned a little, picturing his grandfather with buffalo sauce on his face, which was typical whenever they ate chicken wings and watched college football.

His muscles tensed as he recalled the bruises he endured when his grandfather taught him self-defense. The training sessions in Pahlevani, an ancient form of Iranian mixed martial arts, were especially grueling.

Kirk remembered the second promise he had made to his grandfather—to bury him in the mountains far away from any sand with only freshly cut, green grass. Although the graveyard grass was currently dormant, Kirk knew it would return to green come spring, so he checked that promise off his list.

After detectives determined the timeline of events, they cleared Kirk as a suspect in his grandfather's death and shared some details. The coroner's toxicology report said that Pap had been poisoned with a high dose of sodium hydroxide, mixed in a bottle of lemonade. Sodium hydroxide was commonly found in Drano to burn away clogs in household pipes. They determined that pure sodium hydroxide pellets had been dissolved in his beverage, which ate away at Pap's internal organs, causing blood and bile to form in his intestines while burning his skin, and blackening his lips.

Since no logical human being would poison himself, it was clear that Pap had been murdered. Kirk told the detectives that he knew of no one who would do this to his grandfather, but he was positive that Rasoul Haddadi was responsible.

Kirk's ringing phone snapped him out of his daze.

"Hello?"

"Kirk, it's Richie."

Richie was an acquaintance in the State Department he had met a few years ago while working his private security job in Charlotte.

"Tell me good news, man."

"Look, telling you this could probably end my career if anyone found out, but I know how close you and your grandfather were."

"I appreciate it, Richie. Spill it."

"Haddadi was once a high-ranking member of the Iranian Revolutionary Guard who retired in 2005. If your grandfather knew him, he had some serious enemies."

Kirk didn't know what to say. This information wasn't even in the top ten of things that he expected.

"Kirk?"

"Uh, yeah, I'm here. What about the other photo I sent? The one of the older guy with the beard, smiling next to Pap?"

"That I can't tell you."

"You can't tell me? Come on, Richie. Pap was murdered and I need some fuckin' answers!"

"Sorry, man. Not on this. Good luck."

Kirk threw his phone to the ground. Endearing memories of his grandfather were immediately replaced by a burning rage. He clenched his fists, gritted his teeth and slowly thought back to his grandfather's final words.

Rasoul Haddadi. Iran. You, too.

The first promise he made to his grandfather had now become complicated.

A cardinal landed on top of Pap's headstone, looked Kirk dead in the eyes and chirped.

Rasoul Haddadi. Iran. You, too.

Kirk had repeatedly promised Pap not to go to Iran, but he understood the bird to be a clear sign of the man's final wishes for his grandson.

Fuck it.

To hell with everything else—his job, his friends, his future. No matter what would ultimately happen, Kirk decided right then and there what he had to do. Nothing else mattered. He was going to Iran, and he was going to kill Rasoul Haddadi. Promise be damned.

Chapter Seven

Beth Jenkins folded her arms and paced the floor of the war room inside the CIA's Counter Terrorism Center. When she noticed her reflection in an unlit TV screen, she saw dark circles under her brown eyes from burning the candles at both ends. Her jet black, chin-length hair, usually tucked neatly behind her ears, was unkempt, grimy, and pulled back by a headset. Her aqua blouse needed to be ironed. She shook her head, knowing she needed to take better care of herself, but any fellow agent, male or female, knew that Jenkins was a stone-cold knockout, even on what she perceived to be her worst days. Today may be the exception to the rule, though.

It had been a rough few weeks. Fifteen months ago, she had been the station chief in Riyadh when she received word that *Merlin*, the code name for trusted operative Tom Delang, had disappeared. While Jenkins and Delang would likely never share Thanksgiving dinner, she had been in the same class with him at the Farm and they enjoyed a good, often flirty, relationship. As their respective careers progressed, she knew him to be an exceptional agent with a vast network of contacts who routinely provided status reports. When Delang didn't check in following his meeting with the Saudi ambassador in Dammam, she knew something was wrong. It didn't take long for her to be proven correct. The Saudi ambassador called Jenkins when he couldn't reach Delang. His apprehensive voice was unmistakable. It had been two days since Delang disappeared, and Moz, his reliable source, had also vanished.

The entire Near East division of the CIA went into crisis mode. Every analyst, field agent, ground source, and janitor was committed to locating Delang. Since his disappearance happened under her watch on what she considered to be her own turf, Jenkins resigned her post as Riyadh station chief and volunteered to head the task force, code named *Camelot*, dedicated to tracking down Delang. She and her team had followed dozens of promising leads and worked more all-nighters than there was Red Bull available to keep them awake but kept falling short. Jenkins took each new failure more personally than the last.

Prior to Delang's disappearance, issues regarding a Shiite uprising in Bahrain had become a potential threat to the U.S. Naval base located there. The division chief wanted to send another agent to deal with these issues, but Delang had been dispatched there because of his personal relationship with the Saudi ambassador, which was likely to help resolve the conflict more easily, and it was Jenkins who had insisted, in fact begged, that Delang be the one to go. The guilt of that decision weighed heavier on her each day.

Two months ago, Jenkins got what she believed to be the first credible break in months, when a source walked into the American Embassy in Beirut, requesting to speak with an intelligence officer. Khaled Ajan described how he overheard members of Hezbollah in a mosque, discussing torture methods they had used on an American agent. Jenkins quickly had it confirmed that Mossad had previously used Ajan as a source in an op to assassinate a high-ranking member of Hamas. While there was no way to be sure if Ajan was bona fide, Jenkins and her team decided to roll the dice. Seeing Ajan scared shitless about being seen around the embassy was a good sign.

Jenkins sent a team from the Special Activities Center to check Ajan's story. True to his word, he showed up on time to the embassy and met with the lead agent, Jacob Webb, who had a distinguished record for his missions in the field despite his reputation for acting impulsively. CIA leadership continued to remind him that while instincts were important, disobeying orders and acting on one's gut would ultimately have dangerous consequences.

Following the interrogation, Webb estimated Ajan's credibility at fifty-fifty, but he was surprised at how well he spoke English. Jenkins debated the next move and decided to see where the lead took them.

The next day, Ajan lead them to the mosque in the heart of downtown Beirut and patiently waited for members of Hezbollah to show. After a full day of surveillance in stifling heat, they finally arrived for afternoon prayers. Each man had a soldier's build, but one was especially tall. Webb nicknamed him Tall Boy while the others were named Pint One and Pint Two. Pictures of the men were sent to Langley analysts who confirmed that all three were members of Hezbollah.

After splitting up to follow the men to their respective homes, Webb's team reconvened at the embassy, where Jenkins gave the go-ahead for additional surveillance. Once the homes were empty, the team broke in and planted bugs. Webb and his two stocky team members, Dan McAdams and Wyn McPherson, collectively nicknamed "The Micks," were joined by Ben Thrasher. The veteran agents found the rookie to be quirky and unsocial.

The four men impatiently listened to the households' babble about nothing of substance. The families did not go anywhere significant. For two weeks, they were model citizens. They went to work, ate, played with their children, and prayed.

Three days ago, the team hit pay dirt when Tall Boy was on the phone. Though the team had been able to get close enough to clone his cell phone, he wasn't using it. Instead, he talked on a burner phone the team must have missed when they swept the house and installed the bugs. Webb gave Thrasher a scornful glare because it had been the rookie's job to search for such items. As a result, they could only hear one side of the conversation from another listening device, but Tall Boy's choice of words were interesting.

"Did he give up the name? Mm-hmm. How close do you think the egg is to cracking? Okay. Let's turn up the heat. Change the reservation to the house across the river where we can have more privacy with our American guest, the one close to the bakery. Because it has a basement, you idiot. No, let him rest. We'll meet you for dinner Saturday night,"

Webb called and woke a sleeping Ajan to inquire about this so-called house with a basement. Ajan revealed that the only Hezbollah safe house that he knew of across the river was in the town of Jisr El Bacha. Within fifteen minutes, Webb and the Micks picked up a yawning Ajan who directed them there under the cover of night.

After discussing the incident with Webb, Jenkins met with the Near East division chief and the Deputy Director of Operations to debate the legitimacy of the information. They felt it was less than a fifty percent chance that it was Delang being referenced in Tall Boy's conversation, if in fact he was talking to someone on the phone. The odds weren't in the agency's favor, but Jenkins convinced her uppers to green light the operation to raid the house.

That was sixty hours ago. Jenkins had barely slept since she started scouring intel from Webb's team about the house and relistening to the surveillance recordings, hoping to hear any clues about Delang. Nothing. The raid on the house was a crapshoot at best, and now she was putting more operators' lives at risk.

Jenkins looked at the clock on the wall as she continued to pace. It was 12:03 a.m. Beirut time. The team had been in place for five hours but saw no activity. Webb's team lay armed and camouflaged on the bank of the Beirut River under the veil of a moonless night. The three-story brick villa was in sight through their night vision goggles, as they waited for the "dinner guests" to arrive. The lights were off and there was no sign of anyone inside. As they waited, the putrid smelling river carried the rotting garbage and reeking flow of human waste downstream. Webb, the Micks, and the rookie dry heaved as they struggled to handle the intense stench.

"*Bait Shop*, this is *Mariner*. Lights coming from the east," Webb said, speaking to the crowd at Langley over the comm.

Jenkins snapped to attention. Displayed on the jumbo screen in the center of the war room was the night vision lens of a drone, hovering above. Two minutes later, a grey van stopped in front of the house.

"Two men exiting the vehicle," McAdams said.

When an owl hooted, the two men turned their heads toward the river and Webb's team got a good look at them.

"Pint One and Pint Two are in sight," Thrasher said.

The squat heavy driver, Pint One, slid open the back door of the van and let Tall Boy out.

"Fourth man in the back," McPherson said. "Looks like he has a hood over his head,"

Tall Boy pulled the unknown man from the van. He was barefoot, wearing a brown knit sweater and baggy linen pants. His hands were handcuffed behind his back and Webb could see him having difficulty walking with shackled ankles.

"Bait Shop, please confirm the visual is coming through," Webb said.

"Roger that, Mariner," Jenkins said. "Three tangos and an unknown. Wait until all four are in the house and then engage."

"Negative, Bait Shop. There's no way of knowing what's inside. The man in the hood is Merlin, I know it. We're taking them now. *Anchor One* and *Anchor Two*, secure the package," he said, speaking into a shoulder mic to McAdams and McPherson. "*Anchor Three*," he said, referring to Thrasher, "watch our six."

"Mariner, wait!" said Jenkins.

With the heads of each of the Hezbollah members already in their cross hairs, Webb and the Micks wasted no time pulling the triggers of their silenced M4A1 assault rifles. Tall Boy, Pint One and Pint Two fell to the ground as blood sprayed from their heads onto the van. Although he couldn't see anything, the prisoner jerked his head left and right as he heard the bullets crack his captors' skulls. Their bodies bounced off his on their way to the ground and knocked him backwards onto the floor of the van.

Webb and the Micks approached the hooded, shackled man with caution, rifles raised.

"Cover me," Webb said.

"Tom Delang?"

"Yes! Don't shoot!"

Webb kicked the dead bodies out of his way, flipped up his night vision goggles, and reached forward to help Delang stand. But when he yanked the canvas bag off his head, the last thing Webb and his team saw was the evil eyed, grinning face of Khaled Ajan. Having not yet searched the man he believed to be Delang, Webb had no way of knowing Ajan was wearing a suicide vest full of C-4 explosives beneath his brown sweater and that he was holding the trigger behind him in his handcuffed hands.

"*No!*"

Jenkins screamed at the screen in the Counter Terrorism Center.

The explosion lit up the screen back at Langley and rocked the grounds of the riverfront property in Beirut. Jenkins collapsed. When a fellow colleague attempted to pick her up and comfort her, she angrily shoved him away, thrust open the double doors, and ran down the hall to her office where she slammed the door shut.

***

A half mile away, Moz stood atop the bleachers of the Camille Chamoun soccer stadium that overlooked the river from the opposite side and lowered his night vision binoculars. He watched the fiery blast illuminate the sky and grabbed the railing as the bleachers gyrated from its force. Once it passed, Moz pulled a small vile of cocaine from his pocket, tapped out a little powder on his hand and took a snort. Satisfied that he performed his duty, Moz nodded and pulled the vibrating phone from his pocket.

"Yes?"

"Did your friend follow through?" said a female voice on the other end.

"It's finished."

"No survivors?"

"None. The other half of my payment?"

"On its way. Stay out of sight. I'll be in touch."

Chapter Eight

RUSSIAN CONSULATE
NORTHERN TEHRAN, IRAN
AUGUST 2021

Russian President Maksim Petrov stared at the logs burning in the fireplace of the ambassador's private quarters and grew more annoyed with each pop he heard from the timber. He detested being kept waiting. Under the circumstances, though, he had little choice in the matter. His Prime Minister, Vasily Mosorov, had been making power plays within the party to ensure that Petrov didn't run for re-election. That way, Mosorov could take his place on the ticket. So far, his efforts were succeeding, as Petrov was slowly losing his grip on the throat of the Federation Council members who previously backed him unanimously.

Petrov, though, dapper in his tuxedo with a vodka in hand, had his own moves planned for the political chess board. His Iranian friend, who he had met during his years with the FSB, was vague on details but had offered to give Russia a commanding presence in the Middle East. If true, Petrov could checkmate his opponent, clear the pieces off the board with one swipe of his hand and start a brand-new game.

Hence the reason he was kept waiting. The Iranian wanted Petrov to know who was in control. Petrov scratched the top of his balding head. The only thing worse than being kept waiting was someone else having leverage over him.

The sound of heavy oak doors opening reverberated throughout the room, and in walked Major General Rahim Shirazi, Commander of the Iranian Revolutionary Guard, wearing a black Armani suit with a blue dress shirt and a matching silver tie. The heavy heels of his Salvatore

Ferragamo shoes echoed as he strode across the hardwood floor. Petrov didn't budge. If Shirazi dared to keep him waiting, then he would continue to do so a few more seconds. Once side by side, the two didn't shake hands. Shirazi put his hands behind his back and joined his colleague in staring at the fire.

"Soothing, isn't it?" Petrov said.

"What's that?"

"The sight and sound of a slow burning fire."

"I prefer the beauty of a wildfire. Though it rages uncontrollably, you have to appreciate how it moves with reckless abandonment."

Petrov grunted.

"Thank you for seeing me," Shirazi said.

"You said you had an intriguing offer, but under the circumstances, you gave me little choice."

Petrov noticed that Shirazi's beard had grown thicker.

"But you knew that. If I were to look, would I see communication between you and the Prime Minister that facilitated my current situation?"

Shirazi turned to look Petrov in the eye, which meant he had to look up as he was at least four inches shorter than the president.

"Don't blame me because you've been politically outfoxed. If you acted more like your predecessor, it wouldn't be a problem. Nevertheless, when our plan works, your political rivals will scatter."

Petrov sighed. He was in no mood for a debate, so he picked up a manila envelope from the table beside him and handed it to Shirazi.

"I believe Senator Walsh will find herself persuaded when confronted with this."

Shirazi pulled out the files. When he found what he was looking for on the second page, he gave Petrov a sinister grin.

"You're welcome. The curator of the museum in Cairo owes me a favor, so set your meeting there."

"Excellent. How'd you get her father's DNA?"

"He was an old KGB source," Petrov said. "We kept it on file. Now, let us talk about the plans for the military base."

"First, I need some upgrades to our missiles."

"Excuse me? My country isn't your personal tech support."

"For this mission, you are. If my sources are correct, your navy has been working on an intercontinental missile evasion project capable of low range projectiles that can go undetectable to NATO's radars, yes?"

Petrov felt his blood pressure rising. The project in question was top secret, but there were people with loose lips who needed to be dealt with accordingly.

"And if we have?"

"We need it to avoid detection by the American pigs. If we cannot slip below their radar, we cannot succeed in blowing up the bridge."

"I've already given you a big nugget," Petrov said, pointing to the file. "Something like that, if it *does* exist, won't come cheap."

"I'm not buying. I'm trading."

"What could you possibly offer worth that much?"

Petrov chuckled. Shirazi's eyes widened as he glared at him.

"Don't mock me. Bahrain is *ours*. The land was once part of the great Persian Empire, and it will be again!"

Petrov returned the glare and leered down at Shirazi.

"Not without Russian assistance, it won't. I'll ask again. What are you offering?"

"How about a CIA spy?"

Petrov rolled his eyes.

"Spies are like birds. No one cares if one gets its wings clipped. What makes yours so special?"

"Once we are done purging him of his arrogance, we'll hand him over. You can portray him as a double agent. CIA traitor helps Russia take over U.S. military base in Bahrain."

He swiped his hand across the air to indicate the headlines.

"It will play well in the media."

Petrov said nothing and stared back at the fire. He hadn't thought of that angle, which he admitted was a good idea.

"Support for the CIA in America will once again plummet," he said.

"And while the selfish Americans are absorbed in their own squabbles," said Shirazi, "Iran spreads its influence and takes control of Bahrain—once and for all."

"With Russia's protection at the military base in Bahrain," Petrov said.

Shirazi smiled and nodded.

"Unfortunately, the size of our navy can't yet compare to that of the American swine. But yours can. Our alliance would give both of our countries dominating control in the region and will bring the west to its knees."

The hairs on Petrov's neck rose in attention. He could feel global power in his reach.

"There is something else in it for you," Shirazi said. "Your brother died in the field as an FSB agent, did he not?"

Petrov diverted his gaze. This was a sensitive subject. Against his wishes, his brother had taken a mission to assassinate a fellow agent set to defect to America. When they went to intercept the target, a gunfight ensued, and his brother was killed. Petrov executed the station chief for failing to supply back up, but it did little to make him feel better.

"You know he did," Petrov said. "What's that got to do with anything?"

"The same CIA agent that killed your brother is the one we have in our possession."

"How can you possibly know it's the same man?"

"Our information is solid."

The Russian president stared at his Iranian colleague while he debated the legitimacy of his statement. Petrov had searched long and hard for the man in question, but always came up empty. Revenge would play a part in his decision, but he decided that the narrative of a CIA agent flipping to the other side would play well in the media.

"You have a deal, but you don't get the missile software until I have the spy in hand."

"Agreed. I'll be in touch."

The men shook hands. Petrov would remember this moment as one that would change the legacy of Mother Russia. As Shirazi turned to leave, Petrov gently grabbed his forearm.

"Wait. For this occasion, we drink to our success."

"I am not a drinker," said Shirazi. "Allah forbids it."

"For this mission, you are."

Chapter Nine

CAIRO, EGYPT

Naval Medical Research Unit Three (NAMRU-3) was the central biomedical laboratory operated by the U.S. Navy in North Africa and Middle East. Founded in 1946 to help battle a serious typhus outbreak, its primary objective was researching infectious diseases that could threaten troop deployment in the region so that facility scientists could develop vaccines. By partnering with the State Department, the Centers for Disease Control and Prevention, and the World Health Organization, it could work with host nations to monitor diseases and prevent future outbreaks.

A new strain of influenza that recently hit Afghanistan was squarely on NAMRU-3's radar. When it started affecting American troops at Bagram Airfield, the Senate Armed Service Committee sprung to action and Senator Vivian Walsh (D-PA), Chairwoman of that committee, decided to visit NAMRU-3 to investigate.

Walsh was an impeccably dressed African American woman of mixed lineage midway through her third term in office. After eight years in the House of Representatives, she ran for the Senate seat on a platform of reforming Medicare and healthcare for veterans and she won with fifty-three percent of the vote. Her charisma was noticed by the Chairman of the Armed Services Committee, Raymond Giles (D-FL) and she snagged a seat on the committee. Thanks to some crafty maneuvering on her part, she ousted Giles as chairman and attained the committee's top spot despite never having served in active duty.

Walsh had a second motive for visiting Cairo. One of her biggest campaign contributors was the CFO of a big pharmaceutical company who was looking to make strides on a malaria vaccine. A trip to NAMRU-3 allowed Walsh to inquire about the facility's cutting-edge developments. Any information she brought back would give the company's R&D a leg up on its competition. This was illegal. Corporate espionage was a felony. But at the Congressional level, legalities became more flexible when big pockets had your back.

Having fulfilled her obligations as both Senator and corporate spy, Walsh sat down at a local cafe near the American embassy. When she opened the menu, she saw a note taped inside.

Amir Torabi. Tut. 5pm.

Walsh's eyes widened. Her blood pressure shot up as a cold chill went down her spine. She didn't dare look up from her menu. To hide her surprise, she raised it in front of her face. Who knew? How the hell could they know?

Hours later, the Senator was in King Tutankhamun's burial chamber at the Museum of Egyptian Antiquities, pacing the floor in her Christian Louboutin pumps. The museum kept the temperature inside chilly, but at the rate she was going, Walsh's sweat would seep through her white blouse and her lavender St. John suit. She closed her eyes and took a deep breath to calm her nerves. To avoid having her security detail overhear any conversation, she instructed them to ensure that all over-head security cameras were turned off and to stay outside.

Her eyes opened when she heard footsteps approaching. A lean man with thinning black hair and a thick beard entered the exhibit and stood across from her with the sarcophagus in between them. He locked eyes with Walsh before speaking.

"Your hair looked better when it was, how you say, frizzy," he said.

Walsh was taken aback. Had she met him before?

"Campaign research says that my constituents like it better straight." The man smirked and shook his head.

"Americans are so vain."

"Who are you?"

"It's who I represent that's important to you."

"And that would be?"

"An interested party in the Iranian government."

The man pulled a photo from his pocket and slid it to the Senator over the glass top of the sarcophagus, who leaned in to look.

"Your mother together with Amir Torabi, yes?"

"I only know the name. I've never seen him or this picture before."

"Rest assured; it is him."

"Even if it is true, it doesn't prove anything. My mother was a U.S. diplomat assigned to the Moscow embassy. She socialized with tons of people in her career, including Iranians prior to the '79 revolution."

"Believe this."

He unfolded a piece of paper from his pocket, smoothed it out, and pushed it toward the Senator. She glanced at the document but didn't need to see what it said. She knew.

"A DNA test confirms your blood is a match. Congratulations, you are half Iranian."

The Senator slammed her eyes shut. It was her darkest secret, one that her mother had tried to bury. Her African American mother had met her Caucasian father at a fundraiser during the Kennedy administration, and they were immediately smitten—to hell with racial tensions. Vivian came along two years later. Her father and the press believed that her light skin color came from him, but what neither knew was that her mother had a one-night stand with the Iranian ambassador to the U.S. For the first few months of the pregnancy, Walsh's mother thought that her baby belonged to the man she married, but when her doctor told her the estimated conception date, she counted back the days and knew that she hadn't been with her husband that month, which left one explanation. The man that the Senator called her father wasn't present for that conversation and had no reason to doubt his role in her conception. As Vivian grew older, her mother went to great lengths, including lying to the FBI on her background check, to ensure that her secret, which was now her daughter's, too, would not be uncovered. Until that moment, her mother went to her grave confident that she'd succeeded.

Walsh glared at the man in front of her.

"What do you want?"

"A great deal, Senator. You're going to convince your Defense Secretary to close your naval base in Bahrain."

"Impossible," the Senator said, laughing. "Even if I wanted to, which I don't, the military isn't going to give up their most vital position in the Middle East."

The man smacked his hand on the top of the glass.

"This is no joke! You'll do what we ask or your secret will be released to the media. I'm sure your voters will love knowing that the person with the most legislative oversight of the U.S. military is of Iranian origin. You'll be branded the biggest traitor since Edward Snowden."

Walsh's blood boiled. She wasn't accustomed to being blackmailed, and she'd be damned if she was going to be pushed around by some Iranian thug.

"I'll resign before I let that happen."

"You'll do no such thing."

"Oh, I'm sorry, you seem to be under the impression that you can stop me."

"We don't have to. You'll stay willingly."

The Senator laughed.

"Oh really? Good luck with that!"

She turned to leave, but the man zipped around the sarcophagus, grabbed her by the arm, and threw her back against the wall.

"Listen to me, you despicable whore!" he said, pointing at her face. "Do whatever you have to, but you *will* make it happen. In return, not only will your secret be kept, but when our friends take over the base, they'll hire the construction company run by your brother-in-law to make, shall we say, changes. As a minority shareholder in that company, you will stand to make millions of dollars. We own you, Senator."

"Wait. What friends?"

The man slapped the Senator so hard across the face that the back of her head bounced off the wall. Her knees buckled. She held her cheek and crouched down.

"No talking! Listen! Do what you must. We'll be in touch."

He stood over her a moment before walking out of the exhibit, leaving Walsh rubbing her cheek and in tears. Once outside, he reached for his phone and redialed the last number.

"Is it done?" Shirazi said.

"Hello to you, too, cousin," said the man.

"I asked you if it was done, Asghar."

"Yes, it's done. Iran now owns one of the top seats in the United States Senate."

Chapter Ten

IRANIAN AIRSPACE
OCTOBER 2021

The sound of a fluttering garbage bag woke Kirk from a deep sleep as a flight attendant collected drinks. It was official. The plane had crossed into Iranian airspace and Kirk had broken the promise he'd made to his grandfather.

In the fifteen months since Pap died, Kirk had kept his private security job with the Gregory Group in Charlotte while he spent his nights researching his trip to Iran. The first thing he found was that airfare was expensive. Knowing there was a good chance he wasn't coming back, Kirk decided to treat himself to a business class ticket. The bad part was, a ticket from Charlotte to Dubai plus a jumper to Tehran cost nine grand, so Kirk financed the trip by working overtime, taking side jobs and selling some collectibles and stocks.

Learning to speak Farsi was a challenge. During his research, Kirk was surprised to learn that many Iranians spoke English, but he figured that understanding the local language would give him two advantages. First and foremost, instead of relying on locals for help, he could navigate independently. More important, if anyone assumed that he didn't speak Farsi, he could eavesdrop on their conversations. The process of learning Farsi from scratch was mentally grueling. While he wasn't one hundred percent fluent when he boarded the plane, Kirk felt that he knew enough of the language to get around.

He quickly learned that Americans traveling to Iran must jump through a series of hoops. First, they had to acquire a travel authorization number from the Iranian Ministry of Foreign Affairs and include a rough itinerary. Kirk was squeamish about doing that, but rules were rules. Posing as a tourist, he included sites in Tehran and Isfahan that he wanted to see, if he got through customs. Once he received an authorization number, he sent his passport information to the Iranian Interests desk at the Pakistani Embassy in Washington, D.C. Amazingly, the turnaround time was only two weeks, and his invitation came a month later. He guessed that the Iranian tourism industry wasn't exactly booming, so they were eager to get as many travelers as they could. Either that or the surveillance process on Americans was extremely vigilant. He was probably correct on both counts. To be on the safe side, Kirk deleted his social media accounts in case the Iranians wanted some free information.

The most sobering moment came when Kirk ensured that his affairs were in order. He didn't have anything of substance to leave behind and many belongings he had were sold to finance the trip.

Kirk didn't bother to inform the State Department of his plans. Despite what the ticket said, this was likely a one-way trip. Once he succeeded in killing Haddadi, if caught, he would have to atone for his family's sins. The Iranians probably wouldn't send his body back to the U.S. for burial.

Kirk found that nothing prompts a person to re-evaluate his life more than writing a last will and testament. Not that anyone would visit his grave anyway. Kirk was largely a loner who found out too late in life that the best thing about being a loner was that people left him alone, but the worst part of being a loner was that people left him alone.

His boss and colleagues were bewildered by him quitting his job but chalked it up to grief and didn't inquire further. After offering their condolences, only a few bothered to say good-bye or offer best wishes. Relying on someone on the job, especially in the field of private security, was essential but it didn't necessitate being chummy. Kirk was comfortable in his own skin and had far more acquaintances than friends. In fact, he knew no one he felt he could rely on. His best friend had been murdered by Rasoul Haddadi.

His ride to the airport was filled with melancholy. Each 7-Eleven he passed, each group of people he saw drinking outside a bar, and each girl he saw walking and texting with short shorts and a tank top were signs of how free a country he lived in, and how he'd taken such freedom for granted. He wasn't sure if he would see it again and acknowledged that he hadn't appreciated it the way he should have. After a short flight from Charlotte to New York, Kirk consciously looked at the birds soaring in the United States sky, inhaled one last breath from the Land of the Free, and boarded the plane.

The sixteen-hour plane ride to Dubai allowed Kirk to go over the notes he made about where to go, what to avoid, and little nuances about the local culture that would prove helpful, especially as an American. Iranian men, for example, only wore long pants and considered blowing one's nose in public to be gross and inappropriate. However trivial, Kirk noted these things as he wished to avoid any attention.

The rest of his research took him to personal blogs, conspiracy websites, and what he hoped to be pure gossip about the formidable hatred the Revolutionary Guard soldiers had for Americans. One blog, aptly named *Inside Iran*, wrote about how they had recently kidnapped an American man in broad daylight from a business conference in Saudi Arabia. Written by a local Iranian under the pen name Vince, the blog had grainy stills of the last known security footage, showing the man leaving the conference and stepping into his limousine. It theorized that the kidnapped man was a veteran CIA agent who had been on the Revolutionary Guard's radar for months. The blog was intriguing, but Kirk discarded it for lack of evidence. Fake news was everywhere, and he didn't need it clouding his plans.

Iranian law prohibited Americans from being in country without a local chaperone. Kirk was highly suspicious of this but had no choice. When his plane from New York touched down for the layover in Dubai, he texted his chaperone, Farhad Khorsandi, via the Telegram app to ensure that he was prepared for Kirk's arrival. Apparently, Telegram was how Iranians avoided traditional texting, which was heavily monitored by government authorities.

Kirk had found Farhad in an Iranian chat room and learned that he owned his own business, accompanying tourists. So far, Farhad seemed to have no love for the Iranian government and had been particularly resourceful in helping Kirk track down Rasoul Haddadi. When asked why he needed to track down this man, Kirk confessed that he was of Iranian blood and that it was a family matter.

Trusting Farhad was a huge gamble. For all Kirk knew, he could be a plant for the Revolutionary Guard who would be waiting for him when he stepped off the plane. But Kirk wasn't a government agent, and his State Department contacts wouldn't help him. In the end, he had to trust someone. Fortunately, Farhad was fascinated by Kirk and motivated by his money. So long as Kirk kept paying, Farhad kept helping him. Kirk saw this as an encouraging sign, but there was always a possibility that he could be betrayed.

Their relationship began as a simple business transaction but slowly developed into something personal. Kirk wasn't ready to call them friends, but his rapport with Farhad became warmer the more they corresponded and saw that they shared common interests. On several occasions, their emails back and forth were not about Kirk's upcoming trip but about their different theories about characters in *Star Wars*. Farhad was also a fan of American spy novels, author Brad Thor, in particular. He asked if Kirk would bring him a copy of *The Last Patriot*, which was banned in parts of the Middle East. Anyone caught with it, especially in Iran, would face severe consequences. Kirk wasn't eager to learn what they were and though he was already risking enough, he agreed, thinking that it would help establish trust.

The final four-hour flight from Dubai to Tehran should've been an anxious one for Kirk, but he'd spent so much time going over his own notes, as well as those he'd made from Pap's hidden file, that his brain was overloaded. He fell asleep before takeoff, which would likely be his last good sleep, at least for the next few days, if ever again.

Chapter Eleven

TEHRAN, IRAN

Kirk began to sweat when he heard the captain announce their descent into Tehran. As he entered Imam Khomeini International Airport, he was struck by all the signs in English. He figured the western world was so vilified in Iran that everything would be in Farsi or another foreign language. But as soon as he saw members of the Revolutionary Guard standing post with Heckler & Koch MP5 submachine guns, he realized where he was.

Waiting in line at immigration was unnerving. If Haddadi had tracked down Pap, it stood to reason that the name Kurruthers was in the Iranian customs system, just in case any family member tried to enter Iran. Kirk watched the line moved casually as the agents took their time screening people. Kirk's legs trembled and his palms got sweaty. His chest was thumping so hard he felt as if a gorilla was trying to punch his way out. He tried to remember a trick his golf instructor had taught him to relax.

"Whenever you feel nervous about a shot," he said, "start yawning. It sends oxygen to the brain, which helps you calm down."

Kirk was still yawning when his turn came. The big boned, unshaven customs agent in his fifties glared at Kirk when he saw his American passport. Hopefully, the fact that Kirk's facial features resembled his Vietnamese mother more than his Iranian grandfather would sell his disguise as a tourist.

"Who is your in-country guide?" the agent asked.

Kirk attempted to sell his cover as a tourist by reading from his phone.

"His name is Farhad Khorsandi. He runs a company called 3T: Tehran Tourist Tours."

Per protocol, the agent entered Kirk's name into the computer, which proved that the Iranian government tracked Americans moving in and out of the country. Without another thought, the agent stamped Kirk's passport and waved him through.

"Welcome to Iran."

Silently relieved, Kirk thanked him and went to collect his luggage.

As soon as Kirk was out of sight, the agent called the Revolutionary Guard office to alert them of the American traveling alone.

***

As Kirk descended the escalator, he saw a man with a wiseass smirk on his face, holding a sign, labeled 'B. THOR.'

"Cute," Kirk said. "Farhad, I assume?"

"Yes, that's me," he said, with a beaming smile. "You must loosen up, my friend. Your most recent string of emails felt especially tense."

"I've had a lot on my mind," Kirk replied.

Farhad was slim and relatively clean shaven. His hair was thick, combed to the left, and sported a faded cut on the sides. The twenty-six-year-old Iranian wore jeans and a black *Star Wars* t-shirt featuring Han Solo. He reminded Kirk of a grad student at USC.

"It's a pleasure to finally meet you in person, my friend. Thank you for selecting me to be your host."

Kirk introduced himself and received an enthusiastic handshake. Unsure how he would be received on arrival, Kirk was amazed by Farhad's naturally friendly manner. Either money was the universal language, or his perception of Iranian citizens was way off base. For the moment, he tended to think the former.

Farhad noticed that Kirk was carrying quite a few suitcases.

"How long are you planning on staying?"

"Sorry, I tend to overpack. I get cold easily, so I brought warm shirts for when we're out at night."

"Excellent. I'll make sure we have fun. My car isn't far. Please come."

Farhad helped Kirk load the luggage and Kirk rode shotgun. It seemed odd to him that the steering wheel of Farhad's car was on the American side. He expected cars in Iran to have them on the right, as they do in Europe. He reached into his backpack and handed Farhad the copy of *The Last Patriot* he'd promised to bring. Judging by the excitement on Farhad's face, Kirk could practically hear the chorus singing 'Hallelujah' inside the kid's head.

"You have no idea what this means to me. Thank you, my friend."

Traveling to downtown Tehran in a Suzuki Sidekick that was at least ten years old, Kirk noted that Iran's interstate system was not carpeted with potholes and spray-painted signs or filled with camels mindlessly roaming around. Quite the opposite. He could just as easily have been traveling on I-95. A motorcycle zipped past him to his right.

"Holy shit! Did you see that?"

"What?"

"We're driving north, right?"

"Yes, why?"

"Then why the hell did I see a guy on a motorcycle speeding past us going south?"

"Ah, yes. Traffic is very bad here. Some people take the risk to get where they need to go faster."

Kirk gave Farhad a puzzled look.

What kind of crazy fucking place is this?

"How far to Haddadi's house?"

"It's about an hour outside the city."

"Take me there now."

It's time to get down to business.

"That's not a good idea, my friend. His wife usually stays with him in the afternoons. Besides, even if you manage to do whatever it is you are going to do, flying in and out of Iran on the same day will send up a red flag to the Revolutionary Guard. You *will* be detained."

Kirk grunted. He didn't like what he heard but knew Farhad was right.

"You look stressed, my friend. Take this."

Farhad handed Kirk a beer from his center console.

"I thought alcohol was illegal here."

"It is. The mullahs may run the government, but the black market runs the economy."

"Won't you get in trouble if they find out?"

"Most definitely. Last time, they gave me eighty lashes and took my car for two months."

"Eighty lashes?"

Farhad handed Kirk his phone. He saw pictures of raw flesh from his lashing punishment.

"Holy hell . . ."

Kirk zoomed in on the picture, his first glimpse into Iran's sense of discipline and what could be in store for him if he got caught killing Haddadi.

"So why do it?"

"On the outside, we're servants to the government and constantly watched, but inside my own car and my own home, I am king."

Farhad popped open a beer and raised it to toast his guest.

Kirk smiled. If Farhad was a set-up, it was a good one. This guy was cool. It was also nice to know that Iranians, at least this one, appreciated freedom and weren't a bland people subservient to their religion. Elements of western culture were present.

To help sell his tourist cover, as it was assumed they were being followed, Farhad took Kirk to see a couple landmarks in the middle of downtown Tehran.

The Azadi Square was a sight to behold. Essentially the Eifel Tower of the Middle East, it was built to mark the 2,500-year anniversary of the Imperial State of Iran and was the trademark entrance to Tehran, just as the Arc de Triomphe graces Paris.

Kirk found it a bit ironic that "Azadi" translated to "freedom." Given that the structure was commissioned in the final years of the last Shah's reign, it was as if the tower was one of the last monuments to true freedom in the country before he was exiled. Once the Ayatollah came into power, he implemented a system that kept freedom in shackles, hidden away in an undisclosed prison of solitary confinement. In that sense, the tower symbolized the death of the old nation and the birth of what is seen today.

It was surrounded by a roundabout like those commonly seen in Europe. Walking across the street to get to the Square, though, was like crossing the 405 freeway in Los Angeles in rush hour. Tehran didn't have designated crosswalks. Traffic flowed at thirty miles per hour and lane lines were mere suggestions. Crossing to Azadi Tower meant playing chicken with the cars. More than once, they came within centimeters of Kirk, and just because one car stopped didn't mean the car in the adjacent lane would do the same, even though the driver could plainly see people walking. Trying to cross the road reminded Kirk of the old Atari game *Frogger* whose soundtrack played in his head.

"Let's not do that again," Kirk said.

Farhad smiled.

"Get used to it, my friend. Traffic in Tehran has its own personality and its own rules."

After snapping some pics and posting them to his Instagram account, the only form of western social media allowed in Iran, Farhad took Kirk to Milad Tower, where the upper floors belonged to Islamic Republic of Iran Broadcasting, the national television station. While on the terrace, Kirk purposely attempted to take a picture, knowing that security would stop him because the Revolutionary Guard was concerned with foreign spies. Farhad politely explained to the guard that Kirk was a tourist who didn't know any better, which further legitimized his cover.

Along the observation deck, Kirk was astounded by the hair-raising view from one thousand feet, where he could see the carved landscape of Tehran and snowcapped tops of the Alborz mountains. Pap had once taken Kirk to Rocky Mountain National Park in Colorado, so he was no stranger to a beautiful mountain landscape, but the Alborz Mountains had a more commanding presence than the Rockies. Whereas they begged to be climbed and enjoyed, the Alborz dared you to try. Unofficially, the Alborz served as both guardian and shepherd from the freedom of the Caspian Sea on the other side.

Fixated at the rugged mountain tops, Kirk visualized the face of Rasoul Haddadi. His pulse was slow, but he could feel revenge bubbling in his soul.

Soon.

Farhad noticed that the sun was setting and offered to take Kirk to his hotel so that he could check in and rest for a bit before they went out for the evening. Little did Farhad know that someone from the Revolutionary Guard was already waiting for him at the hotel.

Chapter Twelve

Farhad dropped his American customer off at the Bahar Hotel, only a few miles from the landmarks. Being the polite host, he ensured that his guest checked in without incident and told him that he would be back in a few hours for a small party at his friend Simin's apartment. When he appeared outside, Capt. Azam Aslani of the Revolutionary Guard was waiting for him in full uniform. Panic-stricken, Farhad practically froze mid-stride when he saw the man and nervously gulped when his throat tightened.

Aslani was a Shia believer in the truest sense and worshipped at the feet of the Supreme Leader's every command. He moved up swiftly in the Revolutionary Guard's ranks by arresting and carrying out punishment on those who defied Sharia law. He wasted no time arresting women who didn't cover enough skin or displayed affection in public. His ruthless actions came to the attention of then-Colonel Rahim Shirazi, who decided to groom the up-and-coming soldier despite his often-shortsighted thinking.

Alcohol and drugs were two of Aslani's pet peeves. The Quran strictly forbid them, and he took an exorbitant amount of pleasure in doling out the lashing punishment to those who dared defy the law. This is how he met Farhad. Two years earlier, Aslani was in the middle of berating two women for hugging when Farhad's car flew around the corner at excessive speed and hit a parked motorcycle. When Aslani rushed over to investigate the incident, it was immediately evident that the driver was drunk. Farhad became Aslani's first lashing victim, which was a defining moment for both men. For Farhad, it was his first lashing *and* a personal victory against the government by not revealing where he scored the alcohol. For Aslani, this was a beloved moment in his career when he 'popped his cherry' on this brand of legal punishment. It also gave him his first promotion.

Six months later, he volunteered to serve as public executioner when the courts passed judgment on two gay women. Such an act disgusted him to his core, and he proudly carried out his duty in kicking the stool from underneath the queer whores, an act which gave him his second promotion.

The execution made him proud of his country and himself. Of all the forms of capital punishment, hangings were his favorite and he savored Iran's recent changes to the procedure. Rather than a sudden drop to snap the victim's neck, it now occurred by a gradual asphyxiation, with a crane lifting the victim in the air. Aslani reveled in watching the life extinguish from their eyes. The final looks on the faces of the deceased would give most people nightmares, but Aslani used those images to lull him to sleep. Holding the dead bodies until the families paid for the noose was his way of twisting the knife into the bloodline that raised such sinners.

In the last few months, though many would staunchly disagree, Aslani felt that he'd mellowed. He still hated seeing the indignity of western influence in his beloved country, but he had come to accept some of it because he didn't have the manpower to enforce everything.

Allah chose him for this profession, and he enforced the law. But no matter how many punishments he carried out, he always remembered the first lashing of Farhad. Like an old high school sweetheart, Aslani continued to keep tabs on Farhad from time to time and was elated when he was notified that the drunk was playing in-country host to a particular American.

"Come here," Aslani said, pushing off the lamppost and motioning him over with his forefinger.

Farhad slumped his shoulders and walked over.

"Look at me."

With a hang dog expression, Farhad raised his head and looked into Aslani's piercing eyes. At six-foot-two, he was three inches taller than Farhad, which Aslani used to his advantage to loom over and intimidate the dope standing in front of him.

"What are you doing with the American?"

"He is my guest. I need the money, so I started a company that allows me to be an in-country guide."

"I know that, you idiot. I've been watching your Instagram posts. Has he been up to anything I need to know about?"

"No, he is just on vacation."

Aslani laughed.

"I'm not sure who is more stupid: you or him. What questions has he been asking?"

"Nothing unusual, sir. He was alarmed when the policeman told him not to take pictures outside of Mirad Tower, but that's all."

Aslani grunted. He would have a word with the Tower's security team. The video cameras would corroborate Farhad's statement.

"What else does he want to do while he's here?"

"He wants to see the old U.S. Embassy, the Ayatollah's burial site, and the ancient parts of Isfahan."

"Anything else?"

Farhad grew frustrated and rolled his eyes.

"No, he's just a tourist!"

Aslani belted Farhad across the cheek.

"Don't roll your eyes at me! This American could be a spy, and, if he does anything remotely suspicious, you'd better tell me!"

After stumbling from the hit, Farhad rubbed the side of his face and looked up at Azam.

"Yes, sir . . ."

Aslani grabbed Farhad by the collar and pulled him nose to nose.

"Make no mistake that you're responsible for him, you drunken fool. And if I find out that you're doing anything out of the ordinary, I won't hesitate to throw him in jail and hang you as a conspirator. Is that understood?"

Farhad's chest heaved up and down. His throat was too dry to let words escape his lips.

"*Is that understood?*"

Azam screamed in Farhad's face.

"Yes. Of course . . . sir," Farhad finally replied with a shaky voice.

Azam let go of Farhad's collar and pushed him away.

"Good."

As he opened the door to his car, Azam turned back to Farhad and pointed.

"And don't let me catch you taking him out drinking."

With that, he sped off in his government issued Jeep. Farhad stood helpless on the street corner. Wiping sweat from his brow and trying to calm his nerves, he looked down at his pants and noticed he had wet himself.

Chapter Thirteen

QOM, IRAN

After a brisk two-hour drive from Tehran, Aslani pulled into Kahak Village and parked in front of the Lounge, as the Revolutionary Guard called it. As far as containment centers go, it didn't possess the technological advancements commonly associated with those maintained by western intelligence agencies, but it didn't have to. Iran learned long ago that simplicity helped them stay below the radar in an age of digital surveillance.

The house was more than a hundred years old, but it served the Revolutionary Guard well for interrogations. Despite its domed roof giving the appearance of an astrological observatory, which helped with its disguise, it was dull on the outside but regally gothic inside. Constructed with brick, red clay and stone, its design allowed the sounds of pain from torture within to be contained. For those inside, a lack of windows provided an absence of time. Here at the Lounge, mental anguish was equally as important as physical torture.

The Lounge wasn't without its modern renovations, though. The Supreme Leader saw enough value in the former bathhouse that he allocated a cool two million dollars in upgrades. The inside was gutted and reborn. The holding cells were constructed with steel bars in between two stone walls to prevent prisoner communication and any tunneling, should the hostages be inclined to try. The builders used raised cobblestone pebbles on the floor to make it uncomfortable to stand or lay on. Access to the cells were permitted only via soundproofed solid steel doors, no bars. The prisoners' only link to the outside was a sliding window in the door at eye level, which the guards normally left closed, but could leave open for a variety of reasons.

Recognition of day or night was by way of a half-inch sliver of space separating the walls from the roof, the lone way the rooms were illuminated. Electricity in the holding cells was limited to the night vision cameras on the ceiling that kept a watchful eye on the detainees. None of the holding cells had running water and the toilet was a rusty metal bucket in the corner, which lower ranking guards complained about emptying. The only so-called comforts were a one-inch-thick foam mat and a blanket.

Those who knew about the main interrogation room were in awe of it. For security reasons, knowledge of and access to the Lounge was kept to a minimum. Lining the twenty-foot by thirty-foot dank room was a weapons armory full of various length daggers, knives, and Arabian swords, all of which were shined and sharpened to perfection. The weapons were enclosed behind metal lockers mounted to the wall when not in use, but the locker doors were often left open for intimidation purposes when a prisoner was present and unhooded.

A single whip was used by the guards to perform their duties. Each of the ten, two-foot-long strands were made of braided leather with remnants of skin tissue from previous victims stuck to the knots tied at the end, but they were dipped in goat's blood before a prisoner was brought in and displayed on an oak table for effect. They were never rinsed and carried the stench of at least two skunks.

Though other non-stationary chairs were occasionally used, the primary chair for prisoners was bolted to the floor in the center of the room. Serving as a minivan of misery, the guards could adjust it backward, forward, or lay it flat, depending on their whims of torture.

To ensure that the structure blended in with other houses in the area, a standard oak door, found in any suburban home, adorned the outside.

After unlocking the double deadbolt, Aslani stepped inside, relocked it, and looked up at the security camera above the secondary steel door. After being buzzed in, Aslani didn't return a salute from the sergeant as he made a beeline down the stairway to the guard station outside the interrogation room. There was no two-way mirror, but the fifty-inch monitor displayed the events from the adjacent room via CCTV camera.

"I got a call on my way here," Aslani said, as he charged into the room. "Remember the name of that Libyan colonel that the American gave up? The general told me that their intelligence service threw him off the roof of a building."

"Good. How many is that now?" asked Aslani's right hand man, Lt. Mahmoud Yazdani.

"Seven names, seven kills. What about today? Any progress?"

"Nothing. He's really holding back on anyone he knows in Iraq and has withstood some hard hits. After all that he's experienced, he keeps holding out. Impressive really."

"How hard have you pushed him?"

Mahmoud turned his square-jawed head and sneered at his superior.

"As hard as you've let me. If you would allow me to experiment on him like we did a few months ago, I could get what we need."

"No. The General specifically said that he wants him in fair condition when we hand him over to the Russians, so we can't go overboard."

Aslani spit on the floor.

"But I've got another idea. Did you pick up what I asked for?"

"In the fridge, but here," Yazdani said, tossing Aslani a box of latex gloves. "You should probably put those on."

***

Tom Delang sat upright in the aluminum chair with only a pair of boxers covering him. His chest was riddled with bruises and knife cuts that showed signs of healing. The black hood over his head palpitated as he sucked warm air in and out. His cheeks and jaw were again swollen, but at least his nose wasn't broken this time. Having spit out another tooth from the latest round of strikes, blood was dribbling from his mouth onto his chest. The fractured bones in his wrists from previous sessions had thankfully settled but were strapped to the chair. This beating was mild compared to some others, but pain was pain. It hurt like hell.

However, the bag over his head was a new touch for him, at least while sitting in the chair. Ever since he arrived wherever he was located, he had been able to see his captors during interrogations despite the bright lights. This told him that today's interrogation was foreplay and was about to be cranked up. The metal buckles from the leather straps holding him down jingled as his leg tremored with nervous energy. As the steel door croaked open, a pungent and sharp smell entered the air. Business was about to pick up.

***

Aslani entered with a metal bowl in his now gloved hands and a respirator strapped to his face. Mahmoud entered with him, carrying his own bucket and mimicked his boss's look.

"My colleague tells me that you've been particularly strong today. Good for you."

His sarcastic words were muffled by the respirator but clear.

"Let's put that strength of yours to the test."

Aslani put the bowl below Delang's chin and let the aroma of its contents wiggle up the hood into his sinuses. Delang went into a coughing fit and tears leaked down his cheeks. Aslani laughed.

"That's squashed ghost pepper. One of the hottest of its kind in the world. It's one hundred times hotter than the jalapeño peppers you stupid Americans use on your chicken wings. Our friends in India hang it on fences to keep elephants away."

"Smells better than your mother's pussy," Delang spat back.

The prisoner's comment sparked a rage in Aslani that burned hotter than the peppers he held.

"You'll regret saying that."

Aslani slammed the bowl on the wooden table. He and Mahmoud stepped behind Delang and lifted the bag off his head. Delang was temporarily blinded by the light, but it didn't last long as Aslani replaced the hood with a blindfold that covered only his eyes. Mahmoud pulled a handle on the chair that reclined it backward.

"Get the gag!" Aslani said.

Aslani grabbed Delang by the face and squeezed his cheeks. Delang gritted his teeth to keep from opening his mouth, but the pressure on the spot where he'd lost a tooth just minutes ago was impossible to bare. Mahmoud returned with the metal device and Aslani slid the top and bottom pieces between the prisoner's teeth. Then, he squeezed the levers on the side together and pumped Delang's jaws open. He tried to speak but could only spout gibberish.

In one swoop, Aslani reached into the bowl with a finger's worth of the smooshed ghost pepper and smeared it down the bottom row of Delang's teeth. The scorching sting from the pepper burrowed itself into the empty tooth cavity like a tick and chomped into the nerve. Delang screamed and spasmed in the chair like a wild marlin. The residual nerve pain instantly shot to his other extremities. Aslani and Yazdani's laughs could be heard through their respirators.

"How's that feel my little CIA pig?" said Mahmoud. "Give me the name of one of your contacts in Iraq and we'll give you some milk to smother the heat."

Delang didn't respond. He couldn't. He'd passed out from the pain.

Aslani took some pepper juice from the bowl and wiped a streak across his prisoner's scraggily mustache. Once the robust smell forced him awake, he promptly began screaming again.

"Give me a name or we go again," Aslani said. "This time, I'll stuff the pepper into your open wounds and sew it shut myself!"

Hardly able to form words with his lips, Delang still managed to utter a barely discernable "Fuck you."

Without hesitation, Mahmoud snatched the whip and began lashing at Delang's thighs. The cuts weren't overly deep, but enough to draw blood. Next, he pulled out a pocketknife and tore off the prisoner's underwear, exposing his manhood.

Oh God, Delang thought.

Following his colleague's lead, Aslani dumped the rest of the bowl's contents onto the agent's lap. Not only did the searing heat stake its claim in the open cuts, but the pepper juices leaked into the man's pee pipe.

Delang wailed with all his might and shimmied his hips up and down to get the pepper off him.

"Give me a name! Now!"

Delang thrashed back and forth, trying to make the pain stop, but it grew inside his open skin. He had no choice but to give them the least impactful name he could think of and began yammering unintelligible words until Mahmoud removed the gag.

"Kazeem al-Nashou! Now get this shit off me!"

73

Aslani smirked and nodded at Mahmoud, who grabbed a bucket and slung the milk over the American's pathetic body. The pain was momentarily alleviated until Delang passed out again.

"Get him washed up and give him his clothes," Aslani said. "I'll brief the general and see what I can find on this al-Nashou,"

Aslani turned and left the room.

Chapter Fourteen

TEHRAN, IRAN

Three hours later, Kirk waited outside the hotel with his backpack over one shoulder. He didn't want to leave the file his grandfather left for him in his hotel room. When Farhad picked him up, wearing a new pair of pants, he drove Kirk over to his friend Simin's apartment. When they entered, Simin surprised Kirk when she greeted him with a delicate hug. Kirk guessed that she was a year or two younger than Farhad, but that's not what caught his attention. Kirk was taken aback not only by Simin's resonating beauty, but it was her lack of traditional attire that really got him. The long abaya robe and yoga-like pants that normally covered her legs were gone, along with the hijab, which usually covered her head. Rather, she wore a brand-new black dress that showed off her legs, arms, and wavy brown hair with a streak of blue that hung slightly above her exposed shoulders.

"You look wonderful," Kirk said.

He blurted out the words without thinking.

Simin blushed.

"Thank you," she said.

She tried to hide her smile.

Dufus, Kirk thought.

"Please come in," she said, breaking the awkwardness. "I'll introduce you to everyone."

Like Simin, the other girls in the apartment had shed their classic attire worn in public and were wearing a dress similar to Simin's or jeans with large jagged holes cut into them, exposing parts of their legs, and tight-fitting t-shirts that showed off their upper assets.

The guys were dressed as they would on the street, but some wore cargo shorts instead of jeans. Kirk was shocked that everyone seemed so delighted to have an American as their guest. The music, what Kirk called Arabian rock, blasted through the apartment as the dozen or so Iranians ate sliced fruit and finger foods as they partied in their closeted freedom. It was clear that the influence of the Supreme Leader and Revolutionary Guard stopped at the door of someone's home.

A thunderous knock on the door brought the music to a screeching halt. Simin peered through the peep hole, hoping it was her last expected visitors and not the Gasht-e-Ershad, the Guidance Patrol that enforced the country's religious code. When she swung the door open, everyone was relieved to see it was the bootlegger and his wife, Vahid and Bita. They were greeted happily as they handed out liquor and homemade beer. The Iranians wouldn't post pictures of them drinking to their Instagram accounts for fear of being monitored by the authorities but, absent the booze, they all kept posing for pictures.

The scene reminded Kirk of high school parties where he and his friends snuck around for booze, but his smile quickly dissipated when he realized that those days ended for him when he turned twenty-one. For his new Iranian friends, it was an everyday occurrence.

While Farhad had a serious conversation with Simin, Kirk made his way over to Vahid. He was short, no more than five-foot-five, with thick framed glasses that drew attention away from the gap in his front teeth. Kirk inquired about brewing beer in a country where alcohol is supposedly prohibited.

"It's actually not too difficult," he said. "The state does the hardest part for us by making and selling nonalcoholic beer. All we have to do is add the sugar and brewer's yeast to make it ferment."

Kirk popped the top of a beer bottle and took a long swig.

"Careful, my friend. Don't drink too much at once. By the time it is finished brewing, our beer is about fourteen percent alcohol."

The potency made Kirk cough as soon as he swallowed.

"Yeah," he said, gasping in between coughs. "I think that's a little more than fourteen percent there, bro. If you ever stop bootlegging, that stuff has enough octane to start a truck."

Vahid laughed. He explained that being a brew master was his only source of income, paying about four hundred dollars a month.

"You don't have another job?" Kirk asked.

"Unemployment is high here, between twenty and thirty percent. Most of us make our living below the radar."

Kirk grinned. He respected the man for doing what he needed to get by.

The rest of the night continued like any party anywhere. Everyone drank, danced and made jokes, enjoying the freedom inside their own world that the mullahs would never dream of letting them have beyond those walls.

As Kirk sat by himself in front of an unlit fireplace, deep in thought about his new surroundings, Simin sat next to him and handed him a dessert plate.

"Here, have some bastani sonnati," she said, with a sweet smile.

"Some what?"

"You've never really had ice cream until you've had Persian ice cream."

What a treat. Like most ice cream, it was made with milk, eggs, and sugar, but the Iranians used rose water instead of tap and added in their own mixture of saffron and pieces of pistachio. It was thick as fudge and light as Cool Whip simultaneously, which made it melt in Kirk's mouth like a candy circus peanut. Rather than being served in a cone or cup, it was served as a sandwich between two flat, crisp waffle wafers. Kirk's eyebrows rose in approval.

"I didn't get a chance to tell you earlier, but I love your perfume," said Kirk, as a lovely aroma slithered up his nose. "Is that jasmine with a hint of clementine?"

"Should I be impressed, or have you seen that Al Pacino movie too many times? What was it called? *Scent of a Woman*?"

Kirk was surprised.

"You know that movie?"

"Hoo-ah!" Simin said, smiling, as she quoted Pacino's famous line from the film.

Kirk laughed.

"How do you and Farhad know each other?"

"We work together smuggling alcohol and weed into the country."

"Oh, sorry, I didn't realize you guys were together."

"We're not. We used to be each other's competition, but we figured out that it was easier to combine resources. He knows the best routes to take, and I have the better contact list. It works out better for both of us."

"But you're not dating each other?"

"We did for a little while, but it didn't work out. You know, the whole never mix business with pleasure thing. I even helped him set up his business as a tour guide. I took some classes in web design at the university here in the city."

"He told you I was coming? That's what this party is for?"

"Of course. You're his first American client. He was excited and had to tell someone. I thought it'd be nice to welcome you to the country. Are you angry?"

She suddenly felt offended.

"No, not at all. I guess I'm used to keeping a low profile."

Simin paused to evaluate his answer and consider her own.

"Relax. He didn't tell me much, but I could see he was fired up about you coming. Besides, I think Farhad's content to make the best of his situation here. I dream of getting out of here for good one day."

"Have you ever been to the States?"

"No, no. I don't have any money for something like that. I went to Paris one time with my brother, but that is all."

"Paris, huh? What was your favorite part?"

"Seeing the city lit up at night. Something about it felt magical."

"Any plans on going back? To Paris, I mean. If it's cool with you . . . maybe I could meet you there."

Simin nervously bit her bottom lip.

"Are you sure that's a good idea?"

"Why not?"

"I don't know. An American dating an Iranian? Kind of, how do you say, taboo?

"So, we're already dating?"

Kirk smiled. Simin turned her head away. She didn't want the American to see her blush.

"Don't get ahead of yourself, cowboy."

"Well, little lady . . ." Kirk said, doing his best John Wayne impression.

Simin couldn't contain her laughter as Kirk kept his gaze on her.

"Seriously, wouldn't it be weird for you?" she asked.

"My grandfather once told me that if there is no enemy within, the enemy outside can do you no harm."

"I like that. I wish that was true here."

"One day it will be."

Kirk looked at everyone having fun.

"So, how about it?"

"What?"

"Paris."

"I can see that you don't give up easily."

Kirk sighed.

"Sometimes bad ideas turn into the best memories."

Simin grinned from ear to ear. Though they had just met, this American guy made her feel different. She looked away again, but this time it was to make sure no one was looking at them. When the coast was clear, Simin gave Kirk a sweet peck on the cheek, leaving evidence of her lipstick. Kirk wanted to sport it as a badge of honor for the rest of the night, but Simin embarrassingly wiped it off. Instead, Kirk settled for a selfie of he and Simin, which she promptly posted to Instagram.

A few hours later, the party shifted from a traditional social event to a dance academy when the high-octane beer made Kirk shed his inhibitions and started moonwalking across the floor. Everyone, including Simin, begged him to teach them how to do it. Kirk couldn't refuse. Michael Jackson's *Billy Jean* played on repeat for the next hour. Kirk and Simin continued to exchange flirtatious glances. With each look, Kirk's pain from losing his grandfather faded a little bit more.

Chapter Fifteen

After the party, as Farhad drove Kirk back across town, the American noticed that his guide was still wearing his Han Solo t-shirt from earlier in the day.

"You ever think of forming your own Rebel Alliance to fight the Empire?"

"That's easy for you to say. In America, the John Waynes and Clint Eastwoods of the world are a reality. Here, they are a dream."

"Ayatollah Khomeini was one man and look what he did. See, here's what people don't understand about leadership. Sure, one person is the spokesman for their idea, but an idea without an army of supporters is simply an idea. Leadership isn't convincing everyone that you should be followed. Leadership is getting others to believe in something so strongly that they lead with you."

Farhad's head swayed back and forth.

The American has a point.

"We're here," Farhad said.

He pulled into a complex Kirk didn't recognize.

"Where's here?"

"My apartment. We need to talk."

"Okay . . ." Kirk said, confused.

Farhad lived in a seventh floor, one-bedroom flat in northern Tehran. The taupe-colored walls were bare, and the room was filled with the type of knock-down furniture you'd expect in a single man's home. Only the royal blue couch and forty-inch TV appeared to have value. Kirk was on the terrace, enjoying the remarkable view of a full moon shining over the rolling hills, when Farhad nudged his arm with another beer.

"What's the deal with the brick wall that lines those hills?" Kirk pointed.

"On the other side of that wall, my friend, is Evin Prison. The entrance is about a mile from here."

Farhad's response gave Kirk pause, as it was conceivable he could end up there if he got caught killing Haddadi.

"Let's go inside. There's much to discuss."

Kirk noted that Farhad's normal upbeat tone had turned serious. Inside, they sat across from each other at a round table. Farhad displayed a picture on his phone.

"Your man Haddadi lives here."

Farhad used his fingers to zoom in on the picture.

"The one with the white pillars. It's one of the few suburban areas with houses on the outskirts of Tehran."

Kirk zoomed in and out. The unkept front yard was small with no trees or large bushes for cover. He could easily be seen coming and going.

"What about the neighbors' houses?"

"Some of them gave me curious looks while I took pictures."

Not good, Kirk thought.

"What's the back look like?"

"Swipe to the next couple pics."

A metal fence lined the property and had an arch that welcomed those who walked the brick path through the garden toward a screened-in porch. A wide-branched walnut tree in the center provided additional cover.

"There's no lock on the rear gate," Farhad said.

"He's quite the arborist."

"His wife is. She mostly tends to the vegetables in the garden, but lucky for you they have someone trim the hedges once a month. Based on the past schedule, the guy is due to visit this week."

Farhad picked up a pair of grey coveralls, commonly used by professional gardeners, and held them up for Kirk, noting that he should wear them when he goes in.

"Any pets I need to worry about?"

"No."

"Alarm system?"

"No guarantees, but those are rare here."

"What's the wife's schedule?"

"She usually runs errands around lunch time."

"How do you know he'll be there?"

"I don't, but he's a homebody."

"What if I confront him on the street and force him to come with me?"

"That's one of the things I wanted to talk to you about. First, it seems like he's been off his schedule. I haven't seen him leave the house in about a week. Second, it's going to be tough to get to him in public. What are you going to say? 'Hello, I have a family issue to discuss with you?' No. If you want to talk to this guy, you need to do it at his place. He may have an advantage, but it avoids a public scene."

"Sounds like you did a lot of recon work."

"I did what you paid me to do," Farhad said.

He didn't disclose that he'd had help.

Kirk paused.

"You know, Farhad, you never asked why I needed you to do this."

"Well, I did my own research on Haddadi. He used to be Revolutionary Guard, right? The way I see it, you have your reasons, and if I'm right about what you're going to do, then he'll get what he deserves."

"You'll be an accessory, though. If they track you down, your fate could be the same as mine. I've paid you well, but not enough that it's worth your life. I accepted the risks when I came here. You don't have to do the same."

Farhad exhaled a deep breath through his nose. Turning in this American wasn't a bad idea and the thought had merit. If he alerted Aslani, it could be his ticket to getting the insane Guardsman off his back forever. His back. Highlights of the whipping he endured at Aslani's hands flashed through his mind and sent a frosty shiver down his spine. Other friends of his had experienced the same. No, this American was brave enough to do what he couldn't do himself. If Kirk killed this Haddadi person with his assistance, it would be his own way of extracting a pound of flesh from the evil empire.

"Let's just say that I have my reasons, too."

Kirk nodded.

"Fair enough."

"Here's to the Iranian Rebel Alliance," he said, raising his beer bottle.

Farhad smiled and tapped his bottle in return.

***

Back at the hotel, Kirk stretched out on the bed and thought about the information Farhad had provided, but his gut bothered him. Something felt off. It was as if someone else was in the room even though he was clearly alone.

Kirk pulled the drawers out of the dressers and desk, looked under the furniture and inside the light fixtures, but found nothing. When he looked at a plastered cross beam that ran from one side of the room to the other, presumably to mask the ventilation pipes, he saw an eighteen-inch space between the top of the beam and the ceiling. He pulled the wooden desk from the wall, jumped on top and gazed down the length of the beam. His eyes popped when he saw it: a small listening device the size of a fingernail.

So, it's true. The Iranians are surveilling me.

Kirk didn't know if this was standard government procedure for an American visitor or if he had provoked this. He laid on the bed and stared at the ceiling. Were his newfound Iranian "friends" truly friends or had someone reported him? Farhad was his sole contact. Was he in on it? And who the hell was listening on the other end?

Chapter Sixteen

The Enghelab golf course wasn't much to look at by modern standards. It was the only course in the country with grass, but the landscaping was shoddy, due to lack of maintenance. The rough was especially thick and the greens were as bumpy as broccoli, but it was all Iran had to offer. Aslani couldn't have cared less about that. He truly hated golf and even his own presence on the property. Only the Scottish could invent a game so maddeningly frustrating. Considering Iran's history with the British Empire, the entire property would have been demolished if it were up to him. Thankfully, the military took care of some of that in the mid-1990's when they shortened the course to thirteen holes to make room for parking tanks at the nearby army base.

Regardless, Aslani had no choice but to be there that day. While he despised the game, the Vice Admiral of the navy loved it and when two of his superiors offered to bring him along to play a round with the man next weekend, Aslani knew it would be detrimental to his career to refuse.

The problem was his game stunk. He wasn't worried about his full swings because he could usually hit the ball far off the tee. Given his ability to make it fly straight, he thought that he could make enough of an impression with his superiors on his good shots that the bad ones would be forgotten. His short game, however, was another matter. His approach shots were consistently shy of the greens, no matter what club he used. This meant that he constantly needed to chip or pitch the ball up to the hole, an aspect of the game he struggled to master.

Wearing street clothes, he stood on the chipping green trying to hit his ball close to the hole from twenty-five yards away. But each time, he either hit too far behind the ball resulting in it effectively going nowhere or he hit the ball with the bottom edge of the club and watched it zoom past the hole like a fast putt. Out of thirty balls, he didn't hit one correctly. He was going to be a laughingstock and felt his career flushing away. As his frustration built inside his emotional pressure cooker, he repeatedly slammed the ground with his club head.

"Need some help?" a man said.

Startled, Aslani snapped his head around. He wasn't aware of being watched and he didn't like it.

"Who are you? Why are you watching me?"

"Take it easy, chief. I'm a bit of a golfer, so I walked over."

Aslani inventoried the man up and down. It took a moment before it dawned on him that the person standing in front of him was the American who Farhad was escorting around town.

"What do you want?"

"If you'll let me show you, I think I can help you with your chipping. Do you mind?"

Kirk set down his backpack and reached for the golf club. Aslani glared at him. He wasn't sure if the American was purposely trying to show him up or if he was naively trying to help. Given his miserable situation, he tossed Kirk the club.

Kirk proceeded to show Aslani that he didn't need to flip his hands or swing hard. Instead, he showed him how to slightly lean the club forward and make a putting motion with his arms. The length of the backswing and follow through were always the same, and he recommended using a lower lofted club for longer shots. Kirk handed the club back to Aslani and let him try. Out of the next ten balls, Aslani hit nine of them within three feet of the cup, and the last one went in. Totally dumbfounded, he looked at the American.

Kirk winked.

"Welcome to golf," he said, as he extended a hand to introduce himself.

Since he was not dressed in full uniform, Aslani wasn't about to identify himself as part of the Revolutionary Guard, so he established himself simply as "Azam."

They spoke about some of the sites Kirk claimed that he intended to see during his so-called vacation. Aslani smiled and faked interest for as long as he could before being thankfully interrupted.

"Kirk?"

The voice came from down the street.

"Down here!"

Farhad turned the corner with coffee in his hands and appeared through the gate to see his American friend standing with the brute who had made him wet himself yesterday. He stopped dead in his tracks and instantly felt the blood drain from his face.

"Everything okay?" Kirk asked with a curious look.

"Huh? Oh yes, yes. I didn't know where you went."

"Sorry. I saw the golf course down the street from the hotel, so I decided to take a look while I waited for you. I saw this fine man struggling with his chipping, so I gave him some pointers. He's a quick learner."

Farhad nodded, trying to appear unflustered.

"This is Azam," Kirk said.

He was treating Aslani like some of Farhad's friends from the day before.

"Do you know him?"

Farhad looked stupefied at Aslani, who was slowly and minimally shaking his head. Farhad got the point.

"Uh, no, sorry, I don't. Nice to meet you."

Continuing his phony act of being nice, Aslani decided to try and get some information from the American.

"So, where are you headed today?" he asked.

"I thought about taking a trip to Isfahan, but my in-country guide here is taking me to see the old American Embassy."

Kirk lied like a pro.

"Kirk, I'm afraid we must be going if we want to get to the museum in time for it to open," Farhad said.

"Certainly, go and enjoy yourself," said Aslani.

Kirk picked up his backpack, shook Aslani's hand, and wished him the best of luck for a good round of golf.

"Try not to judge the museum too harshly," Aslani said. "It shows the darker side of Iran. Most Iranians don't feel that way."

As he watched Kirk and Farhad walk away, Aslani displayed a smug smile that was not fake at all. Once they were out of sight, Aslani dropped his club and rushed to his Jeep.

Chapter Seventeen

BASRA, IRAQ

Due to economic sanctions, Iran has been using the drug trade to finance its terrorist activities for years. But the aftermath of the second Gulf War between the U.S. and Saddam Hussein presented a unique opportunity. With the US too busy fighting ISIS, the illegal trade along the southern border of Iraq and Iran had increased by a factor of one hundred. The city of Basra turned into a thriving market for narcotics. Iraqi intelligence services and honest officers did their best to combat both the supply and demand, but they were outnumbered and outgunned by local militias. Iran's firm grip on these areas necessitated that businesses accept only Iranian currency. Unofficially, Iran was slowly invading Iraq by using illegal trade to ooze its way in.

Basra Police Chief Kazeem al-Nashou was not among those accepting bribes and was determined to rid his city of drugs. Two days ago, his trusted informant came to him with information regarding Mustafa Shamekh, a high value target of the Americans. The Syrian born terrorist was responsible for several small pipe bomb attacks across eastern Iraq, but it was his latest actions in the Kurdish city of Sulaymaniyah that landed him on the chief's personal shit list. While Sulaymaniyah had a corrupt local government, it was also relatively tolerant of its westernized tendencies. It was this tolerance that enraged Shamekh, so he initiated a string of suicide bombings during the city's World Music Day celebration. Eighty-five men, women, and children, whose only crime was gathering at a concert hall, lost their lives that day. Shamekh had been on the run ever since.

The chief's informant provided him with strong evidence that Shamekh was headed to his city, and he had a probable location. Al-Nashou immediately called one of his local U.S. military contacts in the area, hoping they would put a drone in the air. The U.S. agreed.

Waiting outside Shamekh's reported location, the chief found his informant's tip to be spot on and discretely followed the terrorist's car from a safe distance. Satisfied that he had his man, it was time to make a call.

***

The Naval Support Activity base in Bahrain was home to the United States Naval Forces Central Command and the U.S. Fifth Fleet. Due to its cornerstone presence for U.S. military activities in the Middle East, the navy embarked on a six hundred-million-dollar project to double the size of the sixty-two-acre facility. Moving the drone station from Umm Al Melh Border Guards Airport in nearby Saudi Arabia to NSA Bahrain was included in the expansion. This was an unprecedented move that didn't please the generals of the Navy or the Air Force, but the Secretary of Defense justified the move because the hellfire missiles were first transported to NSA Bahrain before being trucked over to Saudi Arabia.

The Senate Appropriations Committee saw merging the two facilities as a cost saving initiative and promptly approved the Secretary's request, citing it as an example of government fiscal responsibility in the coming election.

The Secretary's decision to consolidate proved rewarding. Since moving the drone station to Bahrain in 2011, the United States had conducted four hundred seventy-three successful drone strikes across the region, eliminating threats to the homeland with minimal collateral damage. Sometimes, all it takes is a change of scenery.

Sitting in his office at NSA Bahrain was Captain Javier Suarez. Day in and day out, the captain sorted through intelligence provided by CIA and DIA analysts. While these reports were often correct, Suarez had a good nose for which intel did and didn't "fit." He was also a soldier who used to love his time on the ground while serving in Iraq. There, he made many friends and contacts who he still depended on for information in his current position. One of these contacts was Basra Police Chief Kazeem al-Nashou, who had a direct line to the captain's desk.

"Aviation Command, Captain Suarez speaking," the captain said, answering the phone.

"Javier, we have a big opportunity," said the police chief.

"Your man came through?"

"In spades, my friend."

"You have eyes on the target?"

"I'm following him in my car, but it was definitely him I saw coming out of the building. He and his driver are in a blue BMW headed northwest on Alqaed St."

"Excellent. Let me talk to the pilot. Sit tight. I'll get back to you."

Suarez stepped into the Aviation Command Center, which contained ten seventy-inch high definition screens, all projecting images from all drones across the region. He approached Lt. Commander Max Wellman, who was assigned for the day to observation post number nine.

"Whadda we got, Max? The chief said the car is heading northwest. What's in that direction?"

"A whole lot of nothing. Thanks to ISIS, most of the businesses have been cleared out and other buildings have been hit with RPGs."

"Okay, let's talk to the bird."

Suarez picked up a microphoned headset. Wellman connected him to the drone pilot, Petty Officer 1st Class Samantha Bartlett and her co-pilot

Petty Officer 2nd Class Deion Clifton, who were in a soundproof trailer outside.

"RENEGADE1, this is Command, do you copy?"

"Command, this is RENEGADE1, go ahead, sir," Bartlett said.

"Sam, we've got a blue BMW headed towards on Alqaed St. It was last seen leaving the old distribution plant on the corner of Dakeer Rd. Tell me what you see."

After a few seconds, Barlett replied.

"Got it. Sir, heat signatures indicate that there are two individuals in the car."

"What's the damage assessment in the area, Max?"

"Luckily, the car is on the northwest edge of the town. Nothing to its north or immediate west. To the immediate east, there's an old factory. The biggest damage threat is to the immediate south and southwest as this is where the two roads converge. No buildings, but potential civilian casualties driving in their cars."

"The assessment, Max."

"Estimating fifteen to twenty percent casualties outside the target, sir."

Weighing the cost of war was the toughest part of Suarez's job. If the target was confirmed and his team fired the missile, the strike could eliminate dozens of innocent men, women, and children who were going about their daily lives. If he aborted the mission, the innocents would be spared but the target would live to carry out another attack on American soldiers or innocent civilians or both.

"Sir, the car is stopping," Bartlett said, over the comm.

"Max, what's that building they stopped in front of?"

Wellman checked his data.

"It used to be an elementary school, but ISIS didn't like the western influence on the young girls, so they shot the principal. It closed down three months ago."

"Subject exiting the vehicle," Barlett said.

"Pilot, let's have a look at him," Wellman said.

As ordered, Bartlett zoomed in, hoping to catch a positive ID. To everyone's amazement, the man in the backseat stepped out of the vehicle and looked straight up.

"Holy shit, I can't believe he did that," Wellman said.

"Check the ID," Suarez commanded.

The computer ran its facial recognition software against their database. It was a match for Mustafa Shamekh.

"Ninety-one percent, sir."

Suarez crossed his arms and rubbed his chin. In his three years of drone strikes, the intel had never been this good. They knew who the target was, where he was located, and the son of a bitch actually looked directly at them. Something didn't feel right. But he also knew that luck was part of the game and would always take it.

"Sir, the targets have entered the building," Bartlett said.

Suarez snapped out of his daze.

"What's the ID on the other man?"

"Eighty-seven percent that it is Shamekh's right hand man, Abdul Jamil Al-Jayani."

Suarez was familiar with that name, too. He often recruited suicide bombers. Suarez and his team nearly cornered him two years ago but received the intel too late and Al-Jayani was gone.

"Sir, do I have permission to fire?" Bartlett asked.

"Hold fast, pilot," Suarez replied.

"Yes, sir."

Suarez removed his headset, grabbed the hardline phone at the nearest desk, and dialed al-Nashou. The chief picked up on the first ring.

"Kazeem, what's up with that school? Are there any kids there?"

"Not anymore. The building is intact, but kids still go in there from time to time to play football, sorry, soccer."

"So, the school is *not* operational? Not even on weekends?"

"Affirmative."

Suarez stared at the screen, contemplating his decision. There was no time to find an asset on the ground to go into the school to check it out, and he certainly couldn't send the chief in. He had the chance to kill two big-name bad guys at the same time, but his gut gnawed at him. The circumstances seemed too perfect. On the other hand, what would be the cost of him having to tell his superiors that he had the best confirmed intel one could ever hope for in order to make a decision, but didn't do what was necessary based on gut instinct?

"Pilot, report all activity in the surrounding area," Suarez said, via the headset.

Bartlett zoomed out to have a complete aerial view of the building. There was nothing to the back, only cars traveling fifty feet in front of the building, and no one else had entered or left the building.

"No other activity, sir."

"Any other heat signatures in the building?"

"Negative, sir."

"Hold fast, pilot."

Suarez picked the phone back up.

"Kazeem, get out of there. We're pressing forward. I'll call you later."

In Basra, the chief sped away in the opposite direction.

Suarez put his headset back on and gave the pilot his order.

"RENEGADE1, you are a-go. Repeat, you are a-go."

"Copy that, sir."

She looked to her co-pilot.

"Okay, let's run through the checklist."

Clifton grabbed the clipboard and began spouting off the required items while Bartlett verified the status of each time on her dashboard.

"Battery power?"

"Three-quarters."

"Weapons guidance system?"

"Check."

"Targeting system?"

"Check."

"Release system?"

"Check."

"Weapon armed?"

"Check," she said, as she flipped a switch in front of her.

"Damage assessment?"

"Sir, please verify my damage assessment."

"Eighteen percent, pilot," Wellman said.

"Roger that, eighteen percent. Co-pilot, verify my range to target," Bartlett ordered.

"Pilot, your range to target is two-four-eight-one-five feet."

"Sir, the weapon is hot. Awaiting your order."

Suarez took a deep breath.

"Fire."

Bartlett re-gripped the joystick, narrowed her eyes at the screen, and squeezed the trigger.

"Missile away! Missile away! Missile away! Eighty seconds to impact."

All they could do was watch and wait. Like clockwork, precisely eighty seconds later, the building exploded into a fiery cloud of dust. Pieces of the building and chunks of shrapnel flew through the air and dispersed around the area, chaotically but fairly hitting anyone and anything in its away. Two minutes later, the dust settled, and they could see inside the building.

"Pilot, verify that the target was eliminated," came the order from Suarez.

Bartlett focused on the damage but couldn't find the head or body of either target that she saw earlier, entering the building. The bodies she could see in the destruction numbered more than two.

"Sir, I think we have a serious problem."

***

A half mile away, a black Mercedes was parked with the keys in the ignition. Normally, Abdul would've opened the back door for his boss, but time was of the essence. Once he and his boss were securely inside, he raced down the road. He didn't know where he was going on this hot, sunny day and he didn't care, as long as it was far away from here.

A cell phone laid on the back seat with one number preset into it. As soon as he caught his breath, Shamekh picked it up and pressed Send.

"If I am receiving this call, I take it that you made it out," Shirazi said.

Shamekh had met Shirazi during a joint operation between Syrian and Iranian forces against Israel in 1993. Their lives had ended up taking different trajectories, but Shirazi managed to stay in touch and used Shamekh as his go-to guy whenever a dirty deed was required.

"Yes, I survived. The skeleton keys were a nice touch."

"An artist always signs his work," Shirazi boasted.

"I suppose that I owe you?"

"Yes, you do, but I'll collect your debt at a later time. For now, stay out of sight for the next few weeks. I don't want to hear *anything* about *anyone* seeing you *anywhere*. If I hear otherwise, the next bomb will drop on you. Understand?"

"Cleary," Shamekh said.

He didn't take kindly to being threatened.

"Good," Shirazi said.

As he clicked off, Shamekh put the phone back on the seat and exhaled. It had been a close call, his closest yet. From the rear window, he saw a large plume of smoke rising from the ground behind him.

Chapter Eighteen

TEHRAN, IRAN

It was a silent ride to Haddadi's house. Kirk focused. There was no turning back from what he was about to do. Despite his lack of military service, Kirk had killed before. While on duty during the Occupy Wall Street protests in uptown Charlotte, Kirk, his protectee and two other colleagues came under fire while escorting a CEO from the company building to a waiting Lincoln Town Car. Having trained for such a situation, Kirk had no choice but to return fire and kill the female shooter. But that was different. It was self-defense and his job. From this day forward, for however much longer he lived, if he succeeded in killing Haddadi, he would be a murderer. It was a label he'd come to accept, but it took time to get used to.

The picture of Pap sitting around the table with Haddadi and others was folded in his shirt pocket. Kirk double tapped it with his finger as he remembered why he was doing what he was about to do. He knew Pap was an honorable man. No one is perfect. Whatever he did to Haddadi years ago couldn't have been bad enough to be killed over. In Kirk's mind, his retribution was justified, and he was prepared to stand before God for judgment when the time came.

Oddly, he wasn't nervous. He felt relief. The moment he had envisioned for months had finally arrived. The thought of staring down Haddadi was invigorating, to not only having him know who was ending his life but to know that his grandfather would be the one having the last laugh, made Kirk feel triumphant.

Farhad, on the other hand, was a nervous wreck. Sweat formed at the top of his forehead as he sped away from the golf course. He was fidgety and his fingers repeatedly tapped the steering wheel. The tips of his ears were a scarlet color. His blood pressure was in overdrive. Was he getting cold feet? Kirk couldn't have that happen. He needed him calm.

"You okay?" Kirk asked, breaking the silence.

"I can't believe you did that!" Farhad snapped.

"What?"

"You're getting ready to go kill a guy, and I find you wandering around at a golf course?"

Kirk was taken aback by Farhad's unusual hostility.

"Look, you were running late, so I took a walk to help clear my head. I didn't know I was going to run into that guy. What's got you so unglued?"

"It's just that, I never . . . this is a life changing event for me."

Farhad's reply was half-true.

"I get it but settle down."

Farhad nodded.

Forty minutes later, Farhad parked the car down the street from Haddadi's house. He and Kirk remained silent as they studied the front door. Farhad looked at his watch.

"Look, there she is. Right on time," Farhad pointed out.

Kirk watched a pudgy, older woman in her seventies, wearing glasses and a green hijab make her way down the porch steps and into her car.

"Haddadi's wife?"

"Yes. She should be running errands. Normally, she's gone for about an hour, so that's your window. You want me to follow her and text you when she's on her way back?"

"No, stay close by. Matter of fact, pull around back."

Farhad did so while Kirk put on the grey coveralls that were brought for him.

"If this takes an hour, then something went wrong. In that case, you tear ass out of here and run for cover," Kirk said. "Were you able to get it?"

Farhad motioned his head to the glove box as he drove around to the backside of the house. Kirk pulled out the Ruger SP101 9mm revolver and checked it for bullets. He spun the wheel, whipped it back into place, and stuffed it in his waistband.

"Are you sure you don't want to do this at night?" Farhad asked.

"No. I don't want his wife to be there. I want him alone."

"I bought a pair of hedge trimmers at the hardware store this morning," Farhad said, "which is why I was late picking you up. They're on the backseat."

After putting on one of Farhad's black ballcaps displaying the logo of the national soccer team, Kirk pulled the picture of Pap from his shirt pocket and stared at it one more time.

"What's that?" Farhad asked.

"An old picture of my grandfather with Haddadi," Kirk said, flipping the picture around.

An astonished look formed on Farhad's face. He snatched the picture from Kirk.

"Hey!" Kirk barked.

Farhad squinted fixedly at the photo.

"Where did you get this?" Farhad asked.

"It was Pap's old papers. It's what brought me here. What's wrong with you?"

"What was your grandfather's name?"

"Kamran Kabiri, why?"

Farhad shook his head, folded the photo and placed it in his own shirt pocket.

"Nothing. I'll hold on to it for you. A little incentive to come back alive."

Kirk didn't like the idea of not having Pap's photo on him when he killed Haddadi, but Farhad had a point—this was no time to start an argument or to be sentimental.

"Fine, but we go straight to the airport after this, and I want the photo back. You good?"

"I'm good if you're good."

Both looked confident, at least for the moment, and they clasped their hands together in a Hawaiian handshake.

Kirk zipped up his coveralls and checked his surroundings to see if anyone was watching. After giving himself a quick nod in the mirror, he got out, tool in hand and walked casually between the two houses on his way to the Haddadi's back gate, like a guy doing his job.

Visions of Pap flashed in Kirk's head as he opened the gate: his double dimpled smile, the card tricks he could perform for the young kids at the park, how he could never properly remember the words to *Born to Run*. The memories converted to burning rage behind Kirk's eyes. It became the fuel that drove him. The flowery aromas of tulips and jasmine permeated his nose as he made his way through the garden.

Maybe revenge does smell sweet after all.

Thankfully, Haddadi wasn't sitting on the screened-in porch. Kirk came to the latched screen door, which he bypassed by slipping a pen he found in the coveralls through the crack in the door and lifting the hook out of the loop. Once inside, Kirk placed the hedge trimmers on a lounge chair, unzipped his coveralls and pulled the gun from his waistband as he made his way to the main door.

Filled with adrenaline, Kirk twisted the doorknob with maddening strength, unsure if it would be locked. If so, he'd have no choice but to kick down the door and quickly sweep the house, not knowing what could be waiting for him at every turn. Luckily, the door was unlocked. Perhaps Haddadi had been on the porch after all. The cream-colored carpet was grungy and desperately needed to be switched out, but aided him, nonetheless. A creaky wooden floor would have inhibited his ability to be stealthy. Stale air whisked out of the room, but the well-oiled door hinges opened without a peep and Kirk noticed that he was in the dining room. The bare mahogany table was well-polished with six chairs around it. To the right, was a small kitchen that looked like it belonged in an apartment instead of a home. The light was on, but there was no sign of Haddadi.

Gun raised, Kirk crept forward. Straight ahead was the living room. Family pictures hung on the wall, which Kirk ignored. On one side was a desk filled with unopened mail. On the other was an L-shaped couch with a TV hanging above the fireplace. A stink of mothballs filled the humid air, but no one was there.

Kirk turned left, discretely stepping down the hallway and avoiding an ill-placed black console table with fake roses inside a ceramic vase. He scanned the bathroom. Empty. Across the hall was an impressive private office with bookshelves filled from top to bottom. If Kirk didn't have to kill Haddadi, he may have asked him if he could borrow one of his books on Persian military history.

Next was what looked to be a guest room with a pair of twin beds. The window revealed how unkept the room was as curls of dust danced in the sunlight.

The only room remaining was the one at the end of the hall, which could only be the master bedroom. Unless he and Farhad had missed him leave the house earlier, Haddadi had to be in there. Hearing a creak from the floor, Kirk did a sharp one-eighty to ensure that no one was behind him and was relieved to see that was the case. Kirk peered past the door to see an unobstructed floor plan. The armoire was ajar. His wife's oversized vanity mirror and make up counter were front and center. An open closet was to the left. But on the right side of the room, lying in bed asleep, was Haddadi.

Kirk cautiously approached with gun extended, ready to pull the trigger. When he was no more than two feet away, Kirk got a better look at the freckled faced, thin, wrinkly man with an empty bowl of ice cream on his bedside table. He still had most of his hair, but Kirk could tell that he was in his eighties.

Something about him wasn't quite right. The air conditioning was on full blast, but the man was sweating like he had been walking through the desert. His skin complexion was anemic. His breathing was labored. A trash can was at his side next to Kirk's feet, full of what looked like vomit, which explained the putrid, acidic smell in the room.

Am I too late? Is Haddadi already on the verge of dying?

Kirk decided that it didn't matter. Haddadi wasn't going to get the benefit of natural death. He poked the man's head with the barrel of the gun not once but twice before Haddadi awakened. The man's eyes struggled to focus.

"Who . . . who are you?"

Haddadi sounded as groggy as he looked.

Kirk turned on the bedside lamp and tossed the man his wire rimmed glasses.

"Take another look."

Glasses now on, Haddadi sat up on his elbows and inventoried Kirk, but said nothing.

"Still don't know?"

Haddadi shook his head.

"I'm Kamran Kabiri's grandson."

The frail and confused look on Haddadi's face faded to one of shock and anger.

"My men said that they saw you two together. I should've told them to kill both of you when they had the chance and eliminated the coward gene altogether."

His speech was slurred, but the message was clear. Haddadi wasn't even bothering to hide the fact that he had Pap killed.

Kirk back handed Haddadi with his fist.

"He was a lot of things, but my grandfather was no coward!"

Haddadi fell flat to the bed, stunned at being accosted. But as he wiped the blood from his lips, they slowly bent into a depraved grin.

"He never told you, did he?" Haddadi asked.

"I know enough," Kirk said. "I know what kind of man he was. And I know what kind of man you are."

"No, you only *think* you know," Haddadi said.

He quickly went into a coughing spell.

"Enlighten me, old man."

"Did you know that we worked together on the 1953 coup that brought the Shah back to Iran?"

"Yes," Kirk said.

He recalled the paperwork he found in Pap's desk.

"Then you should know that our plan was not to help the CIA. Our plan was to screw them."

"Bullshit."

Haddadi hacked out a laugh.

"I knew that he couldn't have told you. Look in the top drawer of the table next to you. There's a picture on top."

Kirk kept his eyes and gun trained on Haddadi while one hand to open the drawer. He immediately found the picture. It was a yellow tinted, four-by-six, black and white photo with ruffled edges. In the center sat a much younger Ayatollah Khomeini, long before he became Supreme Leader of Iran. Seated on the floor to his left was Haddadi. To his right was a man with a red 'X' marked through his face. Kirk couldn't believe his eyes. He tried to only lower the gun, but the muscles in his hand gave out and it dropped to the floor.

The look of amazement and recognition on Kirk's face aroused Haddadi.

"Yes," the old man said, nodding his head. "Your grandfather and I were once great friends of our dear Supreme Leader. Kamran was also a Twelver of the Shia faith."

"You lie," Kirk said.

"Of course, you must say that. Khomeini may have been a younger man at the time of that photo, but he was always our leader. Together, the three of us molded our philosophies against secularism for years. In many ways, Kamran was more cultivated and passionate on the subject than the Ayatollah himself."

Kirk's stomach dropped as his blood pressure skyrocketed. Haddadi began to sweat even worse, becoming more invigorated as he talked about the past.

"Unfortunately, we never had enough money to accomplish anything," Haddadi continued. "When Khomeini learned that the CIA planned to overthrow Mohammed Mossadegh from his prime minister position, he saw an opportunity. Kamran and I installed ourselves into the CIA plot as on the ground assets and pocketed the money they handed out. We had the CIA agent eating out of our hand. We were going to depose Mossadegh as planned, but rather than reinstall that pathetic Shah, we would kill the CIA agent and his team, allowing Khomeini to come to power and reign Iran."

Kirk was shocked and said nothing.

"But Kamran double crossed us. That's right. Your grandfather was a traitor. He blabbed to the CIA agent, who gave him a large fee for the information. We were arrested and later tortured by the SAVAK. Some of us lived, others didn't. The coup succeeded. Khomeini's reign would have to wait. Because of your grandfather, Iran had to endure the miserable Shah, who lived in opulence for another twenty-six years while the rest of us begged for scraps on the street. Those of us who remained in Khomeini's circle blamed your grandfather. He ran and hid like a cowardly dog, and so are you!"

Haddadi spit at Kirk's face. He was so mesmerized by what Haddadi was telling him that he wasn't paying attention to the man's left-hand inching to the opposite side of the bed. Haddadi turned his body and lunged at Kirk with a nine-inch dagger. Kirk was taken by surprise, but thanks to Haddadi's weakened state, he caught the man's wrist, which stopped him from being stabbed. As he twisted Haddadi's arm backward, the old man cried out in pain. The dagger dropped to the floor, but Haddadi headbutted Kirk in the jaw.

All the anger and hatred that had been simmering below now shot to the surface. The emotion within overtook any sense of logic or morale in Kirk's mind. Without even realizing what he'd done, Kirk punched Haddadi in the nose, swiped up the pillow from underneath his head and smothered the old man's face.

"Die! Please . . . *die!*"

Fueled by visions of his grandfather, Kirk used every ounce of his energy to push the pillow down on the bed. As blood rushed to Kirk's face, the seething hatred he felt made him drool. Haddadi struggled, wiggled, and flailed at Kirk's body, to no avail. The man's motions slowed until there was no more useable air at his disposal and Kirk felt the life drown from underneath the pillow.

Kirk pushed down on the pillow twice more, ensuring that he'd finished the job. When he stood up, he was out of breath. His chest heaved, and he gasped as he swallowed the sour, puke-filled air.

He stared at the now lifeless face of Rasoul Haddadi, his eyes open and mouth agape, but he felt no remorse for his action. But for the first time in his life, Kirk didn't recognize the face he saw in his reflection off the brass bed knob. He wasn't looking at the same man who had entered the room just minutes before.

Having accomplished his mission, Kirk winked at the man looking back at him.

Click.

Kirk's eyes widened at the unmistakable sound of a gun being cocked. His gun.

"Don't move," a voice said from behind him.

The wife?

Had Kirk been so enthralled by Haddadi's story that he missed a text message from Farhad? He raised his hands in the air and slowly turned around. But the person he saw was not Haddadi's chubby wife.

"Azam?"

Chapter Nineteen

Kirk stared at the two guns pointing at him. One was the revolver that Kirk had brought with him and dropped to the floor. The other was Aslani's Browning HP 9mm.

"What is this?" Kirk asked.

"We've been waiting for you," Aslani said.

We?

His eyebrow raised.

"Come again?"

"You can't possibly be stupid enough to think that Kamran Kabiri's grandson could waltz into Iran unnoticed, did you?"

Kirk's stomach dropped. The jig was not only up, but he quickly realized that there had never been one in the first place.

"How'd you get in here?" Kirk asked.

He wondered how he'd missed him when he swept the house.

"I have a key, you moron. Haddadi was a personal friend. You did all the right things on your search, but what you couldn't know was that Haddadi has a hidden room behind his bookcase."

"How'd you beat me here?"

"Your friend Farhad may know every route in the country, but he drives like an old woman—slow and blind."

Farhad?

"How'd you know his name? I didn't introduce you to him at the golf course."

"Shut up," said Aslani. "There's someone who wants to meet you. You will be the guest of *honor* at his home."

A contemptible grin curled at the corner of his mouth.

"Now, move."

Kirk made his way back down the hallway with his hands raised. Whatever was about to happen to him was why his grandfather had been so adamant about him not coming to Iran. He felt that he was as stupid as his grandfather feared he would be.

***

Parked on the street outside, Farhad stared at the photo he'd taken from Kirk, occasionally checking his surroundings for Kirk's return or anything alarming. A million thoughts raced through his head as images from his eyes translated to his brain.

After putting the photo back in his shirt pocket, Farhad reclined his head and was deep in thought when he heard footsteps approaching from behind. His eyes popped when he saw who was holding Kirk held at gunpoint. Aslani shoved Kirk against the side of the car and made him put his hands on the roof before pointing one of the guns at Farhad.

"Out," he instructed.

Farhad did what he was told and stood next to Kirk.

Aslani grinned.

"Thank you, Farhad, for delivering this idiotic American right to me."

"You son-a-bitch! You sold me out!"

Farhad attempted to reply, but Kirk tackled him to the ground.

"I can't believe this! I trusted you!"

Kirk shook Farhad by his collar. He was interrupted when Aslani put the gun to his head.

"Enough!" he said, trying to hide his laughter.

As amusing as it was seeing them squabble like children, they were running late.

"Get up, both of you."

Both men did as instructed but kept their hands raised.

"Farhad, go get my Jeep parked around the corner. You two are going for a ride," Aslani said.

He tossed Farhad the keys. Kirk focused on Aslani's fiendish eyes while Farhad was gone. Not a word was spoken between them. When Farhad pulled up, Aslani sat in the rear with Kirk next to him.

"Where are we going?" Kirk asked.

"Our host insists on giving you one last meal," Aslani said. "So, you better enjoy it."

Chapter Twenty

The drive took about thirty minutes, but Farhad didn't recognize the address. It was a glamourous part of the city he'd never seen on his bootlegging runs. Their destination, a profound high-rise building in the Elahiyeh district, overlooked the city landscape. Whatever impression Kirk had made on whoever Aslani had brought him to see, it was clear that it was someone important. Though he tried not to show it, Farhad was feeling terribly guilt ridden. What was about to happen to Kirk was partially his fault.

Meanwhile, the gears in Kirk's head were grinding and his veins were pumping adrenaline in overdrive. His hands were shaking, the same hands that had just physically killed a man. He'd dreamt about it for months. Revenge was his at last. Perhaps he should've repented because he would ultimately answer for it at his time of judgment, but he didn't. Haddadi had become his mission and that mission was now accomplished.

But his victory was short lived. His thoughts alternated between his concern for what was about to happen and what he would do to Farhad if he managed to get his hands on him alone. It was hard to tell which took priority.

"You have dignified clothes under those coveralls?" Aslani asked Kirk.

Kirk nodded, hoping that his polo shirt and jeans would suffice.

"Good. Take them off."

Aslani put away both his guns but kept a firm grip on his guest's bicep as they walked in the building. It was clear that Kirk wasn't going anywhere. Aslani nodded to the two guards inside the security booth as the three men walked across the jade-colored marble floor of a lavish lobby.

When the elevator dinged on the top floor, Aslani shoved Kirk down the bare white hallway. Upon reaching a lone door, Farhad took the lead and removed his shoes. Despite his current hatred for Farhad, Kirk did likewise to save himself from any further bullying.

The three men were let into the apartment by a male servant dressed in a black and white suit with a gold vest. Kirk was confused. The last thing he expected was an indoor tailgate party for a televised soccer game. He was hit by strong, amazing aromas coming from the kitchen. Positioned around the room between a flat screen TV in the living room and the adjacent dining room of the open floor plan, were two bulky and imposing soldiers, dressed in their combat uniforms, minus their boots, and three skinny women in vivacious red and green chadors.

"Come, join the party," Aslani said.

As Kirk moved in a state of bewilderment, Rahim Shirazi approached him. Farhad recognized him but had never seen him in person.

For someone of his rank, Shirazi was shorter than one would expect, less than six feet. But what he lacked in height, he more than made up for in confidence and authority. His greying beard was thick, but tidy as was his perfectly combed, shiny hair that was peppered with a hint of black. There was a steeliness about him and with a strong build, he walked as if he were bulletproof. His only blemish was a slight receding hairline. But it was Shirazi's fierce yet frosty eyes that grabbed Kirk's attention. The man rarely blinked. It was as if he was trying to gaze through someone during a conversation. Any eye contact with Shirazi conveyed a gathering storm within the man's soul that could break out at any time. Within moments of meeting the general, anyone knew who was in charge of the room and the conversation.

"General," Aslani started, "this is Farhad. I'm sure you remember me talking about him."

Aslani placed his hand on Farhad's shoulder.

"Farhad, this is the esteemed General Rahim Shirazi."

General?

Kirk mumbled to himself.

"Ah, yes, Farhad. Thank you for your assistance," said Shirazi. "Azam tells me that he has big plans for you. Keep up the good work."

Farhad returned the handshake with a wide smile but said nothing. Kirk gritted his teeth so hard at Farhad's betrayal that he was sure his gums would start to bleed.

"And this is the American we've been waiting for," Aslani continued, showing off Kirk like a game show prize.

Shirazi catalogued Kirk but didn't utter a syllable, which was awkward for everyone but him.

"Uh, it's a pleasure to meet you," Kirk hesitantly said.

He extended his hand. His comment sounded more like a question than a statement.

Shirazi finally spoke.

"Haddadi gave me a very storied history of your family's legacy in Iran. It's good of you to join us," he said.

He had an unyielding handshake and a gruff voice.

"I wasn't given much of choice," Kirk said. "Why am I here?"

"We'll get to that. In the meantime, have a look around and enjoy the food. You'll need it."

Shirazi rudely but purposely pushed past Kirk. Aslani followed but not before giving Kirk another cavalier grin. Kirk noticed Farhad's leg's trembling.

"What did he mean by that?" Kirk asked.

"You better eat up," Farhad replied.

Kirk wandered away and observed several vibrant oil paintings on canvas hung from the walls, depicting iridescent Arabian horses racing through the delicate sand dunes under the harsh desert's tangerine sun and crisp neon moonlight. Kirk noted that they must have been painted by Shirazi himself as each one was signed with the initials 'RS' in Farsi.

He studied the variety of color photos on the bookshelves. In all of them, Shirazi posed in his military uniform. In some, he held weapons with a backdrop of an Iranian flag and others with various military colleagues out in the field. But it was the last picture that injected intense fear into Kirk's veins. It showed three men sitting on the floor of a bare room. Shirazi was on the left, apparently in the middle of a conversation when the picture was snapped. On the right, the president of Iran smiled at what he was hearing. And, in the middle, was the Supreme Leader of Iran himself with a blank but stoic look on his face, absorbing the information he was receiving.

"Impressive, isn't it?" Aslani said.

Kirk's shoulders jumped, unaware of Aslani's presence.

"Huh? Oh, uh, yes, very," Kirk said anxiously. "What exactly is Shirazi the general of?"

Aslani smirked.

"Farhad didn't tell you?"

"Tell me what?"

"All of us are Revolutionary Guardsmen. Karim and Bijan," he said pointing to the other two men in the room, "are sergeants. I am their captain. Rahim is the major general in charge."

Aslani sensed the fear emitting from Kirk's body.

"And I suggest you start addressing us by our titles."

Chapter Twenty-One

Shirazi's wife served an array of Iranian delicacies, including two platters of barberry rice and tahdig, which was cooked with lots of butter, and the naturally sour red barberries had been dried then rehydrated to dilute some of the sourness. The tahdig was the crisp and golden-brown rice found at the bottom of a pot, which tasted like popcorn or potato chips, depending on one's taste buds, but it was the key to holding the flavor using basmati rice instead of brown rice.

The main course was a kebab of lamb testicles, a signal not lost on Kirk. However, when basted in butter and saffron, minced with onions, plus salt and pepper, its deliciousness made it easy to forget what part of animal anatomy was being consumed.

Finally, what came with every traditional Iranian meal, was an herb and cheese plate. Fluffy naan bread was torn off and dipped into a bowl of feta cheese, mixed with basil and cilantro. Westerners would usually treat the dish as an appetizer, but Iranians eat it in between bites of other foods.

Having spent a fair amount of time in foodie towns of America's southeast, Kirk was impressed with the spread. If this was to be his last homemade meal, his hosts were certainly making an odd effort to ensure that he wouldn't die hungry.

The seating arrangements made it clear where the battle lines were drawn, per se. Shirazi sat at the head of the table with Aslani and a lieutenant called Mahmoud, to his right. To his left, sat Kirk, Farhad and another lieutenant, named Bijan. The wives sat at the end of the table. Behind them was a series of glass windows with a remarkable high rise view above the city.

As they began eating, the general toyed with Kirk about how the American was liking his country, emphasis on it being *his*.

"Everyone has been gracious to me," Kirk said.

He wanted to add *until I was brought here at gunpoint*, but he held his tongue.

The general noticed that Kirk had barely touched his food.

"You're not eating," he said.

Kirk stared at his plate.

"I don't seem to have much of an appetite right now."

Shirazi exchanged glances with Aslani, who made no effort to hide his menacing smirk. The general leaned over and whispered to Kirk.

"My wife has prepared a fine meal in your honor," he said, "Surely you don't want to disrespect me in my own home. Do you?"

"No, General."

"Then I suggest you eat."

Kirk was momentarily saved by the game on TV when the Iranian national team scored their second goal of the game against Argentina. Everyone else at the table, including Farhad, shouted and banged their fists in excitement. Kirk stayed silent. The general reminded him of a mafia hitman who would hug you before pulling the trigger.

When the excitement died down, Shirazi continued to trifle with Kirk.

"Azam tells me that you helped him at the golf course. Thank you for that. Your lesson will help us in our tournament next week. I take it that you are a golf fan. Do you think that Tiger Woods will ever break Jack Nicklaus's record of winning eighteen majors?"

Kirk had heard enough of the man's bullshit.

"Never doubt a champion," he said. "But is that why you brought me here? To talk golf?"

Shirazi wiped his mouth with a white linen napkin and glanced at Kirk.

"Of course not," he said. "If you insist on pressing the issue, this is a bit of a celebration."

"Celebration?"

"A dual celebration actually."

"Do tell," Kirk said.

This time it was Shirazi's turn to show off a depraved grin.

"You see, my friend Haddadi had been looking for your grandfather for a long time. But while Kamran was hiding like a spineless coward, Haddadi and his team hunted around the globe for the rest of the Iranian traitors involved in the CIA's 1953 coup. Before your grandfather, the last man was eliminated in 1997. For over twenty years, we were unsuccessful in locating Kamran Kabiri's whereabouts. That is, until a few months ago, when we put him down like the dog he was."

"You son a bitch," Kirk said.

Aslani abruptly shoved back his chair and took a step toward Kirk to discipline him for his comment to the general. Shirazi sharply held up his hand, signaling Aslani to stand down.

"I also wanted to say thank you," Shirazi said.

Kirk's temperature suddenly dipped.

"Thank me?"

"Yes. Haddadi was my mentor. From him, I learned everything I needed to know about being an excellent soldier and leader. Even in retirement, he wielded a considerable amount of influence with our current Supreme Leader. He was a devoted advisor to Ayatollah Khomeini, if you recall. Unfortunately, we had a falling out. I wanted to be appointed to the Guardian Council. In fact, I have more than earned it. Alas, he insisted that I wasn't ready and kept blocking my appointment by the Supreme Leader. Thanks to you, he's gone, and *no one* will stand in my way of getting on the Council. So, thank you," he said.

"If you wanted him dead, you should've done it yourself. What did you need me for?"

The soldiers at the table laughed along with Shirazi.

"You really don't understand politics, do you?" Shirazi said. "Haddadi was under the Supreme Leader's protection. It was delegated to me, actually. The man couldn't be touched. Thanks to Haddadi's thoroughness, he had your name added to our immigration database after he had Kamran killed. When our Pakistani friends at the Iranian affairs desk notified us of your desire to visit, I fast tracked your visa approval and kept a watchful eye on the plane manifests. It didn't take a first-class detective to figure out your plan. All I had to do was ensure that the old man would be home. You saw an empty bowl of ice cream at his bedside, didn't you?"

"Yeah, so?"

"Over the last few days, I had Azam poison it with anti-freeze. The old man had a sweet tooth and never noticed. It easily incapacitated him. You did the rest of the work for us."

Aslani stole a glance at Bijan, which did not go unnoticed by Kirk.

"After our man dropped the sodium hydroxide into that pathetic traitor's bottled drink, we planted a note among his papers and forged his name," said the general. "I believe part of it said, 'For the sake of what was once a solid friendship, please let your quest for retribution end with me.' But I'll let you in on a little secret. The note was my idea. Haddadi wanted to kill you both. I talked him out of it. Again, thank you."

The penny dropped and so did Kirk's jaw as he recalled the final moments of his grandfather's life. He suddenly realized that Pap wasn't trying to get to the lock box to show the letter to him. He was trying to rip it up.

119

Kirk's mind replayed the moment of Pap's last words.

Rasoul Haddadi. Iran. You too.

It wasn't what he said but how he'd said it. The 'I' in Iran was pronounced like 'igloo' but Pap had pronounced it like 'iceberg.' Kirk discarded the oversight as the panic of a dying man, but the realization of what Pap was actually trying to say suddenly hit him.

Rasoul Haddadi. Iran. You too.

He wasn't saying that Kirk needed to go to Iran and kill Haddadi before the man had the chance to do the same thing to him. He was saying that he had run away from Rasoul Haddadi before and that Kirk should, too.

He had been set up all along by people he'd never met, but who obviously knew him better than he knew himself. Kirk flashed back to those words again.

Never, ever go to Iran.

"I still won," Kirk said, trying to contain himself. "I killed Haddadi—under your protection. How do you think the Supreme Leader will like that?"

"A minor infraction once I gift wrap you to him, personally. I think he'll be more interested in your family's history of betrayal and find your motive for revenge fascinating. He'll especially like knowing that an American descendant of a homegrown CIA resource is meddling in Iran's affairs. So, please enjoy your meal . . . before he *cuts your fucking head off!*"

Kirk had no time to react. Shirazi moved so fast and with such ferocity that when he walloped him across the jaw, Kirk fell over before it all had a chance to register. The soldiers laughed. No one came to Kirk's aid. Shirazi calmly sat back and finished eating.

Moments later, the cell phone of every soldier at the table came alive with text messages. The broadcast of the soccer game was interrupted by a breaking news bulletin. The state-run news channel ran a story about a United States led drone strike that blew up a school of Shiite children in Iraq. Images of the destruction revealed the bodies of several young children. Each of the newscasters went into a tirade of anti-American rhetoric about how Islam was once again the victim of America's tyranny.

"Do you see what your country does?" Aslani said. "This is what happens to us every day because of America. You kill our children and then dare to call us terrorists!"

While the broadcast was on a break, the station didn't run a standard advertisement for a household product. Instead, it played a regime produced short film showing the American military blatantly attacking Iran. When a missile hit a mosque, its Iranian flag went flying into the air. One Iranian citizen ran to catch the flag from falling to the ground while other villagers joined him, each carrying their own Iranian flag, their weapon of choice. Music and singing commenced. Surprisingly, there were English subtitles.

I own my own armor.
I'm wary of you, as if you were a mine.
If you dare defy me on either land or sea that belong to me,
I will break your legs![*]

As the next missile launched from an aircraft carrier in the gulf, the villagers charged the shore, flags in hand. When they dramatically staked their flags into the water, the symbolism was clear that the love for their country created a tsunami that destroyed the American battle-

---

[*] This commercial from Iranian state-run TV is real.

ships. The final images were of dead American soldiers, an overturned aircraft carrier, and a burning American flag, floating in the water. It concluded with a message:

Stand proud, until the last drop of blood.

Shirazi walked over to the dining room window.

"Come here," he said.

Aslani grabbed Kirk by the arm and yanked him towards the general.

"Do you see that?"

He pointed down to a building.

"The mosque?"

"Yes. That's the Imamzadeh Saleh mosque. It's one of the most popular shrines in northern Iran and the burial site to the son of the seventh of the twelve Imams. Have you heard of the Twelfth Imam?"

"I have."

"Good. Then you know that he is alive and will return to exact the rightful governance of Islam over the earth, including your putrid America."

Shirazi studied Kirk. It didn't matter that the American was a full five inches taller than him. He fixed a laser-like stare at him.

"Your country will pay for this act of cowardice, and you *will* answer for the cowardice of your bloodline. But first, I want you to witness us hasten the welcomed return of the Twelfth Imam by returning the Persian Empire to its glory."

He paused to ensure that his words registered with the American and signaled Aslani.

"Now, get this filth out of my house."

Chapter Twenty-Two

WASHINGTON, D.C.

Senator Walsh had barely eaten all day, but she wasn't hungry. She'd cancelled her afternoon appointments in the Capital building and was laying on her office couch, wearing yesterday's blue blouse and black pantsuit, as she held an ice pack on her head. She had spent her entire time since the trip to Cairo attempting to cash in every chip of political capital in her arsenal to remedy her situation with the Iranians—to no avail. Now, she had a splitting migraine and all she could do was try to rest and reset.

She tried bullying other members of Congress, threatened to out some of their sacred secrets, getting her supporters with deep pockets to try and bribe them, and even slept with two generals at the Pentagon, one of whom was on the Joint Chiefs of Staff, but none of it changed her circumstances. Getting the American military to pull out of the base in Bahrain was impossible. There was no way the country would give up its best strategic advantage in the most unstable region of the world, where such things were difficult to come by.

After a lifetime in Congress, it became more and more likely that her career was over. The power she had accrued seemed gone overnight. She would be investigated, labeled a spy, persecuted at the public level (at the least) and possibly prosecuted in court for treason—all because her mother slept with a man she'd never known or even met.

Walsh's office door burst open.

"Senator, I'm sorry, but you need to see this."

Her chief-of-staff, Latrina Pearl had just marched into the office and seemed frantic.

Walsh groaned, exhausted and in pain.

"What?"

Pearl switched on MSNBC. A breaking news logo flashed on the screen and the scroll said, "U.S. Drone Strike Kills School of Children."

Walsh removed the ice pack from her head and sat upright.

"What the hell?"

"I don't know, but this doesn't look good," Pearl said.

Walsh put her face into her hands. This was the last thing that she wanted to deal with, especially in her circumstances. Her lack of record in the armed forces would be scrutinized, her chairmanship of the committee would be questioned, and the military would have to endure another scandal as *they* were put on trial.

An idea popped into her head, and she sprang up from the couch.

"Latrina, which base was the drone launched from?"

"Can't say for sure, but I'll confirm it for you. Looking at the map, I'm betting it was from NSA Bahrain."

Bingo. Santa had come early this year.

"Do me a favor. Grab the iPad from my desk. How many strikes have been conducted since we moved the drone operations from Saudi Arabia to Bahrain?"

Pearl retrieved the device and provided the information to the Senator.

"And what is the average collateral damage on each of the strikes?" Walsh asked.

While Pearl scrolled through the data, Walsh kept her eyes glued to the news. The aerial footage showed the destruction from the blast and ghoulish images of the young children in the wreckage. This type of media coverage was liquid gold, and she was going to cash in.

"Less than twenty percent. The brass down there is doing a pretty good job of keeping the figures to a minimum. That won't matter now, though."

"Any digital stills of the deceased caught up in the wreckage?"

"Yeah, but your files only go back six months."

"Call that friend of yours at the Pentagon. Pull every damn file from every drone strike launched from that base since its expansion and bring back as much photographic evidence of the collateral damage as you can."

"Why? What are you thinking?"

"Trina, please, just do it! And don't come back without the photos."

"Yes, ma'am," Pearl said.

She put the iPad on the Senator's desk, took her instructions in stride, and left the room.

For the next half hour, Walsh restlessly paced around the room, biting her bottom lip, as she watched the news and got lost in her thoughts. Her mind raced. She didn't know what she was looking at, but for the first time since Cairo, she could see the puzzle pieces on the table. Eventually, a solution would come, and she'd see the whole picture. She needed to make sure that the story wouldn't burn out. For her plan to work, there was no quick fix. She had to play the long game. It needed to be a slow flame that gradually turned into a blazing inferno that raged and spread like a plague, garnering so much attention that the people in power would have no choice but to stand with her and deal with it.

Walsh grabbed her phone, a sinister grin on her face. Before unlocking it, she saw a text message waiting for her from an unknown number.

Your turn, Senator.

Amusing.

She opened her Twitter app, copied the link on the news feed about the drone strike, and tapped away at her phone.

UNACCEPTABLE! THIS ROGUE BEHAVIOR WILL NOT BE TOLERATED!

She closed her post with the slogan that would soon go viral. *#closethebase*

Chapter Twenty-Three

TEHRAN, IRAN

After his men left with Kirk and Farhad, Shirazi settled into his private office, which he loved. It was one of the few sanctuaries available to him where he could strategize or relax without being bothered. Two years earlier, he'd soundproofed the room in case anyone dared to listen in, including his nosy wife. Shirazi leaned back in his leather chair and stared at the large, framed map on the wall, depicting the Persian Empire at the height of its sixth century control.

In due time.

He looked at his Rolex watch and decided that it was time to make the call to Moscow. The recipient answered on the first ring.

"Is the package ready?" asked Russian President Maxim Petrov. He sounded annoyed.

"It is. Make sure that your men are on time tomorrow."

"They'll be there," Petrov said.

"When do I get *my* package?" Shirazi asked.

"It's already in Tehran. Once I receive word that the exchange is complete, I'll have an embassy messenger bring it over."

"Where?"

"Our delicate little location. Make sure that you are there, personally."

Now it was Shirazi's turn to be annoyed. But this was the game. Petrov was referring to the Glass and Ceramic Museum two blocks from the Russian embassy. Their people had met there many times before and were able to hide flash drives containing secret documents among the ceramic souvenirs. Shirazi preferred a dead drop, but given the sensitivity of the software he was receiving, he understood the Russian's desire to do it in person.

"We're going to do beautiful things, my friend," Shirazi said.

"Indeed, but let's not get ahead of ourselves."

The Russian's patience was starting to weigh on Shirazi. He hated the way Russians played political chess, executing their moves by seeing them six moves ahead. Shirazi was more of a checkers player and wanted to double jump his opponent before they knew what hit them and then be kinged.

"Agreed," Shirazi said.

***

Petrov stood up from his desk and watched the snow falling as he visualized how the events would play out over the next weeks. With luck, Russia would have the commanding military advantage in the Middle East within a year, tops. It was an aggressive timeline, but when motivated, politicians in Washington could accomplish anything.

From the TV above his crackling fireplace, CNN displayed a screenshot of a tweet sent by Senator Vivian Walsh. A smile formed on his face. He looked at the cedar timber burning. It was time to throw on another log.

Chapter Twenty-Four

QOM, IRAN

The next morning, Tom Delang was asleep on the floor of his cell when the metal door squealed open. He'd been having a string of so-called good days where he wasn't subjected to physical torture, only the degrading psychological type.

While sore and sensitive, the broken bones in his fingers and hands had mended. He knew that a couple of his ribs were still cracked because he could feel the bones grind together when he moved, but they too were healing. From what he could tell from his reflection in the aluminum bucket that was his toilet, the swelling on his torso and face had gone down. The bruises had faded from purple to a hazy yellow. He'd barely eaten since the ghost pepper incident. His jaw was swollen, and the thought of eating sent nightmarish shivers down his spine.

He knew that his current state of recuperation was temporary. His captors would return and the beatings, too. The only way to get through it all was to think of it as radical fraternity hazing. He began to understand how prisoners in confinement can rationalize anything.

The solitude was its own form of punishment, though. Not only did he have to endure the experience of patiently waiting for his body to heal; the beatings were his only form of human contact. In a way, he looked forward to them. By staying vigilant in repeatedly telling his captors to go fuck themselves, he could keep his wits about him. They could break or extract as many teeth with pliers or slice off as many fingernails with dull pocketknives as they wanted. They could even poison the well of hope in his soul, but they would never overtake his intellect. Whenever it was that death would finally come for him, he would die with his mind intact.

But the long periods of isolation threatened to deprive him of that when the demons of depression visited. Besides not being able to escape, his most troubling issue was with the thorough torture sessions. They were lengthy and he had passed out several times, if he recalled correctly. The most painful incidents were often followed by prolonged sleep deprivation, which the CIA learned in the days after 9/11 were most effective in squeezing terrorists for information. Even Navy Seals broke after they reached a seventy-two-hour threshold.

Delang scrolled through the Rolodex of his mind to take note of all the sources he had given up under duress, but there were many blank spots in his memory. His source in Mossad, Eli Sahar—did he say anything about him? Eli's wife had just given birth to a new baby girl when Delang was snatched. What about the military intelligence officer in Egypt, Omar Mohsen? Omar had been critical in giving him a head's up when protests called on then-president Hosni Mubarak to step down. Delang had promised Omar's wife that he would protect him. And then there was Pakistani ISI agent, Yousuf Bashir. Besides Tariq, Delang had known him the longest.

Tariq. Delang tried not to weep. Somewhere along the way, Delang had been careless in avoiding detection. It was his fault that Tariq was killed. He missed talking to his friend.

As two goons came into his cell, Delang's first thought was that his string of "good days" was coming to an end. He prepared himself as best he could, but his body had become so withered that any effort would make little difference. Prior to his capture, he remembered weighing one hundred and eighty-five pounds. Now, he was probably a buck forty. All that he could do was hope that he survived to see another day.

Rather than lift him up and drag him to the interrogation room and strap him to the chair, which he had come to know as the only constant in his life, one of the gorillas brought an aluminum chair into his cell and tied down his arms. It was useless for Delang to resist. He guessed that today was waterboarding day, but he was wrong. Facing the door of his cell, Delang's jailers surprised him by rolling over a flat screen TV. It was too much to hope that they would let him watch *Seinfeld* reruns.

As his eyes tried to focus, the first thing he saw was the state-run news channel broadcasting a story about a U.S. drone strike killing children at a school in Basra. Considering the news source, he figured that the story was bullshit, but if true, he was about to become the object of "affection" for some very pissed off Muslims. There was a strong possibility that they would finally beat him to death on this very day.

He saw the date on the bottom of the screen. It was October. He had been in captivity over a year, but it felt like five. He had two choices: he could either let the timeline make him depressed or analyze the situation for what it was.

Fortunately, the training chiseled into his brain kicked in. If they had wanted to kill him, they would've done it already. They'd questioned him during hot days and cold nights, sometimes all day. Critics say that people will blurt out anything to make the pain stop and that was true, but all information provided was always checked and rechecked. Bad info meant that the treatment resumed. Ultimately, the only way to help oneself was to talk. He'd done his best to withstand the sessions and not to betray his country, but everyone has their breaking point when it comes to torture. No one is immune. Delang hoped that his weakness hadn't cost any of his colleagues their lives.

He absorbed the footage for useful information, but his vision was blurry and what he could see wasn't worthwhile.

"This is what your country does. It's a machine of murder," Aslani said.

He grabbed Delang by the back of his lice-infested hair and pushed his head forward.

"*Look!* Your country spins its web of lies, telling the world that they are good and then they spill the blood of our children!"

Aslani smacked him in the face. It stung, but all-in-all, Delang had encountered much worse.

"If you say so," he said.

This angered Aslani. He lit a cigarette and blew the smoke directly into the prisoner's face. Naturally, Delang coughed, but it was nothing compared to what happened next. It was then that he saw the Revolutionary Guard patch on the man's uniform. No other jailers had such identifying marks. It didn't confirm for him that he was in Iran, but at least it was clear now who was holding him.

Aslani took a long drag of the cigarette, ensuring that the cherry was large and defined, and twisted it out on top of Delang's left hand. He screamed in agony and smelled the burning flesh as the hot ash pressed into his skin.

Aslani bent down and spoke into Delang's face.

"This is a fraction of what those children felt when your country murdered them. And now, every time you look at your hand, the scar will remind you of them."

Delang groaned in pain but managed to thrust forward and head-butted Aslani above the eyebrow. It was the first victory versus his captors; his first in anything in more than a year.

Aslani fell backward and touched the spot on his brow where he'd been hit. When he saw blood on his hand, it lit a fuse. He tackled Delang onto the floor. The back of Delang's head banged against the cobble-stone, but he had no time to process the pain because the man on top of him had a ruthless grip on his throat and glared at him with raging, red-rimmed eyes.

"You'll pay for that! Your entire country will pay!"

Aslani spat in his face each time he popped his P's.

Due to the lack of oxygen, Delang's eye rolled back into his skull as the room started to go dark. Unexpectedly, his adversary let go and Delang gasped for air, but the relief was short-lived when Aslani stomped on his stomach.

As he stood over his prey, his adrenaline was pumping, and he tried to calm himself. The general had given him specific orders not to kill the American.

"Consider yourself lucky that our friends want you alive. Otherwise, I would skin you myself!"

"You've got friends?" Delang asked.

He laughed as he continued coughing.

Aslani responded by cutting off Delang's air supply, only this time he put his boot on the American's throat.

"Save your energy, you pig. You'll soon witness the power of our country's spirit as we demonstrate to the world America's two-faced cowardice. Rest assured that no one knows where you are, they don't know where you are going, and no one is coming for you. You'll die alone as the traitor you are."

He released his foot and glared down at Delang before deciding to give the repulsive agent one final parting gift. Aslani squatted next to him and whispered into his ear.

"Before you leave, I want you to remember that everything you worked for was for nothing. Your reputation will be tarnished, your friends will be dead, and your country will lose its control of the world. And before you die, I want you to know that we set up the drone strike."

Aslani reached into his back pocket and grabbed a pair of pruning shears that he brought with him to use on one of the other prisoners. After unlocking the spring with a flick of his thumb, he clipped off the top of Delang's left ear before calmly walking away.

Delang screamed in pain and didn't see Aslani leave, but he heard the clang of the door shutting though the sliding window left open. Fighting intense pain, he replayed the images from the TV, showing the Supreme Leader of Iran leading a "Death to America" chant. Whatever was going on, the long simmering cold war between America and Iran was heating up, and he was smack-dab in the middle of it.

***

Outside the cell door, over the sound of Delang's agonizing howls, Aslani spoke to Bijan, who had been waiting outside.

"Give him back his clothes and get him ready to go. The Russians should be here soon. Oh, and keep his door window open. I want the other one to hear his screams."

Chapter Twenty-Five

OUTSIDE QOM, IRAN

Vasily Plaskin and Nikolai Rozovsky were young but experienced agents with the Russian FSB. Vasily was a beast of a man, broad but not fat, with thick, red hair and a full beard. Nikolai was a smidge taller with a wiry frame, a baby face and a blonde buzz cut. Riding in back was their team leader, Luka Volkov. Unlike his junior agents, Volkov was totally bald and sported a fluffy mustache. Due to an underbite, he didn't like to talk, but when he did, it exposed discolored teeth from years of drinking coffee and chain-smoking cigarettes.

The trio had recently extracted a fellow FSB agent from a dire situation in Turkey. The mission didn't go exactly as planned, but they successfully got their man, didn't get killed, and returned safely to Moscow. In the spy world, that was a win. Everything else was details.

Each extraction mission was different, so any intelligence agent would be hard pressed to be called an expert, but their successful achievement in Turkey was their fourth in a row. Heralded for those efforts, their fellow agents awarded them the nickname "Red Tide." When the director of the FSB personally selected them for the handoff of a captured CIA agent from Iran, their egos grew. Their instructions were clear, though. Under no circumstances was the package to be harmed. Gunfights, car crashes, even flying camels were all acceptable factors, as long as the package arrived unscathed in Moscow.

It would require some careful execution on their part, but given the Russian's relationship with the Iranian Revolutionary Guard, they expected the handoff and exit from the country to be smooth. That is, if they could ever get to the handoff location.

The people of the holy city of Qom had an unwavering and unyield-ing allegiance to the Shi'a faith. A hotbed of organized fanaticism, it was home to thousands of clerics and some members of the Guardian Coun-cil, Iran's version of the Supreme Court, which interprets both Islamic law and Iran's constitution in their own extreme way.

At its heart is the Fatima Masumeh Shrine, where twenty million people per year make the pilgrimage to pay homage to the remains of the daughters of both the seventh and ninth Twelve Imams. On an average day, the shrine saw fifty thousand visitors.

The three Russians left their stash house at a time that should have allowed them to arrive at the prearranged meeting place early to perform a final scout of the location. But thanks to the news coverage of the American-led drone strike at the school, the shrine became the site of massive protests all over the city. In the center of the shrine's courtyard, cleric Imam Aymen Shanin stood on a stage, leading the charge of anti-American rhetoric and energizing the mob. His rants were magnified by the courtyard's audio system that carried the words into the middle of traffic.

That's where the Russians were jammed. Their situation was made more annoying by a young lady with blue strands of hair in a white Suzuki Sidekick who was honking and yelling at them in Farsi to get out of the way.

After flipping her the bird and letting her pass, Vasily focused on the cleric. Shanin was wearing an olive-colored cloak over a white robe. He was in his mid-fifties, short and tubby, with a long, stringy, grey beard. He'd lost his right eye as a child soldier in the Iran-Iraq War. The fact that he survived fueled his reputation as being personally spared by Allah.

To his right were two Revolutionary Guardsmen. In front of them was a young mother and her sixteen-year-old son. Both were crying and looked scared shitless. According to the cleric, the boy's father, a soldier for the Basij, had found pornography in his room. It was actually just a *Victoria's Secret* catalogue, something not easy to come by in Iran. Like many prohibited items in Iran, pornography was tolerated behind closed doors. But the boy had taken photos of the magazine with his phone and uploaded them to his friends via the Telegram app. His friends shared the pics with their friends and so on. One of the boys in the chain convinced his girlfriend to pose for some risqué photos that in America would be considered PG-13, but the girl's parents found the photos on her phone. The investigative trail led back to the boy who first sent the photos. Since the husband was working when the pictures were sent, it happened under the nose of the boy's mother. They were convicted of producing and distributing pornography as well as using the materials to solicit sex, both capital crimes.

The trial and judgment took place weeks ago, but the drone strike fueled the hatred of the city's ultra-religious zealots, and they used the case as an example of how America spreads its immorality like a plague to corrupt the Muslim world. They wanted to make an example to demonstrate the consequences of violating Sharia law.

"America spreads its lies and evil across our lands, infecting our children!" Shanin said.

The crowd chanted loudly in between his shouting.

"Death to America! Death to America!"

"The disease has spread to our country, my brothers and sisters, to this woman and her son," he said, pointing at them. "We will not tolerate this! Today, we proclaim that America is the carrier of this immoral virus, and that Islam is the cure!"

"Death to America! Death to America!"

The cleric nodded at the two Revolutionary Guardsmen who placed nooses around the mother and son's necks, followed by a stiff jerk to tighten them. As the guards counted down from three, the mother and son looked at each other one last time before the crane operator raised their bodies in the air. When the rope was stretched to its capacity, the mother and son kicked and struggled for air that wouldn't come until each of them expired. All that remained were two swinging corpses, staring back at the crowd, tongues hanging out above a pile of defecation.

Rozovsky and Plaskin cringed at the sight of it.

"You think they'll still be there?" Rozovsky asked to Volkov from the driver's seat.

Volkov grunted.

"They better be," Plaskin said. "I can't wait to get out of this miserable country."

Chapter Twenty-Six

QOM, IRAN

It was evening when Kirk reached the prison. A hood had been placed over his head upon leaving the general's house and his captors took his phone. When he finally arrived at whatever gothic prison he was located, he was taken down a staircase and shoved into a barbaric cell that was deafening in silence and rich in darkness with just a small crevice of moonlight appearing through near the ceiling to guide him. They even took his shoes so he could feel the discomfort of a frigid floor with raised cobblestones.

Bastards.

With only a foam mat to comfort him, Kirk sat with his head against the stone wall to contemplate all the ways he had been so stupid to come to Iran. He always knew there was a chance of getting caught, but not like this. The last thing he ever expected was for the whole trip to be part of a diabolical general's master plan. His entire life, he had been warned.

Never, ever go to Iran.

The words played over and over in his head until his mind finally slowed, and he went to sleep, never wanting to wake up.

The next morning, he awoke to screams from another man down the hall. Kirk tried to see what was going on through the sliding window at his door, but the hallway was too dark. He trembled with fear.

Moments later, the man he recognized as Karim from the general's house was power walking down the hallway toward his cell with a malicious scowl on his furry face. Seeing him standing at the door, Karim locked eyes with Kirk.

"Move back!" Karim commanded.

Before Kirk had a chance to charge the door and make a run for it, he was pinched by two electric prongs from a ten thousand-volt taser.

The next sensation Kirk felt was ice cold water being thrown in his face. Shaking off the water and the cold, he noticed that his wrists were pinned down to the arms of a metal chair by leather restraints, which he tried to pull away from, to no avail. Raising his head, he saw that he was in a circular room that would make Hannibal Lecter proud. If the weapons on the wall were any indication of what he was in for, his stay in Iran was about to become either quite lengthy or terribly abbreviated. The bloody whip on the table, which stunk to high heaven, wasn't lost on him either. All speculation was pushed to the back of his mind when he saw Karim, Bijan, Azam, and Farhad standing in front of him.

"You!"

He screamed at Farhad.

"When I get out of here, I swear to God, I'm gonna rip your fucking throat out!"

Kirk squirmed in the chair, making every effort to fight his way out of the leather straps, but all that did was prompt laughter among the Revolutionary Guard soldiers. Farhad stared at Kirk, emotionless.

"So, my American friend," Bijan said, walking towards Kirk in the chair, "you think you can just walk into our country and kill one of our beloved brothers? No, no, no. I don't think so. It's time for you to atone for your sins."

"Fuck you!"

Kirk spit on Bijan, who glanced down at the phlegm on his uniform and then back up at Kirk with a look of revulsion. Without asking, Bijan turned back to Aslani and snatched the pruning shears from his boss's hand.

Kirk made every frenzied attempt to get away. Bijan gave him a forceful chop to the throat. Kirk's mouth fell open and he pitched forward, shocked by the impact and desperate for air. Coughing profusely, Bijan grabbed him by the hair and put his right nostril between the clippers' blades. His bloodshot eyes glared at Kirk's. But before he could squeeze the handles, Aslani interrupted.

"Bijan! You can have retribution in a moment. I think our friend needs a more subtle introduction."

Karim joined Bijan and unstrapped Kirk, jerked him forward and kicked his feet out from underneath him before shoving him to the ground, face first. Bijan held Kirk's wrists and placed his knee in Kirk's back. Behind Bijan, Karim held Kirk's ankles.

"Normally, we would use the chair to lay you on your belly and pin you down, but when your pig grandfather betrayed Khomeini and helped restore the Shah, his actions gave birth to the SAVAK. When the Shah wanted to crush any opposition to his reign, he assigned them to whip his adversaries into submission and this is how they did it. You will have the same merciless experience as our ancestors."

Aslani grabbed the skunky whip from the table.

"Farhad, take hold of his right wrist and keep him from moving," Aslani ordered.

With Farhad in place, Bijan knew what to do next without being ordered. He raised Kirk's shirt, exposing his naked back, sparking a reaction in Aslani. Bijan had barely gotten into place when Aslani began whipping Kirk. In two lashings, the skin split open. Once the bleeding started, each lashing was worse than the one before as the leather penetrated deeper into Kirk's skin. He squirmed, wiggled, fought, jerked, and wormed his body in every manner possible, but the Iranians' grips were too strong. His screams echoed against the stone walls and carried down the hallway to the other cells. Kirk lost count at fifteen lashings and was on the verge of passing out when Aslani stopped.

"I hope you enjoyed that because that's as easy as you're going to get it," he said.

After throwing down the whip, he tapped Bijan on the shoulder and motioned for the pruning shears.

"Now, let's take things to the next level. The Supreme Leader will want proof of our ruthless aggression."

Aslani squatted down and put his knee on the top of Kirk's left hand, which flattened out the fingers. Bijan swapped spots with him and Kirk cried out pain as Bijan pressed on the center of the torn flesh on his bloodied back. Aslani placed the base of Kirk's left pinkie between the blades.

"No! Stop! Stop! Please!"

"I thought Americans were tougher than this," Aslani said. "Surely, you won't miss this finger," Aslani cracked.

"Wait," Farhad interrupted. "Let me do it."

Aslani's eyebrows shot up.

"You? You think you're ready for this?"

"If I do this, my debt to you is cleared. Deal?"

So, it's true. Farhad used me as leverage.

Aslani looked to Bijan and Karim, who nodded in approval.

"Deal," Aslani said.

But he lied. He had no intention of letting Farhad off the hook, but he handed him the shears, handle first, anyway.

"I don't think you have the guts to do it."

"Oh, I assure you, I do," said Farhad. "I'm stronger than you give me credit for."

With Aslani holding down Kirk's left wrist, Farhad put his knee into the top of Kirk's right hand and placed the pinkie between the blades. Without as much as a countdown or a warning, Farhad squeezed the handles mightily, bringing the sharp blades together to slice through the cartilage and tendon in the finger.

Kirk writhed on the floor like a wild game fish, spurting every expletive in the book with such ferocity that his throat began to burn with anger, like the force of a strong bourbon. Farhad picked up the disconnected finger and began bending it with his other hand, making it wave at Aslani and the other soldiers.

"Hi, how are you?" he said.

Farhad laughed. The other soldiers joined in.

"Azam, I think your man here is enjoying himself," Karim said.

Aslani studied Farhad's face and recognized a piece of himself as he recalled the first time he had done the same thing to a prisoner. Perhaps there was hope for Farhad, after all.

"Let me do another one!" Farhad begged.

"You've got the taste of it now, haven't you?"

Farhad stared at the severed finger as he absorbed the adrenaline rushing through him and nodded at Aslani, licking his lips.

Chapter Twenty-Seven

"One more," Aslani agreed.

"Before I die, I swear, I'm gonna kill you!" Kirk said, barely able to speak.

Farhad ignored the comment.

"Bijan, you pick this time. Which finger?"

With his knee still in the middle of Kirk's wounded back, Bijan bent over and examined the hand that was gushing blood.

"Cut off his middle finger. That way, he won't be able to flip us off," he laughed. "But the middle finger is quite thick. You sure you can do it?"

"Don't worry," Farhad said.

He looked straight at Kirk.

"I'm good if you're good."

Before Bijan knew what hit him, Farhad stabbed him in the eye with the pruning shears. The soldier threw his hands to his face and roared in pain. After releasing Kirk's wrist, Farhad tackled Aslani.

With both hands now free, Kirk twisted and pushed Bijan off him. Shocked by the sudden turn of events, Karim loosened his grip on Kirk's feet just enough that it allowed Kirk to kick him in the face, knocking him backward. A tooth flew out of his mouth. He attempted to push himself up, but he was met by Kirk's fist smashing against his cheek. When Karim reached for the gun on his belt, Kirk grabbed his wrist, jerked him onto his stomach, and twisted it far beyond forty-five degrees behind his back. Karim yelped when his arm was pulled out of its shoulder socket.

Noticing a knife on his captor's belt, Kirk pulled the blade from its sheath, thrust it into the side of Karim's neck and left it in. The blood pooled immediately as Karim gargled and clung to what was left of his life.

Bijan's stabbing barely registered with Aslani before Farhad vaulted on top of him. Sneak attacks were the most difficult to defend. When being assaulted, the brain's curiosity to identify the attacker overwhelms the body's ability to defend itself. This was a natural reaction that had to be squeezed out of a soldier.

Farhad repeatedly pounded on his nemesis's face. Aslani did his best to block the punches, but some inevitably landed on his swollen brow. Each blow caused his head to bounce off the stone floor. A few more and he would be knocked out. Thankfully, his training kicked in. Aslani made the only choice available and yanked Farhad by his shirt down toward him. Farhad's nose cracked and spewed blood when it rammed into Aslani's forehead.

Stunned by the unexpected move, Farhad instinctively covered his beak with both hands and rolled over in pain. After enduring a fierce kick to the ribs, he dodged the heel of Aslani's boot by rolling to the side. Pushing himself up, Farhad threw the back of his elbow into the side of Aslani's head. He staggered back but tossed Farhad over his shoulder when he saw another punch coming. Farhad landed with a thud and winced in pain. Aslani leered at Farhad, pulled the sidearm from his belt, and pointed it right at him.

"I'm going to enjoy this," Aslani said.

Just as he wrapped his finger around the trigger, Aslani was grabbed by the back of his collar and yanked backward. A shot went off but missed Farhad by a mile. The gun flew out of Aslani's hand when he hit the floor. He kicked Kirk hard in his knee, but somehow the American found the strength to fight on.

Fists were flying, toe to toe, but Aslani was more well-trained than Kirk and landed his punches faster. A solid one-two punch was followed by a stiff uppercut to Kirk's jaw, which dropped him. Out of the corner of his eye, Aslani saw Farhad making a second charge at him, this time with a long dagger he'd grabbed from the arsenal on the wall. Without missing a beat, Aslani pivoted and gave Farhad a solid kick to the stomach. Once Farhad dropped the blade and doubled over, Aslani took a calm step forward and hit Farhad with a ferocious uppercut. Aslani's confidence was building now. It was almost over. He could feel it.

Despite the injury, Bijan sensed that his companions were in danger. The loyal soldier struggled to his feet and pulled his gun. But with one eye now useless and the other clouded by residual blood, Bijan had trouble determining his target.

Seeing Bijan alive and armed, Kirk panicked. But when Aslani's strikes sent him to the ground, he fell onto the whip that had been used on him moments before. He hastily grabbed it and made an awkward reverse move that nailed Aslani. The leather braided tassels smacked him directly in the balls.

With Aslani hunched over from the surging pain, Kirk stood and stomped on Bijan's right forearm, causing him to drop the gun. He cried out in pain, but before Kirk could strike again with the whip, Bijan drove the heel of his left hand upward into Kirk's mouth.

Dazed by the stars he saw, Kirk tripped over Karim. When his eyes refocused, he yanked the knife out of the dead man's neck and threw his shoulder into the center of Bijan's chest as he tried to pick up the gun. Bijan's back flew against the wall. Knife in hand, Kirk approached his grandfather's killer like a rabid wolf. Bijan tried to pull his knife, but Kirk was too quick and rammed the blade between his ribs, directly into the heart. The expression on Bijan's face told Kirk all he needed to know about how Bijan would spend the last moments of his life.

"That's for Pap," Kirk said.

With his privates throbbing, Aslani seized the dagger that Farhad dropped on the floor. Farhad jumped back, trying to avoid the sharp edge slashing toward him, but the tip connected, ripping his shirt and creating a huge gash across his lower rib cage.

Sensing his prey was about to be finished off, Aslani took another slash at Farhad. But the pain in his groin had made him unstable and his legs wobbled when he tried to move. This time, Farhad used Aslani's momentum against him. When Aslani missed, Farhad snagged him by the back of his uniform, let out a therapeutic roar and slammed Aslani's temple into the corner of the oak table. Aslani passed out immediately.

His chest heaving from the heavyweight bout, Farhad stood over his adversary, sweating and bleeding. He snatched the stiletto still in Aslani's hand and prepared himself to do what he knew he had to do. Suddenly, two shots rang out. Farhad opened his eyes and inspected himself for bullets not believing that he wasn't dead. Instead, he saw two more soldiers dead in the doorway after rushing to their boss's aid.

Farhad raised his hands and turned to see smoke curling from the barrel of the gun in Kirk's bloodied hand. His t-shirt was covered in sweat and blood. But it was Kirk's wrathful eyes that concerned Farhad the most. He looked possessed and his veins were pulsing. Considering what Farhad had done to him, it was easy to understand Kirk's desire for revenge.

"If you kill me, we'll never get out of here," Farhad said.

The gun began to shake in Kirk's hand. He had every right to shoot Farhad. He wanted to, but in his gut, he knew Farhad was right and lowered his weapon.

"We'll settle this later. Let's get out of here."

Chapter Twenty-Eight

With his ear still bleeding, Delang put on the clothes that were thrown into his cell. He recognized them as the button-down shirt and suit pants he was wearing the day he was captured. He noted how strange it was seeing something familiar after more than a year in isolation. It was quickly evident how much weight he'd lost. His shirt hung off his shoulders and his pants barely stayed up. Still, it felt good wearing clothes that belonged to him.

He heard the screams of another prisoner down the hall. It was the first time in what he could only guess was months that Delang heard someone else in a similar predicament. The Iranians rarely left the window open in his cell door. He figured they did so now for dramatic effect. For all he knew, there may not be anyone in the chamber room. They could be using a sound system to replay audio from other sessions, probably his own, just to mess with his mind.

But when he heard the gunshot, he knew he was wrong. Delang wasn't sure if he should feel relief for the poor soul who'd been put out of his misery or if he should be fearful that his own time had finally come. Moments later, the screams continued.

Delang raced to his door and inspected every angle outside the window. Nothing. When he heard a second and third shot ring out, he knew something was up. Had the CIA found him? Were special forces here to rescue him? Had his prayers been answered?

"Over here! Help! I'm over here!"

Finally, he saw a bloodied man with a gun running toward him. Was this it? Would the Iranians kill him moments before his rescue? Delang backed away from the door.

As the stranger hustled up to his door and peered through the window, he squinted his eyes and saw the distinctive scar on the side of Delang's face.

"Oh my God, it's *you!*" Kirk said, alarmed.

Delang was dumbstruck by the man's reaction and relieved that he spoke perfect English. He studied the man, but the lack of light made it difficult.

"Who the hell did you think it was? Get me the fuck outta here!"

Kirk searched the door but there was no keyhole. The lock was electronic.

"Farhad! Get to the control room and find the button that opens this door!"

Farhad stared blankly at the control panel in the security room. Not knowing which button to choose, he pressed them all and Delang's cell buzzed open.

"Thank you," Delang said.

He emerged as a free man, at least for the moment, but then he paused outside his door.

"Wait, I know you."

He gazed inquisitively at Kirk's face.

"You're Cameron's grandson. Kirk, right?"

"What? How do you know that?"

Kirk was equally astonished.

"I'll explain later."

Delang saw Kirk's missing digit.

"Are you okay?"

Kirk noted the colorlessness of Delang's skin and thin physique.

"I think I should be asking you that."

Delang grinned.

"No, I'm really not. But I'll be okay eventually. We'll have to cauterize the wound on your finger. Where's the rest of the team?"

"Team?" Kirk said. "It's me and another guy."

Delang was stunned.

"Two guys? I guess the agency didn't put a lot of weight into my rescue."

"Huh? Listen, this isn't what you think it is."

Farhad approached them, holding his nose. Blood continued to drip onto his shirt.

"Holy shit!" Farhad said.

He stared at Delang.

"Yeah, the plot just got a little thicker," Kirk said.

"I'll say," he mumbled.

Farhad stuck out his hand to introduce himself.

"We can do introductions later, kid," Delang said tersely, not returning the handshake. "Now, we gotta get out of here. Another team is on their way for the exchange. Where's your car?"

"What exchange?" Kirk asked.

"They were going to hand me off to another team and they'll probably be here any minute. Now where's your car?"

"Outside," Farhad answered.

"It is?" Kirk asked.

Farhad nodded.

"You're going to have to trust me."

Though his eye was swollen, Kirk saw the knife wound across Farhad's torso.

"Whoa. You gonna be okay with that?"

"Yeah, I think so. It's bleeding like hell, but it doesn't feel very deep."

"Come on, they'll be here soon," Delang insisted.

"They who?"

"I don't know, and I'd rather not find out. All I want to do is get the hell outta here. Are all the other Iranians dead?"

Kirk and Farhad glanced at each other.

"Yeah, I think so," Kirk said.

Delang wasn't satisfied with the answer. Either someone was dead or they weren't, but he didn't have time to argue.

"Fine, you have a gun I can use?"

Kirk handed over Karim's Browning HP 9mm gun, which he had tucked in his waistband.

"Grab whatever ammo and other guns you can find, and let's move!"

Delang brushed past his rescuers, instinctively going into fight or flight mode.

Kirk turned to Farhad with a puzzled look.

"What the hell's going on here?"

"If I'm right, you won't believe it. But if we want to live, we need to do what he says."

After rushing outside, Delang shielded his eyes. It was the first time he'd been in full sunlight since his capture. He squinted as his eyes began to water and he appraised his surroundings. His once bronzed skin had faded to an ash white that could combust from sunburn.

"Who are you?" a voice said.

Delang raised his gun toward the voice. His eyes couldn't make out who it was. Seconds later, Kirk and Farhad emerged from the building and saw who was waiting. Kirk was shocked.

"Simin?"

Chapter Twenty-Nine

Not knowing if she was friend or foe, Delang kept his gun on the woman. Simin's eyes bulged and she instinctively put her hands in the air.

"Who is she?" Delang asked.

Kirk placed his good hand on the barrel of Delang's gun, signaling him to lower his weapon.

"She's cool."

Delang inspected Simin. He was hesitant to trust anyone, but now wasn't the time to dwell on details. If they were leaving, he was sure as hell going with them.

"Simin, what are you doing here?" Kirk asked.

Farhad leaned in to explain.

"After I dropped you off at the hotel, Azam was waiting for me. I knew he was up to something, so I told Simin at the party to track my phone over the next few days. With us constantly going on bootlegging runs, we keep the Find My Phone feature active. That way, she or one of my other friends can keep an eye on me or pick up the car if I had to dump it. Azam may have taken possession of our phones, but I guess he didn't get a chance to destroy them, so the signal was still running. I had a feeling she'd come looking for us. Thanks, by the way."

Simin nodded.

Kirk knew that Farhad had more explaining to do, but it appeared that his in-country guide was in fact on his side.

"I didn't know you'd be here, but it's good to see you again, Kirk," Simin said.

Kirk smiled. Seeing Simin made his body tingle in a way that didn't involve losing one of his limbs.

"It's good to see you too, Simin. But things are about to get extremely dangerous. Can you handle it?"

"Because of him?"

She pointed at Delang.

"Not just him. We killed a bunch of Revolutionary Guard soldiers so someone's going to come looking for us."

"Azam's dead?"

Delang was impatient.

"Excuse me! This little reunion is cute and all, but we need to get out of here *now*. I'm not gonna ask again. Where's the car?"

Simin pointed to Farhad's Sidekick parked fifty feet away.

"I didn't know what this place was or where you'd be, so I wanted to be cautious."

Delang struggled getting to the car, so Farhad helped him. Kirk held up his palm.

"Toss me the keys," he said.

"Kirk, you don't know where you're going. I'll drive."

"No, I've been trained in evasive driving, and I think we're going to need it. You navigate. Hand them over."

Simin didn't argue the point any further. She tossed Kirk the keys and sat shotgun.

Farhad put Delang's arm around his shoulders while clutching his waistband. Bleeding and weak, Delang wobbled as he walked. Just as they made it to the car, the passenger window exploded.

Azam emerged from the building with his backup ankle gun in hand. His head was bleeding profusely, and he was so disoriented from what had to be a concussion that he stumbled around like a drunken man as he fired more shots. The American couldn't be allowed to escape.

"Down!"

Delang's reflexes kicked in as he threw Farhad in the backseat head-first. He aimed his gun and was ready to fire, but his eyes were still adapting.

Uneasy on his feet, a second gunshot made Aslani fall down. The bullet missed, but Delang heard it whiz past his one good ear.

"Drive!"

With everyone secure inside, Kirk tore off down the road.

Azam got off a few more wild shots, but it was no use. The last thing he saw before he passed out was the taillights of Farhad's booze runner. They were gone.

***

Relieved to have finally made it past the mosque, the team of Russians drove the final thirty minutes to the Lounge. As they turned off the main road, they were nearly sideswiped by a white Suzuki Sidekick tearing out of the exit. Vasily slammed on the brakes and cursed in Russian.

"Fucking crazy Iranians!"

If he hadn't been on a mission, the Russian would've followed the driver and shot him in the head. He calmed himself and pressed on to the pick-up point.

Luka sat up in the backseat and positioned himself between the two front seats.

"There," he said, pointing, "the one with the rounded roof."

Pulling up, they saw a soldier's body lying face down. Luka and Nikolai jumped out of the van with their guns drawn. Vasily followed.

"Was another buyer involved?" Nikolai asked.

Luka shook his head.

"No one else knows."

He surveyed the property and saw blood on the ground.

"There was a fight."

A faint moan came from Aslani. Although there was a significant amount of blood surrounding the soldier's head, he wasn't dead, not yet. Vasily kicked him over. His eyes were blinking rapidly.

"What happened here?"

Nikolai lifted Aslani's torso off the ground.

"Three," Aslani mumbled.

"There were three of them?"

Aslani barely nodded.

"Who?" Luka asked.

Aslani tried to respond but the words wouldn't come out. He was on the verge of passing out again, so Nikolai smacked him in the face.

"Who was it?"

"Golfer," Aslani said.

The three Russians looked at each other quizzically.

"Golfer?" Vasily said. "The British did this?"

Aslani shook his head. He knew what he wanted to say, but the words in his mind wouldn't connect with his tongue. Nikolai smacked him in the face twice more, which seemed to help.

"Americans . . . hurt. White car," Aslani finally said.

Vasily and Nikolai glanced at their boss, remembering the white car that almost hit them as they came in.

"They can't be far," Luka said. "Move!"

Nikolai jumped up so fast from his squatted position that Aslani's body slid off his supporting leg and plopped to the ground. He moaned again, but there was no empathy from the Russians. Before getting in the Jeep with his team, Luka stood over Aslani. He had intended to have a callous word with the Iranian but changed his mind. Instead, he struck him in the face with the butt of his gun.

"That's for fucking up," Luka said.

As he walked away, Aslani was out cold.

Chapter Thirty

Half a block from the Fatima Masumeh Shrine, Kirk repeatedly blared the horn at the crowd on Zaer Boulevard while Simin screamed at them to move. The last thing Kirk wanted to do was run anyone over, but he needed to put as much distance between himself and their previous location as he possibly could.

"Go there," Simin said.

She pointed at a gap in the crowd. Kirk turned right onto Tohid Boulevard, a long stretch of urban road filled with markets, banks, fast food restaurants, and cafes. It wasn't ideal, but it had fewer people.

"The on-ramp to Highway 56 is up ahead," she said.

Kirk took his navigator's advice and raced onto the expressway. Never letting off the gas, he merged into traffic and narrowly avoided an accident when he refused to yield to another car. He had no idea where he was going and didn't care. All he wanted was to get away clean so that he could have a Come to Jesus meeting with Farhad and their new companion.

"We've got company!" Farhad called out.

Kirk peered over his shoulder and saw a grey Jeep barreling toward them. It apparently knew their way around Qom better than they did. Seeing that they'd turned on Tohid, the men in the Jeep took a different route over the Dey 9 Bridge and raced to intercept them with total disregard for any innocent bystanders.

The Russians gave chase as Nikolai and Vasily fired their weapons out the windows. Their bullets blasted out the taillights and rear windshield, but luckily for Delang and company, the spare tire mounted on the rear door absorbed or deflected much of the gunfire.

Delang and Farhad did their best to aim at the chasing car as Kirk bobbed and weaved through the chaotic maze of cars. Thankfully, Delang's vision had returned to near normal. Simin fed them spare magazines, but her priority was being Kirk's navigator.

"Talk to me!"

"They're about two hundred yards back!" Delang said.

Kirk slammed the pedal to the floor, but the old car didn't have much pickup. Delang and Farhad continued shooting, but they knew they had to conserve their ammo.

Shooting a gun while hanging out of a car window while flying at eighty miles per hour and threading through traffic wasn't as easy as Hollywood stuntmen made it look. If the twisting and turning to avoid the cars didn't throw off one's aim, the wind did. Fortunately, the scattered driving pattern made it difficult for the car behind them to aim. Due to the extent of his injuries, Delang's body reminded him that he wasn't fully healed as it bounced and twisted from every hard turn and bump in the road.

Bullets from both cars sprayed through the air and hit windows and doors of other cars. Delang could only pray that no bystanders were hit, but the shots caused other drivers to swerve, which created more obstacles for the car behind them, which allowed the Sidekick to gain some distance.

"I'm out of ammo!" Farhad said.

"Me too!" Delang added. "They're coming up fast, Kirk!"

Kirk glanced in his rearview mirror. Their lack of firepower was narrowing the space between them and their hunters.

"What else is on this road?" Kirk asked.

"Nothing much between here and Tehran," Simin said.

The Jeep was rapidly closing the gap. Kirk saw that there was nothing but cars and sand dunes lining each side of the road. An idea popped into his head.

"Buckle up! Things are about to get wild!"

From the far-right lane, Kirk jerked the wheel to the left and engaged the four-wheel drive when the car hit the dune. The sand was surprisingly compact. When Kirk hit the gas, the Sidekick jolted upward faster than expected. As it neared the top, Kirk punched the pedal all the way to the floor. The car went momentarily airborne with the front end vaulting upward. After what seemed like a slow-motion eternity, the front end slammed down on the other side. Everybody inside banged their head on the roof as gravity directed their way back to the sand. Once he got control of the wheel, Kirk steered down the dune and back onto the freeway, but he neglected to mention the next part of his plan.

Chapter Thirty-One

"They're out of bullets!"

Vasily was roaring from the backseat.

As Luka narrowed the gap to about seventy-five meters, he eased his foot off the gas as the car they were chasing veered left and mounted the sand barrier between the northbound and southbound lanes.

"They're turning around!" Nikolai said. "Go, comrade! Go!"

Luka engaged the four-wheel drive to climb up the sand, but the Russians weren't prepared for what they had to do next. Up ahead, the Americans hadn't turned their car around to go southbound once they reached the bottom of the dune. Instead, they continued northbound into *oncoming* traffic, creating total havoc on the highway.

Traffic anarchy followed. The Russians had to avoid a swarm of cars heading directly at them while avoiding the crashes and near collisions caused by Kirk's wild decision in the Sidekick.

Vasily and Nikolai were sweating profusely.

"Go left! Go right!"

They were screaming in unison and at odds with each other as total chaos took over.

Their senior commander was just trying to survive the ordeal.

Left! Right! Right! Left!

This continued for more than a mile. Up until that point, the Americans were somehow successful in creating and evading the unholy traffic, but the Russians were well-trained for such situations. Eventually, the American's luck would run out.

"There! There! They're going back up the dune! Go!"

Vasily was shouting over the roar of the traffic.

"I see! I see!" Luka responded.

"I knew they didn't have the stomach to keep this up," said Vasily.

Two drivers lost control of their cars and crashed right in front of the Russians. Luka barely avoided them by yanking the wheel to the right and driving down the length of the dune at a risky angle. This slowed them down, but they avoided the other cars. The Americans neared the top of the dune again.

"Go down the side now! We can cut them off," Vasily said.

"No, we don't know which way they will go," said Nikolai. "We could lose them! We have to follow their tracks!"

Luka had a decision to make. Both his comrades were correct, but there was only one right answer. Believing the Americans were out of ammo, he followed their path. Once they reached the other side, it was only a matter of time before one of their own bullets would hit the driver and end the entire chase.

The Russians continued until they were halfway up the dune. The rear end of the Jeep skidded when they were forced to climb vertically. Despite the minor slip, Luka kept his foot on the gas, which kept the wheels spinning and avoided a slide down to the bottom. Thankfully, this dune wasn't as steep as the previous one. The horsepower of the newer model Jeep and the strength of the four-wheel drive sent them soaring over the top.

But something massive crashed into the underside of the Jeep before it even landed. The collision sent the car and its passengers, who weren't wearing their seat belts, end over end down the dune. When they reached the asphalt at the bottom, they were trapped in the middle of traffic, where they were met by an unyielding dump truck hauling topsoil. The driver slammed on his brakes but couldn't stop his momentum. The dump truck t-boned the Jeep at seventy miles per hour, sending it soaring in the air. It barrel rolled four times before finally landing on its roof, belly up in the middle of the interstate.

***

As Kirk reached the bottom of the dune, he couldn't believe what he was about to do. His friends shouted at him, wondering if he had gone insane, but they still called out warnings to help him swerve the car out of danger.

"It's the only chance we have!" Kirk said.

"Oh, my God! We're gonna die!"

Simin braced herself between the dashboard and the seat.

"Help now, pray later!"

Kirk hollered and pushed on.

Delang was the most helpful. Kirk didn't know if their mysterious companion had pulled this exact stunt before, but he wasn't about to ask because he needed all the help he could get.

"Swerve right past that green car," Delang said, "and cut left before the black one!"

The Sidekick was barely avoiding major collisions but still swiped the side mirrors off some of the cars they passed. Kirk couldn't help but notice the expressions of those driving past him. Some of their faces were pale, as if death was imminent; some were in shock, and others were bracing their loved ones in the passenger seat. Although they were racing at high speeds, Kirk felt as if he were passing those cars in slow motion, allowing the expressions to be ingrained in his memory for the dark moments ahead when he was by himself.

"Kirk, we can't keep doing this," said Farhad. "Get off this fucking road!"

Kirk knew Farhad was right. He couldn't press their luck much more, and he heard police sirens in the distance. What he didn't know was that the responding police cars had been involved in the accidents he left in his wake. He saw a section of the dunes ahead that might give them a chance to get away clean. It was a wild idea, but it was his only card to play.

"Hang on," Kirk called out, "we're going up and over one more time!"

The Suzuki climbed the dune and catapulted over the top. Upon reaching the bottom, Kirk should've hit the gas and merged into the flowing traffic, but instead he popped a u-ey and mounted the sand dune once again, stopping three-quarters of the way to the top.

His friends were smacking him on the shoulder, vehemently yelling in his ear, perplexed by what he was doing.

"For God's sake, move! Move!" Farhad begged.

"Not yet!" Kirk said. "Buckle up!"

"What the hell are you waiting for?" said Delang.

"Almost . . . almost . . ."

Kirk was mumbling to himself. He glanced over at Simin, who was gripping the door handle with one hand and bracing herself against the dashboard with the other. She knew what was about to happen. The sound was getting louder from the other side of the sand. Kirk tuned out the protest of the others in the car.

"Almost . . . almost . . ." he kept saying.

Now!

Kirk punched the gas, hoping his timing was right. The Jeep hauled ass over the top and rammed into the rear underside of the other car when it catapulted itself over the top of the dune.

Pure wreckage.

The Sidekick went spiraling down the sand. The front end was beyond smashed and all four of those inside, although secure in their seat belts, were bouncing back and forth, arms and heads flailing in all directions like inflatable, waving tube characters in front of a used car dealership. When gravity finally finished working its magic, the Sidekick landed right side up on the side of the freeway with four bloodied, unconscious fugitives inside.

Chapter Thirty-Two

Delang woke up with a bloodied forehead to match his ear and one bitch of a headache. He was groggy, his vision was shaky, but he was alive. He wasn't sure how long he had been out. As he blinked to focus his eyes, he saw a crowd gathering in the middle of the highway. One of his journeymen was out cold, but two others were starting to move. People approached their car.

Bystanders? Has the Revolutionary Guard gotten word?

He smacked himself in the face to break his stupor. When a stranger reached his door, Delang instinctively pulled out his gun and pointed it at the man. He was out of ammo, but the mystery man didn't know that. As his blurred vision cleared, Delang saw the man was a civilian in a grey t-shirt holding his hands up in the air.

The battered CIA operative exited the beat-up car and walked up the interstate through a mass of cars, all at a dead stop. He saw a Glock 19 on the ground that must have flown out the window of the car that had been chasing them. He tossed away his Browning HP, picked up the Glock, released the magazine to check the ammo, and yanked back on the slide after punching the magazine back in.

Up ahead, Delang saw a body face down in a pool of blood. He nudged it to see if the man was alive and then kicked the body over, but he didn't recognize the face. He checked it for identification, which had probably been falsified, but at least he got a picture. Luckily, the man's passport hadn't been lost in the crash. Delang looked it over, put it in his back pocket, and moved on.

The next body was ten yards away, with the man's brains squashed on the street. Delang retrieved the man's ID and headed toward the Jeep that had been pursuing them. Someone was inside. With gun extended,

Delang cautiously approached and found the bloodied man alive, his face covered in glass. He stared at Delang as if he were confirming his identity.

"Who are you?" said Delang. "Who sent you?"

"Brat . . ."

"Who? Brad who?" Delang asked, confused.

The man smiled, shook his head and spat blood on Delang's shoes.

Knowing that he wasn't going to get anything more from the man, Delang finished him off. Blood squirted from his head like a water fountain and the crowd surrounding the car ran back to their cars. Delang searched the Jeep and quickly found what he was looking for—a plastic trunk full of assault weapons, handguns and ammo.

By then, his companions in the Sidekick had come to and had stumbled out of the car to meet him.

"Kirk, do you have any money?" Delang asked.

"What?"

Kirk was still in a daze.

"Money! Do you have any?"

"Yeah, why?"

"Come on, we've got to get out of here," Delang said. "The Guard or the cops will be here soon. Let's move."

Delang approached a frightened woman in a rose-colored chador, sitting in her Nissan Rogue with the windows up and the doors locked. He knocked with his gun and motioned for her to get out. When she didn't comply, he pointed the gun at her. He had no intention of killing her, but he didn't have time to play nice. Delang smirked as she exited the vehicle.

Funny how a gun always makes people agreeable.

Scared out of her wits, the young lady began to sob. When she moved out of his way, Delang reached in through the driver's side door and swiped the FOR SALE sign taped to the rear window. He held it up and showed it to her.

"How much?" he asked in Farsi.

The woman looked at Farhad for help to understand what was going on. She shook her head in disbelief. Delang kept his eyes on her to make sure she didn't have a gun. He reached out in Kirk's direction and repeatedly snapped his brittle fingers. Kirk handed him money. Thumbing through the cash, Delang saw that it was about three hundred Euros. It was a pittance, but it would have to do. He snatched the woman's hand, slapped the bills into it, and dropped the FOR SALE sign at her feet.

"Let's go," he said.

Kirk, Farhad and Simin barely nodded.

"Can you drive?" Delang said to Farhad.

He nodded.

"Good," said Delang. "Let's go."

After loading the plastic case of weapons from the Russian's car into the rear of their new SUV, Delang collapsed into the shotgun seat while the others piled in back.

He turned to Simin.

"I need to take the sim card out of your phone," he said. "Hand it over."

Simin was still disoriented and handed him her phone. Delang removed the sim card, put it in his pocket, leaned his head back and closed his eyes.

Farhad started the car but had no idea where to go. He looked at Delang.

"Where to?"

"North," he said. "Just head north."

Chapter Thirty-Three

QOM, IRAN
VALI-E ASR HOSPITAL

"Can you stay off your feet a few days?" the doctor asked.

Aslani sat up and shook his head slowly, but even that hurt.

"It's a serious concussion. You need as much rest as possible."

Suddenly, the hospital curtain slid open. Shirazi stood in the doorway and glared at Aslani, with a puckered brow, wide daggered eyes and tight lips. He was so apoplectic with rage it looked as if his eyes might pop out of his head.

"Get out!"

He screamed at the doctor, who took one look at the well-known Shirazi and left in a hurry. Shirazi ripped the curtain closed and immediately punched Aslani with a vicious right hook that lifted his body right off the bed. Aslani's fresh stitches busted open, and pain shot through his already bruised, throbbing head.

"I've been calling your phone for hours," Shirazi said. "No answer. I called Bijan. No answer. But I did receive a call from our friend, saying the package was *not* delivered. Now, I see the mess on the highway. You have two minutes to tell me *what the hell happened*!"

Aslani massaged the side of his cheek and sat up to speak to his superior.

"It was the American," he said.

"What American? The CIA tracked you there?"

"The American from last night."

Shirazi was confused.

"Kabiri's grandson? Kurruthers? He escaped with the American agent?"

Aslani reluctantly nodded.

"Bijan and the others are dead, too. General, I . . ."

Aslani didn't get a chance to finish his sentence before Shirazi punched him again. He leaned down, flush with white hot anger and grabbed Aslani by his uniform collar to pull him up to his feet.

"You stupid fool!"

His shouting was followed by a headbutt directly to Aslani's mouth, which was quickly bloodied like the rest of his head. He was certain that one of his teeth had been knocked loose.

"General, please! I swear . . ."

Shirazi squeezed Aslani's cheeks and forced his mouth open. He pulled a Browning HP 9mm from the holster on his belt, shoved the barrel into Aslani's mouth, and cocked back the hammer. Aslani's eyes bulged and sweat poured down his forehead.

"You don't get to talk anymore," Shirazi said, gritting his teeth. "You either nod your head or shake it when I ask you a question."

Aslani nodded as best as he could, considering he had a gun shoved down his throat.

"Did you bug his hotel room?"

He nodded.

"Did you tell *anyone* about the exchange? Even your wife?"

Aslani shook his head, but Shirazi didn't believe him. The gun barrel was so far into his mouth that his eye-teeth were nearly all the way to the hammer and his jaw was so wide open that his tongue touched the trigger guard.

Aslani gagged.

"Don't lie to me!"

Aslani shook his head. He knew that his boss's finger was on the trigger. All he had to do was squeeze. Unexpectedly, Shirazi yanked the gun from Aslani's mouth. His teeth clinked across the top of the barrel as he vomited on the tile floor next to Shirazi's boots.

Shirazi paused to let Aslani finish puking, but he wasn't letting up. He grabbed a tight fistful of his hair, snatched him upward, and tilted his head back until they were face to face.

"Now, you listen to me," Shirazi said.

He was hissing like a poisonous snake about to bite.

"Get checked out of here and return to Tehran immediately. I want all materials regarding the American's travel information and the recording data from the bug delivered to my desk. You have three days to find the Americans and bring them to me. I don't care what you have to do or who you have to kill to make this happen. *Get it done.* Do you understand, you pathetic little worm?"

Aslani nodded.

Shirazi slapped him hard across the cheek.

"Do you understand?!"

The taller Aslani wobbled to his feet and stood.

"Yes, sir," he said, with a salute.

"Good," Shirazi said.

He turned toward the curtain.

"Mahmoud, get in here!"

His guard, who had been standing outside, entered and stood at official attention. "Take Mahmoud with you. He'll help coordinate whatever you need done. Keep me informed at all times. If you need something, you damned well better ask. Do I make myself clear—to the both of you?"

Shirazi pointed his finger from one man to the other.

"Yes, sir!" both men replied.

Shirazi stood silent for a moment, letting his eyes move back and forth between both men to ensure that they understood the gravity of the situation and how serious he was. He put his hand on Mahmoud's shoulder and whispered into his ear. Mahmoud nodded. Then, Shirazi turned back one more time and pointed his finger at Aslani.

"If you come back to me empty handed, I'll ensure that your next hospital visit will be with no hands at all."

Chapter Thirty-Four

KARAJ, IRAN

Two hours after leaving the pandemonium on the interstate, Farhad drove their confiscated car to the nearest metro station. Not only did they need a different set of wheels to avoid detection, Kirk insisted that they drop off Simin, as he thought she had risked enough already and should go no further with them. She, along with her loved ones, was now in grave danger because it wouldn't be long before the Revolutionary Guard discovered her involvement. She needed to escape, albeit on her own.

Farhad pulled into a distant parking spot at Golshahr Metro Station. He and Delang went to find another car to steal while Kirk and Simin said their goodbyes. Once the two men were out of sight, Simin slugged Kirk in the gut.

He doubled over and groaned in pain.

"Do you know what you've done to my life?" she said.

She was yelling and trying not to make a scene at the same time.

"Yeah, I guess I had that coming," Kirk responded. "How's your head?"

Simin's forehead was already swollen from the tumble down the sand dune. Kirk brushed away her blue hair to get a better look at the nasty purple bruise that had already started to form.

"I'll be okay," she said.

She adjusted her hijab to hide the discoloration.

Kirk grimaced. The hijab could not hide enough of the bruising.

"Is there somewhere you and your family can go?" he said. "Iraq? Turkey?"

"I have an aunt in Azerbaijan. I'll call an old smuggling friend who owes me a favor to help me get across the border. He has friends in the government we can pay to look the other way. But why can't I go with you? Why are you abandoning me?"

Kirk grabbed her hand.

"Simin, I know we only just met, but when you're not punching me in the stomach, when I look at you, I feel my soul lift up in a way I've never felt before."

Simin began to blush.

"Something that feels so good can't be bad," he said. "I meant what I said about meeting you in Paris. I promise we'll work something out and meet there some day, but this situation with Shirazi and Aslani isn't done. I don't know what Farhad told you about me being here, but. . ."

"Kirk, stop. There's something I have to tell you."

Kirk was confused. He thought he was the one who needed to do the explaining.

Simin took a long breath.

"Farhad told me about you, and why you were coming."

"Oh, he did, did he?"

"Don't be mad. He had a good reason. Many years ago, my father was part of a protest against the Supreme Leader near Azadi Tower. Haddadi arrested and tortured him. Before he killed him, he raped my mother as part of his punishment. I know that she loved me, but I don't think she ever fully recovered. She died of a stroke when I was fifteen."

A light bulb flipped on in Kirk's head.

"Which would make you . . ."

"Haddadi's daughter."

Kirk stood frozen in front of her, breathless, as his brain processed the information.

173

"Farhad and I didn't know for sure what you wanted with Haddadi, but it didn't take much to connect the dots. I did what I could to help Farhad learn about Haddadi's house, his routine and habits. Is he . . .?"

Kirk nodded as looked down at his hands, reliving the moment he ended Haddadi's life.

"Damn right," he said, with pride.

Simin closed her eyes and leaned her head back as a wave of relief washed over her.

"Did Haddadi know about you all this time?" asked Kirk.

"Yes. He rarely sought me out, but always kept me under his thumb."

"And now?"

Simin didn't answer. Kirk was quickly beginning to understand what kind of person Haddadi had been and why Pap had tried to caution him. He thought about asking Simin why she hadn't told Farhad about the hidden room in the man's library but decided against it. There was no point in rehashing the incident.

"I know more about that man than I'd like to, Kirk. Secrets, contacts, and all. The only thing I can't do is find a way to steal some of the money he has hidden away."

Kirk squinted and gave Simin a skeptical look.

"What money?" said Kirk. "You mean his pension?"

"No, he's siphoned money from arms deals with other countries for years. I can't prove it but there've been rumors and every instinct I have says that the money is tucked away somewhere. Now that you've killed him, I may have a shot at finding it."

Kirk mulled over what he'd heard. It was no wonder Simin helped him.

Sounds like a motive.

"Where will you go?" she asked.

"I'm thinking Turkmenistan, but that's something we have to figure out."

"What do I do?"

"It's time for you to get out of the country."

"How long will I have to be gone?"

"I don't know the answer to that. Based on the target on my back, though, you may not be able to come back."

"This is my home, Kirk. Everything and everyone that I've ever known is here."

Kirk's lips tensed as guilt set in.

"All I can say is, I'm sorry. I knew the risks for myself when I came here, but I never wanted you to become involved. Simin, I wouldn't be able to live with myself if anything happened to you. But if you stay, you'll be branded as conspiring with Americans. If that happens, I think you have a good idea about what they'll do to you."

Kirk paused and looked to the sky, as if it had an answer.

"I feel like I've wrecked your life by just saying hello."

"You didn't wreck my life, Kirk. You saved it."

She gently clutched his face between her hands and gazed adoringly into his brown eyes. He was equally captured, and without looking around to see if anyone was watching, they leaned into each other for a long, soft kiss.

"Simin!"

Farhad yelled from behind Kirk, interrupting their tender moment. He and Simin turned to see that Farhad had commandeered a green Ford Explorer.

"Be sure to call the others," said Farhad. "Tell them what happened and that they need to get out of town. If the Guard gets them under interrogation, a lashing will be the least of their worries."

Simin nodded and turned back to Kirk.

175

"Here," she said, pulling a key off her keyring.

"What's this?"

"Give it to Farhad. He will know what to do with it."

Simin pressed the top of her forehead to Kirk's.

"No matter what," she said, "promise me one thing, that you'll find me again."

"I promise . . ."

She pressed her plump lips against his once more.

"Let's take one more picture together," she said, "just in case."

Kirk laughed. The timing was a little odd, but he wasn't about to say no.

"I don't believe this," Delang said, from inside the car. "They're taking a selfie? Now?"

Farhad shrugged.

"Simin's been like that for as long as I've known her. She wants to remember every moment, especially this one."

When selfie time was over, Simin gave Kirk a little wink and backed away. His heart began to ache with every step she put between them. He desperately wanted to go with her, but he knew he couldn't.

"Kirk!" Farhad said.

Farhad motioned for him to get in the Jeep. When Kirk turned back, Simin was gone.

Chapter Thirty-Five

"Wake up, my friends." Farhad said.

Delang wiped his eyes.

"Where are we?"

"Dizin. Simin's brother is a ski instructor here, but he lets us use his cabin because we help the staff smuggle in booze and weed."

"And where is he?" Kirk asked.

"Simin told me a few days ago that he's on vacation in Greece. Does it matter? We won't be here long, right?"

Delang looked around to see if anyone was observing them or looked suspicious, but there were just a few civilians in the parking lot, unloading their gear. Satisfied that nothing was out of the ordinary, he gave Farhad a pat on the leg.

"Good thinking."

The Revolutionary Guard would have added security at every airport, so escaping that way was out of the question. Delang didn't know much about either of his accomplices, but Farhad was one hell of an in-country asset.

A favorite of the former Shah, the Dizin Ski Resort was a staple in Iran. It was Iran's first established ski resort and still its largest. The highest ski lift reached more than eleven thousand feet, making it one of the highest ski resorts in the world, officially recognized by the International Ski Federation for worldwide competition. Although it was open to the public, it was mostly frequented by a rich client base and their families. Its main season started in December, so it wasn't yet cold enough to allow guests, but deliveries were being made, and the crew was arriving early to make the necessary preparations.

Fortunately for the three fugitives, the resort was liberal in terms of its application of Sharia law. Though the Guidance Patrol was known to make its rounds during ski season, generally speaking, it was a more relaxed environment. Women often showed off their hair, and they allowed dance parties with disc jockeys playing American music. Thanks to smugglers like Farhad and Simin, alcohol and marijuana were openly displayed and passed around. It was also one of the few locations in Iran where it wasn't uncommon to hear people openly criticize the government. In catering to such moneyed clientele, the Revolutionary Guard and Guidance Patrol turned a blind eye to such activity unless it was absolutely necessary to intervene.

For anyone visiting from the West, Dizin offered a little piece of home. For anyone that lived nearby, it was a place where the freedoms they had only read or heard about became a reality. For the American fugitives and their native co-conspirator, it was not only a smart place to lay low while they figured out their next steps; it gave them an advantage in finding others friendly to their cause who might help them get across the border.

After hiding the car behind a shed, the first item on the agenda was food. All three men were famished, so they grabbed some chicken kabobs and wraps from the staff's snack bar. Walking past the tennis courts and down a concrete pathway to the staff cabin area, given their ragged appearance, the men garnered some odd looks from the few passersby. Fortunately, they didn't give it a second thought when they saw Farhad escorting them.

When they reached the cabin, they spotted a flyer in the screen door. Farhad grabbed it.

"Well?" Kirk said.

Farhad flipped the paper around so that Kirk and Delang could see it. The neon red and blue haze background leapt off the page, along with a picture of a base jumper in an orange wingsuit, soaring from the resort mountain top.

Dizin Diving! Coming Soon!

"Looks like they're going to start offering base jumping as a vacation package," Farhad said. "Think we can come back and give it a try?"

Sure, we'll squeeze it in between getting our next finger removed and hanging.

Kirk was famished, but not too much to enjoy a moment of sarcasm.

They entered the fully furnished cabin and gathered at the communal table to devour their meal. Farhad grabbed bottles of water from the pantry and passed them around to the others.

Once he finished, Kirk sat back and stared at Delang who was picking away at his chicken wrap and lamb kabob, shoving pieces in his mouth as quickly as he could tear the food apart. Kirk could tell that he had to force himself to be patient as chewing seemed difficult.

Noticing that his gorging was garnering attention, Delang paused and looked around the table. He wiped his mouth with his sleeve.

"Sorry. It's been a while since I had a decent meal, you know?"

The men nodded. Kirk gave Delang a stern look. It was "Come to Jesus" time and there was plenty of explaining that needed to be done.

"Time to spill the beans, man. Who are you and how the hell did you know my name?" Kirk asked.

"His name is Meadows," Farhad said. "He's a CIA operative who was kidnapped from Riyadh over a year ago."

A stunned silence echoed across the table. Kirk and Delang sat with their jaws agape. Delang couldn't believe that the Iranian knew his details. Kirk was dumbstruck that the article he'd read on the plane, which he'd dismissed as fake news, was in fact true.

"How the fuck did you know that?" Delang asked.

"My friends and I write a blog called *Inside Iran* that tries to expose the government for their actions. One friend's father is in the Revolutionary Guard, and he left some papers around one day. When we thought it was safe, we posted the story. As it turns out, it's about you."

"Wait, you're Vince?" Kirk said.

He remembered the name of the person who'd written the article.

"Vince? Who the hell is Vince?" Delang said.

"It's a pen name that me and my friends collectively use to publish the articles," said Farhad. "I chose it because I'm a fan of Vince Flynn novels."

This dialogue supported what Delang thought to be true all along.

"So, the penny drops. The CIA didn't recruit you to fly in country and ask questions about me because of your heritage."

"Not by a long shot, pal," Kirk responded. "Now, start talking. How'd you know my grandfather?"

"You know that Cameron was part of the 1953 coup, right?"

Kirk nodded.

"Well, assets like that have to stay registered with the CIA. At his age, there wasn't much for either him or I to do, but I became Cameron's handler in 2010. I don't know a ton about you, but whenever I saw him, Cameron couldn't stop talking about you. He showed me all kinds of pictures of you. He even used me as a reference to help get you your private security gig. Now, it's my turn to ask questions. If the agency didn't ask you to come, then what are you doing here? Cameron always said that he'd never allow you to enter Iran."

"He's dead."

"Who? Cameron?"

Kirk nodded.

"When?" Delang said in a low voice.

"A year ago this past July. Rasoul Haddadi tracked him down and had him killed. I came here for retribution. Killed that wrinkly piece of shit myself. Suffocated him in his own bed."

Delang was shocked.

"The entire Mossad couldn't assassinate Rasoul Haddadi, but *you* killed him?"

"You bet your ass I did."

Kirk paused as a thought crept into his head.

"Wait a second. When were you taken?"

"Uh, April eleventh, last year."

"So, you were kidnapped in April. Pap got killed in July. You weak mother fucker. It was you. The Iranians tortured you and you gave him up, didn't you?"

The deviled look on Kirk's face was not lost on Delang. He slowly let his hand fall to the gun in his waistband and scrolled through the memories of his time under duress. Much of it was hazy because of the sleep deprivation, but he couldn't recall anything about Kamran Kabiri.

"No," Delang said. "That's not true."

"Bullshit, I don't believe you," Kirk snapped back.

Delang leaned forward and looked Kirk squarely in the eyes.

"Listen to me, kid . . ."

Kirk likewise leaned forward and returned the man's gaze.

"I'm no fucking kid. Let's get that straight right now."

"Fine. Listen, then. I don't think they ever asked me about Cameron, but even if they did, I did my damnedest to hold back. Do you think you could've withstood *this*?"

Delang lifted up his shirt, exposing random cigarette burns and multiple knife slashes.

"Whoa," said Farhad. "That's some real shit."

181

Kirk didn't believe that Pap's name wasn't surrendered under torture, but as much as he wanted to be angry with the man sitting in front of him, he understood. The body and the mind can only be pushed so far before it breaks.

Delang lowered his shirt.

"And who is he?" he said, pointing at Farhad.

"He's my in-country chaperone."

"You've got to be shittin' me . . ."

"No," Kirk said.

"And how'd you end up at the facility where I was being held?"

Kirk glared at Farhad.

"I got used for bait and was betrayed. Wasn't I, Farhad?" Kirk said.

Farhad stopped chewing his kabob and stared back and forth at the two men. He had a little explaining to do.

"Start talking," Kirk commanded.

Farhad pulled out his phone and flipped to a photo that Kirk had thought he'd seen before. It showed the lashing that Farhad received for drunk driving, but this one included the person delving out the punishment. Having now experienced the same abuse, Kirk made a wry face at the photo.

"Aslani?"

Farhad nodded.

"He's had his talons in me ever since."

"Did he assign you to spy on me?" Kirk asked.

"Not at first. I swear to you, my business is legitimate. I needed the money. I think he found out that I was your in-country guide later. Blind luck on his part, I guess. No matter what I do, he'll never leave me alone."

Kirk didn't like it, but Farhad was in a no-win situation.

"How did Aslani manage to get past you and into Haddadi's house?"

"I'm really not sure. He must have taken a shortcut that I don't know about to get there. I was parked around back, like you asked. Judging by what Shirazi was telling us, I'm guessing he used a key to get in the front."

"Where were you last night while I was locked up?"

"I was locked up, too, my friend. Probably a few cells down from you."

"And how do you explain *this*?"

Kirk held up the bloodied hand that was bandaged with a piece of his t-shirt.

"You were the one that did that to him?" Delang said.

He strengthened the grip on his sidearm. Perhaps Farhad wasn't to be trusted after all.

"I'm truly sorry about that, my friend. It killed me inside to do that to you, but if I hadn't, there was no other way to distract Azam. He *had* to believe that I was turning to the dark side, so to speak."

Kirk stared at Farhad, but the intensity slowly subsided. He knew he was right. In the end, cutting off his finger is what enabled them to escape.

Delang closed his eyes, put his elbows on the table and held up his hands.

"So, let me see if I've got this straight. Presumably, the entire CIA has been looking for me, but they couldn't find me. Yet, I was literally rescued from the hands of the Revolutionary Guard by a globetrotter on a revenge ride and his tour guide who didn't know I was there. Is that about right?"

Kirk and Farhad exchanged looks.

"Pretty much, yeah," they nodded and replied in unison.

The veteran agent sat silently for a moment and then cracked a smile. Then, he chuckled before busting out into full-fledged laughter, and then the others joined in. Delang laughed so hard he was nearly in convulsions as tears came from his eyes. Cramps began to form in his stomach and the cackling agitated his injured ribs. As painful as it was, he ignored the hurt and continued with his therapeutic laughing.

Kirk wanted so badly to stay enraged at both Farhad and Delang, but the laughter was taking effect. A smirk broke through his angry scowl, and he couldn't help but chuckle as the realization of what they'd done together finally sunk in.

"Well, you fellas may not have much in terms of common sense," said Delang, "but you sure as hell have iron balls."

They grinned.

"Thank you."

Kirk and Farhad made their formal introductions with Delang, who shed his Marvin Meadows persona. With the pleasantries out of the way and the truth finally out in the open, each of the men took turns in the shower while the others conversed over a pack of stale cigarettes they found in the kitchen.

The showers provided relief from their recent experience, but it was also a time to take inventory of their injuries. Kirk's eye was swollen and the hot water against his back caused him to let loose a loud hiss from the deep sting, so he turned the water all the way to cold.

Worst of all, his right hand was missing a digit. The bleeding had thankfully stopped, but the wound needed to be sealed. After finding some superglue in a junk drawer, he spread it around the wound where his finger used to be, which stung like the devil. While Farhad did his best to hold Kirk's bulky frame in place, Delang took a heated kitchen knife and cauterized the wound. Kirk bit down on a wooden spoon, but the red-hot metal on the open gash hurt like a son-of-a-bitch. He yelped and squirmed as the pain surged through his body but pushed through it.

Farhad's nose was broken, and dark circles were forming under his eyes. Delang squeezed the nose between his palms and reset it with a crunching sound that would be ingrained in his memory forever. Despite not being able to taste much of anything, he'd live. The slash across his abdomen wasn't as deep as he originally thought, and the superglue helped to seal the wound, but it wouldn't hold long. All he could do was hang in there until he could get to a hospital for stitches.

Delang looked the worst. After stepping out of the shower, he got the first good look of himself in a real mirror since his capture. He had turned scrawny, and bones were protruding from his rib cage. Numerous purple bruises on his back and scars from knife slashes on his torso hadn't fully healed. He gingerly touched the spot where he thought his ribs were broken but didn't press on it for fear of more trouble breathing. He didn't need any bones pressing into his lungs.

He opened his mouth and pulled on his lips with a hooked finger. It wasn't a pretty sight. Besides missing teeth, some were fractured and loose, which made it difficult to eat. Beyond that, he knew he'd need multiple root canals. His gums were so sensitive that he howled like a baby and banged his fist on the table when some mouthwash he found under the sink sent an electric surge of agonizing pain up his jawline causing his hands to involuntarily shake.

Luckily, the cabin wasn't only used as primary housing for the senior ski instructor. In the offseason, it was also used to store extra staff uniforms, so Farhad put one on and passed another of the charcoal grey, long sleeve, quarter zip shirts with the stylized 'D' logo on left breast to Delang. The CIA agent was now dressed like a desk clerk, but at least he was clean. Simin's brother had left a pair of sneakers in the closet, so Delang put them on. They were about a half size too big, but he made do.

Given the state of his back, Kirk had to double up, wearing a t-shirt under the quarter zip. It would soak up some of the blood and would hurt like hell to take off, but he'd deal with the discomfort in the meantime. Once everyone had washed and changed into clean attire, they were in better spirits.

They wanted to avoid any attention from the resort staff and steer clear of anyone that would come looking for them, so they got down to the business of plugging up the cabin. The weapons case from the Russian's car was brought in for inspection and inventory. Delang gave a quick tutorial on how to use the semi-automatic weapons. He wasn't sure if they knew already, but he didn't want to wait until a gunfight to find out. All the blinds were shut, and the curtains were drawn. All the doors were locked. Since most of the tables were made of thick wood, they could be turned over and used for shields if it became necessary.

"Do you know who was chasing us on the highway?" Kirk asked.

"No," Delang said. "I haven't been able to figure that out, but I think Eastern European, judging by one guy's accent."

"Why would anyone from Europe want you?"

"I don't know. I've spent most of my career bouncing around the Middle East. I've done enough ops in Syria and Libya that they'd want to kill me."

"So, what's next?"

"We figure out a way to get the hell out of this country."

"Why not just call your friends at CIA?"

"Because only a handful of people knew where I'd be when I was taken. My boss was so adamant that I make the trip that I can't rule out an inside job. I don't know who I can trust there. If I could call Tariq Al-Masari, I would, but the Iranians killed him after they got me."

"Whoa, did you say Tariq al-Masari? The Saudi ambassador to the US?" Farhad said.

"Yeah, why?" said Delang.

"Tom, he's not dead," Farhad said.

"Huh?"

"He's right," Kirk said. "The Iranians tried to assassinate him on U.S. soil, but the FBI foiled the plot. I remember seeing a story about it on *60 Minutes*."

A wave of shock and relief washed over Delang. He'd known in his gut all along that his friend had to be alive, but all the punishment and isolation had him believing what he'd been told. Once the news sunk in, Delang pounced up and grabbed a phone from the wall in the kitchen.

"Won't they be able to trace the hardline?" Farhad asked.

"Maybe, but I'm betting this resort isn't high on their watch list," Delang said.

He punched in the numbers on the receiver.

"No offense, Tom," said Kirk, "but do you still know who to call? I hope it's standard procedure for the intelligence services to change their contact information regularly."

Delang stopped mid-dial and sneered at Kirk.

"Do you still remember your home phone number from when you were a kid?"

Kirk thought about it for a moment.

"Yeah, why?"

"Then, no offense, but I know who to call. Besides, I'm not calling anyone at the agency."

"Okay, so who are you calling?" Farhad asked.

"Someone I trust."

Chapter Thirty-Six

SERIK, TURKEY
REGNUM CARYA HOTEL CONVENTION CENTRE

Yasser Al-Zoubi hated the G20 Summit. It was selfish for the countries with the world's largest economies to get together and quibble over their role in the world piggy bank. The only wallet they were concerned about was their own. The rest of the world deserved more. The Muslim world in particular deserved more.

Because the conference included the twenty top heads of state and their finance cabinet, security was a nightmare. As the Director of Security for the Saudi Arabian Ambassador to the United States, this problem came once a year, like a cold sore. If anyone thought it was difficult to get twenty heads of state to agree on how to steer the global economy, they should try being in the event's security staff meeting. The host country put their best foot forward to accommodate everyone, but every country set up their security differently because no security agent worth his weight in gold enjoyed deviating from their own advanced planning.

Of course, a plan that worked for one security team was full of flaws to another. There was constant bickering back and forth over procedures, travel routes, and scheduling. All security personnel were naturally short on patience when it came to such issues. It was their way or the highway, except for the week of the G20 Summit. Since the teams making the security decisions were the ones carrying the guns, Yasser was convinced that the summit would one day come to a pulverizing halt when a gunfight broke out over which country's head of state got to go to the bathroom first. If only he were that lucky.

An added annoyance was having to tolerate all the protestors who wanted their fifteen minutes of fame on the news by shouting and spitting their opinions, as if anyone cared, at the summit or anywhere else. Five years earlier in Toronto, the activists started a full-scale riot. No heads of state were harmed, but there was extensive damage to the property. Hundreds of arrests were made. Yasser didn't care about that, but the riots put every security detail on edge. There was nothing like going to the vending machine and having someone shove a fully automatic weapon in your face when the sound of the machine dropping a pack of crackers startled a nearby agent.

Worst of all, Yasser hated it because his boss didn't need to be there. Attendance at the G20 Summit was required by his country's Minister of Finance, not the Ambassador to the United States. However, his boss found the summit useful to meet with his counterparts. While the heads of state argued about the global checkbook, no one paid any attention to the ambassadors, meeting in private to work outside deals. Yasser may have hated the G20 summit, but Tariq Al-Masari loved it. He felt that private negotiations were more productive in the conference's two days than they were in two years otherwise.

For the last forty-five minutes, the ambassador was at a dinner in the hotel's private dining area with the French Ambassador to the U.S., Jean-Louis Vannier. Due to differences over ISIS and America's coddling of Iran, the once rock-solid relationship between the U.S. and Saudi Arabia had become chilly, though it was starting to show mild signs of improvement. France was currently the third largest supplier of military arms to the kingdom, behind only the United States and the United Kingdom, but Tariq saw the opportunity to do more, and the crown prince had authorized him to write a substantial check if he could get the deal done.

This essentially killed two birds with one stone: it gave the kingdom more protection against Iran's growing influence in the region and it prevented interaction with the current White House administration, who as of late wanted to receive more than they were willing to give. While he couldn't be certain, Tariq postulated that the Saudi-U.S. relations could've remained more stable had his friend Tom Delang not been taken.

Tariq managed to get the king to agree to a joint task force with the CIA to help look for Tom, but that request was rejected by the higher ups at CIA for fear that the kidnapping was an inside job within the Saudi royal family, a gesture that wasn't received well by the king. Off the record, Tariq tasked some recent retirees from the General Intelligence Directorate who had gone into private sector to investigate Tom's kidnapping, but they came up empty.

While the two ambassadors were savoring their meal, Yasser felt a vibration in his coat pocket. Thinking that it was rude to answer the phone during discussions with international diplomats, Tariq routinely handed over his phone to his director of security, someone he had known since childhood. During their early teenage years, Yasser stole a car to rush his then schoolmate to the hospital for what turned out to be an emergency appendectomy. The car he stole ended up belonging to one of the many cousins of the Saudi royal family. Tariq's father, a wealthy businessman who owned several Lamborghini dealerships within the kingdom, stepped in to save Yasser from a caning punishment. Tariq knew that he was alive today because of that heroic act. From that moment on, through thick and thin, the two always had each other's back. There was no one whom Tariq trusted more. Not even Tom Delang.

"Yes?"

Yasser answered in Arabic.

"Let me speak to *Moccasin*," the voice said.

Moccasin? There was only one person who used that code name for the ambassador. Yasser's eyes popped open, and he drew a short breath in astonishment. He quickly walked to the delegation's table.

Tariq looked irritated at his head of security. He was making tremendous progress with the French and didn't want to be bothered, but what Yasser whispered in his ear was worth a break in the negotiations.

"Jean-Louis, I'm sorry, I'm going to need a minute with my security detail," Tariq said.

"Certainly," said the Frenchman.

Tariq snatched the phone from Yasser's hand and walked to the other end of the dining hall, where he politely asked the staff to disperse so that the ambassador could have some privacy.

"Hello?" Tariq asked.

"Hello, my friend."

Relief washed over Tariq. He could recognize that voice anywhere. "Tom?"

Yasser grabbed a small notebook and pen from his breast pocket and began scribbling.

"Yes, it's me."

Yasser handed Tariq a handwritten note, which simply read VERIFY.

Tariq was confident he was at long last hearing from his friend, but Yasser had a point. There was a lot at stake on the world stage and he couldn't afford to be fooled by another country's voice alteration software. He thought of a question that only Tom could answer.

"What did we have to eat the first time I dined at your house?"

"Lasagna," he answered without hesitation.

Filled with relief, Tariq's apprehension melted away. It was his friend, after all. He nodded to Yasser that everything was okay, but the security man stayed close by in case he was needed.

"Tom, my God, where have you been? Are you okay?"

"It was touch and go for a while, but I'm fine. I'm in Iran with a story that you absolutely won't believe."

"Iran? Those bastards!"

"Where are you? How did you get away? How can I help you?"

"Tariq, Tariq, calm down. I don't have much time, but I need your help."

"Anything."

"Do you have any agents from the General Intelligence Directorate stationed in Iran?"

"I know that we do, but where they are precisely, I don't know."

"Okay, can you pull a couple of strings and have them meet us at the Dizin Ski Resort?"

"Dizin Ski Resort? Tom this is no time to hit the slopes!"

Delang laughed. Even in a crisis, his old ally had a sense of humor.

"Well, it's been a few years, so I thought I'd drop in between beatings. Can you do it? I will also need a suitcase full of money to bribe our way across the border."

"How much?"

"As much as you think it will take."

"Hang on."

Tariq put the phone to his chest.

"Yasser, track down the Minister of the Defense. I need to speak with him immediately."

Yasser retrieved a phone from his pocket and went to work.

"Tom? Listen, there are things you need to know. There's a big push being made in Washington to close the base in Bahrain."

192

"What? How? There's no way Congress is gonna sign off on that."

"Congress is the one pushing it. The U.S. fired a drone missile launched from the base and killed innocent children at a school in Iraq. They're using the incident as an excuse to close the base and let the region work out its problems on its own."

"Holy shit. There's no way that all of this is a coincidence."

"I can't put all the pieces together, but I agree. I don't think I need to tell you what kind of ramifications there will be for the region, let alone Saudi-U.S. relations if America pulls out of the base."

"Okay, look. Me and my. . .team here are in the staff cabins at the resort. If your guys pick us up by morning with the money in hand, we'll work out an exfil plan."

"Your team? CIA found you? Don't they have an exit strategy?"

"I'll explain later, but deep down something always told me that my kidnapping was an inside job at the Agency. Right now, you're the only one I can trust. Can you do it?"

"I'll get it done," Tariq promised.

"With any luck, I'll be seeing you in a few days."

"Good luck, my friend."

Tariq clicked off and glared down at his phone, clenching it with his fist.

"When this is over, I'm begging you to send me to find Moz so I can personally cut his throat!" Yasser said.

Tariq lifted an eyebrow.

"When this is over, I want you to cut off his balls and bring them back to me in a jar," he said. "For now, go get the car. I'll meet you out front. I need to make another call."

Chapter Thirty-Seven

TEHRAN, IRAN
REVOLUTIONARY GUARD HEADQUARTERS

Aslani sat at his desk, rubbing his temples. His head still throbbed despite the five tablets of aspirin he'd swallowed. He wasn't sure if it hurt more from the beating he'd taken at the hands of the general or from the problem he presently had, but he didn't have time to figure it out. The only way out of his predicament was to find answers, and fast. Unfortunately, they were in short supply.

Aslani pulled Kurruthers's passport information from the customs database and found his home addresses in the States. Thanks to some phone calls to sympathetic local Shiites at mosques in the Charlotte area, he requested a break-in at the address listed to see if anything of substance could be found, but there was no word yet. These things took time, but it was time that he didn't have.

Tick, tock.

Then there was the video footage from the highway chase. After local police arrived on the scene, they encountered a woman who was scouring through the busted-up Sidekick, which he immediately recognized as Farhad's, looking for anything she could steal. Under threat of being tortured for interfering with a crime scene, the woman confessed that a scary man with a scar gave her money for her car, but it wasn't nearly enough, so she was looking to see if they'd left anything behind that she could sell to make up the difference. When pressed for information about her car, she was more than compliant. With the car's description, plus corresponding video, Aslani thought he'd caught his first break.

The highway footage showed the getaway car making its way north toward Tehran, which should've allowed them to be intercepted, but the car disappeared past the city of Karaj. When Aslani saw that Farhad was driving, he knew why. The back roads around Karaj and those headed to Tehran were known as "Bootlegger's Alley."

According to Aslani, drunken booze heads like Farhad and his friends used those roads as their own little trade routes to smuggle alcohol back to Tehran. Getting more cameras installed and breaking the network had been on the Basij's to-do list for a while, but tasks related to crushing America's grasp on the world always seemed to take priority. Knowing what he knew now, Aslani wished that he'd pushed harder for better surveillance in Karaj, but he wasn't about to admit that to the general.

Keeping Farhad in mind, Aslani tried to push aside any daydreams he had about hacking off the drunkard's thick head with a dull blade, as any such thoughts would only waste time he didn't have. Farhad would inevitably pay for his crimes, but it would have to wait.

Meanwhile, he had Farhad's phone. He should've searched it last night but decided to get some much-needed sleep. Being such a disciplinarian about following standard procedure, if the general found out about this little slip up, getting his hands chopped off would be the least of his worries. While he gave the American's phone to the general, he decided that it was for his own good to tell him that he'd thrown Farhad's phone out the window on the way to the Lounge.

He backtracked through Farhad's call history to see if he could find anything to cross reference that may help him locate his fugitives. With a few of his bootlegging associates living in Karaj, there were a couple of promising leads, so he arranged to have those homes searched and the suspects questioned. But while those that had been located admitted to knowing Farhad, the searches and interrogations came up empty in terms of a current location.

Aslani considered them to be accomplices after the fact, so he threw all six of them in jail. Mahmoud was sweating them for answers in the interrogation center downstairs, but as of yet they were only producing tears and pleas of innocence.

Aslani's last chance was Farhad Instagram account, which gave him more of a headache than any beating from the general. He hated the self-worshipping ego of social media. It wasn't enough for people to be happy and enjoy their life. No, they had to snap and post all of their parties, trips, and drunken excursions for all of their other idiot friends to see on a 'look at me, look at me' platform. Such a deranged mentality spread like a pandemic to other weak-minded fools across his beloved country.

To his credit, Farhad hadn't lied to him about where he'd taken the American. There were pictures at the Azadi and Milad Towers, lunch, and a nighttime party with friends.

Having struck out on Instagram, Aslani had no choice but to start combing through the same for their closest known friends. This only made the pounding in his head worse. What a cesspool of garbage.

He found pictures of Kurruthers popping up on other Instagram accounts, but it was more of the same, although he was mesmerized by the backward dance move the American performed. How was it possible to be gliding backward while appearing to move forward?

It appeared that one of Farhad's closest friends, Simin Dehghani, was charmed by Kurruthers.

This could be good.

Aslani hoped for a romantic entanglement between the two. With any luck, the shaggy looking American would have let something slip during his conversations with her, which would help him zero in on a possible search point. He pulled Dehgahni's phone number to trace her cell, but it was a dead end after the highway incident. Obviously, the sim card had been pulled.

Frustrated, Aslani placed a call to the Tehran police to have the woman arrested, but she was not home. Her closets were empty, and by the looks of it, she'd fled in a hurry. Aslani slammed down the phone, cursing his luck.

So, there he sat, massaging his temples. He could keep waiting for the Ministry of Intelligence to get back to him with satellite footage from the highway wreck, but for now, he was out of options. There *had* to be something he missed, a piece of evidence he overlooked. The pieces of the puzzle were there, but he couldn't see the full picture. He was blinded by the idea of the Americans escaping the country and even more blinded by the thought of his own hanging.

Suddenly, the phone on his desk rang, which startled Aslani.

"Yes?"

"Can you do nothing right?"

The female voice on the other end was full of contempt.

Aslani sat up straight in his chair. He knew that voice, but he hadn't heard it in more than a year. While her true identity was unknown to him, she'd first contacted him three years ago with a tip about an Israeli spy that hacked their computer system. At first, Aslani scoffed at the idea and hung up on her. But when it turned out to be true, the voice contacted him again to gloat. On several occasions since, she'd provided him with useful intel.

Oddly, she never wanted to be paid. She only asked for similar favors in return, which ranged from making arrangements at the border to looking the other way at prohibited goods or contact information for black market arms dealers. Because she was so well versed in business,

Aslani assumed that she already had money or would be coming into it soon enough. He codenamed her "The Heiress."

"Excuse me?" he said.

"I gift wrapped the American for you. Now, you let him escape. My faith in you must have been misplaced."

"How could you possibly know about this already?"

"You're not my only source, you imbecile. All you need to know is that my information is solid. How could you be this brainless?"

"There was an unexpected complication."

"Save your excuses for the general. I'm sure he'll love hearing them."

Aslani grew irritated at being continually insulted.

"Do you have information for me or not?"

"I'm not sure you're worthy of it. Perhaps I should use my other sources to not only leak word to the general indirectly but point the finger at your blatant incompetence."

"Go ahead. The general may recapture the American agent, but then he'll kill me, which means you'll lose a valuable asset. If I'm the one to get the American back, it will bode well for both of us."

The Heiress paused. Aslani had a point. Another co-conspirator could be recruited, but the relationship with Aslani had been forged over years. Having to start over with a new asset was not appealing or easy at all to do within the Revolutionary Guard.

"He's hiding at the Dizin Ski Resort, but you need to hurry."

"Where at the resort? I don't have the resources to go rampaging through the entire property."

"Figure it out for yourself, you moron," she said.

The line went dead.

Aslani bit his lip. He knew that the ski resort was only two hours from the location outside Karaj where the last piece of surveillance footage placed the getaway car. But the resort was huge. Even if he sent an entire brigade to surround the property, the slick terrain could still allow the Americans to escape. He needed to whittle down the search grid.

An idea smacked him in the head. He hastily shuffled through the papers on his desk, looking for Farhad's file, and flipped to the section on known associates. Aslani remembered that when he'd first arrested Farhad, he'd been coming from a party. When pressed for further information, Farhad indicated that a friend of his had been promoted to head instructor—at Dizin Ski resort.

Jackpot!

Aslani immediately dialed a friend on the Guidance Patrol who not only owed him a favor but was assigned to keeping the visitors and staff at Dizin under control. After explaining that he was looking for three fugitives believed to be in the area, Aslani texted him both Farhad's mugshot and Kurruthers's passport and waited anxiously for a reply.

Only minutes later, his friend texted back that three scraggily looking men fitting his fugitives' descriptions were seen walking toward the staff cabins.

Chapter Thirty-Eight

Three floors up, Rahim Shirazi was at his desk, listening to the audio surveillance from the American's hotel room. Aslani had been right. There wasn't much to go on. The American hadn't been around very much. What little time he did spend there was spent singing along to music on his phone. Did he know his room was bugged? He played the files three times but came up hollow. When he sent a team of soldiers to search the room, they, too, found nothing.

Shirazi had researched this Kurruthers character long before he'd set the trap for him. Though that prep work had aided him well in getting the American to come to Iran, it was of no help in locating him. The man had no ties to the country; the people he did know were also missing, and since he was in possession of the American's phone, there was nothing to track.

One golden nugget was a backpack left in one of the mangled cars at the highway, which included a file of historical information regarding Kabiri's involvement on the 1953 coup and some notes about Haddadi. Perhaps the old files on the coup could be used as a get-out-of-jail- free- card with the Supreme Leader down the road because the Ayatollah loved having any dirt on the Americans.

Shirazi stopped the recording, tossed the headphones on his desk, and closed his eyes.

It can't come down to this, can it?

For years, Shirazi watched his superiors at the Revolutionary Guard fumble their way through their careers for meager successes, but they never gained any traction on a global level. His career would be differ-ent, he remembered thinking.

As a lover of history, Shirazi enjoyed reading about the Sasanian Empire, which reigned for four hundred years and was a legitimate rival to the neighboring Roman Empire, prior to its own timely downfall. At its height during the Sasanian Persian Empire, the borders of Iran stretched as far east as modern-day Turkey and parts of Egypt, as far north as Azerbaijan, as far west as India, but most importantly south to parts of Saudi Arabia and his beloved Bahrain.

It was a well-guarded secret amongst the Revolutionary Guard and the Guardian Council that Shirazi wasn't native to Iran. He'd been born in Bahrain but taken to Iran when he was nine years old and raised in Isfahan by his parents, who believed it was better for their Shiite faith.

One of his fondest memories as a child was sitting on Marassi Beach in Bahrain, staring out into the Persian Gulf, curious about the glorious future life Allah had in store for him. In his limited time, he used to make the twelve-hour drive from Tehran to Bushehr, where he'd go sit by himself along the rocky coastline and stare back from the home that he'd grown to love, at the homeland he once stared from.

He *used* to make those trips.

Though he could've easily chartered a plane to Bahrain to relive his memories, Shirazi swore that he would never again set foot on Bahrain soil until it was once again part of Iran.

As his career advanced in the Revolutionary Guard, Shirazi first had the honor of being introduced to the Supreme Leader at the rank of Major after successfully negotiating a weapons deal with the Libyan military. While he was delighted to meet the prominent man, their initial conversation was dull. But the Supreme Leader asked him a question to which the man usually received a generalized response, such as "To serve you with honor, Supreme Leader" from all other soldiers.

"What plans do you have for the future?" the Ayatollah asked.

Without hesitating, Shirazi responded.

"To personally see to it that the world once again trembles at Iran's power by stretching our borders as far as the Sasanian Empire, Supreme Leader."

The Supreme Leader had been looking past Shirazi at the next soldier in line but was taken aback by the young soldier's strong response. Upon registering the response, he directed his attention into Shirazi's serious eyes and perceived nothing but confidence.

"Your ambition won't go unnoticed," the Ayatollah replied. "You have my support."

From that day forward, Shirazi considered it his personal mission that Iran become the gatekeeper of the Middle East. He dedicated his career to making contacts all over the region that would someday help him consummate this dream. His hopes were on the rise when his native Shiites of Bahrain revolted against the oppression of the Sunni influence. But those hopes were dashed when Saudi Arabia interfered and squashed the rebellion. The sight of his dead, injured, and tortured brethren was the last straw for Shirazi.

After learning that the Saudi ambassador to the U.S. was meeting with a CIA agent, he decided to personally strike first against America. In his estimation, the CIA never rightfully paid for the coup they created against Mohammed Mossadegh, but this particular CIA agent would.

He didn't care how long the American would be in his possession. Every ounce of pain the SAVAK inflicted on his people would in turn be taken out on the agent. It was more fun than anything else, torturing that man. Pulling off the kidnapping also helped build his expanding confidence. He received a commendation for his efforts.

The commendation was short lived, however. Shirazi's blundered attempt to assassinate the same Saudi ambassador was the only previous occasion he had failed the Supreme Leader. For his flop, he was suspended for a week, but it was little more than a slap on the wrist. Despite his shame in not succeeding, his daring endeavor hadn't been overlooked by his superiors, including the Supreme Leader. In fact, it put more of a spotlight on his relentless determination.

Today, he was so close to achieving his goal that he could practically feel his fingertips touch the leather reins of power. All of the dominos were lined up. The prophecy, his prophecy, was *going* to come true. Except, he'd been selfish. His gut told him not to be in the same province as Kabiri's grandson, but he'd finally put the nail in the coffin on the traitors to the Iranian cause in 1953 and wanted to celebrate by rubbing the American's nose in it.

He should've killed Kabiri and his grandson in America as Haddadi urged, but no, he wanted to go the extra mile and serve a literal, ice-cold dish of revenge. Had one of his soldiers done something so idiotic, Shirazi would've stabbed them in the eyes with his letter opener. Though he wasn't about to inflict such pain upon himself, Shirazi knew that he deserved it.

He clenched his fists until the veins in his forearms bulged and walked to the mirror on the wall. There, full of self-loathing, he punched the image he saw, shattering the mirror into pieces. In an effort to calm himself, he put his hands on each side of the broken mirror, lowered his head, and took a deep breath.

Unless he could catch a break, Shirazi knew that he'd have to answer for his carelessness. He could not present Kabiri's grandson to the Supreme Leader, Haddadi was dead and the CIA operative had escaped, which flushed his plans with the Russians. This wasn't a story that could be spun, and the Supreme Leader rarely gave second chances.

But before he could consider his shattered image, Shirazi felt a cloth full of what smelled like chloroform placed over his mouth. He struggled against the behemoth of a man who had wrapped his arms around him, but it didn't take long for the fumes to take effect. Shirazi's eyes rolled up and went blank.

Chapter Thirty-Nine

THE PENTAGON
WASHINGTON, D.C.

Secretary of Defense Devonte Spinx's ears were burning after finishing a string of video conferences. News footage of the destruction from the drone strike in Iraq was circling the airwaves like a race car and not only were no signs of a pit stop in the immediate future, but its effects were sending shockwaves across the globe, with each one directed at him. He was in full defense mode. It wasn't the type of defense he had in mind when he accepted the position, but apparently, it came with the territory.

Spinx glanced at the clock on the wall. He'd finished his last video conference on time, but his next appointment was late. Though she was only two minutes overdue, the old navy man was a diehard believer in punctuality. *Show up on time or don't show up at all*, he used to tell the sailors under his command. Unfortunately, his personal rule didn't apply to politicians inside the beltway. Instead, a lack of punctuality was often used as a weapon, which wasn't lost on him in this case. Her tardiness was meant to purposely irritate him and serve as a power move to show she had the upper hand.

The Secretary impatiently tapped his pen against the desk when the knock finally came.

"Senator Walsh to see you, sir," his long-time aid, Brian Snider, said.

She strode into his office with such confidence that Spinx felt like he should have rolled out a red carpet.

"Secretary Spinx," Walsh said.

Her handshake was cold.

"Senator. Please, let's have a seat."

She refused to sit until he did the same. With the door open, she didn't want his staff storing an image of a standing Secretary talking down to her while she was seated. Spinx gave it a shot, but the Senator didn't bite. In Washington, optics are everything.

Nice try, she thought.

With the door closed and both having sat simultaneously, Spinx stared at the woman he loathed. Despite her exquisite pantsuits, everything about Walsh was fake and every move she made was a calculated maneuver. Reading her legislative resume, one would think she had a laundry list of accomplishments going into her third term in office. But a deeper look revealed the wretched woman's true colors. Spinx wasn't a fan of term limits, but if he was, Walsh would be his posterchild.

The healthcare reform she touted so much in front of the media was pushed by the corporate donors from the medical world that pulled her strings and contributed to her campaigns. Spinx suspected that Walsh was getting kickbacks from their profits, but he couldn't prove it.

The Senator also liked to claim fiscal responsibility over what she called a bloated military budget and actively worked for better treatment for veterans at VA hospitals. A closer look at her record indicated that the spending cuts she voted for helped create a lower standard of care at the VA. Secretly, Spinx thought that the Senator knew what she was doing and needed the media to catch on to the VA story because it coincided with her play to become Chairman of the Armed Services committee. All it took was a couple of YouTube videos and a segment on *60 Minutes* for her to shore up her image and suddenly she was seen as the "savior" of the VA.

What a joke.

When the last Secretary of Defense made a play to expose Walsh's false image in the media, she beat him to the punch and exposed the man's own indiscretions when he was caught with thumb drives of classified information. The ex-secretary was simply taking work home with him, but the act was technically illegal, and Walsh branded him as irresponsible and a potential traitor. Subsequently, she led a charge to have all thumb drives removed from Pentagon computers. The move against the ex-secretary also sent a clear message that Walsh wasn't to be messed with. While Spinx would be damned if he'd suffer the same fate as his predecessor, until he could hit pay dirt with something to hold over her, Walsh was untouchable.

There was a tact and smoothness at the political level that was required when sitting down with politicians like Vivian Walsh. One would need to be delicately resistant and play the long game. Unfortunately, this wasn't a gene that Spinx was born with and a skill he hadn't yet mastered. He preferred a more direct approach and had paid for it on more than one occasion.

The Senator remained silent as she returned the secretary's contemptible stare.

"So?" Spinx said, breaking the silence.

Walsh hoisted her eyebrows.

"*So?* I came here to talk to you about a U.S. led drone strike that's responsible for killing dozens of innocent children and that's your response?"

Spinx scrunched his lips. Right off the bat, he was in the hole in this conversation and may have created a scandal of his own if the merciless senator Tweeted about it.

"What do you want, Senator?"

Walsh smirked. The question was music to her ears.

"It's time to close the base, Mister Secretary."

Spinx huffed out a laugh.

"If that's what you want, Senator, then you could've saved yourself the trip. The answer is no. And if you're going to leak this conversation to the press, make sure that 'no' is written in caps."

"In all of our time in the Middle East, what have we accomplished?" said Walsh. "Syria and Libya are failed states. Afghanistan is barely better than it was before 9/11. Iraq is a mess. ISIS runs rampant and our grip on Iran hasn't changed in forty years. Did I miss something?"

"I think you're confusing beltway politics with a strategic, geographical advantage," said Spinx. "The base isn't responsible for any of those things. The base is there so that we can respond to defend the homeland in case another 9/11 happens or if we go to war with Iran."

"If the intelligence agencies and the FBI do their jobs," said Walsh, "there won't be another 9/11. If the administration would grow a set of balls, war with Iran can be avoided."

"And if you'd stop slashing our budget and throwing roadblocks in the CIA and FBI's way, they'd have a lot more successes to talk about," Spinx said equally as sternly.

"Mister Secretary, we can go around and around about this all you want because I'm prepared to go ten rounds. The facts of the matter are that the tactical decisions made by our government regarding those countries in the Middle East necessitated a response initiated from NSA Bahrain and the successes don't measure up. If we can't succeed, there's no reason to put American soldiers at risk."

The statement was a ploy, but Spinx wasn't falling for it. He knew darn well that the lives of American soldiers were the Senator's last priority.

"If something does occur, we can always go back in," she added.

"Senator, as a former boxer, I'm prepared to go ten rounds as well. If we have to go back in, as you say, then we've already lost the advantage we had, which then delays any response. And while we work to get resources *back* in place, it's not American soldiers that suffer; its American civilians."

"Why not use another drone strike?" said Walsh. "That seems to have worked well."

"One bad drone strike shouldn't be an indictment of all drone strikes. I could name at least twenty other successful drone strikes that have made this country safer."

"All it takes is one bad apple."

"Senator, what do you think will happen to that base if we pull out? You think it's just going to sit there, abandoned? No, some enemy of ours will take it over and then where will we be? Where does that leave our friends in Israel and Saudi Arabia?"

"Mister Secretary, once we pull out of that base, it won't be our problem."

After swapping verbal punches, the two paused. The cloud of steam coming from both their ears did the talking for them.

"I guess that's it. We're both sticking by our guns," Walsh said.

"I guess so."

The Senator stood and shook the Secretary's hand.

"Be prepared for a Congressional hearing on the drone strike, Mister Secretary. And if I were you, I'd make sure those guns of yours are loaded because mine damn sure will be."

"That's one of the benefits of being Secretary of Defense. My guns are always loaded, Senator, and over a million strong have my back."

"Maybe, but I have the bigger microphone and way more than a million will be listening to what I have to say."

Chapter Forty

DIZIN, IRAN

"Who was that?" Delang asked.

Farhad had just hung up the phone.

"It was my brother. I told them what happened and warned them to get out of the country."

"Please tell me that you didn't call their landline. By now, the Revolutionary Guard has it tapped."

"Don't worry. My brother helps me on my liquor runs and has a burner phone. But I need to go. It'll be at least tomorrow when I'm able to meet them."

"Wait, you're leaving?" Kirk chimed in.

"Kirk, my family is in danger. Thankfully, they made it out of the city. They need me."

"Farhad, you've done more for us than we could've possibly hoped for. But we need you, too, especially now."

"I'm not trying to abandon you, my friend, but you don't have to live here. We do. My being with you puts my family at risk. I have to do what's right for them and get as far away from this situation as possible."

Kirk understood and knew he was wrong for asking Farhad to stay. If he were in the man's shoes, he would probably do the same thing.

"Tom, can you get Farhad and his family asylum in the U.S.?"

Delang shook his head.

"It doesn't work like that. He's not a political prisoner and he's not a soldier wanting to defect. American law *does* allow the CIA to bring up to twenty people to the United States each year, and I'd certainly make the case for them, but there are no guarantees. Remember that doctor in Pakistan who helped the CIA before the bin Laden raid? He got left hanging and went to prison. I don't want that to happen."

Kirk nodded. He remembered that story from the news.

"So, what's next for you, Farhad?" Kirk said.

"They are headed to Turkey. I'll try and meet them halfway. But Iran is all I've ever known. It's my home."

Farhad lowered his eyes at the depressing thought of leaving his country behind. The two Americans exchanged glances. They wouldn't want to be run out of their country either.

Kirk walked over and put both hands on Farhad's shoulders.

"Farhad, look at me."

Farhad raised his eyes to meet Kirk's.

"Even though you cost me a finger, you're one of the ballsiest people I've ever met. You risked your life for people that were total strangers to you a couple of days ago, and you have my respect forever. If you don't want to leave your country, we're in no position to stop you. But if you're going to stay, then make your time here worth it. Do you remember when I talked to you about leadership?"

"Yes. Your words were very inspiring."

"Well, if you decide to stay," said Kirk, "you'll be at the intersection of two roads and you'll have to make a choice. I made mine about coming here, and I have to see it through. Tom and I may not make it to the other side."

He looked at Delang and turned back to Farhad.

"If that's the way it turns out for us then so be it, but we're going down swinging. I'm truly proud to call you my friend, Farhad. And as my friend, I understand if you need to leave and save your family. But if you come back to Iran, fight the good fight that this country needs. Be a leader. Lead the rebellion. Who knows? Maybe you can be the Iranian Han Solo . . ."

Farhad cracked a smile.

Delang took his hand and slowly shook it with his right while covering it with his left, as he had with Tariq. Farhad spoke first.

"I'm sorry about what the Revolutionary Guard did to you. We're not all like that."

"I know," Delang said. "You're a good man, Farhad. Your country is lucky to have you. We're all lucky to have you."

"May I ask you a question?"

"Shoot."

"Do you think that Iran will ever be free like America?"

Delang paused.

"It's a tall order. But the greatest glory comes by overcoming the biggest obstacles. For now, do your best and keep telling yourself and others that it's possible. That's all you can do."

"I understand."

"Can you at least stay until the team comes to pick us up?"

Farhad debated the choice for a moment and decided it was a fair ask.

"Yes," he said, "but once they arrive, I'm gone."

Chapter Forty-One

Ninety minutes later, two men in an SUV pulled up near the cabin. They peered through their dark glasses to examine the surroundings for any potential threats and to survey the landscape for escape routes. Once they were satisfied, they checked the property's perimeter. It took more than thirty minutes to sneak around the cabin area, which was surrounded by towering oak trees and manicured foliage. They were searching for any possible danger while trying to peek inside the windows for their marks.

The front room light was on. The blinds were drawn, but the shadows indicated at least three people inside. The men crept up the steps with their weapons extended.

Delang had his Glock drawn. Kirk slid on his knees to the weapons trunk, loaded up three Glock 17 9mms and tossed one to Farhad as he tucked the last one in his waistband. The Americans split to both sides of the door. Farhad crouched in front of it.

"Identify yourself."

Delang spoke in Arabic.

"Moccasin sent us."

The voice replied in English.

Delang slowly lifted the blind to peek outside. The men were armed, but if they wanted to fire, they would've done so by now.

"Prove it," Delang said.

"He said to tell you that your wife should use less oregano," the voice said.

Delang laughed. He signaled Kirk and Farhad to calm down but kept his weapon behind his back as he opened the door.

"Put 'em down," he said. "We're good."

No one spoke as the men entered and stood in the middle of the living room, staring at the three men with their Glocks hanging at their sides.

"They don't look American," Kirk said.

"They're not," he said. "They're Saudis."

Saudis?

They introduced themselves as Ahmed and Hassan from the GID, Saudi Arabia's version of the CIA. Both were imposing, with muscles bulging from under their cold gear. Ahmed was about six-foot-three, with a narrow face and a short Marine-style haircut. Hassan was a few inches shorter, with high cheekbones, a square jaw, and a thick head of hair. Ahmed was carrying a black aluminum suitcase, which Delang assumed was full of the money he requested from Tariq. Ahmed opened it and Delang nodded.

"Tom, I don't want to seem ungrateful," said Kirk, "but why are two Saudis coming to our rescue instead of CIA?"

"In situations like this, I go with who I can trust. Tariq and I go way back."

"And exactly how far back is that?" Kirk asked.

Delang gave Kirk a menacing look.

"What's it matter to you?"

"Because we're as neck deep in this as you, and I think we've earned the right to know."

Delang looked at Farhad.

"Is he always this pushy?"

Farhad shrugged.

Delang didn't make a habit of discussing his sources, but he was burned anyway, so what difference did it make? He relented and gave Kirk and Farhad a short summary of his friendship with Tariq.

"Happy now, Mister Need-to-Know?" Delang said.

"So why did the Iranians kidnap you first and then try and kill Tariq?" Farhad asked.

Delang thought for a moment.

"The Iranians and the Saudis have been at odds for years. One may not have had anything to do with the other. They obviously knew I would be meeting with him, which tells me they knew his schedule. What crazed Iranian would pass up the chance to snatch a CIA agent?

Tariq is too well-protected inside the kingdom, so if they knew we were friends, they probably also knew that he would visit the U.S., where they could take a shot at him.

They could have killed three birds with one stone: snatch me, kill the ambassador, and pull off a terrorist attack on U.S. soil."

Kirk and Farhad nodded.

"I'm not sure what it adds up to," Delang said, "especially when we add in the exchange they had planned for me, but one thing is for sure, the Iranians are playing for keeps."

Chapter Forty-Two

Delang hated writing anything down, but he had little choice, given that Kirk and Farhad had baptized themselves into the realm of espionage and had limited knowledge of Middle East geography. Figuring it would be easy to burn later, he used the back of the wingsuit diving flyer and a red marker from the kitchen to draw a crude map of Iran and its bordering countries.

The exit strategy was up for debate, but since he was the one who'd been captured, the buck stopped with him on the final decision. Anything through Iraq and Turkey was out of the question. The Revolutionary Guard had too many sources on both sides of those borders. Their chances of slipping through were slim to none.

He marked two sizable Xs over those two countries and circled three potential escape routes.

Ahmed and Hassan made a strong case for driving south to the beach community of Bandar Abbas to meet their contact with a boat who could sail them across the Strait of Hormuz to the shores of the UAE. From there, it was a tolerable two-hour drive to the U.S. Embassy in Abu Dhabi. The fact that Kirk already had a UAE stamp in his passport would make passing through easier, should they be stopped for any reason. Not that it mattered. The Saudi influence was so strong on that side of the Gulf that few problems were anticipated.

But when it came to exfils, Murphy's Law could be depended on like clockwork. With no chance of traveling by plane, Bandar Abbas was a fifteen-hour drive from the cabin. This left plenty of time for a feast of things to go wrong when most of the Revolutionary Guard was looking for them. Delang knew that time was not on their side.

Kirk and Farhad, who decided to stay a little longer, liked the idea of crossing over into Turkmenistan. Looking at the map, the idea was appealing considering that the U.S. Embassy was less than an hour's drive across the border in Ashgabat. With Kirk's impressive driving skills, they could be there in about forty minutes.

However, two issues had to be considered. First was time. The border closest to Ashgabat was more than twelve hours from Dizin. Second, the vast land on the Iran side of Ashgabat was an obstacle. The only resources available in that area were mountains and sand. If cornered, they could hide, but it wouldn't be long before they were found. The Revolutionary Guard were trained soldiers with state-of-the-art technology at their disposal. Delang, meanwhile, knew from past experience that Iran's border station at Bajgarin was well-fortified. They would be easily recognized by anyone looking for them. It was unlikely that bribes would get them through.

He believed that Azerbaijan was their best option. First, it was the shortest drive at seven hours. The less time they spent in Iran, the better. Second, that route would take them through the border city of Astara. Since the two countries shared excellent trade relations, there were markets on both sides that transients crossed every day to shop for local goods.

Prior to his capture, Delang knew that Iran and Azerbaijan had signed an agreement for a railway between the two countries that would connect them to European markets. The CIA had been looking at it in case the Iranians decided to use the railway to smuggle WMD's. If he and his companions were lucky, the construction was ongoing, which provided an opportunity to hide in supply trucks and sneak through undetected if they found a friendly face.

This is where the money came in. In 2010, the Azerbaijan government supported the United States sanctions against Iran, who responded by pouring money into Azerbaijan to support pro-Iranian opposition parties. If Delang's experience in the region told him anything, this would create a hell of a lot of tension for Iranians among Azerbaijan locals. With a suitcase full of money, the odds were in their favor of finding someone willing to risk getting them across. In his view, this was the only spot where the reward outweighed the risk.

"So, that's the plan," Delang concluded.

"What're our odds?" Kirk asked.

"Didn't you see *The Empire Strikes Back*?" said Farhad. "Never ask the odds."

Though he loved the Han Solo reference, Kirk wanted reassurance.

"Look, even if it's a fifty-one to forty-nine split, this is our best shot," Delang said.

He pointed at Azerbaijan on the map and noticed Farhad and Kirk staring at his missing fingernail.

"Yes, they ripped it out. Can we continue?"

"Where's the U.S. Embassy in Azerbaijan?" Kirk said.

"Baku."

"How far a drive is that from the border?"

"Three hours," Hassan.

"The Azers are Shiite, right? Doesn't that put us at risk of Iranian sympathizers?" Kirk inquired.

Delang hadn't made up his mind about Kirk. He was more well-informed than the average Joe, but he seemed like a know-it-all and looked at the glass half empty.

"Try and think positive. We have advantages here that we don't have with other options."

Kirk finally nodded in agreement.

"What do you guys think?" Delang said.

Hassan shrugged and Ahmed opened his mouth to offer his advice, but no words came out. His brains exploded before he could say anything.

Chapter Forty-Three

"One target down," a voice said in Aslani's ear mic.

"Good shot, Green Two. How many did you count in the room?" he said.

"Green One, I counted a total of five shadows, including the one down."

"Roger that. Stand by."

Five targets. Not three. Aslani wondered where the other two were from. Had reinforcements arrived and beaten him to the cabin? Or had the Americans taken hostages?

Mahmoud crouched next to him, a hundred yards from the cabin, looking through his binoculars.

"This whole thing would be over if you'd ordered the entire squad to start firing on the cabin," he said.

"Shut up. The American agent is of no use to the general if he is dead. We have to get him out alive."

"How do you know he wasn't the one who was shot?"

"He's too thin and frail. There's no way that large shadow could've been him."

"Should I give the order to move in?"

"No. They may be armed. I want to see how they react. Cover the rear and wait for my order."

***

"*Get down!*"

Hassan screamed.

The others dropped to the floor, crawled to the weapons cache and scooted into position to defend a window. Hassan peeked through the blinds.

"How bad is it?" Delang asked.

"Surrounded. I count a dozen or so," Hassan said.

Kirk crawled toward the refrigerator, tipped it over with a loud thud, and pushed it below the main window. It would provide some cover for any additional gunfire. A smile crept across Delang's face. Kirk's instincts continued to impress him.

Farhad did the same to the window on the other side, using the heavy oak dining table they'd been standing over only seconds before. Then, they noticed the thick trail of blood on the floor from Ahmed's head. Farhad heard the others talking, but this face of death paralyzed him.

"Farhad!"

Farhad snapped out of his daze.

"Huh?"

"I need you to focus, okay?" Delang said. "We can't do anything for him."

Farhad nodded.

Delang had no idea how they'd been located, but there was no time to figure that out.

"Listen up. We're outgunned with limited ammo, so make your shots count. Got it?"

He didn't worry about Hassan, who knew what he was doing.

"Okay, let's start picking off flies. When you think there's an opening, call it out, and we all run like hell."

Kirk slowly lifted his head to window level and saw one soldier dashing to his right. He wasted no time in breaking the glass with the heel of the Glock and firing at the man who was undoubtedly his enemy.

The bullet struck its target in the side of his head. A burst of blood puffed through the air and the soldier keeled over.

For some reason, when the body dropped, Kirk stared at it through the window. Taking someone's life, no matter who they were, was still not something he could wrap his head around. Hassan yanked him to the floor before a bullet zipped by his head. Multiple pieces of shattered glass slit the side of his cheek. Kirk jerked his head in pain, and as soon as he saw his own blood on his fingers, the queasiness he felt from seeing another dead body passed.

"Mother fuckers!"

He reached through the window and fired several more shots. Bullets scattered in every direction, hitting nothing but tree trunks, dirt, and rocks. Oddly, the attackers didn't fire back. The only movement outside was from ruffling branches in the trees. Otherwise, it was deadly silent. Until it wasn't.

All seven remaining soldiers fired their semi-automatic AK-47's at the cabin. Glass shattered. The thick logs, which had withstood years of rough weather, gave way to the barrage of bullets. Everyone inside remained flat on the floor, hands covering their head. Kirk figured Farhad was now regretting his decision to stay behind.

"They're aiming high! Stay down! Stay down!"

Delang's voice was barely audible over the gunfire.

Suddenly, the commotion abruptly stopped, almost as quickly as it had started. No one moved for a moment. Hassan slowly rose to peer out the window.

"They're advancing!"

He returned fire, retiring two bogeys.

Farhad managed to maim one of the soldiers in the lower leg, but he crawled behind a car. The rest of their fire had little effect. The enemy's strategy was clear: attack, withstand, advance. Eventually, with everyone in the cabin outnumbered and outgunned, the strategy would succeed, and they would coil around them like a killer anaconda. Their capture was imminent.

The air outside clung to another moment of hush. Seizing an opportunity, Farhad jumped up and sprinted out the back door through a mass of wood chips and broken glass. This wasn't what he signed up for.

"Farhad!"

Kirk yelled but Farhad kept moving.

Delang remembered the phone call Farhad had made earlier. Maybe it wasn't to his family after all.

"Did that little bastard sell us out?"

"How the hell should I know?" Kirk snapped back.

Gunfire came from the back door, presumably directed at Farhad, but the sounds were muffled by another swarm of gunfire razing the cabin. All Kirk and Delang could think about was surviving—somehow.

Delang wailed in pain. A bullet had ricocheted off the fridge and hit him in the top of the foot. He cussed up a storm loud enough to be heard over the hail of gunfire. Hassan moved to check on him but slipped on the bloody floor. When he sat up, he exposed part of his head through the window. One split second, one sliver of a target, and one bullet was all it took to splatter his brains across the cabin. As Hassan flopped over, Delang screamed.

"We can't keep this up, Delang," Kirk said. "Think of something fast, will ya? We're in deep shit here!"

Deep shit.

An idea popped into Delang's head. Dragging his bloodied foot, he crawled into the kitchen and opened the cabinet under the sink. He found exactly what he was looking for, and the items had thankfully not been pierced by bullets. His next move required patience and luck. He could only hope that karma was on his side.

***

"We've got a runner," Mahmoud said.

He was speaking to Aslani over the radio.

"Looks like your man, Farhad,"

A wicked grin formed on Aslani's face.

"Roger that. All shooters hold your fire. Mahmoud, go after him and secure the target, alive. Repeat, do not terminate! Advance and hold!"

Aslani smiled as he thought of the first lashing he had given Farhad. That one was considered legal punishment. This time, he thought, it would be . . . fun.

Moving forward meant exposing the men from his team, but it was a necessary risk. Aslani could practically feel his hands tightening around his enemies' throats. The Americans returned fire but inflicted minimal injuries. He wasn't concerned about that. Any fatalities suffered on his end were acceptable as long as he accomplished his mission.

Within five minutes, this entire ordeal would be over. The American agent would be in hand, and he'd be redeemed in Shirazi's eyes. Aslani would personally see to it that Kurruthers was shot in the head and his body left to rot in the Dasht-e Kavir Desert. For Farhad, he would fundamentally redefine the word "torture."

"Fire at will!" he ordered.

Bullets sprayed through the air and penetrated the cabin. The air was engulfed with gun powder and splintered oak chips. Devastation was one of the few elements in life that put a swing in Aslani's stride. The cabin couldn't withstand much more damage, but he delighted in watching it slowly come apart, and as he did, adrenaline pumped even stronger through his veins.

"Hold your fire," Aslani said.

The course hairs in his beard began to tingle. He stared at the cabin and wondered what the Americans were planning. He was about to give an order for the final advance when he heard gunshots from the rear.

"Rear position, report!"

No response.

"Green Six, report!"

Aslani's orders were followed with more gunshots.

"Green Six, confirm that the rear is secure."

"Rear secure. Another target down," a voice said.

Checkmate!

"Fire at will!" Aslani said.

Once again, his team continued to annihilate the cabin. The flurry of gunfire lasted at least two minutes.

"Hold your fire. Send four canisters inside. This ends now."

Three soldiers switched weapons and used air guns to launch black tear gas canisters into the cabin. The Americans were surrounded, their position was compromised, and now their breathing would become labored. In a matter of minutes, they would be faced with two choices: come out voluntarily or Aslani's team was going in.

"There's nowhere to go. Come out now!"

Aslani shouted, but there was no response.

"Breach! Breach! Breach!"

The five remaining soldiers ran toward the house, weapons raised. Any target within their sites would be dead in seconds. A barrel-chested man kicked the door down while another tossed in a flash bang grenade. An explosion was followed by a blinding flash of light and a deafening blast. Then, the heat created inside the cabin ignited a container of flammable gas in the kitchen.

The soldiers nearby were instantly engulfed in flames and the combustion knocked a charging Aslani off his feet. Before blacking out, he knew that the Americans had slipped through his fingers again.

***

Farhad bolted out the back door by then, running toward the woods, dodging bullets that whizzed past his ear. Glancing over his shoulder, he saw a Revolutionary Guardsmen in hot pursuit, firing wildly in his direction. He stumbled over a rock and fell face first in the dirt. Thankfully, he was only a few feet away from his intended destination. Disguised by a camouflaged leaf blanket was a hidden door where he and Simin kept the booze they smuggled into the resort. The hole was barely large enough for him hide in, but it worked.

Though he still had his gun and could fight back, he slammed his eyes shut and covered his ears, shielding himself from the thunderous gunfire. When it stopped, he cracked the overhead door enough to peer out. The soldier who had been in pursuit was gone and he could see that the cabin had been shot to shit. He peeked over the top of a wood pile and saw a slender soldier taking aim at the cabin. As soon as the shooting started up again, he would be able to make a run for it to the ski academy. If he was lucky, he could hitch a ride out of the resort.

But Farhad's moral compass weighed on him. Kirk was in trouble. He'd promised the American that he would not only help him kill Haddadi; he would help him escape the country as well. Could he tell his father that he had a chance to save this man but decided to put his head in the ground like a damned ostrich and then run off to save his own skin? Would he be able to look himself in the mirror knowing what he did? No. He owed this man.

Farhad noticed that the soldier's gun had jammed. Now was his opportunity. For him to live, this man had to die. He pulled the gun from his waistband, took aim and then squeezed the trigger as he popped out of the hole.

The shot successfully hit the man in the neck. He dropped to his knees and fell over. Farhad ran over to confirm the kill and grab his weapon. As he stood over the Guardsman, with his gun extended, he was unnerved by the sight of the man gurgling his own blood. Farhad wondered what was going on inside the man's head as the last seconds of his life ticked away.

Those thoughts were interrupted by a noise coming from the man's earpiece. Farhad tore it off him and put it on.

"Green Six, confirm that the rear is secure,"

He recognized Aslani's voice.

"Rear secure," Farhad said. "Another target down," he replied in a disguised, deeper voice.

Farhad needed to think fast or his minor victory would be short lived. He whirled his head around, desperately searching for an option. Then he saw it. Farhad darted as fast as he could toward a delivery truck parked nearby. He climbed inside, but there were no keys.

"Dammit!"

From the passenger side mirror, he could see the delivery man cowering. He climbed through to the other side and stuck his gun in the man's face. There was no time for pleasantries.

"Keys, now!"

The driver had both hands up, but slowly reached into his pocket and handed the keys to Farhad, who snatched them from the man's hand.

"I'm sorry," Farhad said.

He hopped back into the truck and started the engine. He stepped on the gas and steered the bulky orange truck toward the rear door of what was left of the cabin. By then, there was a thick cloud of white smoke overwhelming the entire structure.

Tear gas.

It glided into Farhad's lungs immediately.

"Get in!"

He screamed as loud as he could between coughs.

Delang and Kirk came hustling through the back door with their shirts raised over their noses. As soon as they jumped in, Farhad slammed his foot on the gas and sped away.

Chapter Forty-Four

As they watched the cabin burst into flames, Farhad hauled ass out of the resort complex and onto Road 425.

"Shit! What the hell was that?" Kirk said.

"*Shit* is right. Nothing unclogs your pipes better than ammonia. When you mix it together with bleach, you get mustard gas. Toxic to breathe and extremely flammable."

"Is everyone okay?" Farhad asked.

"Yeah, thanks to you," Kirk said.

He patted Farhad on the shoulder.

"You are one crazy, ballsy dude, you know that?"

Farhad laughed.

"I'm sorry I ran away. I got scared."

"Given our situation, I can't really say I blame you."

"I couldn't live with myself if I'd left you to die."

"What about your family?"

"They'll be okay. My family takes honor quite seriously. My father would be disappointed in me if I didn't help you get across the border."

"Farhad, pull over," Delang said.

"We need to keep going, my friend. More Revolutionary Guard and police will follow."

"Pull off at the next exit, okay?"

After a few minutes riding in silence, Farhad did what he was asked and pulled the truck into a market parking lot in the neighboring town of Gachsar.

Delang hobbled up from the back of the truck and plopped into the passenger seat. He balanced himself as best as he could and motioned

Farhad to move closer. He reached out for his hand and held it in his own.

"Thank you," Delang said.

He was getting weaker and was bleeding quite a lot.

"You're welcome, my friend."

Farhad went to pull away, but Delang held his grip and pulled him back.

"Hang on, Farhad. One more thing."

"Yes?"

"On behalf of the CIA, I'm sorry for the coup that reinstalled the Shah," Delang said. "That should've never happened. We know what role we played in all this and what it did to your country under the Ayatollah."

"Thank you," Farhad smiled. "That means a lot."

Before he became too emotional, Delang returned to business.

"Where's the money?"

"What money?" said Farhad.

"The suitcase that Ahmed and Hassan brought. You have it, don't you?"

"No, I hauled ass out of the cabin. I thought you had it."

Delang closed his eyes and banged the back of his head against the seat's headrest.

"Shit. I don't know how we get across the border if we can't bribe our way through."

Kirk was noisily rummaging around in the back. He reached up to an overhead shelf containing three plastic cases.

"Farhad, help me out," Kirk said.

They lifted one of the cases from the net guard and set it down. Kirk released the metal clasps, flipped open the top, and foraged through the contents, desperately looking for whatever could be of use to make it across the border. His face contorted in irritation seeing only some thick, orange, polyester fabric until he realized what it was. Of the dozen inside, he grabbed one and held it up in front of him.

"What the . . .?" Farhad said.

"It's a wingsuit," Kirk said.

From the look on Kirk's face, Delang could see the wheels turning in his head.

"What?" he said.

"I've got a crazy idea, but it just might work."

Chapter Forty-Five

ROCKEFELLER CENTER
NEW YORK CITY

"How do I look?" Senator Walsh asked.

"Excellent, Senator. Dynamite suit," her chief of staff replied.

Walsh smirked as she admired herself in the mirror of her make-up table. The money budgeted for the focus group had been well-spent. It *was* a dynamite suit and she looked damned good wearing it. The jacket and pants were black with a thin white pinstripe. The button-down blouse was solid white with the collar slightly open over the lapel of the jacket. The ensemble was accented with the sterling silver cross worn around her neck and a visible emerald-green scarf that popped against the black jacket. Her naturally frizzy hair had been thinned a touch and moderately straightened. Her hairdresser called it a "half and half," giving her the look of a leader and a rebel.

After the news of the drone strike accident broke, the Senator hit pay dirt with her *#closethebase* Tweet. The tagline spread faster than a wildfire over dry timber. It was retweeted and shared more than twelve million times. Twenty-four-hour protests outside military bases across the Middle East and the U.S. East Coast were garnering epic news coverage from an army of media outlets on the never-ending news cycle. And God bless Instagram. Every rant, shouting match, so-called interview, and confrontation with someone of an opposite opinion was shared, liked, and emojied for their world of friends to see. For Walsh, it was the cow that kept on milking.

It didn't take long for seasoned NBC News reporter Elias Pinter to backtrack the origins of the *#closethebase* trend. When he called the

Senator's office, chief of staff Latrina Pearl was eagerly waiting with a silver-tongued response that she'd worked tirelessly to prepare, and she negotiated terms with both Pinter and NBC News. First, the Senator would provide an exclusive quote to Pinter that was to be immediately posted online. The statement read:

> *The U.S. military is the greatest in the world. It led the charge in saving the world from the Nazis during World War II and exacted much needed revenge on al-Qaeda after 9/11. But our military is only as strong as its weakest link and lead by humans that inherently make mistakes. Everyone makes mistakes, but some mistakes are worse than others. We must all ultimately pay for our errors and confront the sins of our past. For too long, the United States has been involved in the Middle East crisis with little to no progress in resolving any conflicts. It's been worse than a strategy of containment. It's been a strategy of not making the situation worse because it's been impossible to make the situation better. There was a time when the Naval Support Activity base in Bahrain served the interests of the United States with great honor, purpose, and prestige. It's obvious that time has passed. While we will always need to defend our nation from the evils in the world, the time has come to close the base.*

The second condition was that the Senator would give a full national interview on the *TODAY* show in front of a live audience at Rockefeller Center. Considering that the Senator was elected from Pennsylvania and not New York, the move was a risky one for NBC producers. With the election cycle not far away, they didn't want to turn the *TODAY* show into a potential campaign rally for the Senator's presidential aspirations.

But the Senator's light was sparkling too bright to miss such a chance. Situations where the Chairperson of the Senate Armed Services Committee received widespread global attention were scarce. Counting the hosts of the show, the image of three strong women onstage would also play well among their demographics. The producers agreed.

It was a chilly November morning in New York City, and there was an extra nip in the air. The crowd was dressed in skull caps, gloves, and their warmest coats, as were the producers, cameramen, and hosts onstage. Off stage, Walsh kept warm in a wool coat. She didn't have on a beanie hat as it would create static in her hair, and she used hand warmers in her coat pockets in lieu of wearing gloves. Her limited winter attire would allow her to slip the coat off her shoulders, energetically walk on stage and get mic'd up within thirty seconds. She had no intention of wearing her coat during the interview. Walsh had always remembered the image of Ronald Reagan beaming with American masculinity by not wearing a coat in the Reykjavik winter to shake hands with Mikhail Gorbachev, who was wearing an overcoat and should have been accustomed to cold winters.

In Hollywood and politics, image was everything.

As the call went out for thirty seconds, the producers queued the Senator on stage. She shrugged off the coat as planned, let it plop to the ground, clipped on her microphone, and fluffed her hair one last time before watching the producer count them down.

Three . . . two . . . one.

The crowd cheered and clapped as hosts Hoda Kotb and Savannah Guthrie welcomed the audience at home back from a commercial.

"Welcome back to the *TODAY* show! We have the pleasure of being joined by someone who has no qualms about creating waves in Washington or on social media. Please welcome the Chairwoman of the

Senate Armed Services Committee, Senator Vivian Walsh!" Guthrie said.

The crowd popped and the camera focused on a smiling Walsh who had her hands folded together in front of her.

"So, Senator, there's been a lot in the news lately," Kotb said.

"There certainly has been," said Walsh.

"As the elected official chairing the Armed Services Committee, how do you put the recent tragedy of the drone strike into words and how do you try and mitigate the damage with our allies in the Middle East?"

"Well, I'm not sure that I or anyone else can say anything that will make the situation any better. First, our hearts and prayers go out to the families of the children lost in this terrible event. Second, America shouldn't be judged only by its mistakes and our military isn't the monster it is being portrayed to be in the overseas media. That being said, the soldiers and their commanding officers involved in this event must be and will be held accountable."

The crowd cheered. Walsh had them eating out of the palm of her hand.

"Senator, you also sent a controversial Tweet about potentially closing the base in Bahrain, which now has many people in Washington nervous," Guthrie said. "Do you stand behind your words?"

"Absolutely."

The live audience once again rocked with spontaneous applause.

"But this base is the home to the Fifth Fleet," Kotb said, "and it is the command center for all operations in the Middle East. Don't you think that we'd be leaving behind a strategic advantage that could be detrimental to our national interests?"

"I think that the time has come for the people of the Middle East to determine their own fate. We've been involved in Middle East politics and conflicts for fifty years. What do we have to show for it? Next to nothing. We can go back into the Middle East at any time by way of an aircraft carrier or fly into local bases supplied by our allies if a conflict arises."

"What about our Saudi Arabia allies?" said Kotb. "What will they say if we pull out of the base?"

"The Saudis make enough money from their oil fields to buy all possible means of defense and ammunitions necessary to protect themselves from a possible attack. This isn't 1990. They have been, and always will be, one of our greatest allies in the region, but just because we're their friend doesn't mean that we need to constantly pitch a tent in their backyard. Friends stand side by side with one another in a fight. We don't come charging in when they whistle for us at will. They need to stand on their own two feet. And the time has come for the United States to CLOSE THE BASE."

Walsh was baiting the mob and they bit right on cue.

"CLOSE-THE-BASE! CLOSE-THE-BASE! CLOSE-THE-BASE!"

Walsh turned back to the crowd with open arms then swung back to the camera with a wickedly beguiling grin on her face.

Chapter Forty-Six

BASRA, IRAQ

Ben Thrasher, one of the CIA's newest and brightest agents in the field, looked like he came right out of central casting for a biker movie. At six-foot-two and an athletic one hundred and ninety pounds, with spikey dark hair, his colorful tattoos of gargoyles and evil clowns running the lengths of both arms were the first things you'd notice about him. His deep blue eyes were rarely seen under his Arnette sunglasses. When he spoke, his no-nonsense, often confrontational attitude made him difficult to enjoy being around, and even those most familiar with Thrasher found him moody at best. Despite his loud, quirky personality, it was Thrasher's investigative instincts at bombing scenes and uncanny memory that garnered the attention of the upper level CIA hierarchy.

His memory, though, had a downside as he lacked the ability to let things go and move on. Psychologists at the CIA had warned him and management in the Special Activities Center that it could have adverse effects on his career and mental state if the issue wasn't addressed.

While he was willing to acknowledge his so-called impairment, Thrasher didn't view it that way. Instead, he used it as motivation. After surviving a suicide bomb attack in Beirut little more than a year ago, he'd been obsessed with never facing such an incident again. The event resulted in the deaths of three colleagues, one of whom had thought enough of Thrasher's abilities to take him under his wing for the mission.

Ever since the bombing, Thrasher had lived with survivor's guilt. Had he performed a more thorough search of one of the suspect's home, he would've found the phone that was used to set up the bombing. The burn marks on his hands and neck were a constant reminder of the dangers of what can happen when you don't pay enough attention to detail.

Thrasher was investigating a suicide bombing near a café frequented by U.S. servicemen in Lebanon when he was notified about the Basra drone strike. An hour later, he was on the first DOD plane to Iraq. He was met at the airport by local military personnel and joined by Basra Police Chief Kazeem al-Nashou, who had originally alerted DOD about the high value target in the area.

"*Jaybird*?" the chief asked.

Thrasher nodded, acknowledging his code name, as he stepped into the Humvee and looked over the chief.

The gentlemanly chief shook hands with his contact, and easily assessed from his strong grip and stony face that the man lacked conventional social decorum when meeting new people.

"Show me where you were sitting," Thrasher said.

This was no time to exchange pleasantries.

After driving to the bombing scene, the chief pointed to the location adjacent to a bus stop two hundred yards from the former schoolhouse where he had sat in his car days before.

"Right over there," he pointed out.

Thrasher deliberated over the man's vantage point. The chief would've had a clear line of sight to anyone entering or exiting the building.

"Good spot," he said. "Who gave you the tip?"

"A guy I've used several times. His intel had never let me down before, but I'm having trouble tracking him down. I think we both know why."

Thrasher pursed his lips in disgust and nodded.

"Introduce me to whoever is in charge of the excavation."

The chief walked him over to meet Agent John Brady of the U.S. Army Criminal Investigation Command (CID) unit. A former sniper, the prematurely grey Brady had a sharp eye and excelled at organizing a chaotic military crime scene into one that was manageable to assess from the ground and the air. He was also known for the high-pitched whistle in his speech when using words with a 's'.

"Are you the CIA guy I've been waiting for?" Brady asked.

Thrasher nodded.

"I want to show you something."

Brady walked Thrasher and the chief over to a table inside a blue evidence tent.

"Among the dead bodies, we found these."

He picked up one of the items and handed it to Thrasher. It was heavy and a little mangled from the explosion, but he recognized it immediately.

"Skeleton key?"

"Yup. Found about dozen so far."

Thrasher rubbed the piece of steel between his fingers while he recalled the chief's previous vantage point.

"And then there's that," Brady said.

He pointed out a large, bent sheet of metal.

"What am I looking at? A piece of a wall or a big ass freezer?"

"A three-inch thick, lead door. Doesn't fit. Doesn't belong in that building."

Thrasher's eyes darted back and forth as he contemplated how this piece fit the puzzle.

"There's something else," Brady said.

Brady walked them over to two computer monitors on the opposite side of the tent.

"Now that most of the smoke has cleared, we've got the before and after images of the bombing," he said. "Notice anything?"

Thrasher studied the screenshots but the photos from the drone weren't high definition.

"What's this dirt formation here? The soil looks disturbed, almost softer."

The chief felt a sickening feeling in his stomach.

"That's it," he unintentionally said aloud.

"What?" Brady asked.

"I think that's a smuggling tunnel. I've known that the Iranians were running drugs into the city using a tunnel, but I've never been able to prove it."

"Are you fucking kidding me?" Thrasher said. "You knew about this thing and didn't think to mention it to Colonel Suarez before he launched a God damned missile?"

Thrasher got up in the chief's face. Sensing the anger in his voice and tension in his body language, the chief stepped back.

"I said that I knew a tunnel existed, not that it was here," the chief said. "Besides, your military knew the tunnel existed, too, but we could never find it."

Thrasher looked to Brady, who acknowledged the chief's statement with a nod.

"I heard the rumors," he said.

This satisfied Thrasher for the moment, but he'd call Suarez to verify.

"Please tell me that you've got the crew digging out the northwest side of the blast," Thrasher said to Brady.

"They started on it ten minutes before you got here."

"They just started?"

"In case you haven't noticed, tough guy, we've been a little busy pulling the bodies of dead kids out of the rubble!"

Thrasher backed off, conceding the point.

"Lemme see where they're at."

Brady exited the tent and was heard whistling and barking orders outside. Hearing commotion, Thrasher peeked out to see what was going on and saw Brady motioning him over. He rushed out of the tent without saying a word to the puzzled chief, who followed behind him.

Unfortunately, the chief's theory was proven correct. A quarter mile down from the bombing, the tunnel had crumbled from the effects of the missile strike. But as force of the explosion lost energy, the tunnel's wooden structure maintained its integrity as it moved farther away from the school.

After a backhoe unearthed a section that was still intact, Brady retrieved a ladder and he, the chief, and Thrasher climbed down to walk the remaining length of the tunnel. Thrasher and Brady used the mini flashlights on their belts to aid their navigation. At the end of the tunnel was a set of stairs leading to a second abandoned building and the main road heading out of town.

"And that's how they did it," Thrasher said.

"Well, I'll be damned," said Brady.

The chief was shocked. For more than a year, he'd been trying to break the drug operation in his city, and the key to doing so had been in front of him the entire time. He never thought the drug traffickers would stoop low enough to use a children's school as cover.

How could I have not known about the tunnel? Was I that stupid or have I trusted the wrong men in my own department?

Outrage built up inside him. The veins on his forehead started to protrude and throb.

"Chief, this area is known to have earthquakes, right?" Thrasher asked.

"What?"

The chief looked confused.

"Earthquakes. They're common around here, aren't they?"

"Yes, since the late seventies."

"That's when the school was built, right?"

"I'm not sure, but I remember it being there in the eighties. What are you getting at?"

"Do you know anyone who was a teacher there before ISIS sunk their claws into it?"

"Sure do."

"Call them. See if the school had an underground bunker."

The chief grabbed a phone from his pocket, scrolled through his extensive contact list, and tapped the number of his source. Upon hearing the answer to his question, the chief turned to Thrasher with a dismal look and nodded.

"Son of a bitch!" said Thrasher.

He charged toward the chief, slapped the phone out of his hand, and pushed him against the wall. Grabbing his throat, Thrasher came nose-to-nose with him, his eyes livid with rage.

"Hey!" Brady shouted.

He lunged to grab Thrasher and pull him off the chief, but Thrasher was too strong.

"Now, you listen," he said. "I'm only going to ask you this once, so you'd better think twice about lying to me."

Thrasher held his gaze and tightened his grip on the chief. Brady stood by, just hoping he wouldn't choke the man out.

"Who was your source? Who gave you the tip about Mustafa Shamekh?"

The chief struggled to answer.

"Mazen Al-Jafari," he wheezed. "People call him. . . Moz."

Stunned, Thrasher released his grip on the chief, who dropped to the ground, hacking and coughing as he tried to regain his breath. Thrasher brushed past Brady.

"Whoa," said Brady, "where are you going?"

Thrasher didn't answer. He pulled the phone from his pocket and dialed his boss at Langley. What he had to say couldn't wait.

Chapter Forty-Seven

SERIK, TURKEY

Across town from the G20 Summit, Yasser entered Tariq's hotel room and saw the ambassador leaning against the full-length glass window that had a bird's-eye view of the Turkish landscape. He was worried about his boss. Usually calm and levelheaded, it was rare to see him so tense. The sky was a breathtaking peach color as the sun set over the calm waters of the Mediterranean, but Tariq paid no attention as he twirled his cell in the palm of his hand.

"Tariq, here's your tea," he said.

Yasser set the tray on the desk and poured his boss a cup.

Tariq was so lost in thought he hadn't even heard Yasser come in.

"Thank you," he said. "Did you bring the extra strength Tylenol?"

Yasser handed Tariq the pills. His boss's palms were sweaty.

"I take it there's been no word?" Yasser said.

"No. I'm expecting a call from the Director of Intelligence, but the seconds are ticking away like hours."

"Anything from Tom?"

Tariq gave Yasser a sharp, angry look.

"If I'd heard from him, do you think I'd be this stressed?" he snapped.

Yasser stared at his friend. It didn't happen often, but being a verbal punching bag sometimes came with the job.

Tariq put his hands on the desk and exhaled a deep, much needed breath.

"Sorry."

"It's okay."

Tariq nodded, sipped his tea and flipped the Tylenol in his mouth.

"You know, you never told me how the two of you met. Whenever I've asked, you only said that the two of you go way back."

Tariq's mouth belied a smile.

"When Hezbollah bombed Khobar Towers, I was an up-and-comer in the diplomatic service, but I knew that if we let them get away with bombing us once, it would happen again. Changes to our technological infrastructure needed to be made and that ingenuity *had* to come from the west, so I started attending technology conferences around the region. At one of them, I met this American with slicked back hair who looked like a Wall Street tycoon. I was no stranger to businessmen who tried to seduce me with their words to make a sale, but there was a kindness to Tom that struck me as genuine. That introduction was the foundation of what is now the Saudi Telecom Company, which led to upgrades in our country's security measures."

"If he was a salesman, what happened to make him join the CIA?"

"9/11 happened. Despite other applicants ten years his junior, Tom did what he felt he had to do. Using his Arabic skills and Middle East contacts from his previous business dealings, it didn't take him long to move up the food chain."

"And you were his first phone call."

Tariq nodded.

"What started as a strictly business association blossomed over time into a tremendous friendship. He even left his Bahamas vacation to attend my mother's funeral in Riyadh. I never forgot that. By 2015, I became the ambassador to the U.S. and Tom was the most trusted agent in the CIA's Near East division. He could've been promoted from within and had a legitimate shot at becoming Deputy Director of Operations, but the powers that be decided he was more valuable in the field."

"And the two of you have been watching over the world ever since."

"Apparently not well enough."

"Tariq, I probably shouldn't ask this, but if Tom makes it out of there, what do you think will happen when he finds out about the back-channel deal you made with the Iranians?"

The ambassador set his cup down and drummed his fingers on the desk. Before Tariq could reply, his phone finally rang. Ignoring that Yasser's phone buzzed nearly simultaneously, he snatched it up and answered before the first ring was complete.

"Yes?"

Glancing up from his phone, Yasser watched his boss's reaction. From Tariq's wide-eyed look, it was clear that whatever he was being told was not good news.

"What about the other thing I asked you about? Thank you. I understand."

Tariq flipped the phone on the desk and put his hands on his hips.

"Well?" Yasser said.

"Both of the men we sent to Dizin are dead."

"Confirmed?"

"No photos yet, but according to his sources in the local police department, it's them."

Tariq couldn't contain his frustration. He grabbed the teacup and threw it against the wall, splintering the porcelain into a dozen pieces.

"And Tom?"

Tariq shook his head.

"Nothing."

"You think they got him again?"

"I don't know. Anything from your end?"

"Excuse me?"

"Your phone. It buzzed as I received the call. Any follow-up from your contacts in the Ministry of Defense?"

"Oh. Unfortunately, no. It was an update regarding tomorrow's security protocols."

Massaging his temples, Tariq thought about calling the director back with some follow up questions, but his battery was near dead, and he decided against it.

"Sir, don't take this the wrong way, but you look terrible. You should get some rest."

Yasser was right. Tariq wasn't going to do anyone, including himself, any good if he couldn't focus. He attempted to charge his phone, but was so distracted he couldn't manage to plug the cord into the jack. Yasser stepped in to help.

"Here, let me take care of that for you," he said.

Tariq wiped his eyes.

"I'm going to get some shut eye, but make sure to get me if it rings, understood?"

Yasser nodded and Tariq disappeared into the bedroom. There was something 'off' about Tariq that Yasser couldn't put his finger on. His boss had always maintained a certain level of calm and laser focus in stressful situations.

Although he knew he shouldn't, Yasser entered his boss's passcode and started searching. He had to be hiding something, but he found nothing. He decided that Tariq should not be undisturbed, so Yasser disobeyed his boss's order and put the phone into airplane mode. Whatever news was forthcoming would have to wait. He would check back when the phone was finished charging.

Chapter Forty-Eight

TABRIZ, IRAN

Simin sat at a café in El Goli Park in southeast Tabriz, sipping her sugary tea and waiting for her ice cream. The lake was her favorite spot in Iran. She didn't know what she loved more: the lavish, apricot-colored sunset over the rolling hills or the beaming moonlight over the soft ripples in the water with the Pars-El-Goli Hotel illuminated in the background.

As she enjoyed the atmosphere, she couldn't help but notice all the couples romantically huddled together in booths and swan shaped paddle boats. Her thoughts drifted to Kirk. While she didn't know what he and Farhad were planning, she knew that whatever it was would carry dire consequences if they were caught by the Revolutionary Guard. She understood why Kirk had to say goodbye, but, oh, that last kiss . . . it had to mean something.

In Iran, it was remarkably common for a woman to be told she was in love when her parents arranged the marriage or when she convinced herself she was in love because of her need to be supported. Simin wanted no part of either approach. Having just celebrated her twenty-fourth birthday, she didn't know if she'd ever find love by traditional means. Like any young woman, she dreamed of it. She wasn't immune to such fantasies, but in those divine trances she never thought it would be with an American. For obvious reasons, it wasn't common to see them in Iran. Further, she'd been told by her friends who had interacted with them in other countries how they made themselves appear high and mighty.

"It's in their DNA," one friend told her.

But this wasn't true with Kirk. He never once talked about his possessions or boasted about any of his accomplishments, but it wouldn't have mattered to Simin if there were none to brag about at all. She loved his outgoing personality and the smile that stretched across his handsome face when he made his deep belly laugh. Most important, despite his family's history with Haddadi, Kirk didn't judge her for hers. Any sane man would have run in the opposite direction. While she had spent so little time with him, hours really, every ounce of her heart felt a deep connection.

As she watched a couple paddle by in the swan boat, the idea of doing the same with Kirk, in Paris or anywhere else, brought a smile and a tear to her eye.

"Are you okay, miss?" the waiter said.

As he placed the ice cream in front of her, he noticed the bruise on her forehead.

"Yes, I'm fine," she said.

She brushed the hair back under her hajib and wiped the tears from her eyes.

"Have a nice evening," he said.

"You as well."

When she ordered the ice cream, she hadn't realized that it was the same bastani sonnati that she'd shared with Kirk at her apartment a few days ago. She stared at the melting vanilla on the waffle crisps and languished in her thoughts about the dreamy American. Since she wouldn't be crossing the Armenian border until tomorrow, she knew that she should stay off her phone, but she wanted to let him know that she was thinking about him. She needed him to know. If he'd made it to wherever he was going, perhaps he would reply. She hoped he was okay.

With the new sim card she'd bought from a local vendor at the train station, Simin logged into Instagram and squatted down to capture the ice cream with the glow from the setting sun, glimmering across the lake. She had a caption ready, too: *Waiting for You.*

"What are you doing?" a voice said from behind her.

Simin turned to see the friend she'd called to help get her out of the country.

"Oh, hey. Nothing," she said. "Thanks for coming, Moz."

Simin stood up to give him a hug.

"I was surprised to hear from you," said Moz, "but a deal's a deal. If it wasn't for you, I'd have never gotten that truckload of weed into the country a year ago. That border agent really had it out for me."

"That tends to happen when you sleep with someone's sister behind their back."

"Yeah, I suppose so," he said.

He laughed.

"Anyway, without your personal charm, I couldn't have gotten through customs. It was a big score for me. The least I can do is help get you out of the country. Besides, out of everyone I trade with, you're the one that almost never has a problem, so I knew it was important."

Moz took a seat across from Simin. He sniffed, as if something was bothering his nose.

"You got here faster than I thought. I wasn't expecting you for at least another hour."

"I was already a few hours outside out of Basra when you called."

Simin was aware of the drone strike in Basra. She knew that Moz worked with various agents of Middle East governments, but she was smart enough to never ask too many questions.

"Should I bother asking?"

"Not if you expect me to answer," Moz said.

Simin nodded. She knew she should've known better. Moz sniffed again.

"Are you okay? You seem to have the sniffles. Sand get in your nose?"

"Oh, that. No, I think I caught something while traveling. It should clear up in another day or so."

"Right," she said.

For some reason, Simin doubted his response. Moz tilted his head and squinted at her.

"What?" she said.

"There's a glow about you," he said. "Did I interrupt something?"

"No, not at all. I've been sitting here staring off into space, thinking."

"About?"

Simin tried to contain her smile, but her thoughts about Kirk caused her face to crack.

"Oh, I get it. You met someone, didn't you?"

"Yeah, I did," she said, blushing.

"Well, well, well. Looks like the pony with a steel heart is a softie after all."

"Don't say that. A girl needs to be careful with her heart. Women in this part of the world don't get a lot of choices when it comes to relationships. You know that. I'm adamant about protecting mine."

"I guess I can understand that," Moz said.

He remembered her turning him down flat a year ago.

"Do you want to see a picture of him?"

"Absolutely. I've gotta see the Prince Charming that has you all gooey."

Simin opened her camera roll, swiped to the picture of her and Kirk at the train station, and handed it to Moz.

Moz studied Kirk's face for a second.

"Not a bad looking guy. But the shiner on his cheek and the bruise on the side of your head makes me think that he's not the nice guy you're making him out to be."

"No. That's a long story."

Moz was about to hand the phone back to her when he noticed something in the foreground of the photo. More specifically, someone. He widened the image to get a better look at the scruffy looking man sitting in the car. His eyes popped open, and his stomach dropped when he realized who it was.

"Who's this other guy sitting in the car?" he said.

He sniffed again, appearing anxious.

"I don't know much about him, but he's part of the reason I need you to get me across the border as soon as possible."

Moz's eyes twitched. His mind raced with a thousand thoughts.

"Are you okay?" Simin asked.

She was concerned about Moz's sudden change in demeanor.

"Yes, fine. Simin, I need you to tell me why you need to get out of the country."

"Come on, Moz, I can't do that. Our deal is no questions asked."

Moz pulled a pistol from his waistband and pointed it at Simin. In nanoseconds, his expression snapped from a caring friend to a hardened mercenary.

"I insist."

Chapter Forty-Nine

DIZIN, IRAN

"Sir! Sir, are you okay?"

Aslani blinked rapidly as he struggled to regain consciousness. Leaning over him were two soldiers who he didn't immediately recognize.

"Who? Who are you?"

"Sergeants Khaden and Mohsen, sir. You brought us here with you, remember? The rest of our team is dead."

Aslani pushed himself up to his elbows, but the blood instantly rushed to his head, which began throbbing. It hurt like hell. He groaned.

"Where is Mahmoud?"

"Who?" Mohsen asked.

"Lieutenant Yazdani! He was here, dammit! Have you seen him?" Aslani held his head in his hands.

"Yes, sir. He's talking to one of the firefighters," Mohsen said.

He looked at Khaden and flicked his head in Mahmoud's direction. Khaden jogged off to retrieve the lieutenant. Moments later, he returned with Mahmoud.

"Where'd they go?" Aslani said.

"I don't know. I ran off to catch Farhad. I may have winged him, but he somehow lost me. I came running back when I heard the explosion."

"What caused it?"

"Someone in there knew how to mix the right cleaning products to make the wrong combination. They dumped all of it, and I mean *all* of it, into a tall trash can. When the flash bang ignited, the fumes from the chemicals were already mixed and in the air. Kaboom."

Aslani let out an exasperated sigh. These Americans were a major thorn in his side. Seeing that the ground was littered with paper money, he picked one up and held it in front of him. It was a Saudi riyal with a one hundred denomination.

"What's all this?" said Aslani.

"Whoever met the Americans at the cabin must have brought cash. I guess they were in such a hurry to escape they forgot the suitcase."

Mohsen pointed to the opened, empty suitcase on the ground.

"Wherever they're going, they won't get far."

Aslani smiled at this tidbit of fortunate news.

"Excellent. What else?"

"I found this under one of the bodies," Mahmoud said

He pulled a piece of paper from his pocket. Aslani studied it for a moment. Stained with blood and a little charred on the sides, it was a makeshift drawing of Iran and its surrounding countries. He saw arrows pointing around the country's border. A sense of relief tingled down his spine. He carefully stood up and patted Mahmoud on the shoulder.

"It looks like their exit plan. Good job," he said.

Aslani's phone rang.

"Yes?"

As he listened, he grew excited.

"Excellent," he said. "Take care of it immediately. I'll text you my location."

A depraved grin extended across his face. His luck was turning around.

"What is it?" Mahmoud said.

"Allah is with us."

"Should we call the general?"

"Soon, but not right now," Aslani said.

He pointed at Khaden and Mohsen.

"You two, get the cars. You're coming with us."

Khaden and Mohsen looked at each other, confused.

"Where are we going?" Khaden asked.

"To skin a few pigs."

Chapter Fifty

QOM, IRAN

Shirazi had been summoned. Well, not so much summoned as kidnapped. After smashing his office mirror, he remembered being placed into a wrestling hold and passing out, thanks to the fumes from a cloth held over his mouth. He had no memory of the two-hour ride that followed.

When he awoke, Shirazi got a sharp look at the two men he assumed were his captors. The first appeared to be in his mid-thirties, with a completely shaven head, a long, thick beard, and what looked to be a glass eye. The second man seemed to be the same age, with slicked back hair and a scraggly beard to match his furry unibrow. Shirazi vaguely remembered seeing the glass-eyed man in the mirror before he passed out.

Lying on a couch, Shirazi recognized the room. It was large, with dark wood paneled walls, probably soundproofed, a glass coffee table, a heavy oak desk in the corner with the Iranian flag on one side, the Hezbollah flag on the other, and blue mats on the floor. Hanging on the wall were two photos: one of the legendary Ayatollah Khomeini and the other of the current Supreme Leader.

Shirazi was back in Qom, in the same room where he'd taken his oath to be the leader of the IRGC. The meeting that was about to transpire couldn't possibly be good for him.

Marzban Shir-Del gracefully strolled into the room with a blank, emotionless look on his face, his enforcers in tow. He scantily glanced at Shirazi as he walked past him.

"Come," he said, barely above a whisper.

Iran's Guardian Council was comprised of twelve members. All were experts on Islamic Shariah Law, and their main purpose was to interpret the country's constitution. Six of them had been personally chosen by the Supreme Leader to evaluate all current legal issues that may threaten Iranian way of life. The other six were so-called specialists on specific areas of the law and were elected by the Parliament. Collectively, they were the brain trust charged with ensuring that Ayatollah Khomeini's vision for Iran would never be disrupted. Their decisions were trumped only by the Supreme Leader himself who would hand-pick one of the Guardians to succeed him upon his passing.

Of the sitting Guardians, no one wielded more power and had more influence than Marzban Shir-Del. He was ruthless when he had to be and fair when he needed to be. There was a quietness in his outward appearance, but it veiled his dark side. When the Supreme Leader needed to discuss matters requiring discretion, Shir-Del was dispatched to serve as a buffer and messenger. While they hadn't grown up together, Shir-Del had become a close friend of the Supreme Leader after he took up the mantle following Khomeini's passing. He had his ear on all issues of relevant importance and was a sure bet to be the next Supreme Leader. This was fitting because the man's given name literally meant "Guardian of Persia." In effect, speaking to Shir-Del meant one was also speaking to the Supreme Leader.

Shir-Del and Shirazi seated themselves cross-legged on the blue mats. Not a word was spoken while an assistant poured tea. Shir-Del stared at Shirazi as he waited to hear the door close. He allowed a moment of awkward silence to hang in the air before speaking, which served to heighten the general's nerves. His bodyguards stood behind Shirazi.

"I believe you made promises," Shir-Del said in a measured tone.

"Yes, my Guardian."

Shirazi responded with the customary title when speaking to one of the members of the Guardian Council.

Shir-Del held up his hand.

"You promised that you would cut off Saudi Arabia's military aid to Bahrain by using the Russians new, untraceable missiles to blow up the Kind Fahd Bridge between the two countries, did you not?"

"Yes, my Guardian."

"You promised that the American swine would abandon their military base in Bahrain, and our relationship with our Russian friends would be forever forged when we allowed them to take over the base, did you not?"

"Yes, my Guardian."

Shir-Del calmly sipped his tea.

"And all of this was dependent on trading the filthy American agent, yes?"

"Yes, my Guardian," Shirazi said.

"If my sources are correct, I understand my dear friend Rasoul Haddadi was murdered while under your protection, correct?"

Shirazi hesitated. In his planning for Haddadi's death, he'd only considered the Supreme Leader's response. Haddadi and Shir-Del grew up together. Shir-Del's feelings didn't factor into his decision to lure Kabiri's grandson into killing Haddadi. Fear began to set in.

"Yes, my Guardian."

"The Supreme Leader thinks you're a man of your word. Has his faith been misplaced?"

"No, my Guardian."

Shir-Del smacked his palm on top of the table with such force that it caused tea to spill over the sides of both cups.

"Then why is it that we hear the American not only got away, but had help?"

Shirazi had no idea how word had reached the Supreme Leader or his dog, but it didn't matter. Shir-Del's pale brown eyes were bulging, and his normally emotionless, freckled face was fading from its tan color to a deep red.

"My Guardian, my men . . ."

"Your men?" Shir-Del interrupted. "Your men are bungling fools. You should've chosen your soldiers for this mission more wisely."

Shirazi sighed. His own anger at being insulted was building, but he couldn't afford to lose his temper. Not at Shir-Del.

"Yes, my Guardian."

Shir-Del turned his eyes to his two guards. Without uttering a word, one grabbed Shirazi's arms and pinned them behind his back while the other gripped the back of his neck, slammed his head against the table, and held it there with his forearm. Shirazi could only grit his teeth in pain.

"I suggest you adjust your tone when addressing me. Is that understood?"

"Yes, my Guardian," Shirazi uttered as he fought back being handled.

"What is being done to amend our situation?"

Shirazi hesitated. He didn't have an answer. All he could do was stall.

"Progress is being made on the base," he said. "The Senator will be holding hearings about the drone strike any day."

Shir-Del glanced at the man with the glass eye who responded by grinding his forearm against the side of Shirazi's head, compressing it against the glass. Shirazi growled in agony.

"I know that," said Shir-Del. "I'm referring to the American agent. I won't ask again."

He took another sip of his tea.

Shirazi stammered. Shir-Del was about to look at his guards again when Shirazi's cell phone rang. Unibrow man reached into Shirazi's pocket and showed him the screen.

"That's my asset. Please, I'll get you answers!"

Shir-Del nodded at his guards who promptly released him.

Shirazi shrugged them off and answered the phone, hoping to be saved by good news.

"You'd better have good news for me."

"We know where they're going. It is one of three spots along the border." Aslani said. "I'm headed toward one and have dispatched two teams each to the other locations."

Shirazi wanted to scream at Aslani for not having caught them yet, but he decided that his current predicament prevented him from doing so.

"Get it done." said Shirazi. "I'll make another call to provide additional help. You have two days left and your clock is ticking."

Shir-Del stared at Shirazi, waiting for an answer. Shirazi filled him in on the situation and prayed that it would be enough to spare him any more affliction. The sixty-four-year-old man stroked his long, course beard.

"General, if you want a seat on the Guardian Council someday, you'd better keep your promise. Do I make myself clear?"

"Yes, my Guardian," said Shirazi.

Shir-Del nodded at unibrow man who promptly delivered a high-octane punch across the general's cheek. Shirazi saw stars as he fell over.

"That's for Rasoul," Shir-Del added.

He stood up to exit the room as calmly as he'd entered but stopped at the doorway.

"Oh, and General?"

"Yes, my Guardian?"

"Your clock is ticking, too."

Chapter Fifty-One

MOSCOW, RUSSIA

Maxim Petrov was finished with his meetings for the day, but he wasn't ready to go home. He informed his security detail that he wanted to catch up on some FSB reports and that he wasn't to be disturbed. In fact, he needed to think. Sitting in his favorite chair behind his desk, he watched the snow fall. In one hand was a glass of premium vodka and in the other he twirled a thumb drive. A television on the wall was turned on but muted.

His Iranian colleague hadn't delivered on his promise, and Petrov was deliberating his options. Shirazi was useful and had proven his value on prior occasions, but the stakes were now considerably higher. If the plan to secure the base didn't go flawlessly, there would be little he could do to avoid political ruin. Of course, he could eliminate his troubles by killing those who challenged him, but after word of Russia's involvement in the failed plan broke, there would be too many eyes watching him.

Getting his hands on the base in Bahrain would solve all of his problems. It would ensure that Russia would be a power player in the region, which would keep him politically stable for years, and most important, it would secure his legacy.

Petrov wondered if the plan was a set-up. The information he'd been given on the illustrious Senator Walsh was one of his most closely guarded pieces of intelligence to use against the U.S. His contacts in the pharmaceutical industry told him that she was feeding product information to one of her richest supporters prior to it being available to the public. Petrov later confirmed this via wiretaps on the pharma executive's phone. This act of corporate espionage, coupled with his knowledge of her Iranian heritage, would've proven advantageous to him when he needed to leverage the U.S. military's position in the Balkans to stave off the Prime Minister's challenge for his current position.

That opportunity was now gone. On top of that, the thumb drive was full of missile software that cost millions of dollars to research and perfect. If he could secure the base, it would be worth surrendering.

If.

Too many other dominoes needed to fall correctly for that to happen. The fact that his FSB Director was unable to reach the extraction team in Iran didn't help. He doubted that the CIA had gotten wind of the extraction plan, but it was a possibility he had to consider. Had they intercepted the handoff and killed his men? He hated not knowing. After another long sip of Beluga Noble, he clenched his jaw and crushed the ice with his teeth at the thought of being put in such a vulnerable position.

He had to hand it to Shirazi. The man dangled the right piece of bait in front of him. Though he doubted that Shirazi knew how long Petrov had been searching for the American agent, he certainly knew how desperately he wanted him.

Petrov's brother, Bogdan, had only been a second-year field agent when he was killed. He was ambitious and showed great promise, thanks to his natural instincts, but was far too impulsive and abrasive to his fellow agents and the FSB leadership.

As Deputy Director, Petrov had monitored his brother's career with great care and did his best to ensure his survival by giving him cupcake assignments. One day, his brother barged into his office and kicked everyone out of a meeting. The two brothers had an obscene screaming match regarding Bodgan's assignments. He thought he was ready for a big mission while Petrov told him to be patient. Star agents were built over time and charging into danger like a cowboy with something to prove was a good way to end up dead. But Bodgan's mind was made up and he wasn't taking no for an answer.

"Fine! You want an assignment, you arrogant shit? Here!"

Petrov threw a file at his brother.

"There's an agent planning to defect to America. The meet is a week from now in Bucharest. Take care of it or don't come back!"

Bogdan thumbed through the pages, nodded with a satisfied grin, and calmly walked out the door. The next time Petrov saw his brother was on a slab at the morgue after his body was flown back to Moscow. Holding back the tears, Petrov kissed his brother's cold forehead and whispered in his ear, swearing revenge.

For years, he'd been haunted by the surveillance footage of Meadows, or whatever his name was, shooting his brother. The mere thought of watching Meadows be tortured under his orders excited him. The first thing he would do was burn his genitals with a hot poker.

His cell phone woke him from his daze. It was Shirazi.

"Yes?"

"There have been developments."

"Do tell," Petrov said.

Shirazi filled him in on the details he knew of the American's escape.

"And the men I sent to Qom to pick up the American agent?" Petrov said.

"Dead."

Petrov threw his glass of vodka against the wall.

"This was a simple exchange! If your men aren't dead yet, I'll kill them myself!"

"There's no time for that, Maxim! We can still get them!"

"Them?"

Shirazi paused. It was a slip of the tongue in the heat of the moment. He told Petrov about the American escaping but had left out any part about assistance from inside his borders.

"The American had help," he said.

"CIA?"

"I think so, yes."

Shirazi lied. Petrov kicked his chair toward the window but said nothing.

"Maxim, I need your help. I know where they're going."

Petrov scoffed at the idea.

"I've given you enough and have received nothing in return."

"Do you want the base or not?"

Petrov tried to collect himself.

"Of course, I want the base, you idiot. But I expect to be compensated for the loss of my men. Thirty million. Ten for each man."

Shirazi dropped the phone and let loose a string of profanities. He couldn't believe that the Russian was talking about money at a time of such urgency, but he was hardly in a position to argue.

"Done. I'll find a way to get it to you. Now, can you help or not?"

"Yes. And lucky for you, I have an idea."

Petrov explained his strategy to Shirazi who surprisingly agreed. After they hung up, Petrov was pleased to see Senator Walsh on CNN, ready to address a reporter. He unmuted the TV.

"Senator Walsh! Senator Walsh! What can we expect from the upcoming hearings about the drone strike in Iraq?"

"We're going to get to the truth. The soldiers piloting the drone and their commanding officer will answer for their actions to the American people and the people of Iraq."

"What punishments will the soldiers face if they're found guilty?"

"I'm sorry, but I cannot discuss that at this time. However, I can tell you that actions have consequences, and I will personally ensure that they are held accountable."

Petrov chewed his lip. If Shirazi was right and their plan worked, everything would be fine. Still, Shirazi's failures gave him pause. He needed some insurance, so he called his energetic assistant.

"Yes, Mr. President? The security detail said you weren't to be disturbed. Is everything all right?"

"Yes, Anna, I'm fine. Would you inform the Foreign Minister that I need to see him in my office right away?"

Chapter Fifty-Two

RAZAVI KHORASAN PROVINCE
NORTHEAST IRAN

After leaving Dizin, Kirk called an audible. Crossing the border outside Ashgabat, Turkmenistan was their best shot. Delang protested and called the idea ludicrous, but Kirk won him over. Chances were slim that they wouldn't draw attention, banged up as they were and asking questions about sneaking across the border. Delang conceded the point and while he still thought the plan was risky and hare-brained, it might be crazy enough to work. Besides, with Ahmed and Hassan now dead, he couldn't trust that their plan to get out via Bandar Abbas hadn't been compromised.

Kirk and Farhad took a look at Delang's gunshot wound. Unfortunately, the bullet was lodged into the top of his foot and had to be removed. They didn't have any medical devices to pull it out, so they had to make do with two flat head screw drivers they found in the back of the truck. Thankfully, the previous driver of the truck was a drinker and had left a bottle of vodka under his seat, which would sterilize the wound.

Kirk restrained Delang, and while it took several tries, Farhad managed to remove the bullet. Delang passed out during the "procedure." With nothing to stitch up the wound, all they could do was wrap it with pieces from their t-shirts and hope for the best.

Since the delivery truck was conspicuous, the three men stopped in Behshahr, a tourist town along the Caspian Sea, to steal another car. Delang hotwired a Toyota Land Cruiser while Farhad disabled a phone, which had been left inside the car and rigged it up so they could use it. Two minutes later, they were on their way.

The trip to Bardar was long. Stopping was risky so Kirk and Farhad took turns driving and sleeping. Delang couldn't be depended on to not pass out, so he wasn't driving. By mid-afternoon, they got off the highway in Sharhroud and found a general store near the village of Negarman. Farhad was the natural choice to buy munchies and supplies they needed for their climb through the mountains. Even so, his broken nose and dark circles under his eyes made him ripe for questions from the cashier.

Delang took note of the man's appearance.

"Ask about his watch."

"Why?" Farhad said.

Delang passed along one of his trusted espionage tactics.

"There's no better way to avoid having to talk about yourself than making someone else talk about themselves."

Farhad wanted to remember that one. A few minutes later, he returned with four bags.

"Any trouble?" Delang said.

"No, it was a cakewalk. The old guy at the counter asked where we were headed, but the watch trick worked like a charm."

Kirk finished pumping gas.

"What'd you get?"

"I think I got what we needed, but our money is pretty much gone."

"You didn't think that spending nearly two hundred Euros would look suspicious?"

"Oh, I'm sorry, did we have enough time to make a second trip tomorrow?" Farhad said.

Kirk took inventory. Water, crackers, sweatshirts and sweatpants, a home medical kit for Delang, a lighter, flashlights, plastic binoculars, and cheap looking backpacks—everything grown men needed to escape a country of deranged terrorists. Kirk held one of the backpacks up with one finger. It wasn't so much a backpack as a canvas laundry sack with a drawstring. He looked at it skeptically before glancing back at Farhad.

"Hey, man, I did the best I could," he said.

When they got back on the road, Farhad slept in the back while Kirk drove, with Delang riding shotgun, though he was barely conscious. Kirk noticed how much blood he'd lost and hoped that he could make it the rest of the way. A tough climb was ahead tomorrow.

By midnight, they reached the village of Bardar, with its unpaved roads and some small, brick houses scattered in the hills. Delang wasn't sure if they even had running water.

The pitch-black night made it difficult to navigate but thankfully, the sky was clear, and the moon provided added visibility. After searching for a place to stop, they came upon an abandoned barn, which was so rundown it looked as if a stiff wind might collapse it at any moment.

"This thing looks like a bunch of sand spiders holding hands," Delang said.

"Maybe, but it'll work for a few hours," said Kirk.

They all needed some sleep.

Once inside, Kirk and Farhad attempted to clean Delang's foot using mouthwash purchased from the general store. Delang cringed as the alcohol stung his open wound, but on the bright side, as Kirk pointed out, his foot smelled minty and fresh. Kirk re-wrapped the wound as best he could with cotton balls and gauze from the medical kit. All that Delang could do was elevate it to keep the swelling down, which he did by propping the heel of his foot on the ledge of the window after lying down in the back seat to get some shut eye.

Kirk and Farhad let Delang sleep in the car. As shot as their nerves were from their recent experiences, they should've conked out as soon as their heads hit the dirt, but this wasn't the case. They stared up at the sky. Blinking and breathing. Blinking and breathing. Wondering if they would make it to the embassy across the border.

Something else tugged at Kirk's gut.

"Farhad?"

"Yes?"

"Why'd you come back for me?"

"I told you, honor is a big deal in my family."

"And I appreciate that, but the loyalty you've shown to me is off the charts. There's something else, isn't there?"

Farhad sighed. The jig was up. He reached into his pocket and pulled out the old picture of Kirk's grandfather the one he'd taken from him in the car outside Haddadi's house.

"Remember this?"

Kirk squinted at the photo. His eyes popped when he recognized it.

"You held on to it," Kirk said.

"See the man near the end of the table? Second from the left with the thick glasses?"

"What about him?"

"That was my mother's grandfather. My great-grandfather."

The answer hit Kirk like a tidal wave.

"I guess our worlds aren't that far apart after all."

"No. But if my ancestor chose to fight alongside yours, then I can fight alongside you."

Kirk smiled. Honor *did* run deep in Farhad's family.

"Tell me about him. Your great-grandfather. What was his name? I can't see the print on the picture."

"Saeed. I never knew him. He died in the mid-seventies when Haddadi's hit squad found him, but my mother told me lots of stories about him. One I remember. The day of the coup, there was a lot of rioting and he got caught up in it. While one of the local mullahs berated him, another man tried to sneak up and stab him, but a man named Kamran saw what was about to happen and hit the man with a baseball bat. So, in a way, I owe my life to your grandfather because without his interference that day, I may not be here."

Goosebumps washed over Kirk's body. Pap never told him that story.

"Consider your debt paid in full, my friend."

Delang missed Farhad's story as he laid in the backseat of the Toyota, pondering the day's events. How did the Revolutionary Guard find them so quickly? If they were monitoring Farhad's family's phones, they could've traced them. After all, the call was made from a landline. But it was also the second time Delang had been put in danger after speaking to Tariq. Could it really be that his friend sold him out? While rotting in his cell, he hadn't wanted to believe it, but anything was possible. Prior to being captured, Delang recalled Tariq mentioning a back-door deal with the Iranians that he wouldn't want to know about.

He powered up the cell phone in the console and noticed that the screen read NO SERVICE, which wasn't surprising, considering they were in the middle of nowhere. Still, he tried to get a message out and hoped that tomorrow they would find reception.

After debating what to say, Delang typed a message in three emojis that he hoped his friend would understand:

Dinosaur + Azerbaijan flag + U.S. flag.

He sent it to Tariq's phone. Given the stakes and recent history, this was a huge gamble. All Delang could do was hope he was right about his friend.

Chapter Fifty-Three

At sunrise, the three fugitives began their hike through the mountains to a peak of more than ten thousand feet. They only had to trek two miles, but it was more strenuous than anticipated, especially for Delang, who did his best on his injured foot. Kirk and Farhad alternated helping him and carrying the gear. One would support at least half of his weight while the other carried the gear. To his credit, despite slipping on the slopes and enduring agonizing pain from pressure on his open wound, Delang pushed onward.

His complaints about hunger and fatigue were another matter. At first, he seemed larger than life and able to ignore pain. But his lengthy imprisonment had taken a toll on his body and his psyche. Super-agent or not, he was human. Regardless, his whining was becoming intolerable, particularly for Kirk.

The temperature was in the mid-sixties, but there wasn't a cloud in the sky and the sun beat down on them. Kirk realized that hiking through the Kopet Dag mountains wasn't the same as trekking through the Blue Ridge mountains of North Carolina. Navigating ravines caused by earthquakes was an unexpected, laborious complication. They were depleting their water supply, so they had no choice but to ration what they had.

One benefit they found was an abundance of wild grapes and apples, which provided much needed sustenance. After four hours, it was time for a short break. Kirk and Farhad let Delang rest while they collected the fruit. When they returned, they gathered around their feast, fit for a trio of rabbits.

"Tom, if we make it, what will happen to you?" Kirk said.

Delang sighed.

"I'm sure I'll get the usual medal for bravery, but it'll be after they spend months debriefing me. I'll be grilled to the point of being extra well done."

"Grilled for what? You'll be an American hero, for God's sake."

Delang lifted his shirt and exposed the evidence of his beatings.

"Even heroes have their breaking point. I resisted the best I could, but having a ghost pepper pressed into an open wound could make a mute person confess to the Kennedy assassination. The difference with me was that I actually knew operational secrets in the region. There's only so much one person can bear. In the end, everyone talks. The Iranians know this better than anyone. They practically perfected it."

"Meaning what?"

Delang stared at the half-eaten apple in his hand. This was a sensitive subject.

"Meaning I put other agents and assets in jeopardy. These people put their lives on the line to help protect our country. They trusted me. And there's a good chance they're dead simply because . . . I wasn't strong enough."

"People like Pap?"

"I told you. I never gave him up."

"Uh huh," Kirk said.

He still didn't believe him.

"It doesn't matter. The right government lawyer could have me branded a traitor."

"That's not gonna happen."

"Maybe, maybe not. I knew the dangers of what I'd be facing when I signed up for this job and that's what they'll argue. Spies don't get fairytale endings. We usually get killed, labeled a traitor, or given a new assignment. That's just the way it is."

Farhad noticed the tan line on Delang's ring finger where a wedding ring used to be.

"What about your wife?" he said.

Delang's mind wandered to his beloved Abby. He missed things about her he never thought he would: her cute laugh, listening to her terrible singing in the shower, the way she never picked up her socks, how she needed a blanket outside when it was seventy-five degrees with a slight breeze, but kept the air conditioning on full blast in her car.

The Iranians could never take those memories from him. Would she be waiting for him or had the government declared him dead and she remarried? Knowing her the way he did, Delang believed that she wouldn't rest until she'd gotten answers about him, but it was possible. Despite his renewed freedom, these dark thoughts still haunted him.

"I really don't know," he said.

As they talked and ate their meal, all three were oblivious to the half dozen sheep and goats wandering around them. Startled when one of the goats bellowed, Kirk picked up a thick branch and held it like a baseball bat.

"Where there are goats and sheep, hyenas and leopards are close by," Farhad said.

Kirk pointed at Delang's injured foot then held up his hand that was missing a finger.

"They must smell our wounds. We better keep moving."

Chapter Fifty-Four

By late afternoon, according to the spotty GPS service they were receiving on the cell phone, they'd reached a range of peaks closest to the Turkmenistan border.

Farhad stayed behind with Delang while Kirk climbed the last hundred feet to check out the situation. Pain from shin splints shot up his calves and his quadriceps burned, but he pressed on and pulled out his plastic binoculars to study the border station and their potential flight path down the mountain range to ground level.

Kirk had no way of knowing if the flurry of activity he saw was normal or due to heightened security. Cars were backed up twenty deep. Even from his elevated position, he could hear drivers blaring their horns. In the Middle East, honking horns in traffic was part of the culture, if not a language of its own.

While they'd been fortunate not to run into any IRGC soldiers patrolling the border on their side of the mountains, the other side was another story. He didn't see any border agents hiking in the mountains, but he saw them roaming the foot of the mountain. Kirk estimated that about thirty to forty soldiers spread fifty feet apart and all of them carried sub machine guns.

The good news was that there a clear path to the ground. If they jumped from his precise spot, they could soar straight toward the main highway leading into Ashgabat. The landing zone would be between two dirt hills, but at least they wouldn't have to navigate through any jagged mountains or tall trees. The flight could go smoothly.

The highest risk would come once they had to deploy the parachutes. Recalling his on-site training on a team building retreat near the North Carolina-Tennessee border four years ago, the average parachute was pulled at three thousand feet. While that was a safe altitude for the float down to the ground, the hangtime in the air from the moment of deployment allowed for more than enough time for them to be shot by border agents before touching down.

Call the Guinness Book of World Records, Kirk thought. They were going to raise the bar for the biggest learning curve ever.

He gritted his teeth and shook his head. Would they make it? It was a fifty-fifty shot at best. Turning back down the mountain, his muscles became stiff. The temperature had dropped, and purple clouds were rolling in.

Great. On top of not getting shot, we may have to dodge lightning and battle the rain.

When Kirk got back, they all started shivering from the temperature drop. Delang's skin looked particularly ashen.

"How's it look up there?" he said.

Kirk explained what he saw, including the coming rainstorm.

"Can we create enough distance in the air to make it?" Farhad said.

Kirk mumbled to himself as he converted meters to feet in his head while considering the distance and their projected rate of descent.

"We need to fly about one point five miles," he said.

"Will that be enough from where we are?" said Delang.

Kirk stared back at the top of the mountain and winced.

"It's time to find out."

Chapter Fifty-Five

It started pouring as they began their final ascent. Their trek to that point had been hard enough in sneakers, but the dirt and sand was quickly turning into mud, which added more adversity. All three slipped and fell several times. It was as if the Iranian soil was trying to keep them there.

Upon reaching the summit, Kirk pulled the wingsuits out of the duffle bag and handed them out. Only then did they notice how neon orange they were. With the sky getting darker by the second, they may as well wear signs, saying "Shoot Here."

Kirk grabbed some cinnamon-colored mud and spread it on the front of his suit. He didn't know if it would help to camouflage them, but it was better than nothing. Delang and Farhad did the same.

"That'll have to do. Goggles on!"

Kirk yelled as thunder boomed. Farhad and Delang looked at each other, bewildered.

"How's this work?" Delang said.

It was one hell of a time for a crash course in wingsuit flying, especially since they had no helmets. As the rain fell harder, Kirk explained that they had to jump headfirst. Once they dropped fifty feet, they could spread their wings to level out and gravity would do the rest, but they needed to ensure that their arms and legs were spread as wide as possible and that the nylon material was as tight as it could get. Anything loose would allow the wings to drag in the air, which would cause them to lose control mid-flight. With an airspeed of about a hundred miles per hour, no inexperienced jumper would be able to regain control.

What Kirk didn't tell them was that his previous wingsuit jump was from an airplane and not the top of a mountain. Being in a plane provided choices in terms of approach angles. Doing it from the ground, even from an elevated position, meant that there was less time to establish any angle at all. The first fifty feet were critical if they were to glide their way to safety.

When Kirk finished explaining, Delang's heart was punching through his chest, but he nodded that he understood. Farhad nervously did the same.

"You'll have to use your best judgment in the air, but you pull the cord at about two thousand feet."

"How the hell am I supposed to know when that is?" Farhad said.

"We're at roughly ten thousand feet. At the speed you'll be going, you'll need to count to one hundred and fifty. But don't count too fast and don't lose count. When you can start making out the specific rock formations and the land doesn't look like a bunch of squares, you should be safe enough pull it."

"Should?" Farhad said.

"How fast will we be flying?" said Delang.

"With the wind and the rain, about eighty miles an hour. Maybe a little faster."

Kirk could tell by the fear in their faces that the reality of the situation had set in.

"I don't know about this, Kirk. I still get jet lagged from a long flight!" said Delang.

"Me, too," Farhad said.

"Are you fucking kidding me?" Kirk said. "This is the only way! We have to do this!"

The rain was pouring down more and more.

"What's the alternative?" said Kirk. "How do you intend to deal with soldiers patrolling the other side with machine guns? Plus, Tom might not make it down on his bad foot. We don't have a choice!"

"There's gotta be another way," Delang said.

Kirk had heard enough. He grabbed Delang and Farhad by the collars of their wingsuits and yanked them to his face.

"Now listen to me! Those guys down there won't hesitate to kill our asses. We're not going back, and we won't make it by foot. We got all the way up this fucking shithole mountain so we could do this. There are no other options. This is what we decided. We are *doing* this! Got it?"

"Yes, okay," Farhad said.

Delang nodded.

Kirk released his hold on them.

"Farhad, you lead us off," Kirk said.

It was more of an order than a question. Farhad hesitated, but then nodded.

"Tom, you go next. Be sure to follow Farhad's exact flight path. Do everything he does and do *not* pull the parachute earlier than him. Understand?"

Delang nodded as a lightning bolt tore across the sky, followed by a thunderous boom.

"Where are we headed?" Farhad said.

Kirk put his hand around Farhad's shoulder and pointed toward their designated landing.

With rain pelting down, the three men flashed a nervous look at each other. There was nothing to say. It was do or die time. They gave each other a firm nod and lined up for the jump.

Farhad stared straight down.

"Fuck me," he said.

"What's the matter?" Kirk said.

"It's one thing to talk about jumping from ten thousand feet, but it's another thing to stare it in the face!"

A gust of wind suddenly created an accordion affect, causing the men to stumble into one another and nearly fall back down the mountain. Kirk staggered, but he caught his balance and grabbed his companions.

"You can do this! Be fearless!"

Kirk was shouting over the torrential rain.

Farhad took one last look at his homeland. Despite the danger of the immense challenge he was confronting, he took in a long, slow breath, ignoring the rain, as he imagined the freedom of being rid of Azam and fighting for what was right in his country. But first, he needed to live. This was about to be a real leap of faith. Farhad bent his knees and vaulted off the mountain top.

Delang stepped up and made the same mistake Farhad did as he gazed down and felt a bolt of fear shoot through his body. As he watched Farhad sail down, another bolt of lightning streaked across the purple sky; its electric tentacles reached out and struck one of the mountains roughly a half mile to his left. Delang remained frozen as he eyeballed the crushed boulders tumbling down the mountain. He knew that he had to get out of this country, but now that he was confronted with the moment of escape, one he'd spent more than a year imagining, nose-diving down to near death wasn't the way he wanted to try it.

Kirk had to think fast. The weather was getting worse, and every moment spent deliberating was a potential wasted moment of safety. He placed both hands on Delang's shoulder, leaned forward and spoke into the man's ear.

"Tom, heroes aren't born. They are molded over time by what they overcome. I don't know if the government will label you a hero or not and you may not get a fairy tale ending, but after everything you've been through, why die a hero when you can live as a legend?"

With the rain rolling down his face, Delang felt the inspiration surge up his spine.

You didn't come this far to only come this far.

He reached up and patted Kirk on his hand, acknowledging that he understood.

"You've got this! Go! Go!"

Delang's heavy breathing was evident by the air vaping from his face. His eyes stared down the mountain as every horrendous memory of being beaten motivated him and he plunged into the air that would lead him to his safe haven.

Kirk watched him descend until he spread his arms and followed Farhad. The sight of both men flying in near synchronized fashion through the storm-filled sky filled him with confidence. Though he wasn't Catholic, he performed the up, down, left, right motion of the Holy Cross on his chest.

Please, God, let this work.

He took one last look at the country of his roots, which he'd promised not to visit. Though it was tangled in complexity, he loved it and hated it all at once. He pondered whether wonderful, misunderstood people like Farhad and Simin would ever know freedom or if they would have to endure the fist of submission by the Ayatollah for the rest of their lives.

Simin. His mind briefly wandered to Paris where he wanted to kiss her in front of the Eiffel Tower, a promise he intended to keep, but the only way to do that was to jump.

A bolt of lightning struck the mountain less than thirty feet from Kirk. The violent crackle startled him, and the ground began to shake underneath him. Kirk waved his arms to regain his balance, and as he did, he slipped. Instead of making a precise nose-dive toward the ground, Kirk fell awkwardly over the edge.

Chapter Fifty-Six

Aslani had been waiting at the Bajgiran border station for hours with no sign of the Americans. He was physically exhausted, his patience had worn onion skin thin, and his head was still throbbing. The constant rain did nothing to improve his mood. He stepped into his Humvee and surveyed the map that the Americans drew inside the cabin before tossing it on the adjacent seat. He figured there was no way he could've missed them, that he and Mahmoud had been there long enough.

Even though he knew they would find nothing, he instructed Mahmoud to check in with their counterparts near the Azerbaijan border and Bandar Abbas. Most important, he'd received a text from his trusted source, informing him that the Americans would be attempting to cross the border into Turkmenistan. Given the heightened security, he was extremely confident that he'd be able to catch them.

Shirazi gave him explicit orders that the American agent wasn't to be harmed, but he didn't say anything about Kabiri's grandson. Aslani couldn't wait to put a bullet in his brain. The mere thought of watching the life suffocate from his eyes gave Aslani as cozy a feeling as hot coffee on a cold morning. He could practically feel the weight being lifted from his shoulders. Afterward, he'd concentrate his efforts on Farhad, who wouldn't get the benefit of a swift death. Aslani would spend his every waking moment ensuring that the drunken fool would slowly feel every inch of the blade that he intended to sink into his flesh. He even had the weapon picked out, an ancient dagger with an eight-inch steel blade and a bronze handle from the Safavids dynasty of the Persian Empire, given to him by his uncle. Aslani would see to it personally that Farhad had a gradual and agonizing death.

"Captain?"

The voice came over his radio.

"Aslani here."

"Sir, this is Sergeant Ghoddos. My team and I are in the foothills of the mountains roughly one mile west of your location. We're seeing strange activity."

"Strange? What activity?"

"Well, sir, my men saw large orange birds flying over the border."

"Large birds? Why are you bothering me with this nonsense? Get back to your post. I don't want to hear your voice again unless you have the Americans in custody!"

"Sir, please, these birds have parachutes."

"What did you say?"

Aslani could barely hear the man over the fuzzy reception and noise from the rain.

"Parachutes, sir! They have parachutes. We see them over the border."

Birds with parachutes? What in the world is he talking about?

Ghoddos wasn't making sense. Aslani tried to visualize what his soldier was seeing when he realized what happened. He snatched the map that the Americans had drawn, turned it over and stared at the advertisement for sky diving—in orange suits.

Aslani grabbed his binoculars and shoved the car door open. Despite the downpour, he searched the sky, cursed the rain for blocking his view, but finally detected a white parachute opening above a hill just over the border in Turkmenistan.

He grabbed the radio.

"Sergeant, how many parachutes did your men see?"

"Three, Sir. The last one is landing now."

Aslani didn't bother finishing the conversation.

"Mahmoud! Get in the car, now!"

***

Farhad had made it to the landing spot and was unzipping himself from the soaking wet wingsuit when he spotted Delang floating down behind him. Pumped from all the adrenaline, he sprinted to Delang, who landed awkwardly as his damaged foot could not support his weight. He tried to use his opposite leg for balance but ended up dislocating his ankle. As Farhad uncovered him from the parachute, he saw Delang's foot mangled in the mud. The sight of it was enough to make him vomit.

"Are you okay?" Farhad said.

"Yeah, hang on," said Delang, grimacing.

Farhad's jaw dropped as he watched Delang use his knuckles to violently pop the joint back into place.

"That should do it," Delang said. "Help me up, will you?"

Delang extended his arm to Farhad. As he stood, the pain hit.

"You made it out, Tom. Welcome to Turkmenistan," Farhad said.

Delang grinned as the torrential downpour continued.

"That was one hell of a ride! Where's Kirk?"

"There!"

Farhad pointed up.

"Shouldn't he have pulled the chute by now?"

"Oh no, something's wrong. He's not stable."

"Pull it! Pull it!"

Delang screamed, seeing Kirk less than a thousand feet above them. As Kirk sailed over his friends, Farhad ran after him and Delang followed as best he could. When Kirk was about five hundred feet above them, he pulled the chute and somehow got yanked backward and upside down as the wind caught his chute and deposited him in a nearby mud pit. He was barely moving as Farhad reached him.

"Kirk! Are you okay?" he yelled as he tugged the parachute away.

Kirk groaned in pain.

"Yeah, I think the mud cushioned my landing."

"What the hell happened?"

Kirk told him about the lightning and how he fell from the top of the mountain.

"It took a few hundred feet before I could regain whatever balance I could. I had to cannonball down before I could snap the wings out. Once I got control, I was already lower than your trajectory ahead of me, so I had to delay pulling the chute in order to make up the distance."

Kirk grabbed his knee as he stood.

"You all right?" Delang said.

"Well, my long jumping days are behind me, but I'll live," he said. "Tom, you still have your gun on you, right?"

"Yeah, right here."

Delang pulled it out from his waistband.

"Good, come on. We need to grab another ride."

"One more and the carjacking union is gonna file a grievance," Farhad said.

The three fugitives hightailed it on foot toward the Gaudan Highway that would take them into Ashgabat. They didn't have to wait long before a minivan came at them at a lower speed than the other cars. Kirk stepped into the middle of the road and fired a warning shot over the vehicle before aiming at the driver. The van slammed its brakes to a stop. A chubby bald man put his palms in the air above the steering wheel. Kirk ripped opened his door.

"Out!"

Scared out of his wits, the man froze. Traffic piled up behind as onlookers noticed what was going on.

"Now!"

Kirk pulled him outside and hopped in. Delang and Farhad jumped in the back.

"Next stop, the American Embassy!" Kirk said.

***

Minutes later, Aslani jumped out of the car and ran toward where he had last seen a parachute float to the ground. All he found was an orange jumpsuit in the mud. He picked it up, curious how it worked, until he noticed the herd of footprints that hadn't yet disappeared in the rain. He cursed and headed toward the highway.

Chapter Fifty-Seven

"There!" Mahmoud pointed. "That has to be them in the van, weaving in and out of traffic."

"Stay back, but don't lose them. I need to call the general."

After bribing their way past the Turkmenistan border, Aslani and Mahmoud plowed through traffic. Though they had no jurisdiction, they had to re-capture the Americans, no matter what it would take. Aslani braced himself against the dashboard as Mahmoud swayed left and right through a line of cars.

"What is it?" Shirazi answered, curtly.

"Sir, we found them! They are fifty meters ahead of us on the freeway leading into Ashgabat."

"Excellent. I've placed a call to a friend at the local police. For a small fee, he has agreed to look the other way as long as you keep the damage to a minimum. How many men do you have with you?"

"Mahmoud and I are in pursuit in the lead car, but I have another car right behind us."

"Perfect. They're headed toward the embassy. Continue the pursuit and *do not* engage them until they get inside the city limits. Push them toward the embassy, but don't let them out of your sight and don't you dare let them get inside."

"Yes, sir."

"And Azam, you remember what I told you at the hospital, don't you?"

"Of course, sir."

"Good. Keep it in mind. The next time I hear from you, the American agent had better be in your custody."

Shirazi clicked off. Aslani repeatedly flexed his free hand. He knew Shirazi was deadly serious about making good on his threat.

"Don't stay in their lane," Aslani said. "Just keep them within eyesight."

***

Inside the van, Kirk had a case of the jitters. They looked everywhere for any sign they were being followed or for an ambush up ahead. Farhad took special notice of Delang's weakened state and heard an audible growl from his stomach.

"You okay, Tom?"

Delang closed his eyes as his breathing slowed.

"Yeah, barely, but the first thing I'm getting is a burger."

"I think we've got company," Kirk said. "There's a Humvee less than a hundred yards back. I don't like the way it keeps weaving in and out of traffic."

Delang turned around and squinted to see through the rear windshield.

"Dammit! It's gotta be Aslani. Does that fucker never die? How much farther?"

Farhad glanced at the map on the phone.

"Thirteen miles."

Lucky thirteen.

"Kirk, step on it. We don't have much time."

"Tom, I'm going as fast I can."

"Step on it!"

***

Russian FSB agent Anton Chalov and his team members, Yuri Zobnin and Sergei Gazinsky, had been rotating their positions all day around the American Embassy in Ashgabat. Fatigue was setting in and they were starting to cough profusely from a mix of their own chain smoking and the exhaust fumes from the vehicles passing by. To stay sharp, Chalov sat his husky frame at an outdoor table in front of a local café while Zobnin and Gazinsky maintained their foot patrol around the one-block area. He was downing an Espresso when his phone rang.

"Chalov," he said.

"They're headed your way," Petrov said. "Don't disappoint me."

Chalov slid his phone into his belt clip and shoved the Bluetooth device into his ear.

"Stay sharp, comrades," he said. "We're about to see some action."

***

Inside the embassy, Beth Jenkins enjoyed a rare quiet moment at her desk during yet another hectic day. After a failed rescue attempt that cost the agency the lives of three operatives, she had been immediately transferred to another post, despite her strenuous objections. The task force formed to look for Tom Delang was still technically operational but was now run by a man whose lips could reach the director's ass from ten miles away and couldn't find snow in Siberia.

That was a year ago. Today, as the station chief in Ashgabat, Jenkins once again made the acquaintance of the brash agent, Thrasher, whose last name fit the bill as he continually disrupted her meetings with his unfiltered reporting from the drone strike in Iraq.

She knew in advance that he had a high-functioning brain with a low functioning personality, which had gotten worse since their first meeting. Looking at him was also a painful reminder of the men she'd lost under a plan she had personally approved. Thankfully, Thrasher would only be her problem for a few more days.

Jenkins glanced at her reflection in the mirror. The dark circles under her eyes were gone, and her skin was working on golden brown tan. She may have looked put together on the outside, but inside, that was far from true. The guilt from never finding Tom Delang had not stopped eating at her soul. But thanks to the agency's training, she hid it well. After all, that's what spies are supposed to do.

When her cell phone rang for the millionth time that day, she was annoyed at having her "me" time interrupted, but of course she picked it up. The number looked familiar, but she didn't immediately recognize it.

"Hello?"

"Elizabeth?" the voice said, panicked.

While she hadn't recognized the number, she instantly recognized the gentle yet husky voice of Tariq Al-Masari, whom she had come to know reasonably well from her time in Riyadh.

"Mr. Ambassador? It's been quite a while since we've spoken. What can I . . ."

"Elizabeth, I don't mean to be rude, but we can catch up another time. There's an urgent issue that you *must* know about."

Jenkins's eyes widened. When the call ended, she tore open her office door.

"Thrasher! Load up and meet me out front, *right now!*"

***

"Come on! We gotta move!" Kirk yelled.

Kirk wasn't sure if it was from fatigue, the bullet wound in his foot, lack of exercise during his time in captivity or all of the above, but Delang was struggling big time. Kirk and Farhad did their best to keep him awake, but his breathing was labored as they tried to evade the Revolutionary Guard.

The van hit bumper to bumper traffic not long after entering the city center. The Humvee was hot on their tail, less than a hundred yards back. Judging by their uniforms, they were Revolutionary Guardsmen. Farhad couldn't make a positive ID, but Kirk was sure it was Aslani. The man was absolutely relentless. He had no idea how Aslani knew where to wait for them, but the questions would have to wait. With no other choice, they abandoned the van and made a run for it.

"They're still back there!"

Farhad looked over his shoulder as they scrambled through the crowded street.

"Pick up your feet! We have to keep moving!" Kirk screamed at Delang.

Sweat was dripping down Kirk's spine. A wheezing Delang could pass out anytime.

After angering a group of locals by interrupting their soccer game in a park, they passed the South Korean Embassy.

"We've gotta be close," Farhad said to himself as he continued to look back and forth between the skyline and the cell phone in his hand.

They could practically feel Uncle Sam extending his gloved hand, but the battery on the cell phone was at three percent. It displayed the all too familiar spinning pinwheel of death as the GPS tried to find their location.

"Dammit!" Farhad said.

He tossed the phone. They pressed forward, keeping an eye out for the American flag, flapping in the air to announce their freedom.

"Look, there it is!"

Farhad pointed at the stars and stripes, flying from a flagpole. It was less than a half mile away, but Delang wasn't going to make it under his own power. Kirk lifted him over his shoulders in a fireman's carry.

"Lead the way, Farhad, go!" Kirk said.

Farhad cleared the sidewalk of any onlookers.

"Move! Move! Injured man coming through!"

He shoved people to the side.

"Look, there's an alley. Cut down there!" Kirk said.

The gates of the Embassy were in their sights, but Kirk could see Aslani closing the distance. He was less than fifty yards back. Carrying Delang was slowing them down.

"Farhad, we need to lose them if we're gonna make it!"

Farhad spotted a dumpster. He ran toward the putrid metal can and dropped down on the other side of it and motioned for Kirk to follow. After setting Delang down as easily as he could, Kirk joined Farhad and glued their backs to the brick building behind them.

"Let's hope they go past us," Farhad said.

They waited a moment but didn't hear any movement. Kirk slowly raised up from his crouched position to have a look.

***

Aslani and Mahmoud were still a short distance away.

"Stay visible," Aslani said. "Make sure we stay in their sights!"

"I can take a shot," Mahmoud said. "Let's just shoot them now!"

"Not yet!" Aslani said.

As they jogged to keep up with the Americans, ducking between locals on the street, Aslani's phone rang.

"Aslani."

"Where are you?"

A Russian voice spoke to him.

"We're on Kemine Street, headed to the embassy."

"Push them toward the theater. We'll meet you there," the man said.

"Mahmoud, close the distance! The trap is set!"

Suddenly, Mahmoud stopped in front of an alley and swiveled his head left and right. Aslani caught up seconds later and did the same.

"Did you lose them?" Aslani said.

Noticing two heads rise over a dumpster, an evil grin spread across Aslani's face. He walked with steadfast purpose down the alley. This was it. The Americans were caught.

Chapter Fifty-Eight

"Shit, they saw us. Run!"

Kirk screamed and grabbed a reeling Delang by the front of his shirt and dragged him down the alley. They had barely gone ten feet when they were met by three imposing white men with guns pointed at them.

"Freeze!" one of the men said.

Delang recognized the language as Russian.

The three fugitives stopped dead in their tracks. They backtracked a few steps and turned around to see more men pointing guns at them. They were sandwiched between two sets of firing squads. The Iranians were at one end of the alley, the Russians at the other. Both stepped toward them, boxing them in. Delang reached for his gun but it had fallen next to the dumpster. It wouldn't have mattered. There were too many targets, too little time, and not enough bullets. No chance of escape. It was over.

"There's nowhere else for you to run, my American. . .friends," Aslani said with a seething glare. "That trash you took from me will go now with his new captors."

He gestured toward Delang.

"Before they take him, I have a goodbye gift for you."

Kirk and Farhad looked nervously at each other while Aslani used his phone to give their location to someone on the other end. Thirty seconds later, two more of Aslani's bearded IRGC henchmen appeared in the alley, and they weren't alone. One of them violently yanked a young woman by her arm, stopping only to harness her in front of him. Tears ran down her cheeks as her lower lip quivered.

"Simin!" Kirk screamed.

Aslani laughed.

"Ah, so, you *did* fall for this miserable bitch."

Farhad tried to grab Kirk's arm as he stepped forward, but he smacked it away as he approached Aslani with clenched fists. Aslani cocked back the hammer on his Browning HP, forcing the American to stop.

"Azam, this is about us, not her," Kirk gritted through his teeth. "Let her go."

Aslani tilted his head and looked at him curiously.

"No."

A shot rang out and smoke from the barrel of Aslani's gun twisted in the air. Kirk didn't realize what had happened until he felt warm liquid oozing through his shirt. Only then did he understand he'd been shot in the abdomen.

"*Kirk!*"

Simin squirmed to get away, but the soldier jerked her back and pressed a sharp blade to her throat.

Farhad tried to rush to his friend's aid until he felt the metal nose of a Makarov pistol pressed into the back of his head.

Kirk stumbled backward until he fell. He made a feeble attempt to put pressure on the wound, but the blood seeped through his fingers. His face turned pasty as the shock kicked in. Aslani stepped forward, crouched down, and smacked him in the face to get his attention. Grabbing him by the hair, he drew close and whispered to the meddling American.

"I want you to know that you'll have the honor of being the last to die. But first, you'll come to appreciate true pain. You'll watch the life fizzle from your idiot friend's face when I splatter his brains on that wall. Then, you'll watch me repeatedly ravage that little whore of yours until there is no spirit left in her, and she is bleeding from my domination. Only when I'm done and you're begging for death, will you and your American arrogance receive the gift of my mercy."

All Kirk could do was helplessly look up at Aslani and shake his head.

"Line them up against the wall!" he yelled while keeping his eyes locked on Kirk.

No one moved and Aslani took notice.

"I said line them up against . . ."

He suddenly saw the Russians with barrels of Heckler & Kock HK416 assault weapons glued to the back of their heads, held strong by what looked to be five Americans, three of them soldiers. When he turned back to his own men, he saw each of them also held at gunpoint. But those men weren't Americans. They were Arabs.

"Hand over the guns," Thrasher said.

Zobnin and Gazinsky turned to Chalov, who nodded, as he knew they were beaten. The Russians passed their guns to the Americans.

"Drop them!" a Saudi Royal Guardsmen said.

"Don't you dare do it! That's a direct order!"

Aslani shouted to Mahmoud and his other men. The two younger IRGC soldiers, Khaden and Mohsen, looked to Mahmoud for guidance. He stared at Aslani as he dropped his weapon. Khaden released Simin, who ran to Kirk. She removed her hijab and held the satin material against his wound with one hand and placed the other against his cheek.

"Hoo-ah . . ."

Kirk managed to mumble and almost smile as he looked up at her.

With tears dripping down her face, Simin smiled at him.

"It's going to be okay, Kirk," she said.

Farhad also rushed to his side.

"Hang in there, my friend. We've got you," Farhad said.

Clasping Farhad's hand, Kirk considered their situation. This was a version of a Mexican standoff he'd never seen.

Iranians, Americans, and Arabs, oh my.

Behind the Russians, he saw a dark-haired woman talking to one of her men.

"You got 'em?" Jenkins said.

"I got 'em," said Thrasher. "Go."

Jenkins holstered her Sig Sauer M11 and stepped forward, but Aslani raised his gun.

"Stay where you are!" he said.

Before he had the chance to fire, Aslani was hit in the leg. The bullet from Thrasher's gun blew off his kneecap and he collapsed, screaming in pain. His gun tumbled to the ground where Jenkins kicked it away before hustling over to Delang.

"Tom! Are you okay?"

He looked at her strangely.

"Beth?"

"It's me, Tom. Come on, let's get you out of here."

She put her arm around him and walked him out of the alley with one of the soldiers.

"Wait, wait," Delang said.

He motioned toward Kirk, Farhad, and Simin.

"They're my friends and they're coming, too."

Farhad and Simin gingerly pulled Kirk to his feet. He was now bleeding profusely and on the verge of passing out as they did their best to carry him to safety.

Thrasher and the Marines followed, but not before putting the Russians flat against the wall and slowly backing away with their guns still pointed at them. They didn't want to kill them but would if they had to.

297

The Saudi Royal Guardsmen grabbed Aslani and the other Iranians and jerked them away as Farhad and the Americans walked past.

"You fucking weasel," Aslani said, "I should've killed you years ago."

Farhad couldn't contain himself any longer. He reared back, let loose a therapeutic grunt and gave Aslani a field goal kick to the head, spitting on him as he fell to add insult to injury. All Aslani could do was watch his targets walk toward the embassy gates.

"No!" Aslani begged. "Mahmoud, do something!"

But it was too late. The Americans had slipped away for the last time. When they crossed onto sovereign American soil, Mahmoud cautiously picked his sidearm off the ground. Unsure what he was doing, the Saudis kept their M16's pointed at him, but he had no intent of harming them or trying to escape. Instead, it was time for him to settle a score of his own. Recalling what the general told him back at the hospital, he pointed his gun at Aslani, who stared at him in bewilderment and raised a bloody hand.

"Mahmoud, what the hell are you doing?!"

"Following orders," he said.

Mahmoud pulled the trigger and shot Aslani in the face.

Chapter Fifty-Nine

S.A. NIYAZOV INTERNATIONAL MEDICAL CENTER
ASHGABAT, TURKMENTISTAN

"Tom, can you hear me?"

Delang blinked his eyes. As they focused, he recognized Jenkins.

"Hey, girlie," he said.

Jenkins smirked. Delang's nickname for her was good to hear. First and foremost, it meant the man's memory was at least somewhat intact. Second, his term of endearment warmed her heart and helped melt away some of the guilt of having never found him.

"Where am I?"

"Hospital. Down the street from the Turkmenistan Embassy."

Delang let out an audible breath of relief. He hadn't hallucinated. They'd made it. He felt the plastic oxygen line hooked to his nostrils and looked down at the IV in his forearm.

"It's fluid. The nurse said you were massively dehydrated."

Delang nodded and surveyed the depressingly beige room but saw no one else.

"Where are they?"

"Who?"

"The guys who were with me. They helped me escape."

"*They* helped *you* escape? One of them said he was a tourist!"

"It's a long story. Where are they?"

"Down the hall. The doctors are doing what they can for the one who was shot."

"Okay, good."

Delang noticed a TV on the wall, tuned to CSPAN. It was broadcasting a congressional hearing.

"What's going on?" he said.

"A lot. DOD ordered a drone strike from the base in Bahrain on a high value target in Iraq but ended up killing a bunch of innocent kids. The bodies were everywhere, and the images went viral. Congress is using it as an excuse to close the base. It looks like the esteemed Senator Walsh is grilling the commanding officer right now."

The base. Tariq had told Delang about it over the phone a few days ago. Even if the U.S. abandoned it, there was no one else in the region with the military power to occupy it. There was no way the Iranians or the Libyans could pull that off. Their fleets were too small and any superiority they intended to have in the Gulf would be short-lived.

Delang hoped Kirk and Farhad would pull through. The last thing he remembered was running down an alley toward the embassy before being confronted by a team of vulgar looking Europeans. What was it the one man said? "Freeze." But he said it with a Russian accent. He'd heard the same accent recently, but where? Images of being chased on the highway replayed in his head. After tumbling down the sand dune, he had checked on the people in the other car. One man called himself Brad in what sounded like a Russian accent, but who the hell was Brad?

"Beth, you spent a little time on the Russia desk, right?"

"A few months. It didn't stick. Why?"

"What does 'brat' mean in Russian?"

"Brother. It means brother. Why?"

Delang's bloodshot eyes shot open. The pieces quickly came together for Delang. He knew why the Russians were involved and why they wanted him so badly.

"I know that look on your face. What is it?"

"I'm not sure if you know this, but I was in Bucharest three years ago."

"Bucharest? You spent your entire career in the Middle East. Why Bucharest?"

"Just listen. The agency received word that an FSB agent had some major intel about Russia's involvement in Syria's nerve gas attack in eastern Ghouta. Remember?"

"Yes, 2013 if I recall. The Syrian government wanted to crush the opposition."

"Right. Well, this agent had evidence that Russia supplied Syria with nerve gas, but he wouldn't go any further than Bucharest. Given my experience in Syria, they sent me in to juice him for intel. Unfortunately, another team was waiting when we arrived. A shootout ensued and the target was gravely wounded. I wasn't able to get much out of him before he died. But I managed to put a bullet in his shooter's head before he got away. I snapped a picture of what was left of the guy's face. While I didn't know it at the time, one of the agency analysts identified him."

"And?"

"Beth, it was Bogdan Petrov. President Maxim Petrov's brother."

Beth excused herself and ran back to the embassy. What Delang just said matched up perfectly with Thrasher's report from Iraq.

Chapter Sixty

Later that day, Farhad and Simin bull rushed the doctor as soon as they saw him push through the waiting room doors. The surgery had been tough, and he confessed that Kirk had flatlined, but the staff resuscitated him. Ultimately, the bullet cost him a kidney. All things considered, it could've been worse, but he needed to stay in the hospital for at least another week followed by at least a month to fully recover.

In the recovery room, Farhad and Simin were shocked to see their vibrant friend so lifeless looking and vulnerable. Simin glanced back at Farhad as if to ask permission to go see him. Farhad nodded. He knew that seeing Simin would be the best thing for Kirk's spirits.

She stood at his bedside. Not knowing what else to do, she clasped his hand and was astonished by how frigid it felt.

"Kirk?" she said.

However frosty his hands may have felt to her, the warmth from her hands reverberated up his arm and her voice was music to his ears. Kirk tried to focus, as he knew who was standing next to him. Though he'd seen her without her hijab at the party in Tehran, he was awestruck by her thick and wavy caramel-colored hair.

"Hey," he said.

Simin grasped his face between her hands and pressed her pillowy lips against his. Gunshot or not, it was the type of kiss that brought men out of comas.

"Hey, yourself," she responded.

She combed her fingers through his hair.

"He didn't hurt you, did he?"

Simin hesitated. She had been slapped more than once by Aslani and his goons, but thankfully not raped.

"No more than he did to you."

"Simin, I'm sorry you got involved in all of this. I didn't mean . . ."

"Shhh. It's okay," she said.

She put her finger to his lips. Kirk cupped her hand and gently kissed it. He placed her hand on his chest. As she heard the heart monitor machine beeping, she felt Kirk's heart literally thumping against her hand.

"You really had me scared, you know."

"When I saw that they had you, I just . . . nothing else mattered except getting to you."

Tears welled up in her eyes.

"Kirk, what happens now?"

"After I recover? I go home, I guess."

Simin felt flushed and worried, which Kirk noticed.

"But first we go to Paris," he said. "I could use a *real* vacation."

He smiled at Simin the way he first had back in Tehran. She leaned down and pressed her forehead against his, knowing that they'd be okay. Kirk leaned over and saw Farhad loitering at the door.

"Well, don't just stand there," he said.

After a brotherly hug, Farhad broke the bad news to Kirk.

"Doc said they had to remove your kidney."

Kirk looked down at his abdomen.

"Tell 'em I'm not coming back for it."

Farhad and Simin looked at each other and shook their heads. He was going to be fine.

"Got room for another visitor?" a voice said from the door.

They turned to see Delang being pushed in a wheelchair.

"I'll take it from here," he said to the orderly.

Delang rolled his chair over to Kirk's bedside, where he exchanged hugs with everyone.

"You gonna be okay, young man?" Delang asked.

"Yeah, you?"

"I'll make it, but I may be leaving soon. There are things back home I have to sort out."

Kirk nodded. He wanted to know what those things were but decided not to ask. He'd had enough of the spy business for a while.

"So, what's next for you guys, and lady?" Delang said.

"I have a couple of requests," Kirk said.

"Name it."

"You think that you can help with Simin and Farhad's passports so they can come to the States with me?"

"I'll take care of it. What else?"

"Actually, Kirk, that's something I wanted to talk to you about. I'm going to stay."

They all stared at Farhad as if he had octopus arms coming out of his ears.

"What? Why?" Kirk asked.

"Someone has to stay and fight the regime. I have a small victory against them now. I want another, no matter what the cost might be."

Delang smiled.

"Let's stay in touch, Farhad. I think we can do great things together."

"I'd like that. Thank you."

"What about me?" Kirk said. "You're bailing on me after all?"

Farhad clutched Kirk's injured hand.

"Never, my friend. You good?"

"I'm good if you're good," Kirk replied, trying to hold back the tears.

"Tom, would you mind taking a picture of us?"

Simin pulled out her phone.

"Actually, if you don't mind, I'd like to be in it, too."

Technically, he was still an undercover CIA operative, but he knew it wouldn't last. Kirk and Farhad saved his life. But more important, after a year of solitude where he thought no one was coming for him, his wild adventure gave birth to new friendships that he intended to keep.

They gathered around Kirk's bed and Simin tried to get all of them in frame.

"Are you ready?"

They nodded.

"Three . . . two . . . one . . ."

Simin snapped the picture.

"That's it for me, guys. I need to get going," Delang said.

"We'll see you again, right?" Kirk said.

Delang grinned.

"I'm CIA. I know how to find you."

Kirk winked at him.

"I'm counting on it."

"Wait. Before you leave, I have something that'll make all of you feel better," Simin said.

"Oh, yeah? What's that?" Delang asked.

She stood back from the foot of the bed. Kirk pressed the button to elevate himself so he could see her better. After slipping off her shoes, Simin turned on her phone and began gliding her feet back along the floor to the music of *Billy Jean* with a sparkling smile that targeted Kirk's eyes with her every move.

"Moonwalking Iranians," said Delang. "Now, I've seen it all."

"Oh, *now* you've seen it all?" Kirk said.

Farhad, Kirk, and Delang laughed as Simin garnered all their attention. Kirk held his side and grimaced in pain.

"Please don't make me laugh," he said.

Chapter Sixty-One

ARLINGTON, VIRGINIA
ONE WEEK LATER

Secretary of Defense Devonte Spinx had to hand it to Senator Walsh. She'd really outdone herself by grilling the drone strike commanding officer and pilot. Not only had she intentionally created civil unrest with her *Close the Base* movement, she'd also managed to unintentionally coin another phrase during the course of the hearing. Spinx would never forget it.

"This whole thing *stinks* of immorality and flagrant disregard for the community within the target zone!" she said.

She punctuated that claim by slamming a file on the table.

Within an hour, protestors were lined up around the Pentagon and in front of the Congressional steps with colorful signs labeled SPINX STINX. It was juvenile, but clever. The protests grew and the signs multiplied like cockroaches. The narrow-minded protesters swarmed the Capitol walkway to collect their pound of flesh from him as he made his way into the building to provide his own testimony.

Spinx did his best to reinforce the testimonies of Col. Suarez and Lt. Bartlett and provided footage of the hours prior to the drone strike, which clearly indicated that there was no evidence of children present at the site in question, but Walsh wouldn't hear of it. According to her, innocent children were dead, and it was the U.S. military's fault. End of discussion. She deflected from his evidence and launched into a tirade regarding other drone strikes conducted from NSA Bahrain that led to what she deemed unnecessary collateral damage.

These optics played well for the political pageant she was hosting in front of the cameras. She cared little about the lives saved by the drone strikes successfully killing their intended targets. Instead, she focused solely on the damage and what it could do for her political ambitions.

"War isn't perfect, Senator," Spinx said.

"That's true, Mr. Secretary. But our military is held to a higher standard throughout the world. If there is even a one percent chance that something like this could happen, don't you think we should be?"

She optimized the moment by holding up a photo of a decapitated child at the wreckage.

Touché.

Spinx knew that Walsh played her cards well. Every line had been rehearsed and polished to perfection. It was almost as if she was playing with a stacked deck, but Spinx couldn't figure out how she did it.

The next day, Spinx was feeling a bit of hope when it came to cracking Walsh's code. The director of the CIA had briefed him on an operative who'd been kidnapped more than a year ago who was believed to be dead but had escaped custody and shown up at the U.S. Embassy in Ashgabat. He had a well-formed theory about the events, which lined up with a report received from the bomb site. But it was just that, a theory. It made sense and Spinx wanted to believe it, but in the world of geopolitics, truth is only what you can prove. For what seemed like an eternity, it can evade a person and often slip right through one's fingers worse than a lathered bar of soap, but once it's established, it can be the gift that keeps on giving.

Spinx's security detail had received a discreet message while standing post outside his home. Apparently, Aleksey Barinov, the Russian ambassador's second in command, had information for Spinx that would be well worth his time. Internal security measures prevented them from being friends, but in the few meetings they attended together, the two men developed a bond over their mutual love for deer hunting with a bow and arrow.

Spinx paced back and forth at Arlington National Cemetery, in front of the Pan Am 103 Memorial, as requested. Why there of all places, Spinx had no idea. Thankfully, there was no one around. While waiting, he examined patches of psoriasis on his hands. He'd suffered from the condition for years, and stress made it flare up.

He looked up and saw Aleksey being searched by a member of his security detail.

"Good morning, Vonte," he said.

"Aleksey. To what do I owe the pleasure?"

"I have a gift for you," he said.

He handed Spinx a manila envelope. The Secretary was hesitant to accept such a thing in public from a Russian official. If anyone was watching, one picture would be all it would take to create an espionage charge, which was the last thing he needed.

"I think you'll want to see what is in it," he promised.

Though he thought he might end up regretting it, Spinx opened the file. As he thumbed through it, he tried to contain his excitement. It could be a trap.

"Why give this to me?" he said. "In political currency, this is worth more than all the diamonds in Africa."

"Our president believes that a man should be able to keep his promises."

"I'm not sure that means a lot coming from him, but what's it got to do with me?"

"I think he wants our country's recent entanglements to be settled privately."

Spinx got the hint. The file was an olive branch in exchange for keeping Russia's involvement with the Iranians out of the press.

"I hope you find the information useful," said Barinov. "I'd love to show you my new bow sometime."

As he walked away, Spinx tapped his fingers on the envelope, wondering if he should make use of its contents.

Chapter Sixty-Two

U.S. CAPITOL
WASHINGTON, D.C.

Senator Walsh banged her gavel to bring the committee to order. Spinx took his seat and folded his hands in front of him.

"Good morning, Mr. Secretary. I take it that you've given a great deal of thought to our time together yesterday?"

"I have indeed, Madam Chairman. Things are becoming much clearer."

Walsh squinted at Spinx, puzzled by his statement.

"Meaning what, Mr. Secretary?"

"I'm glad you asked, Senator. I've come into possession of some evidence that I think will shed great light on these proceedings and will vindicate our military in the context of this horrendous tragedy."

"New evidence, Mr. Secretary?"

Walsh looked at her fellow committee members.

"Why has this evidence not been brought forth until now?"

"Madam Chairman, this information was just made available to me. There was no time to disclose it to the committee prior to my arrival. However, I'd personally like to assure you, the committee, and the American public that it will be worth our time here today. May I proceed?"

Walsh's colleagues nodded, but every instinct in her bones told her that what was about to unfold couldn't be good for her.

"Proceed, Mr. Secretary," she said.

"As this committee pointed out, the wreckage site was littered with body parts of small children. This is a tragedy. But among the body parts and fallen rubble were mangled pieces of steel, believed at the time to be part of the debris. We now know this isn't the case."

He motioned for his aide to display photos of three skeleton keys from the wreckage. They were largely unscathed, despite damage from the missile.

"These keys are believed to have been worn by the children who died in the incident."

"Keys, Mr. Secretary? They appear to be simply garbage collected in the attack. What's this have to do with these proceedings?"

Walsh knew exactly what the keys were but couldn't believe that the Iranians would be so stupid as to pull such a symbolic stunt.

"If I may, Madam Chairman, I'll make everything clear."

He didn't wait for her permission.

"Also found at the site is what is believed to be a tunnel for smuggling drugs, leading from the school to a building nearly half a mile away with direct access to the main road leading out of town and toward the Iranian border."

"Please make your point, Mr. Secretary," Walsh said, hoping that rushing him might throw him off his game.

"Of course, Madam Chairman. The drone footage shows the terrorist Mustafa Shamekh entering the building."

"Allegedly," Walsh interrupted.

"No, Madam Chairman. As Captain Suarez testified, facial recognition software puts the ID at ninety-one percent."

"So, there's a chance it could be wrong?" Walsh said.

She was grasping at straws.

"We have full confidence in the software. It's our belief that Shamekh was instructed to be there by elements inside the Iranian government."

Gasps of surprise filled the gallery. Walsh banged her gavel for order.

"The Iranians, Mr. Secretary? That's quite an accusation. Can you offer any proof?"

"Those skeleton keys are the proof, Madam Chairman. During the Iran-Iraq war, the Iranian government placed such keys around the necks of innocent children, such as those killed in this incident. The children were sent running in the mine fields to plow the way for its infantry. The keys were used as symbols for the children to enter Heaven. We believe that the Iranians leaked information about Shamekh's whereabouts, knowing that our military would be monitoring with the drone, and they used these children as pawns in the unofficial war they've declared on America."

The media in the gallery was in an uproar and were taking pictures of the confident Secretary.

"Order! Order!" Walsh said.

She banged her gavel, as if it could stamp out these new revelations.

"Mr. Secretary, three keys don't make a firm case for interference by a foreign power! Do you have any additional evidence of such an outrageous accusation?"

Spinx smirked. The trap was set.

"I do indeed, Madam Chairman."

He motioned to an aide to change the slide to a picture of an Iranian official. The Senator recognized him instantly and her stomach tightened.

"Thanks to our friends in Israeli intelligence, the man in the photo has been identified as Asghar Moharrami, the third cousin of Major General Rahim Shirazi, commander of the Iranian Revolutionary Guard. And this is surveillance footage of you, Senator, meeting him in a museum in Cairo."

Everyone in the room gasped as the new slide came up,

Son of a bitch.

Walsh had specifically instructed her security team to have the museum cut all its camera feeds in that room. Little did she know that thanks to an unrelated graffiti issue, the museum had just installed a new camera inside the sarcophagus.

All eyes were on the Senator. The rapid clicks from the camera sounded like a swarm of bats, flapping their wings. C-SPAN zoomed in on her face. Her slack jawed image would come to define her years in public service.

"That . . . that's not me," she muttered into the mic.

Spinx asked his assistant to turn up the volume so Walsh's words were clear.

Congratulations Senator, you're half Iranian.

The press wasted no time popping up from their chairs, shouting questions at the Senator. Each member of the committee who had aligned with her tried to discreetly meet with their assorted aides to discuss how they could run for political cover and distance themselves from her. All Walsh could do was put her hand over her eyes. While the committee tried to continue, Spinx's new chief of staff, Zoe O'Brien, pushed through the doors of the chamber and made a beeline for her boss. Spinx wondered what could be so important to interrupt him at this pivotal moment. She leaned her tall, red headed frame down to whisper into her boss's ear and pointed back to the door.

"Are you sure?" Spinx said. "There are no do-overs in here, Zoe."

"I think it's worth rolling the dice," she said.

Gambles like this often didn't pay off in politics. Spinx remembered all too well, Colin Powell's speech in front of the United Nations talking about the 'firsthand intelligence' of Saddam Hussein's nuclear weapons program when in fact no American operative had spoken to the Iraqi source. He had to decide fast, but he needed to put a nail in the coffin.

"Senator, one more thing," he said. "My chief of staff has informed me that a witness has come forward and would like to testify."

Everyone waited for the Senator's response, but Walsh's throat was paralyzed.

"Madam Chairman, I'd like to be recognized to answer that," said Senator Dwayne Laskin (R-MI).

Laskin was also chairman of the Senate Committee on Government Affairs, which had oversight authority over the Justice Department and congressional figures.

Walsh, overwhelmed by the moment and unable to speak, just nodded.

"Mr. Secretary," Laskin said in his appealing voice. "Who is this witness?"

"Senator, the witness would like to explain that for himself, and if you're willing to grant me a little latitude, everything will become crystal clear."

Senator Laskin recognized an opportunity to rid himself of Senator Walsh for good.

"Please ask the witness to come forward and be sworn in," Laskin said.

He didn't wait for any other committee members to agree.

When the doors opened, a sharply dressed man strolled into the chamber, leaning on a cane. For Senator Walsh, still dumbstruck, the echo of his heels on the marble floor sounded like the slow tick of a doomsday clock, growing louder with each step, and sounding a death knell on her career.

Spinx moved over to make room for the man to raise his hand to take the oath.

"Please state your name for the record."

"Tom Delang," he said.

The operative looked refreshed and confident.

Over the next two hours, Delang shared his tale of being captured, tortured and his unlikely escape. Having reviewed the scenario surrounding the drone strike with Jenkins, including the school's underground bunker, originally built as protection from earthquakes, he explained how human traffickers and drug dealers added a tunnel leading away from the school. He also disclosed his reveal under torturous circumstances the name of the Basra police chief. Unbeknownst to Delang, he and the chief shared a relationship with Moz, who betrayed them both.

"Having obtained this information from me, the Iranians collected innocent children and smuggled them underground from the other end of the tunnel, rendering them undetectable to the drone's infrared scanners. Once the lead door in the school was opened, which aided their concealment, the children were led inside where they unknowingly awaited certain death. My primary captor admitted this to me on my final day of captivity."

This, he believed, solidified his theory about how this appalling act was used to trigger events that would call this committee to order in hopes of getting the United States to abandon NSA Bahrain. Per O'Brien's request, he didn't mention the Russians by name, only that an unknown third party was interested in his exchange.

When Delang finished, Spinx wasn't sure who was more stunned: Walsh, the committee, himself, or the media.

Spinx cleared his throat.

"I ask you now, Madam Chairman, is it still your desire to close the base?"

Walsh was slumped in her chair and either unwilling or unable to speak.

"The committee would like to further review the evidence in private," Laskin said, "but I can speak for the rest of my fellow members in saying that we expect Captain Suarez and Petty Officer Bartlett to be cleared of any charges."

"I will be sure to communicate that to them, Senator," said Spinx, "but I was asking specifically about the base."

Laskin gazed down at the other seven Senators, minus Walsh, who nodded decisively.

"Please inform our friends in Bahrain that the United States will remain there."

"Thank you, Senator. I'll do just that."

"And Madam Chairman," Laskin said, staring down at Walsh, "I believe the FBI will have some questions for you."

Chapter Sixty-Three

KARACHI, PAKISTAN
THREE MONTHS LATER
1 P.M., LOCAL TIME

With sweat beaded on his forehead, Moz took a long drag of his cigarette as he waited nervously in his car across the street from the Wazir Mansion Railway Station. He saw on the news that the CIA man he'd betrayed more than a year ago was alive and well, having returned to the United States. Already a marked man, this news raised the stakes significantly for Moz, as he knew that Meadows would seek revenge. This only heightened his paranoia, since he narrowly escaped an assassination attempt by an Iraqi police chief he'd betrayed months later.

Originally, he wrestled with the decision of his betrayal. Meadows had always treated him well, but there was a big difference between being paid reasonably for his services and being paid handsomely. Unexpectedly, a mysterious female voice tracked him down by phone and offered to pay him well above Meadows's going rate to give the man up to the Iranians. While he was skeptical at first, once the voice wired a good faith payment of ten thousand dollars to his account, it didn't take long for Moz to decide. He was tired of living on table scraps. Two hundred and fifty thousand dollars went a long way in his world, but as it turned out, not as far as he'd thought.

True to her word, the source came through with the rest of the cash. Moz started blowing his money on high-end prostitutes. But he quickly realized that his erotic experiences were much more pleasurable and put the women in more agreeable moods with drugs on hand. What started out as an innocent cocaine habit snowballed into full blown addiction.

The money dried up in four months. Back at square one with bloody nostrils to go along with his bouts of withdrawal, Moz tiptoed back to some of his old sources, looking for work as an informant. While he found enough to keep his head above water, his sources could see that he'd become an addict and labeled him unreliable. The only steady work he could find was as a forklift operator at Port Qasim Terminal in Pakistan.

When his source called him with a new opportunity, Moz jumped at the chance. He desperately needed the money to pay back some drug dealers who supported his habit. Still, Moz needed to watch his back. Fighting his habit was bad enough. Adding a price to his head put his paranoia into overdrive, which was further intensified by the fact that the female voice wanted to meet in person. Moz kept his sweaty palm gripped on the Walther PPK at his side. He wouldn't be double crossed.

An hour of skittish waiting and half a pack of cigarettes later, his source approached the car wearing a black suit with a button-down olive dress shirt, and got in.

"What are you doing here?" Moz said, astonished.

He instantly recognized the face from his travels with Meadows and knew the person's name, but the individual sitting next to him was *not* female.

Yasser smiled and tapped on the voice modification app on his phone.

"You don't seem happy to see me," he said with the device exporting a female voice.

"No, I just didn't know it was you. It's good to see you again," Moz said with a twitchy handshake.

Yasser stared at him.

"I would ask if you kicked your habit, but one look at you and I know the answer. This was a mistake. You can't be trusted."

The head of security for the Saudi ambassador put his hand on the door handle, but Moz squeezed his arm.

"Wait, wait! Please! I need the money. I can do whatever you need me to do. I promise!"

Yasser glared down at Moz's hand on his arm and gave him a "don't do that" look before settling back in his seat.

"The Iranians have offered a bounty on the American agent. I want to use you as bait to draw him out."

"Does the ambassador know?"

"No. He's as blind now as he was before, but after this, I'll need to disappear."

"How much are they giving you this time?"

"Me? Two million."

"How much for me?"

"Same as last time."

Moz was insulted.

"I will be taking a lot more risk this time. I want double that," he said.

"Don't even try to renegotiate with me. I . . ."

Yasser didn't get to finish his sentence. An explosion hoisted Moz's car in the air and into a fiery ball of shrapnel and body parts. Two hundred feet away, Kazeem al-Nashou stepped out from the shadows and approached the mangled remnants of the car. Given the extent of the blast, while he felt it was overkill, his new boss was emphatic that he confirm both kills. He surveyed the damage and saw Yasser's head laying in the dirt not twenty meters from that of his snitch.

The former Basra police chief turned and handed the grenade launcher back to Jaybird.

"Thanks for letting me do the honors," he said.

Thrasher nodded as he accepted the weapon.

"We good now?" the chief asked.

Thrasher glanced at the grenade launcher before returning his handshake.

"Yeah, we're fine. You need a ride back?"

"Yes, but let me make a call first."

As al-Nashou took a moment of privacy, Thrasher made a call of his own.

"Good news?" the voice said.

"Your cockroach problem in Camelot is no longer an issue."

"Thanks. See you soon."

Back in Washington, Beth Jenkins hung up the phone. Gazing up to the heavens from the back porch of her Georgetown apartment, she thanked God that her nightmare was over.

Chapter Sixty-Four

BETHESDA, MARYLAND
TOM DELANG'S HOME

"Hello?" Tariq said.

"It's done," said the chief.

"Thank you, Kazeem. Please return home immediately."

"Yes, sir."

Tariq glanced up at Delang, who was sitting in a leather club chair in the middle of his private office. He nodded at his friend, acknowledging that the task was complete.

"Thanks for taking care of that," Delang said. "I appreciate you giving the chief a job."

"Under the circumstances, the position was obviously vacant."

"I was hoping you'd understand the dinosaur reference when I texted you."

"Are you kidding? *Jurassic Park* is your favorite movie. I'm glad I was notified. I'm sorry that Yasser saw it first and that I saw it so late."

"When did you know he was the inside man?"

"After you called the first time, he mentioned Moz by name, so I got curious and had the Ministry of Defense clone his phone. As it turns out, Yasser had already cloned my phone. When I got your text, he also got it. Even though he deleted it from my phone, the analysts at the Ministry of Defense saw it. But his fate was sealed when he called your former asset a week ago. I never told him about Moz. Tom if I'd known . . ."

"Tariq, please. It's not necessary."

"My negligence cost you over a year of your life. I'm not sure how I atone for that."

Delang walked over to his friend and put his hand on his shoulder. Of all the experiences he and Tariq had shared, they now shared the common bond of being betrayed by people they trusted.

"I was the one that got sloppy, Tariq. I trusted that little shit way too much. It's not your fault. It's part of the war we fight."

"Is that what you told Abagail when you finally saw her?"

Delang grinned.

"Well, let's just say that we've been making up for lost time and we haven't done a whole lot of talking."

For the first time all night, Tariq laughed.

"Oh, so that's why she won't let you leave town?"

"That and she's a little timid about letting me out of her sight right now."

Delang smiled, exposing his teeth.

"I can't say I blame her. How's your mouth? Did things work out with the dentist?"

Delang rubbed his jaw.

"I'm a little sore, but the agency guy did a good job."

He wasn't sure whether to ask his next question but knew he had to.

"Tariq, before I was taken, you spoke about a back-channel deal that you made with the Iranians. What was it?"

Tariq looked out the window at a crescent moon glowing in the clear sky among a blanket of twinkling stars. He had been hoping to avoid this conversation.

"The rebellion in Bahrain really shook the king to his core. Under no circumstances was he going to let the Shiites invade our shores. He knew the Iranians were behind the insurgency. So, in exchange for a pledge not to invade the kingdom, he gave them plans for a secret missile system that the Ministry of Defense had been working on. It probably would've been used against Israel, but the kingdom would be safe."

Delang was stunned.

"Tariq, are you serious? You know how unstable that would've made the region. It could've started a war of apocalyptic proportions! The U.S. would've had no choice but to intervene."

"That's why he asked me to do it. He figured I could reason with the American diplomats and press our friends in Bahrain to refuse U.S. assistance. I had no choice, Tom. When the king gives an order, you do it. But at great risk to myself, I went outside his authority and had our engineers make changes to the plans. I arranged for any engineer we knew about on the Iranian side to be taken care of. With faulty plans and no one with experience to study them, the Iranians may as well have been looking at schematics for a pinball machine. I think that's why they tried to assassinate me in Washington."

Delang stood in silence. On the one hand, his friend had nearly enabled a war. On the other hand, his unauthorized decision had nearly cost him his life. And if the king found out what Tariq did behind his back, never mind the Iranians, he would've had him killed.

"You know, Tom, I meant to tell you that I'm thinking about getting out of the game. I've grown so weary of the war in the Middle East."

Delang half-expected this.

"It takes its toll on all of us. I know that better than most. And, if you are serious, I won't try and talk you out of it. But please keep in mind that bad things happen when good men do nothing. We may not have the power to stop the war, but could we really live with ourselves if we sat idly by on the sidelines?"

Tariq sighed. Tom was right, but nobility didn't make him feel any less exhausted.

"I'll give it some thought. For now, let's have a drink."

Delang was taken aback. Tariq wasn't known to be much of a drinker.

"Since when do you drink bourbon?"

"Since my friend was kidnapped," Tariq said.

Tariq set up the high ball glasses on his desk, poured three fingers into each, and handed one to Delang.

"We have a lot to be thankful for. What should we toast to?" Tariq asked.

Delang smiled and clinked his friend's glass.

"To friendship."

Epilogue

NAGS HEAD, NORTH CAROLINA
TWO DAYS LATER

The Outer Banks Fishing Pier was a staple of Nags Head, a town in the Outer Banks of North Carolina. Built in 1957, it was six hundred fifty feet long and sixteen feet wide on the eighteen-and-a-half mile post. The wooden planks of the deck had weathered over the years, but only added to its character. Fishing rods lined the colored walls of the quaint, old-style tackle shop. Black and white photos of the pier hung behind the register. A solid stink of squid bait mixed with the salty ocean, which served as every fisherman's official cologne, hit you immediately when walking through the door. The recently added oceanfront grill was quickly becoming a hidden gem. It was basic, not glamorous in the least, but when matched with a breathtaking sunset and the music of the Atlantic's waves crashing against the pillars below, it was a good place to start or end a first date.

For kids, it was a place to hang out and play the claw arcade game while their parents fished. For local wives, it was a place where they could banish their husbands until they were ready to hear an apology. For their husbands, it was often a place to clear their minds and think about that apology.

For the dedicated fishermen of the area, though, the pier had a presence. In a strange way, they had a better relationship with the pier than they had with anyone else in their lives. Some days, the pier would smile on them and grant them the gift of a good catch. Other days, the pier gave them the gift of peace and quiet with a cold beer. Whether it was Croaker, Spot, Puppy Drums or Budweiser, it didn't matter because there was never a bad day at the pier. They understood the pier and the pier understood them. Day after day, season after season, year after year, there was the pier. Just sitting. Always waiting for them and always eager for their return.

Every man has his own private place of solace to clear his head and find some much-needed rejuvenation from the hustle and bustle of everyday life. For Kirk, it was the pier. Hours upon hours, he would stare at the ocean, listening to the waves break against the shore, and feel the wind blowing against him, alone.

But today, Simin stood next to him, wrapped in a winter coat, her arm hooked around his, her head leaning against his shoulder as they watched the sunset.

"You know, Kirk, we could've gone to Paris straight from Turkmenistan. After some rest, it would've been easier than coming to the States first."

"You're probably right, but I didn't want to go galivanting around one of the best cities in the world while nursing a gunshot wound. I want to enjoy it. After everything I went through, I wanted to come home."

"I understand, but why is this place so special?"

"It's where Pap taught me to fish. I don't know what it is. This old pier somehow makes me think of him. Plus, I figured we could lay low and have some quiet time before we head to the airport. I know there's a nip in the air. We don't have to stay long."

"It's fine. But I'm going to go inside and get us a cup of coffee, okay?"

Simin gave Kirk a peck on the cheek and walked back to the bait shop.

As Kirk stared at the sun setting along the horizon, he thought about his adventures in Iran. Had he done the right thing by going? Was he right to avenge Pap? Would Pap be proud of him or want to smack him upside the head for doing something so idiotic?

"Nice view."

Kirk turned to politely reply, but before he could speak, he felt the soreness of his bullet wound that was still healing.

"Still on the mend, I see."

"Miss Jenkins? What are you doing here?" Kirk asked.

"Please call me Beth."

She extended her hand to Kirk, which he graciously accepted.

"Okay, how'd you find me?"

Jenkins gave him an awkward look.

"Right," Kirk said. "CIA."

He laughed, realizing the stupidity of his question.

"Is Tom with you?"

"He apologizes for not being here in person, but as you can imagine, his testimony has placed him in the spotlight. The day after his testimony, Hollywood producers were lined up at the CIA's door, trying to get the rights for his story. I hear that Tom Cruise is interested, but Nicholas Cage is pushing hard for the role."

Hollywood never ceases to surprise me.

"I appreciate Tom leaving me out of his testimony and only referring to Farhad when he was asked about his escape."

"Well, he didn't leave you out. That would be lying to Congress. He just didn't mention you while the cameras were rolling. He did, however, have to include you when he spoke to the committee behind closed doors."

"Still, I appreciate it. Will Tom be okay? He said something about being grilled about revealing his sources when he was being tortured."

"That may come, but right now, he's front-page news and the agency is getting some good press. If the rumors are true, the director will be awarding him the Distinguished Intelligence Medal. I think it'll be hard for them to rake him over the coals after that."

"Okay, so, why'd he send you?"

"I have an update," she said.

Jenkins pulled out her phone and showed Kirk a picture of a man in a *Star Wars* t-shirt at the center of the photo, leading a protest demonstration.

"Your friend Farhad has joined up with the PMOI."

"What's that?"

"People's Mujahedeen of Iran. They're the only formalized rebellion against the Ayatollah regime. Khomeini tried to kill them all after the revolution, so most of them fled to Europe, but they're still around to make trouble for the mullahs."

Kirk smirked. It seemed that Farhad had joined his own rebel alliance after all.

"From what I understand, he's well-liked within the group and could rise in the ranks pretty fast."

"Any chance that they'll be successful?"

Jenkins shrugged.

"Too early to tell. What counts is that his joining up has rejuvenated the group's leadership. I also wanted to tell you that Rahim Shirazi has disappeared. He went to have a meeting with the Supreme Leader and hasn't been heard from since."

"That's a relief."

Kirk eyed Jenkins curiously.

"Washington could have sent anyone to tell me this or no one at all. I don't think you drove six hours from Langley just to deliver that news."

"You're right, I didn't. Tom said that the reason you were in Iran was to settle some family business. He's not the type to let that sort of information slip. I did some research, and the results were rather enlightening."

"I'm all ears."

"I'm sure you remember that Kermit Roosevelt, Jr. was the brainchild and architect of the 1953 coup in Iran, right?"

"I read about him."

"Well, if there was ever a list of the greatest CIA operatives, he would be at the top. At the same time, if there was ever a list of the greatest CIA assets, your grandfather would hold the same spot. He was Roosevelt's right hand on that op. After the coup was over, Roosevelt got him out of the country. He was incredibly protective of Cameron and did everything in his power to keep him hidden from the Ayatollah. Even when Roosevelt retired, he regularly checked in on him. When Roosevelt died in 2000, Cameron's file was passed around, but no one at the agency gave it the affection that Roosevelt did until it was given to Tom."

"And that's how the Iranians tracked him down? Careless bureaucracy?"

"No. That's the other reason I came to see you. You were wrong about Tom."

"How so?"

"He didn't give the Iranians your grandfather's name under torture. We don't think that they even asked him about Cameron."

"Is that right?" he said. "So how, may I ask, did they find Pap?"

"They didn't find him. He found them."

"Excuse me?"

"Think what you want about Tom, but there are two things about him that separate him from other agents. For one, when he says that he's going to meet you at a certain time and place, you can bet he'll be there.

Second, he believes in the power of a personal touch and can connect with people on an intimate level better than anyone I've ever seen."

"What's that got to do with Pap?"

"When Tom didn't show for his six-month check-in with Cameron, I think your grandfather knew something was up. Tom's reports said that the man had good instincts. Despite everything that I'm sure was against his better judgment, I believe that he felt as responsible for Tom as Tom did for him. Cameron may have made his life here in the U.S., but there was always a piece of him that remained Iranian. Anyway, the forensics on his computer verified that he ended up chatting online to the wrong person with the right connections in the Revolutionary Guard. After that, it was only a matter of time. Since Tom was already in their custody, the fact that he was your grandfather's handler was pure coincidence."

Though it was difficult to hear, Kirk understood his grandfather's feelings as he'd felt the same responsibility for Tom up on the mountain.

"Beth, while you're here, there's something I need to ask you," Kirk said. "Haddadi said that Pap was an Imam Twelver. Do you know if that was true?"

"I read his file. It's half true. Did your grandfather ever tell you about his parents?"

Kirk had to think about it.

"Actually, no. Never."

"His father was a strict Shiite and very much a Twelver. It's true that Cameron started out being raised that way."

"So, what changed?"

"I think it was because he met Roosevelt. Because Roosevelt was such a private person, it's not really clear when the two met, but apparently, they had quite a friendship. Sometimes, people come into our lives and have such an impact that it changes our lives forever. Haven't you ever experienced that?"

Kirk immediately thought of Farhad and looked down the pier at Simin, who was walking toward them with two coffees in hand.

"I have now."

Jenkins smiled.

"Come work for me."

Kirk laughed.

"What? Thanks, but no thanks. I've had my fill of Middle East adventures."

"Kirk, do you know how difficult it is to escape from Iran?"

"I know how hard it was for me. Otherwise, I have no idea."

"Well, dozens of my people have died trying, but you pulled it off. The Iranians have placed additional security along the Turkmenistan border because of you. Tom can't speak highly enough about you and the agency could use someone with your ingenuity and quick thinking."

"I don't know. It was dumb luck. Besides," he said staring at Simin, "I've got a lot going on right here."

"I know it's a big ask, but between you, me, Farhad, and Tom, I think we change the world for the better. Just think about it. Here's my card."

Kirk put it in his pocket. Jenkins nodded and walked off.

"Enjoy your trip," she said to Simin.

"Was that the lady from the embassy?" she said.

Simin handed Kirk his coffee.

"Yeah."

"What did she want?"

As Kirk debated telling Simin the truth, a red cardinal flew onto the pier railing in front of them. He looked at its beady eyes staring back at him, and the bird chirped. Kirk grinned.

Okay, Pap. I understand now. I promise.

"Friendship is the hardest thing in the world to explain.

It's not something that you learn in school.

But, if you haven't learned the meaning of friendship,

You really haven't learned anything."

—Muhammad Ali

Author's Note

While I am aware that some authors in a variety of genres have chosen to begin including the COVID-19 pandemic into their storylines, I have chosen to avoid it. This is an adventure novel and I want the readers to be able to escape the realities of the pandemic as you spend your time with me.

The events regarding the Shiite uprising in Bahrain and Iran's attempted assassination of the Saudi ambassador by Iran are real, both having occurred in 2011.

Russia's claims to have missiles capable of beating NATO's radar detection system were noted by the media in early 2018.

I have taken creative license with these events and placed them in present day.

Acknowledgments

Some people discover early what their dream or purpose is in life and relentlessly pursue it at a young age. Others wait either patiently or lazily for that moment of discovery. I fall into the latter category. I never thought that I could write a novel. Because of summer reading requirements in school, I never used to like to read. In fact, I hated it. As I began what would ultimately become a spectacularly mediocre career in logistics, I needed to get away from my desk and out of the office during my lunch break, which is where my love affair with reading began. Coupling my naturally creative instincts with my repository of geopolitical knowledge enabled me to finally write this book. Sometimes one's whole life comes down to a single decision. I'd like to thank the following people who helped me along the way.

To **my wife, a.k.a. "Fireball."** You believed in me when at times I didn't believe in myself. Without your encouragement and faith in me, this novel wouldn't have been possible.

To **my mother and father**. Thank you for all the sacrifices you made for me over the years and for supporting, encouraging, and enabling my creativity as a kid. It's carried over well to my adult life.

To **Jason Gregory, Jake Webb, Josh "Krutch" Kinnison, Dan McAdams, Wyn McPherson and all my closest friends**. There is no greater gift than friendship and I am eternally grateful for yours. I'm good if you're good.

Special thanks to **Alan Scott, Martha Scott, Kathy Patel, Anne Goodwin, and Josh Lanier** for being my beta readers during my literary journey and providing me the feedback that I needed to hear. You guys are awesome!

To the **Hampden-Sydney rhetoric program**. While I believe that I've always had a natural talent for writing, the school's program honed my skills and gave it precision without which this novel wouldn't have been possible.

To **Caroline Tolley**. Your edits of my first draft and allowed me to learn how a novel should be molded from the lump of mud that it was to what it eventually became. For me, your advice and experience is worth more than all the whiskey on St. Patty's Day. Thank you.

To **Les Brown**, **Gary Vaynerchuk**, **Mel Robbins**, and **Tom Bilyeu**. Your motivational words pushed me to pursue my dream. I'm forever in your debts.

To **Meg LaTorre**. The iWriterly You Tube channel guided me on every step of my literary journey and provided me with invaluable tips that would've been difficult for me to find otherwise.

To **Stephen King**. Your book *On Writing* paved the road for me to write an honest novel. Whenever I was stuck, I always referred to that book.

To **Dan Brown**. *The Da Vinci Code* brought me back to the world of reading. In way, my journey to this novel started there. I've tried my best to learn from your writings and I hope you enjoy reading mine.

To **Vince Flynn**. While Dan Brown's *The Da Vinci Code* brought me back to the literary world, your novels ensured that I stayed there. I loved every single one of your novels. From you I learned how to create strong villains and stronger dialogue. You were a true force in the literary world and are dearly missed.

To **Jack Carr**. First, thank you for your service to our country. Second, I once told you on Instagram that I believe that you are the next Vince Flynn and I stand by that statement. Thank you for showing me how an author should interact with his fans. See you on Instagram!

To **David Baldacci**. You may not remember, but we met at a book signing you hosted in Williamsburg, VA for your *Long Road to Mercy* release. When it was my turn at the table, since I would be turning forty-years-old in those coming months, I asked you if forty was too old to start writing a novel. Your response of "Oh, hell no" lit the fire under me to take the risk to write this novel. Thank you.

To **Brad Thor**. You are the undisputed champion of the political spy thriller genre and everything that a thriller writer should be: creative, talented, well-informed, incredibly friendly, and true gentleman. While we previously met at your book signing for *Foreign Agent*, I can only hope that our paths cross again. Until that day, I hope you find my work worthy of being in the same arena as yours.

To **Dan Lawton**. Thank you for your patience and guidance during this initial literary journey. I hope that we will continue to stay in touch!

Coming Soon!

MATT SCOTT
SURVIVING THE LION'S DEN SERIES
BOOK 2

THE IRANIAN DECEPTION

Beth Jenkins wakes to a call in the middle of the night from her source inside Iran, Farhad. The Supreme Leader of Iran is dead. Within three hours, the Assembly of Experts names his replacement. Will he bring change to Iran's relationship with the west, or will he be their next nightmare? As the world waits, the new Supreme Leader plans to lift the economic sanctions against Iran once and for all…

For more information
visit: www.SpeakingVolumes.us

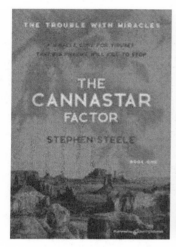
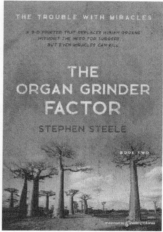

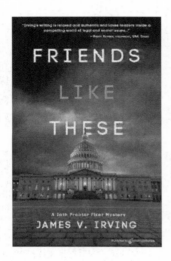 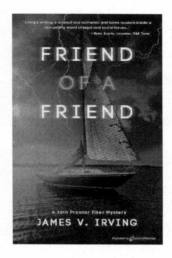

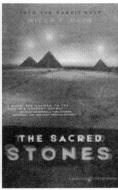

Join Our Mailing List

Be the First to Know

FREE Books, eBooks, Audiobooks and More offered every week just for being a loyal Speaking Volumes customer. Subscribe to our email newsletter and be notified of our latest titles from our award-winning and best-selling authors.

Sign Up Now for Free!

Made in the USA
Columbia, SC
22 August 2022

65848246R00212